# MIDNIGHT BLUES

This book is a work of fiction. Any references to historical events, real people, or real places are used fictitiously. Other names, characters, places, and events are products of the author's imagination, and any resemblance to actual events, places, or persons, living or dead, is entirely coincidental.

Lead Editor: Sara Walker

Copy Editor: Jeremy Taylor

Story developed by J. Paul Adams, K.E. Taylor, and J. Taylor (author)

Cover Design and Interior Formatting by Nuno Moreira, NM DESIGN

ISBNs

ISBN: 978-1-7377482-2-9

ISBN (ebook): 978-1-7377482-3-6

First Edition, Published by LS Prestige

For inquiries or collaborations, please connect with the author
via social media: @jtexpressive

# MIDNIGHT BLUES

### J. TAYLOR

For the lovers of a good story

Thank you for giving this one a chance.

# CHAPTER 1:
# A MURDER

"A good enemy is better than a false friend." — Silky

Frankie stood alone on the back terrace, the crisp winter air brushing against his skin as he looked at the well-manicured lawn stretching before him.

Inside, the staff bustled about, a flurry of activity aimed at perfection for tonight's gathering. Unlike last year's wild extravaganza, Frankie had opted for something more intimate for his thirtieth birthday—a quiet evening with close friends and family.

He reminisced about the previous year's chaos, a smirk playing on his lips, wondering if a quieter celebration would suit him. Frankie was determined to go legit, and the debut of his new hit, "Midnight Blues," would set things in motion.

Lost in thought about his future and the changes he yearned to make, Frankie was pulled back to the present by the sound of a car pulling up. He sauntered back inside, barefoot, his interest piqued as he felt the cold grass give way to the cool floorboards.

Bell, his wife and confidante, had left in a mysterious manner, and her refusal to disclose her destination only fueled his curiosity. Perhaps she was back with some surprise in tow for his birthday.

Frankie peered through the window as he made his way toward the front door, his brow narrowing in surprise. Jimmie stood there composing himself—uninvited, unexpected.

Pulling the door open, Frankie walked out. He had a way of putting people at ease, even when they had reason to be angry with him. As Frankie calmly approached, Jimmie rehearsed his confrontation speech under his breath. Frankie greeted him with a cautious smile, intrigued by this unannounced visit.

However, Jimmie's arrival was no coincidence. He had come with an agenda to confront Frankie about the burglary at his warehouse that had cleaned him out. Jimmie was livid.

"I know it was you, Frankie! I can't prove it, but I know it was you!"

The accusation hung in the air.

Frankie raised his hands in mock surrender, a disarming smile on his lips. "Alright, you got me. But come on, Jimmie… you didn't really think we'd let you move in on the business without sending a message, did you?"

Jimmie's expression hardened as he stepped closer, his voice dropping to a frantic whisper. "Frankie, you don't understand. This is serious. The people I owe that money to… they don't mess around." His voice cracked, desperation bleeding into his tone. "I need that money, Frankie. Look, I'm sorry, okay? I got greedy. But I need that fuckin' money."

Frankie's smile faltered for a split second before he regained his composure. He shrugged, his tone steady, but the weight of Jimmie's words lingered. "Alright. I'll admit, things got messy, and for that, I owe you more than an apology."

Jimmie let out a sharp breath, his frustration bubbling over. "An apology? Frankie, this isn't some petty squabble. You have no idea what I'm dealing with here."

Frankie studied him for a moment, then nodded slowly. "You want my side of the track? Fine—you can sell there, but you do it under my protection and my rules. You get your stash back, and we both walk away clean. That's my offer."

Frankie let the silence stretch before locking onto Jimmie's wary expression. "Here's how I see it—the big man forced your hand, and now you're stuck working with me. Lucky for you, I've been looking for a way out."

Initially, Jimmie bristled with resentment, his posture rigid. Sensing the brewing storm, Frankie maintained his composure, aware of the evening's significance and the need for calm.

As Frankie spoke, Jimmie's anger dissolved into contemplation, then acceptance. The men settled into a deeper conversation about the terms, and the tension dissipated.

Before long, Jimmie found himself inside the house, sitting in a plush chair, sipping a drink, and listening to Frankie explain that they now had only one common enemy. Jimmie's previous anger faded, and he relaxed.

Frankie invited Jimmie to stay, and after some insistence, Jimmie relented.

As Frankie and Jimmie sat there conversing, the front door opened. Their dialogue was interrupted by the arrival of Chubbs, Frankie's best friend and business partner.

Chubbs, who had arrived early to assist with the party, arched an eyebrow at Jimmie. "What brings you here?" he asked, distrust evident in his voice.

Jimmie, about to retort, was cut off by Frankie.

"Gentlemen. Let's not sour the evening," Frankie interjected smoothly. "Jimmie's just here to extend his birthday wishes."

Not entirely convinced, Chubbs let the matter drop.

The staff moved gracefully, continuing to set the scene for the night as Frankie's mind wandered. He pondered his life, the roads taken and those yet to be explored. He often glanced at Jimmie and Chubbs as he considered the intricate web of relationships and loyalties binding them. Each guest brought their history, their stories intertwining with his in unpredictable ways.

The night progressed, and the ambiance in the house grew denser with the laughter and chatter of arriving guests. Frankie moved among them, the perfect host, even as his mind was elsewhere. Soft music played in the background, its gentle melodies weaving through the clinking of glasses, filling the air with tranquility.

With a determined stride, Kenya approached Frankie from the side and whispered into his ear, "We need to talk." She had a knack for knowing when things needed attention.

Frankie's face, usually a mask of composure, tightened at her words. He felt a familiar surge of anger, a tide he had been struggling to keep at bay. Their last conversation was sour, and he dreaded another round of it. Despite his rising irritation, Frankie managed a brief sign of agreement.

"Alright, Kenya," he said, his voice strained but controlled. "Let's talk in the sunroom. It's secluded enough."

He led Kenya away from the other guests. The sunroom, usually filled with soft light, was now illuminated by the setting sun and the glow of candlelight. With the faint scent of jasmine and lavender under their noses, Frankie turned to face Kenya.

"So, what's on your mind?" he asked, his voice filled with frustration.

Kenya, her back straight, eyes forward, took a deep breath. "I need that fresh start, Frankie. I'm planning to leave town."

The words hit Frankie like a physical blow. He shook his head in desperation. "Here we go again. K, we talked about this."

Frankie paced before stopping and turning back to her. "No! Kenya, you can't. You're essential to me here," he implored, his voice carrying a rare vulnerability.

"But I can't just stay here, tethered to this…life," Kenya's voice rose, tinged with a hint of sadness. "This place feels suffocating, and so does our situation. I want to explore, find my own path, find my voice."

Frankie's heart raced. The thought of losing Kenya was unbearable. "You're like my soulmate, Kenya. Losing you…" His voice trailed off, the words too painful to finish.

Kenya's face softened. "I know what I mean to you, Frankie, but I need more than this." Her hand reached out, touching his arm gently.

The revelation struck a chord in Frankie and slightly annoyed him. He knew their relationship was unconventional—a delicate balance of power, history, and affection. "Don't leave, Kenya. There's got to be a way to make this work," he pleaded.

Kenya shook her head. "I need to do this, Frankie. For me."

Frankie, his emotions swirling, stepped closer, his demeanor intense as he grabbed her arm. "You think it's that easy to walk away?" he said, his voice rising. "To leave everything behind? To leave me behind!"

He pulled her closer. "You're going to abandon me just like everyone else!"

Kenya recoiled slightly, snatching her arm away. "I have to try, Frankie. I can't keep following in your footsteps forever."

The mood was somber, a silent standoff between two strong wills. Frankie's look softened as he regarded her, his anger giving way.

"Alright," he said, sighing heavily. "If you have to go, then go. But remember, it's unforgiving out there, especially for a Black woman. Do you think the world will accept you? The world barely accepts me."

His attention drifted to the window, where Cal, his loyal bodyguard, was visible, momentarily chasing away squirrels in a light-hearted effort to maintain complete order on the premises. Frankie smiled softly, the scene a brief break from the intensity of their conversation.

Returning his focus to Kenya, he proposed a compromise. "What if you stayed and continued working with me, but I supported your dreams, too? No more strings attached. There's nothing for you out there."

Kenya was brimming with tears. "Do you mean that, Frankie? Truly?"

"I do," Frankie affirmed, pulling her into a reassuring embrace. "We'll start fresh, Kenya. When we walk out of this door, we are leaving our old lives and mistakes behind. A new chapter for both of us."

Kenya smiled. "I'd like that, Frankie. More than you know."

Frankie held her close, placing a brotherly kiss on her forehead. Then, with a playful smirk, he added, "But I'm going to miss... you know."

Kenya gently pushed him away. "Oh, Frankie, always trying your luck. You men always get sexual at the worst time. Let's get back to the party."

As they stepped into the hallway, the doorbell rang, its sharp tone cutting through the muffled laughter and music. Frankie excused himself from Kenya and strode to the door, where he was greeted by the sight of Dr. Williams. Frankie put on a big smile, enveloping him in a warm, hearty hug.

"Hey there, old sport," said Dr. Williams, returning the embrace. As they walked into the living room, Dr. Williams, a man of peculiar habits, pulled a bronze flask from his pocket.

"Care for a drink?" he offered, his grin widening.

Frankie, with a polite wave of his hand, declined. "Thanks, we've got plenty."

Dr. Williams shrugged nonchalantly and put the flask away. "Suit yourself," he said. "Let's head to the bar so I can make myself a proper drink since you're not indulging."

Frankie couldn't help but laugh. "A proper drink?" he asked.

"Absolutely. I can be classy. I'm assuming that's why you turned down my flask," the doctor quipped. His presence brought a new dynamic to the party.

As he sipped his carefully concocted beverage, Frankie asked, "So, how's the medical business?"

With a contented sigh, the doctor replied, "Ah, the same old routine. You know, battling the ailments, saving lives, and overcharging for it."

Frankie caught the wink from Dr. Williams. "Do your patients appreciate your humor as much as your medical skills?" he asked.

"Hmm…not really. Most patients tell me I have terrible bedside manners, but I don't care. I'm old, so I can say what I damn well please." The doctor laughed, his voice rich and full.

Their conversation was suddenly interrupted as the door swung open, revealing Mississippi Red—a figure known for his flamboyant style and erratic behavior.

"Look who decided to show up," the doctor observed, taking note of Red's extravagant attire.

"What's up, fellas?" Red slurred, his words painting his inebriated state.

"You seem to have been enjoying yourself prior to showing up,"

Frankie commented, trying to keep the mood light, but Red's presence made it difficult.

"Yeah, yeah, I'm living it up. It's New Year's Eve, baby!" Red exclaimed, slightly unfocused.

With a look of concern, the doctor noted the glazed look on Red's face. "You look like you've been hitting the bottle or something else pretty hard, my friend."

Mississippi Red brushed off the doctor's concern with a shrug. "Just having some fun, that's all."

Feeling the potential for trouble, Frankie leaned in and whispered a warning to Red. "Let's keep it cool tonight, alright?"

But Sip, as he was known to his immediate family and friends, retorted with a wicked tone. "Oh, Daddy, I plan to put on quite the show tonight!"

At that moment, Chubbs reentered the room, lifting the mood. "Hey! What's the excitement about?" he said, greeting everyone with his usual enthusiasm.

"Red's planning to entertain us," Frankie replied dryly, watching Chubbs approach Red.

"My main man!" Red said, giving Chubbs a hug. Then he turned toward Frankie, eyeing him in disgust.

Frankie interrupted, "Listen, Red, you still got a problem? You got something to say to me? It's my fucking party, and I'm not playing these games tonight."

Red replied, sounding annoyed. "I'm here to party, man. But you, Frankie, you're the one with that wicked vibe. The things you've done aren't sitting right with your spirit, and it's clear."

Trying to calm things down, Chubbs said to Red, "Man, you look tired. You need to rest up if you gonna make it through the night. You know it's gonna be a long one."

He continued, "But in the meantime, why don't you tell me about that new track you've been working on? I'd love to hear about it."

Red looked at him skeptically for a moment before nodding his head. As they walked away, Frankie leaned over to the doctor and whispered, "You know, he may be a pain in the ass, but he sure does know how to make things interesting."

They clinked their glasses together and took a sip of their drinks.

Frankie smirked as the two made their way to the couch. They continued chatting and catching up, occasionally glancing over to check on Red and Chubbs.

The intimate party was becoming lively. The tunes of down-home blues and jazz continued to fill the room, setting the perfect rhythmic backdrop to the evening's festivities.

The doorbell sounded, and Frankie was momentarily drawn away from the conversations. With a swift stride, he reached the door and pulled it open. There stood Silky, a wide smile on his face and a cane in his hand.

"Nephew! How you doing, baby boy?" Silky's raspy voice resonated with a warmth familiar to Frankie.

"It's good to see you, Unc," Frankie replied, hugging him.

Following closely behind Silky was Kristine, his partner and elegance personified. "Kristine, you look beautiful as always," Frankie said, receiving a graceful smile and a kiss on the cheek in return.

As Silky and Kristine made their way into the living room, they were accompanied by four glamorous women dressed in fine bedazzled silk, adding a touch of extravagance to the evening.

"Birthday boy, I brought you some presents," Silky announced, half joking as he gestured toward the women.

Frankie laughed it off. "Unc, you know I don't play that game at home," he replied, reflecting the more reserved side of his social position.

Silky's laughter filled the room, his demeanor radiating charisma.

The doctor approached, extending a firm handshake to Silky.

"How have you been, old sport?" he inquired, his tone carrying a casual affability.

"Just keeping up with these young ones and keeping my stable tight," Silky replied, eliciting an eye roll from Kristine, who was accustomed to his antics.

Observing the scene, Frankie felt a sense of pride watching his uncle. Despite his flamboyant exterior, Silky was a deeply passionate man and a pillar in Frankie's life, often reminding him of his heritage and the greatness within.

Silky stood there and preached to every Black person in attendance. "You folks were kings and queens in a past life, and don't you forget it." He pointed his finger at each person as he spoke, and everyone listened respectfully.

"Before we turn my nephew's party upside down, take this with you: Start walking in your greatness—you don't have nearly as much time as you think on this earth. Take your life seriously, and be better than the generation before you."

The group looked at him intently as he concluded. "My old ass is a pimp, and that's all I will ever be. You all have a good life in front of you. Now, let's take a shot and forget the night. Tomorrow, wake up and get after it. Cheers to the new year!"

As the party's tempo picked up, the doctor's sharp wit and Silky's commanding presence captivated the guests. At the same time, Jimmie's easy Italian charm worked its magic, complementing the other rambunctious storytellers.

The three men told raunchy stories and drank as the party continued. People gathered around them, entertained by their embellishments and infectious energy.

Meanwhile, Red was in a deep slumber beside the sound system, oblivious to the lively party around him. The doctor, Jimmie, and a few others were drawn to one of Silky's acquaintances, her allure undeniable in the bustling room.

"And who is this lovely lady that decided to join us?" the doctor asked, concluding his final story.

Jimmie looked at Cyn, captivated by her beauty and sensuous aura. He stepped in and said to the doctor, "This is my friend Cyn. She's one of Silky's top girls."

Cyn gave an innocent smile. "I don't think we've met, but I'm flattered that you already consider me a friend."

Kristine interrupted, "Cyn, don't pay Jimmie any attention—he's a troublemaker."

Jimmie replied, "Whoa, Kris… Come on… Trouble maker? Some girls like a little trouble, ya know."

He surveyed Cyn from head to toe, his eyes lingering longer than necessary, clearly attracted to her.

Kristine interjected once more. "Well, this one doesn't like trouble. She likes money."

Jimmie backed off as Cyn laughed softly. "Now Cyn, this is Doctor Williams. He's an old friend of mine," Kristine said, gesturing toward him.

Cyn sized him up and extended her hand. "It's a pleasure to meet you."

"The pleasure is all mine, my dear," the doctor replied, kissing her hand gently.

The music thumped as the party hit its stride, with Frankie fully immersed in the festivities.

Just then, he spotted Detective Tony Marlow and his partner, Junior, making a discreet entrance. Nearby, two women murmured curiously to each other, speculating about the newcomers.

Seeing an opportunity to engage, Frankie approached with a friendly tone. "Ladies, I couldn't help but overhear—are you wondering about those two gentlemen over there?"

The women smiled in agreement, their interest piqued.

Smiling back, Frankie continued, "They're detectives and top-notch ones at that. Tony's a great guy and a close friend, and Junior is his partner. Let's treat them like family, shall we?"

Wide-eyed and new to the aristocratic party scene, Junior was quickly drawn into Silky's magnetic orbit. Silky's booming voice and larger-than-life personality captivated him, and before long, Junior was laughing at his jokes and flirting with every girl who would entertain him.

Marlow, on the other hand, kept to himself. He remained a silent observer, taking in every detail and interaction while constantly checking his wristwatch.

He was social enough with the guests to avoid suspicion, ensuring they didn't think he was watching them—although he clearly was.

Frankie noticed from afar that Detective Marlow seemed more preoccupied than usual. Wanting to ask him about his distant demeanor, Frankie approached and said, "Hey Tony, you look like you have a lot on your mind. Everything alright?" His tone was filled with genuine concern.

Marlow let out a sigh that spoke volumes. "Yeah, I'm fine, Frankie. Thanks for asking." He reassured him before continuing, "It's the job… Hard to switch off, even on a night like this." His words reflected his profession, a constant search for trouble even amid celebration.

Frankie responded sympathetically, "I can imagine that must be tough. Hey, how about we get some fresh air?"

Marlow agreed and followed Frankie's lead. The two stepped outside, entering a quiet place away from the party. Frankie leaned against one of the pillars and observed the starlit sky. "What's on your mind, Marlow?" he asked.

Marlow opened up about the burdens of his job, the pressures he faced, and the conflict between duty and personal desire that waged war within him. He took a deep breath. "It's the shitty side of the job. I'm always looking for the bad in people. It's not a pleasant feeling."

He continued, a depressed look on his face. "Let's be honest. It's your birthday, and instead of enjoying it, I'm watching people." He sipped his drink. "But I love it. I actually love it too much. I love the chase and the thrill of catching criminals. I love looking into other people's minds and uncovering the clues they never knew existed."

Marlow shook his head and added, "I'm obsessed, and my career is going to be the death of me."

Frankie stepped closer to Marlow and rested his hand on his shoulder. "Don't let the pressure get to you, Tony."

Marlow smiled faintly. "Thanks, Frankie. I appreciate it. It's good to talk about it. I don't get to do that much."

Frankie affirmed and said reassuringly, "You're a good man, Tony. And a damn good detective."

Marlow's smile hinted at how seldom he experienced such candid conversations. That moment outside was a brief interlude of honesty in an evening filled with superficial joys.

The exchange between the two men momentarily faded into the background as a car pulled up. Frankie's heart sank as he realized the vehicle belonged to Judge Kincaid, a symbol of cynicism and arrogance.

When the car parked, Kincaid stepped out and eventually came toward Frankie, flanked by his roughneck bodyguard, Hogg. The judge exuded an air of entitlement as he approached.

"Frankie, my boy," Kincaid sneered in his southern Creole drawl, extending an envelope to him.

Frankie's stomach churned at the court documents, a looming reminder of the trumped-up charges Kincaid held over him. Frankie thought that if he was going to stand up to the judge, tonight would be the night.

"Judge, let's talk privately," Frankie suggested, masking his anxiety as he handed the documents back to the judge.

"Seems you are having yourself a ball. How about you make good on your payment, and I'll get on out of here so you can enjoy your night," the judge smiled.

"I think you will want to hear what I have to say," Frankie added.

Judge Kincaid stroked his dirty beard. "Well, lead the way, son."

Detective Marlow, picking up on the underlying hostility, inquired about Frankie's well-being.

Frankie responded with a cool, "I'm handling it," signaling that he was in control.

They made their way through the home and entered the Cashmere Room.

Once they were inside, the ambiance shifted, and Frankie broke the ice. "Should we have a drink before we get started?"

Kincaid looked to his bodyguard. "Hogg, whatcha say we stay for a couple of drinks?"

Hogg pulled on his belt and replied, "Well, boss…"

The judge interrupted. "You right, Hogg! I think we should celebrate Frankie tonight. You don't see a problem with that, do you?"

Frankie looked at him sternly, then softened into a smile at the rhetorical question. "Not at all. What'll you have?"

Kincaid took a seat. "Hogg and I will take a couple of Old Fashioneds," he said with a long drawl and quickly added, "And use the good bourbon, son."

Frankie's hands were steady as he began preparing the drinks at the minibar in the corner, his back to Kincaid. "Judge, I might as well stop procrastinating… I won't be making any more payments," he declared, leaving an awkward silence.

After a long pause, Kincaid laughed deeply. "Son, you can't be serious. We just spoke about this. With the charges I have on you, you'll be indebted to me for as long as I say you are."

Frankie stopped making the drinks and handed Kincaid a folder, its contents obscured from Hogg's view. Kincaid's face flashed concern. Frankie took notice and returned to the minibar, deliberately prolonging the moment.

Kincaid tossed the papers on the table in a dismissive manner before yelling, "What the hell is this?"

Frankie continued pouring the bourbon with precision. "Your honor, I did a little digging of my own, and as you can see, I've learned something that could get in the way of your gubernatorial aspirations."

As he began to wrap up the cocktails, Frankie continued. "Governor of Louisiana. Whew! That's a big move, Judge. I've always heard you have to be squeaky clean to pull that off. And let's just say we both know that the information you just saw could complicate your campaign."

Kincaid's face twisted in anger. "You wouldn't dare."

Frankie shrugged while garnishing the two drinks with bitters. "I'm just looking out for myself, Judge. But if you don't want me to go public with this information, I suggest we call our debt slick."

Frankie remained cool, a slight smirk playing on his lips.

"And what if…?" Kincaid challenged.

Frankie returned to the table and set the drinks down. He stepped closer to Kincaid with confidence. "Then the truth mysteriously comes out from an anonymous source," he replied, his voice low but firm. "But for now, just enjoy the drinks."

He turned back to the bar, a large smile on his face. "Two Old Fashioneds for two old men," he joked, his laughter masking the significance of their exchange.

Kincaid's face went pale, and his composure faltered as he processed the implications. Abruptly, he stormed out of the room, Hogg in tow.

Frankie's mind was racing with the possibilities; he knew he had just crossed a dangerous man. Outside the door, Kincaid muttered a veiled threat to Hogg. Frankie tried to listen, but the judge's agitation was the only thing that was clear.

After a moment, Frankie stopped eavesdropping and paced. The door slowly reopened, revealing Kincaid once more. His anger had given way to a grudging respect.

"You are a slick one, Frankie Keys," Kincaid conceded quickly, with a hint of humor. "Seems you have a future governor in your back pocket. Keep my secret to yourself, and Louisiana's law won't touch or apply to you."

Frankie replied, "What exactly are you saying?"

The judge studied him for a moment. "You will never catch a charge in this state as long as I'm around, my boy."

With a handshake to seal the deal, Kincaid requested permission to stick around the party for a bit.

"Hell, I oughta be able to stay for a few drinks. You just took me out back and gave me an old-fashioned butt whipping. What do you say?"

Frankie obliged the judge's request because he saw it as a way to keep his new enemy close for the night. Kincaid joined the party, leaving Frankie alone with his thoughts. The encounter, a dance of power and wits, had ended in Frankie's favor, but at what cost? He knew he had challenged a formidable opponent and that the game was far from over.

Frankie lingered for a while, his confrontation with Judge Kincaid pressing heavily on his mind. Silky's words echoed in his ears: "A good enemy is better than a false friend."

Yet, as he ventured back and forth down the hall, a sense of unease unfurled within him. The laughter and music from the party seemed distant, muffled by his racing thoughts.

Realizing he was not ready to return to the party, he decided to head back to his sanctuary to clear his mind.

As he reentered the Cashmere Room, now tainted by the night's revelations, Frankie noticed the air felt colder and denser. He stopped, sensing a presence.

From the shadows, a figure emerged, two glasses in hand.

"Shit, you scared me," Frankie exclaimed, a nervous twitch escaping him as he recognized the face. "What are we drinking?" he asked, attempting to shake off the chill that ran down his spine.

"Bourbon. Your favorite. I'll pour; you relax," the tone warm, the comfort in the voice betraying its intent.

As the time passed, the countdown to midnight began. Everyone gathered in the main living area, waiting for the clock to strike twelve. Laughter and chatter filled the air.

Chubbs and Silky were deep in conversation at the bar, their voices low and serious.

Kristine lounged elegantly on the couch, her conversation with the judge hushed and discreet.

Still unconscious by the sound system, Mississippi Red remained oblivious to the shifting tides.

Jimmie was involved in a high-stakes gambling match, taking frequent smoke breaks to calm his nerves.

Junior was smitten with a small group of ladies, and Kenya was on the dance floor, cutting loose.

But Bell was still notably absent, her whereabouts unknown.

Amid the celebrations and constant movement, Cal patrolled the perimeter for his routine sweep. Halting at the sight of an open window, a sense of concern crept through him. Cutting his route short, he moved toward the house.

As he advanced from the back to the front, a sudden crash from inside echoed through the halls, halting the party's momentum.

"What the hell was that?" Kristine's voice cut through the confusion. Heads turned as everyone searched for the source.

Hollywood Red stirred, his slumber disrupted, while Doctor Williams briefly emerged, peeking down the hall looking bewildered.

Cal burst into the room and began pushing people aside, scanning the space until his eyes locked on a guest holding the remnants of a vase.

Apologies filled the air, but the damage was done. The guest apologized fervently, begging Cal not to remove her.

He surveyed the damage and tried to calm her down. As he did so, Detective Marlow rushed into the room, having heard the sound of the crash and the resulting commotion.

He looked around the room, taking in the scene before him. "What's going on here?" he asked.

Cal quickly answered, "Just a broken vase, Tony. All clear."

The music was turned back up and continued to blare in the background. Junior had joined Kenya on the dance floor, his childlike demeanor drawing laughter from the onlookers as he showed off his awkward dance moves.

Just as the party began to recover, a piercing scream shattered the fragile calm. Kenya, suspended in terror, raced toward the source, Junior trailing behind her.

As Kenya reached the doorway, her scream joined the chorus of chaos. They found Cal frantic; his cries had sent a wave of panic through the party. Junior stood frozen, his body rigid with shock as he stared at the scene before him.

Frankie was on the ground, contorted in agony. His face, usually composed and in control, was twisted in pain.

Cal hovered over him, desperation evident in his every move. The room spun for Frankie, his vision blurring as he struggled to breathe.

Cal was now holding his head, trying desperately to keep him alive, but it was clear that he was fading fast.

Detective Marlow and Chubbs entered the scene simultaneously. Marlow's detective instincts kicked in as he took in the sight before him. The passive detective from earlier was gone.

"Someone go find the damn doctor!" he demanded, his voice cutting through the noise and screams.

Chubbs's sprint down the corridor was a blur of motion, his urgency revealed as he dodged guests and furniture alike. The sound of his heart pounding in his ears drowned out the distant cries.

As he burst into the doctor's room, the sight that greeted him caused a momentary shock—the doctor was laid up with Cyn in bed.

"Doctor, now! Frankie's in trouble!" Chubbs's voice broke through the haze of passion, urgency overriding the doctor's embarrassment.

The doctor, startled, stumbled from the bed, his mind struggling to adjust from the warmth of the sheets to the cold reality awaiting him.

Clad only in his underwear, knee-high socks, and a sleeveless undershirt, he sprinted toward the commotion, his dignity forgotten as his medical instincts seized control.

The doctor rushed into the room, his heart sinking at the sight before him. Frankie was gasping for air, his breaths coming in ragged, shallow gulps.

The doctor's hands shook as he knelt beside him, immediately noticing the sweat beading on Frankie's forehead. When Frankie grabbed his hand, the doctor felt the clamminess of his skin, cold and damp.

Frankie's lips moved, struggling to whisper something. The doctor leaned in, straining to catch the words, but they were incoherent. As he focused on Frankie's face, he noticed his pupils were unnaturally dilated.

"There's a chance this is lethal!" the doctor screamed, pulling back as foam began to form at the corners of Frankie's mouth.

"I need my bag!" he yelled, shooting out of the room, desperately searching for his medical supplies. "My bag! Where's my bag?" he cried out, panic rising as he rummaged through cabinets and drawers.

It suddenly dawned on him—his medical bag was gone. It was nowhere to be found.

In desperation, the doctor rushed back to Frankie and made a crude attempt to induce vomiting. He turned Frankie to the side and stuck a finger down his throat, a futile effort to expel any potential poison. But as Frankie's body went limp and his breathing ceased, the doctor knew it was too late.

He slumped against the wall, tears of frustration welling up. "What's the time?" he choked out, his voice barely a whisper.

Standing in the doorway, numb and disbelieving, Chubbs replied, "Ten thirty-six."

Crying, the doctor said, "The official time of death is ten thirty-six."

Detective Marlow, his demeanor grim, took control of the scene. "Everyone out, now!" he commanded, scanning the room as he noted every detail, every potential clue.

As the others filed out, the burden of the night settled on Marlow's shoulders. This was no longer a celebration; it was a potential crime scene.

With the room cleared, Marlow turned to the doctor, who was still slumped on the floor, a broken man. "What happened?" Marlow asked, his voice steady but concerned.

The doctor shook his head, his professional composure shattered. "I don't know… I didn't have what I needed… It was too late."

Marlow stepped out into the hallway, his mind already piecing together the fragments of the evening. He knew the suspects weren't just the ones in the room but anyone who had crossed paths with Frankie.

"Cal, sweep the house and keep everyone in the living room," Marlow instructed, his voice carrying the authority of his badge. "Junior, you start with light questioning. If there is anyone you don't feel good about, hold them. Do not let them leave."

Junior replied, "Ten-four. Looks like we have a real whodunit on our hands here... And I hate whodunnits!"

It wasn't long before Cal confirmed the house was clear. All the guests had been escorted out except those Junior deemed suspects.

As the men and women in question sat impatiently in the living room, a tense and somber air replaced the earlier merriment.

Things took an unexpected twist when Bell and Hogg walked into the home together, drawing the attention of every person in question. They were greeted not by music and laughter but by a suffocating silence.

Bell held a small bag, her smile fading as Junior relayed the grim message.

"A *murder!*" Bell exclaimed, her eyes widening in shock. "In our home?" she yelled, her voice trembling with disbelief.

The room was filled with whispers and nervous glances as everyone struggled to process the moment.

Detective Marlow stepped forward, taking in each face in turn. "Folks, this is now a murder investigation," he announced. "I need everyone's cooperation as we try to piece together what happened."

As the clock continued its relentless march toward midnight, the party that had promised so much joy and celebration had instead delivered a mystery wrapped in tragedy, with Frankie at its center.

CHAPTER 2:

# ON THE LAM

"What would Jesus Do?" — First Lady

Chicago, IL 1929

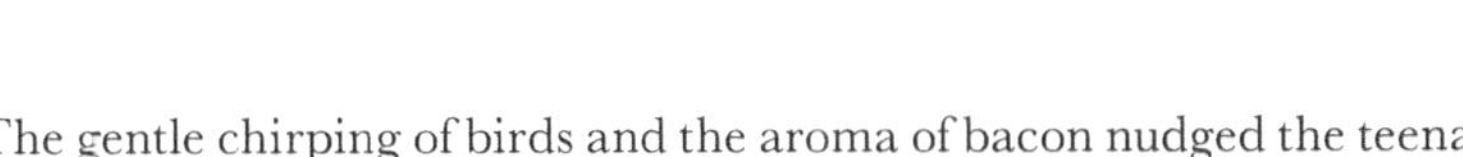

The gentle chirping of birds and the aroma of bacon nudged the teenage boy awake. The familiar sight of his bedroom ceiling came into focus.

In the comfort of his bed, he teetered on the edge of sleep once more, only to be jolted awake by his grandmother's voice echoing through the house. "Luckey! Time to rise, child. You've got a whole town to cross to get to school on time."

His response was sluggish—a rhythmic tapping of his foot against the squeaky floorboards, mimicking the sound of movement while he remained in bed. "Yes, ma'am, getting up now."

He considered pushing his luck for a few more minutes of sleep but thought better of it. Over the years, his grandmother had established a standard of discipline that brooked no sass or backtalk. A misstep often prompted his grandmother to deliver the swift sting of a finely crafted switch.

Lately, however, Luckey had noticed a subtle change in her. She wanted to talk more. Time and health had begun to wear down her stern exterior, revealing a softer side.

Nevertheless, as he hesitated, her voice rang out again, sharper this time. "Luckey! Don't test me today, boy. Up now, or I'll come in there myself!"

He quickly clambered out of bed, slipping into dusty pants that bore the marks of a hard day's labor and worn shoes that had seen better days. His shirt, now snug against his growing frame, reminded him of their modest means.

Bounding out of the room, he greeted his grandmother with a playful charm. "Grandma, you must've found the fountain of youth overnight—looking mighty fine there!"

He reached for a strip of bacon, only to have his hand swatted away.

"Luckey! Wash those hands before you touch God's food. And you know the rule. No breakfast till you play me some music," she said, admonishing him with a warm smile.

The piano, a relic from his father, stood in the corner, carrying a legacy of music and memories. An underworld musician of repute, his father had insisted on a strict daily practice for young Luckey, embedding a consistent routine of morning and evening sessions at the keys. Faithfully upheld by his grandmother, this ritual was her way of preserving his father's dream for him. He wanted his son to become a notable figure in the music world, someone who could hold his own in any circle or club.

Seating himself at the instrument, Luckey announced with a confident smile, "This one's going to be a special treat." His fingers danced across the keys, slow, beautiful chords carrying the soulful essence of a Sunday morning. He began to sing "Amazing Grace." His voice was soft yet resonant, filling the room with warmth.

His grandmother, unable to hide her delight, beamed with pride. "Alright now, come and eat. You have your daddy's gift—that smooth voice."

As he savored his breakfast of toast, bacon, eggs, and grits, Luckey asked, "Grandma, how'd you learn to cook like this?"

Between bites, she recounted her youth in Mississippi, a life that started on a plantation near Yazoo and led her to Chicago during the Great Migration. "It's the soul of the South in every bite, baby," she said with a nostalgic smile.

Luckey finished his meal and made a beeline for the door, stopping to kiss his grandmother's cheek. "See you later. Love you, old lady!" he called out.

She responded, "A coat, Luckey. That wind is going to be whipping later."

"I'll be fine. I won't be out late," he replied.

She shook her head as he walked away, following him out the door. She whispered softly, "Be good, Luckey. God, keep that baby safe for me."

The words lingered in the air, a silent prayer for the day ahead.

As Luckey set out on his walk to school, his mind wandered to grand dreams of performing music for a diverse audience, his talent transcending the limitations of his race. He reveled in the fantasy of being an acclaimed musician, so skilled that no one could deny his gift.

A vivid memory surfaced amid his daydreams: the night his father snuck him into a speakeasy to see Duke Ellington. The exhilaration of the music and Duke's announcement of moving to New York were still vivid, as was his mother's anger when they returned.

"Negroes shouldn't be out so late, especially not with a child!" she had said, scolding Luckey's father.

When he arrived at school, Luckey's thoughts shifted as he encountered Rene, a girl whose beauty captivated him. She was dark-skinned with full lips and bright eyes. She had a presence about her that made his heart palpitate.

"I spent all night trying to write a song for you, but all I could come up with was…" Luckey paused, searching for the right words.

Noticing his hesitation, Rene couldn't resist teasing him. "You getting stage fright? I thought you were going to be a superstar. Big time! That's what you told me."

Luckey blushed, embarrassment and affection showing on his face.

Their playful banter continued and finally ended with Luckey proposing a walk to the general store for candy after school, an offer Rene immediately accepted. She quickly let Luckey know that the only treat he would be getting would be the candy from the store.

"My candy shop ain't open," she said, "so don't get any ideas."

Luckey kissed her on the cheek, a goofy grin spreading across his face. The day seemed to pass slowly as Luckey counted each second, eager to walk Rene home. She knew Luckey well and encouraged him to dream.

Quietly, the boy was in love.

After school, they set off for the store, a journey they often shared because there were no school buses where they lived. Their friendship had blossomed over these walks, with Luckey asserting his role as her protector.

"I'm not afraid of anyone or anything," he'd often declare with youthful bravado.

As they reached the store, Luckey took the lead and confidently walked through the door. "Want anything?" he asked Rene.

"Some gum, please," she replied.

Their closeness and Luckey's confidence were evident to all, including the owner's wife, Mrs. Trammel, who welcomed their visits. She indulged Luckey from time to time because she found him to be rather handsome and charming for a negro. She saw him as someone who was going places in life.

At the store, Luckey's playful demeanor continued.

"Nice to see you, Luckey," Mrs. Trammel said, greeting the teenagers.

Luckey replied, "Likewise, Ma'am. I'll have two sticks of gum. One for me, and one for my girlfriend."

Rene immediately retorted, "Oh please, I am not your girlfriend."

Luckey smiled and said, "Fine then. Mrs. Trammel, will you be my girlfriend?"

When he turned his charm toward Mrs. Trammel, her response was stern and uncharacteristic, sharply different from her usual lighthearted banter. "Don't be absurd! Here's your change."

Luckey had gotten too comfortable, and a sudden interruption intensified the mood. From the back emerged Mr. Trammel, his presence unexpected.

"What did you just say, boy?" he bellowed, his threatening voice making Luckey's heart skip a beat. Mr. Trammel, a police officer, was seldom around during the day, and Luckey found himself at a loss for words.

"I... I'm so sorry, sir," Luckey stammered, his bravado dissolving into fear.

Mrs. Trammel quickly intervened, her voice firm as she addressed her husband. "That's enough, Jeff." With a firm push, she guided him back, her attention returning to Luckey. "You best be going now, Luckey. And remember your manners next time," she said, her tone softening.

Luckey gave a quick nod and a respectful bow. "Sorry, Mrs. Trammel. Won't happen again."

Leaving the store, the encounter lingered in his mind—a sharp reminder of the trouble his quick tongue could spark. As they walked home, Rene's voice broke the silence. "Mr. Trammel looked like he would have hurt you, Luckey. He had the look of a man that could kill."

Luckey brushed off her fears, but the intensity of Mr. Trammel's stare lingered in his mind. "Let's just forget about it and enjoy the walk," he said, seeking solace in Rene's presence.

Arriving at her home, Luckey asked her father for a few more minutes. Pastor TK, who had known Luckey all his life, was hard on him for good reason. Before he became a preacher, he and Luckey's father were "thick as thieves," running the streets together before TK turned his life over to the church.

He showed sternness at Luckey's request before breaking into a warm, teasing laugh. "Alright, ten minutes, but no funny business," he joked, giving Luckey a brief, paternal embrace.

Luckey savored these moments. He loved to hang out at Rene's place, not just for the company but also because her home backed up to a train track and a nearby station.

As the trains eased into motion, he would ask, "Where do you think they're headed?" Watching those locomotives ride off into the dark intrigued him, making the world seem much bigger than Chicago. For Luckey, these trains symbolized a world beyond, full of possibilities and dreams.

With dusk settling over the streets, it was time to part. Luckey told Rene he'd take the long way home, a detour to savor the time they'd shared. The hours had slipped by too quickly, and disappointment flickered in his chest as Rene's mom poked her head out the door.

"Nae! Tell your friend goodnight."

Rene gave him a quick kiss and a seductive look. "Goodnight, friend."

Her mom called out, "Nae Nae! Don't get cute."

Luckey laughed. "Goodnight, First Lady. See you tomorrow."

With a quick peck on Rene's cheek, Luckey set off on the long walk home. His mind was a whirlwind of thoughts under the setting sun.

Luckey replayed the day's events, his thoughts circling back to Rene. There was a warmth in how he cherished her, a feeling his grandmother often reinforced with stories about Rene's family. She spoke highly of Rene's father, Pastor TK, and often reminded Luckey that his own father had once risked his life for the man. Those tales of courage and loyalty were the foundation of who Luckey had become.

During his walk, a subtle unease began to creep over him—the distinct sensation of being watched. He slowed, glancing over his shoulder and scanning the shadows for anything out of place. Nothing. Still, his instincts refused to settle, the tension prickling at the back of his neck.

Suddenly, the quiet of the night was shattered by the sound of a police siren. Luckey's heart leaped into his throat as he stepped off the road, watching a police car slowly approach and stop. The car's lights flashed ominously in the dark.

The loudspeaker crackled to life with a voice Luckey recognized all too well. It was Mr. Trammel.

"Luckey, get on the ground!" His voice slurred through the speaker.

With a sinking feeling in his stomach, Luckey complied. He saw Mr. Trammel exit the car, his walk unsteady. "Out awfully late ain't ya?" Mr. Trammel sneered, approaching him.

Fighting the urge to flee, Luckey managed a nervous response. "I'm just headed home, sir. No trouble."

Mr. Trammel's smile was forced. "The way you were talking to my wife earlier... Seems to me like you're itching for trouble." His tone was heavy with malice.

Luckey felt a surge of fear but tried to remain calm. He pleaded to be let go, but the officer refused to release him.

Fueled by anger and alcohol, Trammel struck Luckey with his nightstick, the blow sending waves of pain through his body.

As Luckey writhed on the ground, the off-duty cop loomed over him, nightstick in hand, his voice a venomous hiss.

"My wife told me to let this go. I told her that dogs need to be trained," he spat, each word punctuated by another blow. The pain was blinding.

Clutching his side, Luckey remembered his grandmother's wisdom—avoid eye contact. But Mr. Trammel wasn't done.

He forced Luckey's chin up with the nightstick, demanding he look at him. "You thought you were slick, talking to my wife like that?" he huffed disdainfully, delivering another gut-wrenching blow.

Each strike felt like a hammer, the physical pain compounded by Luckey's realization of the deep-seated hatred and bigotry he faced.

"I asked around about you. Your daddy was bold once too... thought he could stand up to us. But we showed him his place," Mr. Trammel said, taunting Luckey.

His words cut deeper than his nightstick, revealing a cruel connection to Luckey's father's past. "I was supposed to be there that night. They beat him and that preacher friend of his half to death. They are lucky one of the churchgoin' cops caught a weak stomach and let them go; probably saved their life that night."

The revelation left Luckey breathless. Even his foolish words couldn't justify what was happening to him. Like his father, he was caught in a cruel game played by corrupt men in uniform.

In a moment of defiant desperation, Luckey spat back, "My father was ten times the man you'll ever be."

"Get up!" Mr. Trammel yelled at Luckey.

"Look at me the way you looked at my wife." The policeman gut-checked him again with the nightstick and continued to swing another four or five times, striking Luckey in the side and gashing his head.

As he knelt on the ground in pain, Luckey spat out venom of his own. "You're weak, and you are just like the rest of the white cowards in this world. You hide behind that badge and that stick. You know I could crush you with my bare hands if this was a fair fight."

Mr. Trammel threw the nightstick aside and charged at Luckey, spearing him to the ground. The two were now in an all-out brawl, punches flying and heavy knees exchanged.

In a last-effort tussle, Luckey jarred Trammel's gun loose. The two wrestled fiercely for control of the weapon, a desperate bid for survival.

Finally, with a combination of adrenaline and sheer will, Luckey managed to gain control of the gun.

The world seemed to freeze as Luckey stood, his hand shaking as he pointed the gun at Mr. Trammel. The once intimidating policeman now looked back with evident fear, trying to mask his anxiety and maintain his composure.

"Boy! Think long and hard," Trammel implored, his voice quivering. "Shooting a cop? That's a death sentence. You don't go to prison for that—you'll pay for that with your life. They won't rest until they hunt you down."

Luckey knew he was right. He felt the cold metal of the gun pressed against his sweaty palm.

The reality was paralyzing—he was on the precipice of a decision that would alter the course of his life forever.

"Hand over the gun, son. We can call it a misunderstanding," Trammel offered, attempting to negotiate. But his sincerity was questionable.

Luckey felt pulled between fear and the overwhelming urge to survive. Mr. Trammel's voice was a distant echo, his pleas falling fruitlessly to the ground.

The only sound that mattered to Luckey was the beating of his own heart.

Mr. Trammel grew frustrated. "Give me the fucking gun!"

Luckey's mind raced as he processed his options. But Trammel, sensing Luckey's hesitation, made a sudden move to regain control.

In a split-second reaction, a gunshot echoed through the night, shattering the silence.

Mr. Trammel fell to the ground, his face contorted with pain and shock. Luckey, the gun still smoking in his hand, stood frozen, staring at the fallen officer. He slowly walked over, hovering over him, contemplating whether to finish the job as the officer lay on the cold ground.

"Call for help... I'm dying..." escaped Trammel's lips in a hoarse whisper.

Gripped by a wave of panic, Luckey suddenly understood the irreversible nature of his actions.

With each passing second, Luckey's window to escape narrowed. He glanced around, ensuring no witnesses were present. Driven by primal instincts, he fled into the darkness of the night, the gun still clutched in his hand and the echo of the gunshot still ringing in his ears.

His mind was a whirlwind of thoughts—where to go, how to escape. The night was his only ally now, shrouding him in its embrace as he ran through the empty streets, a fugitive on the run from a crime that would alter his life forever.

He was no longer just a boy with dreams of music and love; he was now a young man marked by violence and haunted by the choices he had made. The path ahead was uncertain, filled with danger and desperation.

Panting and disoriented, Luckey bolted toward Rene's house, the only safe place he could think of. As he emerged from the bushes, he ran into Pastor TK, who was startled to see him out so late.

"What in the world happened to you, boy?" Pastor TK exclaimed.

Still reeling from the night's events, Luckey struggled to articulate his predicament. Pastor TK quickly ushered him inside for safety and a place to gather his thoughts. He turned back briefly to check if anyone had seen Luckey arrive.

Inside, Pastor TK yelled for his wife. Hearing her father, Rene rushed in, worry etched across her face as she saw the welts on Luckey.

"Who did this to you?" she asked frantically.

Barely audible, Luckey mumbled, "Mr. Trammel."

The room fell into a stunned silence as Luckey's trembling hand removed the gun from his waistline and placed it on the table.

"I shot him," he confessed.

Pastor TK's face hardened. "Son, you've got to leave now! You're bringing danger to our doorstep!" he said sternly.

"My grandmother said you were the only one she trusted to help me if I was ever in serious trouble. I was scared. I didn't know what to do," Luckey sobbed, the weight of his actions crushing him.

As Luckey contemplated his bleak future, Pastor TK's wife intervened. She instructed him to change into their late son's clothes, a poignant reminder of police brutality just two years earlier. She then quickly disposed of Luckey's blood-stained garments in the roaring fireplace, the flames consuming the evidence and erasing any immediate traces of the night's events.

Stunned by what was transpiring, the pastor finally broke his silence. "You got to go. I love your grandmother and your daddy, lords know I do, but I can't be part of this. I'm sorry, son, but you got to run far away from here."

Devastated, Luckey dropped to his knees, grabbing the gun and briefly contemplating taking his own life.

The pastor's wife urgently said, "We have to help him, TK."

Pastor TK began pacing, his hands jittering with fear. "Why?" he responded swiftly. "We've already lost one son. You know what will happen if they find out we helped him."

The First Lady took a breath, pleading. "But we also know what will happen if we don't help him! What would Jesus do?" she asked her husband.

The room was spinning as Pastor TK continued to pace, formulating a plan. He stopped and pulled Luckey up from his knees.

"You'll hide in the outhouse until the coast is clear. When it's safe, you run down the track to the train station and hop on the last car," he instructed, his voice firm and compassionate.

Luckey had a blank stare on his face as Pastor TK continued. "Get on that train and ride it as far as it goes. Your new life starts wherever you step off. Don't tell a soul about tonight, and don't use your real name. It's the only plan I can think of. All the black folk are moving North, so ain't nobody gonna be expecting a negro to run down South."

Luckey listened intently as if his life depended on every word, because it did.

"The South ain't like the North, son. Keep ya eyes straight and ya mouth shut. I'll tell your grandmother when the coast is clear. You can't ever write her. Not for a long time."

Heartbroken, Luckey realized the finality of Pastor TK's words. He would never see his grandmother again. His life as he knew it was over. Luckey's face dropped.

Pastor TK yelled at him, "Damn it, boy! Listen!"

Startled, Luckey said, "Tell her I love her, and I'm going to make her proud with my music."

As the night deepened, Luckey sat in the outhouse, preparing for his departure. The distant sound of the approaching train was a call to a new, unknown future.

Pastor TK ran out, his breath visible in the cold night air, offering a final piece of advice—part warning, part fatherly concern. "When it's time... keep low, stay quiet, and make something of yourself. You're on your own now, boy."

He lingered for a moment, his stern expression softening briefly before he turned and quickly made his way back inside the home.

Despite his panic, Pastor TK took a deep breath and composed himself. He knew he would need to keep his cool until Luckey was on that train and out of Chicago.

Two loud knocks at the door suddenly shattered the stillness of the night. *Bam! Bam!*

"It's Coon!" Police Chief Boe Coon stood outside, his imposing figure barely contained by the doorway.

"Evening, Pastor," he said when the minister opened the door. "Seen that young negro Luckey by chance?" His voice carried an air of deceptive casualness.

Pastor TK, steadying his voice, replied with ignorance. "No, sir. Can't say I have."

Leaning forward on the porch, the police chief spat tobacco onto the pastor's shoe. "Sorry about that. You wouldn't be lying to me now, would you, Pastor? The Lord wouldn't take kindly to that."

Before Pastor TK could react, Chief Coon barged into the house. "Lovely place you have here," he remarked, his eyes scrutinizing the room.

The pastor, recalling a past where he had nearly lost his life standing up for what was right, felt a surge of protectiveness. Chief Coon continued. "Just tell me where the boy is, Pastor. Don't make me call the dogs down here to find him."

TK briefly considered giving up Luckey to protect his family but remembered his wife's earlier words.

"Chief, Luckey was here earlier. He dropped off my daughter because they are friends. He left, went that way," he said, pointing, "and he ain't come back. We ain't seen him since."

Chief Coon looked at him with skepticism, his eyes narrowing as he began his inspection. Cabinets were opened and items displaced with a callous disregard, each move like a predator stalking its prey.

Then, without warning, he pulled out his gun and aimed it directly at Rene.

"Where's the boy? Tell me, now!" Chief Coon bellowed.

The pastor focused on his daughter, seeing in her the same resolve he'd once had at her age.

Chief Coon yelled again, louder this time. "Somebody better start talking!"

Pastor TK's heart was beating out of his chest. "She doesn't know, Chief. I wouldn't lie to an officer of the law," he pleaded.

There was a deafening silence as Chief Coon pondered his next move.

"Very well," he said, cocking the hammer on his revolver.

The pastor beseeched him. "Please! I've told you we don't know!"

He dropped to his knees, joined by his wife, then slowly followed by Rene. The police chief stepped closer, placing the gun to Rene's head, letting the threat hang in the air.

"You sure about that, Pastor?" Chief Coon aggressively questioned.

Pastor TK, his wife, and Rene began to pray, their voices shuddering with fear and faith.

After a long moment, the chief finally lowered the gun. "Alright then. Let's pray you're telling the truth."

Seemingly convinced, the chief walked toward the kitchen. "That supper smells good," Chief Coon commented casually, grabbing a piece of meat from the stove before exiting.

The family remained on the floor, enveloped in relief and disbelief.

Once the chief had gone, Rene hugged her father tightly. "Thank you, Daddy," she whispered, her voice choked with gratitude. Her feelings for Luckey were clear; she had been willing to risk everything for him.

The pastor walked out into the backyard to check that nothing looked suspicious. Thankfully, Chief Coon was gone, and the night was quiet again.

TK made his way to the outhouse. Standing there, he lit a cigarette, a habit he hadn't indulged in for a couple of years. He spoke through the wooden door.

"Son, I don't understand what you did tonight, but pretty soon, every cop in this town will be looking for you." He exhaled the smoke slowly. "My daughter sacrificed her life to keep from giving you up. I wanted to tell that cop where he could find you, but she would have rather been shot down than have me hand you over."

Luckey began to cry. "I'm sorry, sir. Can I see her one last time?"

TK pulled a final drag from his cigarette before returning to the house. Moments later, Rene sprinted out and ran directly for the outhouse.

As the pastor stood outside in the background, the distant sound of the train mingled with his thoughts. He knew the police would return, and when they did, they wouldn't let him deflect their interrogation so easily.

Luckey and Rene shared a moment of desperate farewell, their kisses marked by the bitterness of imminent separation.

"I love you, Luckey," Rene whispered, tears streaming down her face.

Luckey smiled through his sorrow. "I thought you didn't want to be my girlfriend, Rene."

She returned the smile and said, "You're right. I wanted to be your wife."

Luckey's heart sank before he replied, "I love you, Nae…" his voice heavy with unspoken promises.

The train's approaching whistle cut through the night, breaking their moment. Pastor TK approached and double-tapped on the outhouse to alert the boy. "It's time, son. You've got a train to catch and a life to live."

The train's whistle grew louder, signaling that Luckey's time in Chicago was quickly coming to an end.

"Luckey," said Rene, "promise me one thing."

He replied, "Anything."

She softly kissed him and said, "Re-create yourself and do something with your music. Use that gift."

He gave Rene one last kiss and said, "I promise."

Rene came out first, while the pastor's head was on a swivel, ensuring nobody had seen her. Luckey attempted to step out as the train approached, but Pastor TK pushed him back in.

"Listen to me, son. Don't forget what I told you. You ride that train until it stops. I think that's Jackson, Mississippi. They treat blacks different down there, so keep your mouth shut and your eyes straight."

Luckey listened closely as Pastor TK continued. "Get into one of them schools and keep learning. Don't ever come back to Chicago; you're not welcome here. You're on the lam now."

Luckey looked confused. "What does that mean, sir?"

The two exchanged an unspoken moment. TK enlightened him, "On the lam means you're on the run from the law, son."

The pastor handed Luckey ten dollars and said, "If anyone asks questions, don't talk; just offer them the money. Remember this: White folk treat you different when you talk good. So when you're jammed up, talk good. If you ain't jammed up, don't talk good—just listen."

He hugged Luckey tightly and added, "Make your daddy proud, boy."

Luckey stepped out of the outhouse, breathing heavily and looking back nervously as he moved along the tracks.

With only ten dollars and his clothes, he stealthily made his way to the train station. He snuck onto the last car and hid among the luggage, his heart pounding as he waited for the train to continue on its way.

As the brakes released with a loud hiss, Luckey understood the depth of his predicament.

"This is it," he whispered as the train began to move.

He was leaving behind his old life, stepping into a world of uncertainty. The train's rumble became the backdrop to his new beginning.

Popping his head up as the train rolled past the outhouse, Luckey caught sight of the pastor and Rene. She was crying on her father's shoulder, while he stood there, silent and still.

TK whispered a prayer for the boy who had become like a son to him.

Just before disappearing into the darkness, Luckey caught one last glimpse of the old man, who tipped his hat in farewell.

# CHAPTER 3:
# UNLIKELY ALLIES

"A person with nothing to lose is always dangerous." — Kristine

The screeching brakes pulled Luckey from his restless slumber. Hidden among the darkness of the luggage car, he felt the train stop after what seemed like an eternity. In reality, it had only been about thirty hours since he left Chicago.

The long journey south, marked by the rhythmic clatter of the tracks and occasional stops, was finally ending.

A porter, grumbling about stowaways, mumbled, "Another darn sneaker," before delivering a sharp kick to Luckey's feet.

"Alright, kid, this is the last stop. Off you go."

Luckey's breath formed a light cloud in the chilly morning air as he stumbled to his feet.

"God, it's cold," he thought, regretting that he'd dismissed his grandmother's warning about the sneaky chill of the season.

Jumping off the train, he landed on the ground, unsure of his exact location but relieved to have finally arrived. The mission to reinvent himself began with an urgent need: find a coat.

His sight fell on a red bench outside the train station, where an old gray-haired Black man sat, hunched against the morning chill.

As Luckey wandered into the station, the idea of a lost and found sparked hope.

Approaching the counter, he was slightly caught off guard to see a Black woman behind it—a rare sight in roles typically dominated by whites.

"I'm looking for my jacket, ma'am. Did anyone turn it in?" he ventured, his voice hopeful.

The woman eyed the beaten boy, skepticism briefly crossing her features. "Could you describe the coat to me?" she asked.

Exhausted from the previous night's ordeal and the lack of food,

Luckey felt a soft shiver permeate his body before he replied, "I believe it was dark blue."

"You believe?" she responded quickly, shooting him a doubtful glance. But seeing the exhaustion and desperation in his demeanor softened her.

"Ah! As a matter of fact, someone did," she said, retrieving a tan coat from the back.

It was snug on Luckey but welcome nonetheless. "Thank you, ma'am. I love this coat," Luckey said, wrapping it around himself to ward off the biting cold.

As he left the counter, Luckey made an observation. The station was bustling, its corridors filled with polite people, mostly Black. It was a stark contrast to the horrors his grandmother and Pastor TK had painted of the South.

He thought back to Pastor TK's advice: "Keep ya eyes straight and ya mouth shut," followed by his grandmother's warning: "Baby, they don't take no sass in the South. You give them white folk all the respect you got." Stories of hate, oppression, and segregation were all that Luckey had heard about the South.

However, the scene before him was different. The station was filled with baggage handlers of various backgrounds slinging luggage and trying to earn a buck. People moved at a slower pace than in the big city he was accustomed to, but this was not the South he had imagined.

The smell of coal upset his stomach, signaling it was time to move on and start his new life.

Stepping into the morning, the cold gnawed through his too-small shirt and new jacket, his nose raw from the razor-like wind. Seeking refuge, Luckey found an alley where warm pipes provided some comfort.

Excited, he sat on the cold concrete, his back against the hard wall. Doubts swirled—how to find food, a place to sleep, and the consequences of his abrupt departure.

"I'm sure Grandma is worried sick," he thought, the pang of guilt sharp against the backdrop of his uncertain future. His heart pounded harder as he continued to fret.

"I have nothing to my name, no money, or even an extra pair of drawers." Leaning his head against the wall, he closed his eyes and began to pray. He was lost in prayer when commotion from afar returned him to reality.

"Stop, you little thief!" a voice bellowed. "You didn't pay for that!"

From a distance, Luckey spotted a chubby kid barreling down the alley, his coat and arms overflowing, items falling with every step.

Momentarily paralyzed by the unfolding chaos, Luckey's long legs became an unforeseen obstacle. In a desperate attempt to evade his pursuer, the boy slipped and crashed, scattering a loaf of bread, sandwich meat, and drinks around them.

Red-faced and panting, the store owner caught up, grabbing the kid by his coat collar and lifting him from the ground.

"Boy! I oughta put something on your little fat ass. You got me all winded!" the cashier huffed, gasping for air.

"Who's your mama? I'm going to tell her you're stealing and let her deal with you, ya hear?"

Luckey looked on in awe as the standoff unfolded in front of him.

The boy, whom Luckey now identified as Chubbs, concocted a quick lie, his voice full of passion.

"I was only stealing this to feed me and my buddy. We don't have any family," Chubbs declared, pointing to Luckey as his "friend."

The words took Luckey by surprise, resonating deeply and thrusting him into an unexpected role.

The store owner could barely talk as he tried to catch his breath.

"If that's your friend," he wheezed, taking a big gulp of air, "then what's his name?"

Luckey hesitated for a moment before replying, "Uhh...Frankie, sir."

The store owner directed his attention to "Frankie" and snapped, "I wasn't talking to you, boy."

Luckey looked back at him and said, "Sorry, sir. I understand, but I'm still hungry."

The older man glared at the two boys in disgust. "Just what this town needs…another pair of thieves."

He snatched the bread and reluctantly tossed them a pack of bologna before turning away. "You two better not come back to my store, or next time, I'm calling the cops!"

The man walked off, muttering to himself and holding his back.

Chubbs turned to Luckey with a mix of curiosity and admiration. "Is your name really Frankie?"

Luckey smirked. "Hell, it is now."

And just like that, an unforeseen alliance was formed, along with a new name for Luckey.

Chubbs quickly accepted Frankie's new identity and asked, "Are you hungry?"

"Yeah, boss. I'm starving. I haven't had anything to eat since I made it to Mississippi," Frankie replied.

Chubbs looked at Frankie strangely. "Mississippi? Are you okay in the head?"

Confused by the questioning, Frankie gave his new friend some context.

"Yeah, Daddy, I couldn't be better," Frankie said confidently. "My uncle put me on this train to come visit my family. He told me to get off when the train stops, so I did."

Chubbs broke out in a roaring laugh, his voice echoing off the surrounding buildings. "Daddy, this ain't Mississippi. You're in New Port, Louisiana."

Frankie felt dizzy with confusion as Chubbs continued to laugh.

"The Jackson stop is four hours away. That's as close as you'll get to Mississippi from here... At least by train. You must have overslept."

Frankie's legs went limp, and he fell back against the wall, his mind racing.

Chubbs kept talking. "This is where the midnight trains come for maintenance and storage. It's literally the last stop."

Frankie's world began to spin. He was more nervous than ever.

"No one can find me here," he thought. "My existence seems destined to fade away. How long before they stop looking for me? How long can I survive?"

His young mind struggled to process what his newfound friend was telling him.

Chubbs touched his arm gently, and Frankie jumped.

"You okay, brother? It's all good here," Chubbs said, his voice soft with reassurance.

"I can tell you one thing," Chubbs continued. "You're much better off here than you would've been in Mississippi. This town is full of all types. It's pretty much all Black with some Creole, Cajuns, and a few whites and Italians hiding out."

Frankie took a deep breath as Chubbs kept talking.

"Our police, clerks, doctors, and musicians are all our people," Chubbs said, his voice brimming with pride.

Frankie's nerves were starting to settle.

"Well, Frankie, you sure as hell ain't in Jackson. I guess this is the right moment to say: welcome to New Port, my boy," Chubbs added with a silly smile.

Frankie interrupted, his tone serious. "Look, Chubbs, I got on that train with the intention of visiting family in Mississippi. I don't have any money for food, clothes, or a place to stay."

Chubbs signaled his understanding with a quick nod.

"Don't worry, Frankie. I got the perfect place. There's a diner I always go to when I'm tight on cash. Follow me."

As they set off toward the diner, Frankie began to sense how New Port might offer the reinvention he sought—albeit not in the way he had imagined.

"So, where are you from?" Chubbs asked, his curiosity barely contained as they walked.

"Up north," Frankie replied in a dull tone.

"Where up north?" Chubbs probed deeper. "I like hearing about new places anytime I meet someone from the outside. Never left New Port myself."

"Detroit," Frankie said, his focus drifting to the horizon as if he could see the city of his past.

Chubbs's smile widened, revealing his teeth. "Detroit, huh? Heard good stories about that place. Hope to see it myself one day."

The distance from Luckey's hometown seemed to stretch further with each step.

"It's a beautiful city. I'm going to miss it," Frankie admitted, his tone somber.

"Miss it?" Chubbs inquired. "You don't plan on going back? Thought you were just visiting family in Mississippi."

Frankie could feel Chubbs's scrutiny, sharp with skepticism and a growing sense of doubt.

"I'm not sure when I'll be back," he said, deflecting. "It was supposed to be a surprise visit, but plans changed. Let's focus on getting to that diner."

Chubbs smiled, pointing ahead. "Relax, city boy. It's right there on the corner."

Entering the diner, Frankie was enveloped by a surprising warmth and sense of community, unusual for such an early hour.

The clink of cutlery against plates and the cheerful ring of the kitchen bell were music to his ears. Patrons engaged in lively conversations, sharing jokes and stories, while a few swayed to the soft tunes of the jukebox, lost in the moment.

Chubbs nudged him, pointing to Kenya, a waitress who moved with a grace and confidence that seemed to capture the spirit of New Port.

"She's beautiful, huh?" Chubbs said, his mouth open as he admired her at work.

Frankie couldn't help but agree. Kenya stood about five foot six, with full hips and lips. Her bronze brown skin had a natural glow, and she moved with effortless confidence, making the boys melt.

As Frankie watched her, he thought back to Rene but quickly reminded himself that life was behind him.

"Kenya!" Chubbs called out, attempting to flirt, but she ignored him.

"Kenya!" he called out again. "I know you heard me."

She huffed and made her way to the table. "Where's my hug, baby?" Chubbs teased.

Kenya replied, putting her wit on full display, "Hug? Ha! That's for paying customers, Woodard."

Frankie interjected, "Woodard?"

Kenya glanced at Frankie. "Yeah, that's his name. Who are you? I haven't seen you around here before."

"This here is my homeboy Frankie. He's from Detroit," Chubbs quickly reinserted himself into the conversation, a hint of pride in his voice.

Kenya showcased a brief flash of interest as she looked at Frankie. He couldn't help but feel the same spark of curiosity and attraction.

Chubbs, noticing the exchange, felt a subtle pang of jealousy but quickly masked it with a smile.

Kenya, still looking at Frankie, asked, "Detroit, huh? What brings you to New Port?"

The moment was ruined by a rude demand slicing through the diner.

"Kenya! Bring your ass on and take my order, goddamnit. I'm hungry!"

The ungracious interruption darkened the mood in the diner, exposing the town's hidden complexities and power struggles. Kenya sighed deeply, her posture deflating.

"I'll be back," she said, her tone laced with resignation.

Frankie, intrigued by the man's audacity, turned to Chubbs.

"Who is that?"

"That's Silky," Chubbs replied with a smirk. "He's a pimp."

Kenya approached Silky's table with a measured stride, her patience wearing thin.

"What's it gonna be, Silky?"

Silky sat there rubbing his hands impatiently. "You alright?" he asked. "You okay? Do you have a fever? What took you so long, baby? I'm gonna lose thirty pounds waiting on you."

Kenya was unamused. "You are so doggone dramatic, Silky. What do you want?"

Silky sat back and crossed his legs, his tone dripping with exaggerated charm. "Well, for starters, I want you to work for me. I told you I can make you way more scratch than this place. What do you say, baby?"

Unimpressed, Kenya replied sharply, "The same thing I always say, nigga… no! Now, are you gonna order or what? I got tables to work."

Silky's deep laugh rang out through the diner obnoxiously, but no one ever confronted him.

"I guess my woman is right; my pimpin ain't what it used to be," he said, elbowing his old lady, Kristine. Leaning back in the chair, he added, "Give me the Cowboy Breakfast and make sure my eggs are like my women: wet."

Kenya shook her head in disgust. "Anything else, Silky?"

He cracked his knuckles, smirking. "That's all for me, but make sure you get my baby whatever she wants. I gotta keep that body nourished."

Kenya gave him a fake smile. "What'll you have, Kristine?"

Kristine replied, "Just my usual: black coffee with an order of flapjacks and extra syrup."

Silky chimed in again, leaning back further in his chair. "Walk off slow, baby, and make sure you bring Kris that ticket. I don't even want to touch it."

As Silky raised his lanky frame from his seat, he sauntered over to the jukebox. "These tunes are weak. I need to hear something I can feel."

Frankie watched with curiosity as Silky slowly pulled a penny from his pocket and inserted it into the machine.

"Kris! Get over here, let's dance," Silky yelled.

Kristine denied the invitation with a dismissive wave. Kenya, eager to return to the boys, shifted her focus to Frankie as soon as Silky turned his attention elsewhere.

"So, you're from Detroit, huh? You a city boy!"

Frankie smirked, his tone smooth and low. "That's right. I'm Detroit's finest."

Kenya blinked slowly, gazing at him. "Is that right? So how did Detroit's finest end up here?"

Frankie rubbed his chin, leaning back slightly. "Long story short, I'm hungry. Got an extra menu?"

Both Chubbs and Kenya shared a simultaneous laugh.

Chubbs enlightened Frankie, "They don't have a menu, Daddy; you got three options: the Cowboy Breakfast, the Texas Steak, or Mama's Gumbo and Fried Chicken."

Frankie said to them, "Some menu."

His snide remark was met with one from Kenya, who quipped, "Well, if you don't like it, just go back to Detroit, city boy."

Frankie relented with a chuckle. "Alright, alright. I guess I'll have—"

Before he could finish, Silky yelled from the dance floor, "Kenya! My lady's coffee is getting cold. Get it together!"

Kenya leaned in close to the boys, her voice low with frustration. "I swear 'fore God, I want to kill him sometimes."

Frankie looked at Kenya, then at Silky, his pride swelling. He wanted to stand up for Kenya, partly to impress her and partly because he couldn't stomach Silky's arrogance.

Gathering his courage, Frankie called out with a firm, resolute voice, "Hey, Daddy! Pipe down! You ain't the only table she's working."

The restaurant fell silent. Every neck twisted, and even the kitchen staff peeked out to watch the commotion unfold.

Silky froze, his face a mask of disbelief. "What the fuck did you just say, little boy? You better stay in a kid's place, son."

Kristine shot up from her seat, quickly heading straight for Silky. She whispered urgently, "Be cool, Silky. Can't you see he's just trying to impress the girl?"

Silky raised his hand to silence her, the light reflecting off his pinky ring.

"Sit yo' ass down, woman! Can't you see two men talking?"

The tension thickened as Silky slowly walked over to Frankie's table, his lanky frame moving deliberately with each step.

"Look here. I'm gonna let you slide because I ain't seen you around here before, and trust me when I say I've seen everybody in this town."

Silky sucked his teeth, leaning over the table as he jabbed a finger at Frankie's chest, sniffing dismissively.

"I can tell you're new around here, and you don't know who the fuck I am."

Frankie immediately stood up, his chest puffed out, retorting, "Don't point your finger at me! And I ain't your son."

Silky laughed quietly to himself, as the restaurant watched the confrontation with bated breath.

"Chubby," Silky drawled, turning his gaze to Chubbs. "Where did you find this nigga? If he wasn't with you, his jaw would already be broken."

Frankie's fury boiled over as he stepped closer to Silky. "Nigga, I'm from Chicago!" he yelled, his voice echoing through the diner.

Kenya and Chubbs exchanged bewildered glances. Kenya's brow shot up in surprise while Chubbs scratched his head, both clearly taken aback by Frankie's sudden revelation.

Frankie pressed on, undeterred. "You ain't nothing but a smooth-talking wanna-be pimp. My Uncle Bubba done pimped more hos than you'll ever meet in yo life."

Silky's jaw tightened, his eyes narrowing at the audacity. Internally, he was floored by the boy's courage. Externally, he maintained his composure, knowing that appearance was everything.

With a swift motion, Silky cocked his right hand, poised to strike Frankie.

Before the blow could land, Chubbs forced his way between them. "Listen, Silky, it's all good, Daddy. He's new around here. Let us talk to him."

Kenya also rushed to Frankie's defense, her voice firm. "He's right, Silky—let us talk to him."

Silky's stare was intense, but the young bull didn't flinch. Frankie met the older man's eyes with unwavering defiance until Silky finally looked away, a smirk curling on his lips.

"Yeah, talk to him," Silky said, his tone dripping with condescension. "Judging by them little-ass clothes and those scars, it looks like you came from Chicago broke and beaten. Ha!"

The room seemed to hold its breath as Silky's words hung in the air. Frankie's fists clenched, his body tense but unyielding, as a simmering silence settled over the diner.

Chubbs and Kenya quickly stepped in, steering Frankie back into the booth. Their voices dropped to hushed tones, urgency thick in their whispers.

"You must wanna meet God!" Chubbs began, his eyes darting around the room as though even the walls might overhear. "Nobody has ever stood up to Silky, and I think that's for good reason. Don't do that again, Frankie."

Kenya leaned in closer, her voice sharp. "Some things you just don't do here. Not only is he a pimp, he's a gangster and the biggest bootlegger in the city."

Their stern expressions bore into Frankie as Kenya snapped her fingers in his face, breaking the heavy silence.

"Are you listening?" she demanded, her tone leaving no room for argument.

"Yeah," Frankie replied, his aggression softening into a determined resolve. "I don't have a history with this guy, and he won't intimidate me. Look, I came here with nothing. No family, no friends, no money. I got nothing to lose," he declared, his voice thick with emotion. "So excuse me for standing up to some aging pimp who thinks he can run over me. Hell, you guys really saved him from me!" Frankie clamped his mouth shut, his expression hardening into a mask of defiance.

Meanwhile, in a secluded corner of the diner, Silky sat visibly shaken, venting his frustration to Kristine.

"Can you believe that little nigga?" he seethed, his anger bubbling over. "He thinks he can step to me! I keep telling you, these young guns have lost respect!"

He pounded the table, causing the plates to shake. "I'd be dead right now if I ever bucked Sweet like that."

Kristine met his outburst with a neutral expression, her response calm and measured. "Calm down, baby."

But Silky was far from calm. "I'm Silky! I ain't been stepped to since I put something on Busta Brown's ass back in Clarksdale," he spat, the cracks in his untouchable facade showing for the first time.

Frustration took hold as Silky suddenly yelled, "These motherfuckin tunes are weak! And these eggs ain't wet!"

With a sharp slap, he sent the plate flying, eggs scattering across the diner. The room froze, all eyes turning toward him. Silky tried to pull himself together, straightening his shirt as he grumbled, "I need to play some shit I can feel! Some shit to calm my nerves. That joker got me spun up."

He smoothed his demeanor and stood, exhaling slowly. "I'm good. I'm Silky, baby."

Kristine didn't flinch. "That's right," she replied with a small smile. "Play something slow for me, Silk."

Attempting to regain his composure, Silky approached the jukebox with deliberate calmness, selecting a slow song to soothe the storm within. "I need to calm down," he murmured, his agitation still evident. As the gentle music filled the diner, a temporary peace seemed to settle over the room.

"Join me, baby. I need a slow drag," Silky called out to Kristine, his voice low and inviting. She obliged, and the two began to sway rhythmically to the easy tunes. The melody cast a soothing spell over the diner, but beneath the surface, Silky's thoughts still churned.

"I just can't believe this…" he murmured, his mind replaying Frankie's bold defiance.

"Stop, Silky. Just dance," Kristine urged, her voice soft, pulling him back into the moment.

Guided by the music, Silky's movements became poetry in motion. Fingers clasped in Kristine's, he glided across the dance floor with a smooth shuffle, his feet barely brushing the ground. Shifting his weight to his heels, he spun effortlessly, his toes pointing toward the sky in an elegant arc.

With each step, his right foot swept in front of his back like a skater on ice, his motions fluid and seamless. The cool breeze wafting through the room seemed to move with them, enhancing the tranquil ambiance.

Catching the rhythm, Silky chuckled, his voice tinged with both pride and nostalgia. "See, this here is wine and caviar, baby. How these young boys dance is more like beer and pizza."

She smiled and laid her head on his shoulder, seizing the opportunity to offer wisdom. "You know… how many people have ever stood up to you? Maybe it's time to see this from a different angle."

To Kristine, Frankie's boldness wasn't mere insolence; it was a sign of raw, untamed courage. "His judgment is off, Silk," she added. "That's a sign of youth. Plus, look at how little his clothes are. It's clear he doesn't have anything. A person with nothing to lose is always dangerous."

Silky dipped Kristine mid-dance, her words clearly landing. She could tell she was getting through to him, his resistance softening as he considered her perspective.

"The fat one clearly has his back," Kristine noted, observing Chubbs's unwavering loyalty. Silky exhaled deeply, his mind drifting to Chubbs's past. "I know that fat one. His mom wouldn't trick for me; she had smarts," Silky reflected somberly, a rare flicker of empathy in his voice. "It's tragic how it all ended for her."

Pulling Kristine tightly into his arms, Silky's tone shifted. "You might be on to something, Kris. Perhaps there's a way to leverage this courage to our advantage."

Kristine leaned in closer, her voice pragmatic. "Think about it, Silky. You're in need of some help, and those two could certainly use the cash."

Meanwhile, Kenya returned to the booth where Frankie and Chubbs sat, her irritation evident. Tasked with cleaning up Silky's mess, she sighed heavily.

"I've got to take care of Silky's crap first. I'll sneak your order in afterward," she announced, her tone weary.

As she walked away, Frankie leaned in to whisper to Chubbs, his skepticism clear. "Is she really going to help us after all this?"

Chubbs nodded reassuringly. "Kenya might be rattled, but she won't let us down. She's one of us. She doesn't really have anybody or anywhere to go."

His voice dropped lower as he continued. "She hates this place. She only works here because the old man who runs the joint knew her uncle. He pays her pennies but lets her keep the tips."

Frankie listened intently, a newfound trust forming as Chubbs shared Kenya's story.

"One of us?" Frankie thought, the phrase stirring something within him—a flicker of belonging he hadn't felt since his arrival.

But his skepticism lingered. Frankie's eyes narrowed slightly as he studied Chubbs, trying to piece together his motives. "What's his angle?" he wondered silently, the question nagging at him even as he nodded along.

Chubbs, gathering his courage, ventured into more personal territory. "Frankie, I need to ask you something, and I hope you'll hear me out." His voice trembled slightly, revealing the depth of his vulnerability.

Frankie nodded. "Shoot. At this point, you can ask me anything."

Chubbs sighed deeply, his eyes fixed on the table. "I don't like being lied to, man. I can't take it. When my mom killed herself..."

"Killed herself?" Frankie interjected, his tone a mix of shock and concern.

Chubbs held up a finger, signaling for patience. "Yeah, but let me finish," he said, his voice tightening with emotion. "My mom's death... it left scars. My dad, he was a monster to her, to me. He used to beat her—bad."

Frankie, unable to contain his reaction, interrupted again. "Beat her?"

Chubbs's jaw clenched, his frustration bubbling to the surface. "Yes! Beat her," he said sharply, his voice quivering with restrained anger. "And then, one day, she just... couldn't take it anymore."

As Frankie parted his lips to ask another poorly timed question, Chubbs slammed his hands on the table, the sound reverberating through the diner. "I ain't done yet! Let me finish my story, Frankie!" His voice was firm, almost pleading, as the room momentarily stilled, all eyes on them.

Startled, Frankie froze, his tone turning careful. "Chill, Daddy. I'm back quiet."

From across the room, Silky's booming voice cut through the tension. "You two need to pipe down. I'm trying to eat."

Chubbs's shoulders stiffened, but he refused to let the moment slip away. Without looking at Silky, he said curtly, "We're cool, Silky. Just leave it."

In the early morning light of the diner, Chubbs began to share his tale of loss and betrayal. "My mom never came to get me. She killed my no-good daddy, then killed herself." Tears crawled down his face. "My grandmother lied to me about it for months." The revelation underscored the pain that had silently shaped him. "Ever since that day, if I feel like I'm being lied to or find out I was lied to, I lose control and blackout," he admitted, revealing the raw scars of his past to Frankie, his newfound confidante.

Frankie looked to Chubbs for permission to speak, wondering if Chubbs was done with his story. "Damn. That's heavy, brother," Frankie said softly. "I really appreciate you sharing that with me." Frankie took a moment to absorb Chubbs's words before continuing. "But I have to ask, what does that have to do with what you wanna know from me?" he inquired, navigating the delicate balance between curiosity and respect.

Chubbs's stare, steadfast and piercing, sought the truth from Frankie. "Are you from Chicago or Detroit, Frankie? And why are you really here?"

Frankie's heart raced as he contemplated his next words. He felt torn between the urge to conceal the truth and the desire to honor the trust Chubbs had shown by sharing his own story.

"I'm from Chicago, Wood," Frankie began, hoping for a genuine connection. "I came down because I got into it with the law, and before I knew it…"

His confession, however, was cut short by an unexpected interruption.

Kenya returned to Frankie and Chubbs, her demeanor noticeably upbeat. "Silky's covering your meal," she announced, her voice carrying an undertone of surprise. "He said to order whatever you want."

Chubbs couldn't contain his joy, his gratitude resonating loudly in the diner. "Thanks, Silky! That's real smooth, Daddy."

Frankie, however, remained cautious. "Thanks, but what's this gonna cost me? My daddy always told me there's no such thing as a free meal."

Silky didn't immediately answer the question but moved toward their table with a panther-like stride. "That's one hell of a question, kid. I actually respect it," Silky admitted, his voice carrying an unexpected warmth.

"Today ain't gonna cost you nothing, but tomorrow is a different story," he continued, locked with Frankie in unspoken understanding.

"But let me tell you something," Silky added, leaning in slightly. "I don't give a fuck if you eat or not, but Kristine," he said, motioning toward her, "cared enough to persuade me to offer. The choice is yours. Don't let that little pride of yours starve you." Silky conceded, offering a glimpse into his complex character.

Chubbs broke first. "Kenya, I'm hungry as hell. I'll have the Cowboy Breakfast with a side of chicken and a swimming pool of sweet tea."

Frankie looked at Chubbs and said, "Damn, Wood, you're going to run up a ticket in front of the man. Have some class."

Silky smirked at Frankie's etiquette before adding, "If you two need anything, you know my name. I'm not hard to find."

After their conversation, Silky did a smooth skip away from the table, which was right on beat with the music playing from the jukebox. The song happened to be one of Frankie's favorites. As Silky continued to walk away, Frankie called out, his tone balancing humor and seriousness. "Hey, Slick! What do you know about this tune?"

Silky did an about-face on his heel and gave Frankie a cautionary look before he commented. "Don't misjudge my southern hospitality for weakness—it's Silky. Don't ever misspeak that again."

Frankie could tell it was time for him to stop poking the bear. "Sorry, Silky," he said, "That's one of my favorite records. I love to play it."

"Play it?" Silky said.

Frankie replied, "Yeah, I play, Daddy. I tickle the keys. What's it to you?"

Silky felt a passing curiosity and a quiet intrigue about how Frankie might fit into his plans. "Are you any good?" Silky inquired.

Frankie confidently responded, "Rest my daddy's soul. He said I'll be the next Duke Ellington."

Frankie's claim was met with laughter as Silky attempted to belittle Frankie's dream. "Son, you have heart and confidence; I'll give you that... But you ain't gonna be no damn Duke Ellington. You wouldn't need me to buy your food if you were that good."

Frankie rose to his feet. "I'm serious! I can prove it; I stroke the keys!"

Silky couldn't resist and looked at Kenya. "Bring these two by the house later tonight. I got an old grand I used to stroke back in the day. Let's see what all this 'Duke' talk is about," Silky proposed.

The hours seemed to blur together after their eventful morning at the diner. Frankie and Chubbs spent the afternoon exploring New Port, sharing stories and getting to know each other better. As the sun dipped below the horizon and the evening settled in, the chill of the night air wrapped around them once more. They returned to the diner to meet Kenya and then made their way to Silky's place. Their camaraderie had only grown stronger throughout the day, and Kenya noticed.

"You two are best friends now. How cute," she teased.

Frankie replied, "No reason to be jealous, Kenya. You're one of the guys, too."

Kenya shot back, "No thanks. I don't know if you two are bright enough for me to hitch my wagon."

The group erupted in laughter, the sound carrying through the chilly evening air.

Reaching Silky's doorstep, the trio paused, absorbing the moment's tranquility. Frankie stepped forward and knocked on the door, the sound echoing softly in the quiet night. Silky greeted them, his demeanor softened by the intimacy of his home. Inside, his record collection—reflecting his life's journey—drew Frankie in, each album a story waiting to be told.

"These are some heavy hitters," Frankie marveled at the impeccable condition of the records.

Silky basked in the praise. "I've just lived more life than you. Keep living; yours will be ten times better than mine." He made his way to the living area and seated himself regally among his eclectic decor. Silky reached for a slim joint of reefer he called "gangsta." Striking a match, he lit it with a steady hand, took a long drag, and exhaled the smoke in a slow, deliberate stream.

"I respect you," Silky said to Frankie, ashing the stick. "I don't let people know where I stay, and you need to keep it that way." Frankie felt a wave of strength and assurance flow through his body. Silky continued, "If you can stand up to me, you can stand up to anybody. Make yourselves comfortable. I want to hear you play… Duke."

As they settled in, soft music filled the air. In this moment, Frankie and Kenya found themselves caught in a delicate and revealing conversation. "What's the deal with you and Chubbs?" Frankie asked, his voice casual but laced with curiosity.

Kenya sighed, her eyes briefly darting to the side. "I've known Chubbs has liked me for years, but the feelings have never been reciprocated." Her hesitation lingered before she added, "But I like you." Her confession hung in the air, complex and vulnerable.

Frankie, despite the weight of her words, leaned in for a kiss, drawn by the undeniable connection between them. Just as their lips met, Kristine entered the room. "Am I interrupting?" she asked, her voice sharp but laced with intrigue. "Silky's looking for you."

Frankie and Kenya quickly straightened up, exchanging flustered glances before returning to the living room, now rejoined by Chubbs. Silky was seated, exuding authority and anticipation. "Alright, kid, let's hear it. I'm tired of you stalling."

As the final notes from the record player faded into the background, all attention turned to Frankie. He sat at the grand piano and began to play, but the notes lacked the fire he had claimed to possess. The group exchanged awkward glances, the room heavy with an uncomfortable silence. Frankie's nerves were running wild. He looked down at his hands twitching over the keys, his confidence dwindling with every uninspired note.

Silky's eyes narrowed, his patience thinning but his curiosity still alive. "Kristine," he called, "chill two shots of moonshine." She moved swiftly, returning moments later with the drinks.

Silky looked at Frankie and held up the shot. "Relax," he said with a knowing smile. Silky threw the shot back effortlessly, and Frankie followed suit. The fiery liquid hit his throat, causing his nostrils to flare and his face to twist in discomfort.

"Now, let's try that again, Duke," Silky said, his tone a mix of challenge and encouragement.

Frankie took a deep breath, the warmth of the moonshine settling his nerves. He placed his hands back on the keys, ready to prove himself.

The room filled with a blend of soulful melodies and energetic rhythms. Frankie's fingers danced across the keys, effortlessly shifting between different styles of music. The small group couldn't help but move to the beat as Frankie wailed and scatted, his voice weaving in and out of the music.

He was performative, playing with one hand, shaking his head, and fanning himself with his other hand, fully immersed in his own world of sound. The group was speechless; the boy was a star.

Silky immediately promised: "I'm getting you a residency in town. You are starting tomorrow." Within the hour, the talks went from vague concepts to a concrete plan, marking the beginning of another new chapter for Frankie.

As the night went on, Frankie could no longer control his tongue.

He began recounting his past to Silky, Kristine, Kenya, and Chubbs. "I'm on the lam, and to be honest… I'm here looking for redemption. I want to be something. I want to prove to myself that I can do it." Silky was moved by Frankie's openness and talent. He decided to extend an offer of housing.

"You know," Silky began, "I almost didn't come to the diner this morning. And now I'm offering you a place to stay. God has a funny way of connecting us with the people we need when we need them most." Silky went on, "I'll help you get on your feet, and you'll help me with a few things."

Frankie looked around the room, seeing the supportive faces of his newfound friends, and felt a surge of hope. Silky extended his hand, a gesture that Frankie countered. "One condition," Frankie said, his voice steady. Silky gave him an inquisitive look. "Are you really negotiating when you don't have a place to sleep?" Frankie met Silky's regard without flinching. "If Chubbs can't stay, I can't stay." The room fell silent, Frankie's words hanging in the air. Silky studied Frankie for a moment, eventually relenting. "I'll make it work, but you two have to earn your keep."

Frankie's resolve didn't waver as he shook Silky's hand, solidifying their new arrangement. This was the first time he stood up for Chubbs, and the significance of that act was not lost on anyone in the room. As the night drew to a close, Frankie, Chubbs, and Kenya found themselves laid out in the basement, their laughter and fatigue blending into the early hours. A bond was forged in that moment, setting the stage for a future none of them could have imagined.

# CHAPTER 4

# TURNING THE PAGE

"The road is fast, and it will swallow you whole." — Frankie

Dec 31, 1940

As the evening unfolded, the once unassuming house in New Port transformed into a grand spectacle of glamour. Two stone-carved lions sat majestically on platforms, flanking the winding driveway that disappeared behind a line of mature trees. The meticulously groomed lawn, a masterpiece of precision, seamlessly blended with dramatic statues that seemed to capture motion in their abstract forms.

From hidden speakers nestled in the bushes, a smooth tune whispered through the evening, blending with the scent of cashmere amber and inviting guests into Frankie's world. This secluded yet opulent setting became a gathering hub for the social elite, a scene echoing exclusivity and allure.

Stepping inside, guests were greeted by careful curation and unabashed luxury. Marble accents and heavy, ornate furniture filled the expansive rooms, attended to by a diligent staff that anticipated every whim. The guest list read like a who's who of the time—judges mingling with Mob bosses, accountants alongside madams, and club owners conversing with activists, some of whom were fugitives in their own right.

The gathering celebrated the twenty-ninth birthday of jazz prodigy and bandleader Frankie Keys, showcasing his growing influence that now stretched far beyond the Mason-Dixon Line.

Amid the chaos, a shiny red pickup truck gleamed under the streetlights as a tall, quirky man stepped onto the curb. With a quick motion, he pulled a handkerchief from his pocket and scrubbed his teeth, using the car window to inspect his reflection. "You look like a soldier!" he declared.

As he composed himself, his eyes caught two admiring women nearby. He approached them with an easy confidence, the kind that comes from familiarity. "After you, beautiful ladies," he said, holding the door open.

One of the women blushed. "Aww, thank you! What's your name, and how do you know Frankie?"

He smiled broadly. "Aren't you inquisitive? I'm Doctor Williams, and I'd say Frankie and I are good friends. You two have a lovely night."

With that, he stepped into the house, where his arrival sparked an immediate exchange with Bell, the wife of the illustrious homeowner.

"How about it, Bell? You look gorgeous as always. Where's that husband of yours?"

She offered a wry smile. "He's around here somewhere, getting dressed or still sleeping." Rolling her eyes, she added, "He and the boys had a late night, so he's a little, how shall I say…hungover."

Dr. Williams let out a deep belly laugh. "That doggone, Frankie. That joker loves to party." He shook his head, still grinning. "I got my stuff in the truck; I'll help whip him back into shape."

Bell's expression softened, and she smiled with a sigh of relief. "Thank you, Doctor," she said sincerely.

As Dr. Williams began to walk away, Bell called after him. "Oh Doctor...Just so you know, Frankie's about to go on tour in a few months. He's been putting off his check-up, claiming he feels fine."

Dr. Williams paused, stroking his mustache thoughtfully. "He hasn't mentioned it, but I'll speak with him and have my secretary schedule something."

Bell adjusted her hair, her voice soft but insistent. "Please do... What are you drinking, Doctor? I'll have it sent to the Cashmere Room— you'll probably find Frankie there."

The doctor smirked, his charm ever-present. "Anything stiff!"

Their exchange carried an unspoken loyalty, a bond that underscored their shared determination to protect Frankie at all costs.

Bell lingered near the threshold, observing the arriving guests as she calmly tracked the headcount in her mind. Each name and face registered effortlessly, a skill honed through years of hosting.

Her concentration broke as a deep, familiar voice spoke from behind. "Counting heads again?" The teasing warmth in the tone drew a smile to her lips.

Turning, she faced Chubbs. Once the pudgy kid of their circle, his frame was now solid, his strength evident in the broad set of his shoulders. He carried himself with an easy confidence to go along with his rugged handsomeness.

"Yes, Chubbs, I am. Is that okay with you?" Bell replied, her voice dripping with sarcasm.

"It's your house—do what you want. But you know nothing will ever happen to Frankie here, right?"

Bell continued counting, her tone sharp. "You're right. It is my house." Her features softened slightly as she added, "And since it's my house, I have a task for you. Fix Doctor Williams a drink. He's in the Cashmere Room trying to resurrect Frankie from the depths of whatever you all got into last night."

Chubbs's laughter boomed, filling the space between them. "That's gonna be quite the mission. Frankie's been in and out all day."

Bell's retort came quick, her words playful but edged. "And who's to blame for that, Woodard?"

Chubbs threw his hands up in mock defense. "Whoa, don't put that shit on me."

She snapped back without missing a beat. "Yes, it is on you! I'm the one stuck entertaining our… eclectic guests… while you and Frankie sneak off for your usual late-night mischief."

Chubbs rubbed his forehead, shaking his head with exaggerated exasperation. "You know what? I don't have time for this." Adjusting his collar, he added with a dramatic southern drawl, "I best get to fixin' dat drank, Miss!"

Bell put on a sarcastic smile, her voice sugar-coated but pointed. "Don't get cute, Wood."

Their lighthearted banter was abruptly ended by the shrill ring of the telephone. Chubbs excused himself, his stride confident as he moved to answer the call, leaving Bell to her thoughts.

"Hello, Wood speaking," Chubbs's deep voice echoed as he answered. The line crackled before Jimmie's hesitant voice emerged, stumbling over his words. "Uhhh… Shit. Hey, it's Jimmie. For Frankie."

Chubbs scoffed. "Well, you got me. Talk."

The conversation that followed was evasive. "Listen, Chubbs… I've been thinking 'bout you guys. Good things, ya know. But, uh, tell Frankie I can't make it tonight. Things are… crazy."

Chubbs's patience wore to a thread. "Frankie needed you here, Jimmie. He said you two had important business to discuss. Now you're bailing?"

Jimmie couldn't complete a sentence as his nerves continued to unravel. "I, uh… I'll have to tell you about it. Tell him happy birthday from me, won't you? And sing him a good tune for me."

Chubbs was fuming with anger as he replied, "Jimmie! Frankie told you a month ago…"

Jimmie interrupted, desperation creeping into his voice. "Hey, pal. Man, I'm really sorry, but I gotta go." His excuses grew increasingly absurd, and his stutters were a telltale sign of his desperation to escape the call. "I…uh, gotta go, man. My fish—yeah, my fish needs to use the phone."

The absurdity of Jimmie's excuse was not lost on Chubbs, who could barely contain his frustration. "Jimmie! What the fuck are you talking about?"

"I really can't hear you that good anymore. This wire is crap. I'll have to call you back, brother. Alright, I'll call you back. Ahh, 'kay, ok-ok."

Chubbs screamed, "Don't you dare hang up—"

But it was too late. The line went dead, leaving Chubbs staring at the receiver.

Chubbs forcefully hung up the phone, his frustration bubbling over into a curse. "I don't like that guy! Fuck!" He took a deep breath, trying to steady himself. With simmering irritation, he meticulously prepared the drink. By the time he returned to Bell, his earlier laughter had faded, replaced by a cloud of unease.

Ever perceptive, Bell noticed the shift in Chubbs's demeanor. "Want to talk about it?" she offered, her voice calm and laced with concern.

Despite his initial reluctance, Chubbs found himself opening up. "That was Jimmie. It's just... I still don't trust him. I think he's up to something."

Bell frowned, her brow creasing as her intuition aligned with his suspicions. "Follow your gut... Don't trust Jimmie. Everyone around town knows he's a fraud and a forger."

Her words landed with weight, confirming what Chubbs had already known deep down.

The night, which had started as a celebration, was overshadowed by unspoken friction. Chubbs leaned in and kissed Bell on the cheek—a gesture of gratitude for her listening ear. He then proceeded to the room, gently knocking before entering. "Frankie?" he said, his voice carrying into the spacious room.

"Come on," Frankie responded from near the window, where he stood half-dressed, deep in conversation with Dr. Williams.

Chubbs approached, handing the drink to the doctor. "Bell said this was for you."

Dr. Williams accepted the glass with a glint of anticipation. "Ah, yes. Just what the doctor ordered," he remarked, a smile tugging at the corners of his mouth as he savored the first sip.

"Glad for the drink, but I'm even happier I ran into Bell earlier.

Heard you're hitting the road?"

Chubbs stiffened slightly, an exposed look flashing across his face, as though the secret had slipped out. "I'm headed back to the party. I'll leave you guys to it."

The doctor's inquiry seemed casual, but there was an unmistakable undercurrent of concern in his tone. Taking another sip, he added, "Surely you planned to swing by the office first?"

Frankie sought to deflect the conversation. "Doc, it's the night before my birthday. I'm not in the mood for that medical talk right now." His voice held a mixture of weariness and avoidance, a sign of the burdens he carried. Taking a deep gulp of water, he shifted the focus. "Right now, I just need to shake off this hangover."

Recognizing the unspoken plea, Dr. Williams gave a subtle gesture of agreement: "As you wish, Frankie." His tone was gentle, mixing professional concern with personal care.

After the doctor finished treating Frankie's hangover, Frankie promised, "I'll swing by your office, Doc. I'll let you test my state of mind and my nerves since you keep hounding me about it."

Just then, Bell breezed into the room, urgency in her step. "Are you ready? Your 'little' party is starting to come alive."

With a mock frown, Frankie quipped, "Little? You've seen the guest list. And wasn't this shindig your grand idea?" He continued teasingly, "Need I remind you, I wanted something small and quaint. You were the one who pushed for this grand affair—not just to celebrate, but to stir the pot and watch the sparks fly."

His tone carried a playful edge, acknowledging Bell's pivotal role in orchestrating the evening's grandeur.

Bell and Frankie descended the staircase, the open walkway ensuring all eyes were on them as they entered the party. The crowd's whispers swelled into a chorus of admiration and anticipation, their presence commanding the room's attention.

Their grand entrance had barely concluded when an eager couple, close friends of Bell, approached with a gift in hand. Just as they began to exchange greetings, a pair of fans, driven by their enthusiasm, rudely pushed past the couple. One of them, grinning ear to ear, exclaimed to Frankie, "Hey! You're Frankie Keys! Your last record turned me every way but loose. You're a legend!"

Bell's eyes narrowed slightly as the fans gushed over Frankie, her displeasure at the disruption evident in the subtle squint. The moment weighed on her nerves as a caterer appeared at her side, urgently seeking direction amid the growing chaos. With a resigned sigh, Bell stepped away, leaving Frankie to bask in his admirers' praise as she turned her attention back to the demands of the evening.

As Frankie attempted to extricate himself from the persistent praise, Kenya swept in with a perfectly timed intervention. "Gentlemen, my apologies for the interruption. Frankie, there's an urgent matter that requires your attention."

Grateful for the escape, Frankie offered a polite smile as he excused himself. "I'm sorry that I can't chat longer. Enjoy the party, and thank you for your support."

Kenya's deft maneuver created a brief reprieve, giving Frankie a moment to catch his breath amid the swirling celebration. Her quick interference reflected their unspoken bond, a seamless give-and-take that kept the night flowing smoothly.

Frankie's voice, low and suggestive, broke the silence. "Let's sneak off. I wanna see you beyond this dress."

Kenya's smile was warm but carried a trace of sadness, a subtle acknowledgment of their complex relationship. "Let's focus on getting through the night. And besides, your wife is right across the room. Let's not complicate things more than they already are." Her tone hinted at the deeper entanglements of their long-term affair. She added pointedly, "As if continuing to sleep together doesn't complicate things enough."

Frustration flared in Frankie's voice. "After all we've done, tonight is where you draw the line?"

Kenya's response was firm, a reminder of the reality they shared. "I value what we have, Frankie, but I'm not here for your flattery—tonight, that's a privilege reserved for your wife."

Frankie sighed, the weight of her words settling heavily. "Why even bring that up?"

Unyielding, Kenya pressed on, her voice steady but edged with resolve. "Just because you shower me with jewelry and take me to nice places doesn't mean I'm confused about what this is. At the end of it all, I know I'm just your late night."

From a distance, Bell observed the interaction with discernment. Tonight, her role extended beyond that of a mere host; she was the guardian of their collective image, ensuring the evening's success while deftly navigating the undercurrents of her husband's indiscretions. She watched Frankie and Kenya for a moment before she turned back to the swirl of guests, her mind always calculating, always a step ahead in preserving their social standing.

As Frankie pondered his conversation with Kenya, his choices settled heavily on his shoulders. The thrill of the night, music, and adoration all faded into the background as he considered the future. He reflected on the unsustainable nature of his affair with Kenya and the conflicting roles he had taken on.

For all its glamour, the night was a tightrope walk of appearances, desires, and obligations. Caught between two worlds represented by Kenya's spontaneity and Bell's consistency, Frankie found himself at a crossroads. As the evening unfolded, the trio navigated their shared space with caution and abandon, fully aware of the delicate balance upon which Frankie's happiness and image hinged.

The evening wore on, with each new interaction that Frankie navigated adding to the night's complexity. The room filled with new faces and clinking shot glasses. Yet, Frankie's mind was full of complex thoughts, momentarily anchored by each handshake and fake smile.

During a rare moment of quiet reflection, Frankie's thoughts were abruptly interrupted by Judge Kincaid's commanding presence. His voice, a distinctive blend of Creole and Southern accents, cut through the haze of the evening. "Frankie? Right?" he inquired, emerging from the assembly with an assertiveness that seemed to part the crowd before him.

Kincaid, the epitome of ambition, was poised to succeed Judge DuPont—a long-standing ally on Frankie's intricate payroll and a vital cog in his network of influence. Yet, whispers swirled that Kincaid's aspirations extended far beyond the modest ambitions of his predecessor. Power, control, and wealth—he pursued them with a relentless hunger that was impossible to ignore.

As they exchanged greetings, Frankie couldn't shake the weight of realization. Maintaining his influence over the judge's seat would be far more challenging than he had anticipated.

This pas de deux was abruptly disrupted by the arrival of Silky and Kristine. Time seemed to have frozen for Kristine—her beauty untouched by the years—while Silky leaned heavily on a polished wooden cane, more for show than necessity. Over the last decade, Silky's outlook on life had shifted, though not entirely. He was still a pimp, but only because it was the profession he had dedicated his life to. In his mind, it was too late to turn back, and his stubborn pride wouldn't allow it.

"A pimp that has pimped as long as I've been pimping has to pimp until his last breath," Silky often liked to say.

His entrance carried that same intensity. Silky's voice boomed across the room. "Frankie! What do you say, Nephew! You got some high-profile suits up in here tonight," he called, his grin wide and greedy.

Leaning toward Kristine, he lowered his voice. "Go get them girls and tell them it's time to eat."

Kristine slipped away without a word, her movements a soft whisper against the lively backdrop of the party.

Frankie, turning to the judge with a small shrug, offered a polite apology. "You'll have to excuse my uncle. He can be a bit brash at times."

On a mission, Silky made his way over to Frankie. Watching the two was like a comparative study in poise. Where Frankie was polished and tightly restrained, Silky embodied unfiltered passion and urgency.

"Frankie, ditch this square. We need to talk," Silky slurred, his stance defiant.

Frankie's frustration simmered beneath the surface. "Silk, not now. I'm networking," he hissed, a plea for understanding evident in his voice. He then turned briefly to Judge Kincaid. "Excuse me for a moment, please," he said with a practiced smile.

The judge returned the smile, though it was clearly forced. "Of course. Take your time."

Satisfied with the judge's response, Frankie stepped aside, positioning himself more privately with Silky.

Silky, however, was undeterred. His tone turned scornful. "Oh, I see how it is… You forget about your people for these suits." He didn't pause, his words flowing with a biting rhythm. "He must be some big shot to make you forget about two hundred and forty-six years of slavery."

Scoffing, Silky gave Frankie a pointed look. "What's with all this pulling me to the side shit? Acting like I'm interrupting, like I'm embarrassing you. I ain't doing nothing but being Silky, baby!"

Frankie remained stern. "Silk! You need to chill." He made a subtle gesture with his head toward Kincaid. "That's the new judge."

The revelation caused a shift in Silky. His earlier bravado dissolved into calculated curiosity. "That's him?" he mused, his tone a mix of intrigue and caution. "I heard he's not cheap. But everyone has a price."

Seizing the shift in mood, Frankie saw a chance to tactfully divert

Silky, especially as the judge's growing impatience became apparent. Leaning in, he teased, "I heard something earlier that you won't believe. Red has been boasting that he's the only dice shooter to fear, claiming you've lost your edge."

Frankie let the words hang in the air, watching as Silky's expression shifted. Sensing the hook, he continued, "His words, not mine. He's so confident that he's willing to bet anything. Anything!" The emphasis carried weight, igniting Silky's competitive spirit.

Silky's reaction was instantaneous. "He said *what?*" Disbelief spilled from his mouth as he quickly took the bait. "You need me for something, nephew? I've got a young gun to school. Seems the end of the rainbow is right over there." He jabbed a finger toward Mississippi Red.

Frankie chuckled, keeping the tone light. "Silk, take it easy on him, will ya? I'm letting him perform tonight. That's the young cat I've been thinking about taking on the road."

The mention of Mississippi Red performing sparked recognition in Silky's eyes. "Oh yeah, I remember now." A grin spread across his face as he straightened his cane. "Let me go break him in and test his mettle. I'll give you a full report afterward," he declared, already moving toward his target.

Frankie quickly pivoted his attention back to Judge Kincaid, who had unintentionally witnessed the quiet exchange. The judge's irritation was palpable, his patience evidently worn thin by the evening's unpredictabilities.

"Let me apologize for that, Judge," Frankie said, his voice laced with remorse and charm.

The judge responded with a tight, insincere smile before turning his back to Frankie and making his way toward the door. Frankie caught up quickly, matching the judge's pace. "I hope the evening hasn't been too much of a bother," he added, his tone light but intent.

"Just the usual circus, I suppose," the judge replied, his irritation still evident. But as Frankie persisted, Judge Kincaid's demeanor began to soften. "Frankie, my boy," he said, his voice carrying the weight of wisdom and experience. "I've seen my share of lively nights, and the old judge still loves them. But I reckon it's time I head out. Better to leave too early than too late."

As they stepped outside, Frankie seized the moment to broach a topic of mutual interest. His tone was measured and cautious. "Judge, I hoped we might discuss a little business before you go. Something that could benefit us both," he ventured, his words carefully chosen to spark the judge's interest without overstepping.

The judge, however, stopped in his tracks and turned to face Frankie with a look that blended mentorship with reprimand. "Son," he said, his voice filled with arrogance, "I never discuss business after I've had a drink, especially not with all these people around. That's a lesson best learned early—it saves you from a world of regret."

Before Frankie could respond, a familiar figure approached, interrupting the moment between the two men. Detective Marlow arrived, as if synchronized with the unpredictable rhythm of the evening.

"Frankie, I couldn't pass through without stopping to wish you a happy birthday," Marlow announced, his tone light.

"Much appreciated, Marlow. I didn't expect to see you tonight," Frankie replied, his smile genuine.

Judge Kincaid, observing the exchange, adjusted his cuffs with deliberate precision. "Detective Marlow, I wasn't aware you were acquainted with Frankie. Are you staying for the festivities?"

"Unfortunately not. Just making a quick stop," Marlow replied in a straightforward tone. "I'm on duty tonight—got the rookie, Junior, waiting in the car. We're off to check out a lead across town. Thought I'd say hello since I was passing through the neighborhood."

The judge's smile appeared polite but strained, a detail Marlow didn't miss. Frankie, meanwhile, studied Marlow and the judge with a thoughtful look. The casual chatter stirred a sense of gratitude as he recalled a past incident when Marlow had stepped in to help him out of a tight spot. Even then, with fewer accolades to his name, Marlow's sharp instincts and unwavering loyalty had been clear—a side of the detective that Frankie had always respected.

Marlow gestured toward the car, his focus returning to his duties. "I should get back to it, gentlemen. Didn't mean to interrupt. Take care," he said, disappearing as quickly as he had arrived.

Frankie turned to the judge, hoping the momentary distraction had diffused the tension. "Shall I have your car pulled, Judge?" he offered, his tone measured, a quiet attempt to make amends for the evening's earlier disruptions.

"That'd be good, Frankie," the judge replied with a curt nod, signaling his approval.

The two stood in awkward silence as they waited for the car to arrive. When it finally pulled up, Judge Kincaid turned, his expression firm but not unkind. "Stay out of trouble tonight. Judge DuPont warned me about your three a.m. calls."

Frankie responded with a soft, practiced smile. "I've changed, Judge."

The judge gave Frankie a skeptical look, clasping his shoulder. "Remember what I said about business, drinking, and those roaming eyes," he cautioned, his voice heavy with the weight of seasoned advice. Without waiting for a response, he stepped into the car and disappeared into the night.

As the taillights faded, Frankie remained rooted in place, the burden of the evening pressing on him. Each interaction, each exchange, seemed to weave further into the complex web of power and influence that defined his world.

As he stepped back inside, Frankie ran into Kenya, who wasted no time offering high praise for the host. "You're quite the topic tonight, more than usual," she said, updating Frankie on his social standing.

"Most of the ladies are hoping for more than just a shot with you, while the men would do just about anything to get next to you."

Frankie nodded, flattered but distracted, his mind elsewhere. Before he could respond, he spotted Mississippi Red gloating across the room. "Finally! Need to catch up with Red. We'll talk later, Kenya," Frankie said, excusing himself as he swiftly navigated through the room.

Red stood out, draped in an oversized black fur coat that dragged along the floor, almost swallowing him whole. The glazed look in his eyes and the faint scent of reefer clinging to him told Frankie all he needed to know—Red had indulged in more than just alcohol.

"So let me get this straight… You're drunk and high? Do you realize the magnitude of the opportunity I'm giving you?" Frankie asked, his voice sharp with frustration and disbelief.

Red chuckled, entirely unfazed. "Ease up, Daddy. I was just out back schooling Silky in dice. Got a little carried away. You know I won this fur off him, right? Feels like they *JUST* skinned the bear! I told you I came to step. He can't see me—I'm the future, baby!"

Red laughed at his own joke, but Frankie wasn't amused. His demeanor was serious as he laid out the stakes: "Listen, Redmond, I want you on tour with me. But I need to know you can keep it together. The road is fast and will swallow you whole if you're not careful."

Red's grin faded as he listened intently, absorbing every word. Frankie didn't ease up. "Tonight's performance is make or break for you."

The weight of Frankie's words caused a shift in Red's attitude. Humility replaced his earlier bravado. "I know I can get a bit carried away, but I'm truly thankful for this opportunity, Frankie. It's an honor to perform at one of your parties. I don't take that for granted."

The sharp buzz of the doorbell suddenly cut through their conversation, startling everyone at the party. All heads turned toward the entrance.

Kenya approached the door and opened it to find Ralph, a stern-looking Italian man holding a package. His entitled demeanor was unmistakable as he declared, "I'm here to deliver a gift from Jimmie to Frankie. It can't be handed over to anyone else."

When Kenya extended her hand to take the package, Ralph refused. His stubbornness escalated in an instant. Without warning, he pushed past her into the house, the force of his intrusion sending her stumbling to the ground. The act of aggression reverberated through the party, drawing gasps and igniting immediate outrage among the guests.

From across the room, Chubbs and Silky sprang into action. Always ready to defend their own, they pushed through the crowd with purpose. Silky's razor appeared with a flick of his wrist.

Chubbs, however, took control, his voice booming with authority. "Put that shit away, Silk," he commanded, his tone leaving no room for argument.

Ralph, unfazed, responded with an unsettling ease, his words dripping with insult. "Take it easy, fellas. Are the spooks on this side of town always this scary? Like I told the lady, I'm here to deliver a gift to Frankie on behalf of Jimmie."

Chubbs glanced at Frankie and caught a subtle nod, urging him to handle the situation. Silky was the first to react, his anger barely contained. "Listen here, mug man. Fuck that gift! You pushed the wrong lady to the ground. Apologize!"

Ralph turned to face Silky, but before he could respond, Chubbs's patience snapped. In one swift motion, he grabbed a fistful of Ralph's shirt and yanked him close, their faces just inches apart.

The shift in Ralph's demeanor was immediate. Submission and fear washed over him as Chubbs's piercing glare seemed to bore straight into his soul. In a low, forceful whisper, Chubbs growled, "Don't get it twisted, white boy. We work with the Italians, not for them. You better read the room and recognize where you at before I take you out back."

With a firm shove, Chubbs sent Ralph stumbling backward. Straightening up, Chubbs shouted in front of the stunned crowd, "Apologize!"

The room held its breath as Chubbs forced Ralph to apologize. Under Chubbs' penetrating look, Ralph blurted out, "Shit! I'm really sorry, miss. I get a little carried away with my orders!" Everyone's attention was fixed, waiting to see what would unfold next.

Red tapped Frankie. "This is getting tense, baby. We'll finish the tour talk after I rock my set."

Amid the rising tension, Mississippi Red saw his moment to reclaim the night. Moving to the center of the room, he immediately drew all eyes to him, his presence magnetic. With a performer's instinct to shift the mood, he raised his arms, addressing the crowd with charismatic ease.

"Alright… Crazy night, *BUT*… thankfully, I'm still here! Let's make this a night to remember. Hit me!"

The music swept through the room like a tidal wave as they began to play. Red sang, danced, and played his trumpet, delivering a performance that impressed and captivated everyone in attendance.

In the aftermath of his performance, Red's demeanor underwent a striking transformation. The wave of adulation that followed seemed to inflate his ego with every chant of his name. Swaggering over to Frankie, basking in the applause, Red's attitude was noticeably different.

"Damn, Frankie baby. Do you hear them calling for me? Shit, Daddy, I might have to take this thang over for you," he boasted, his newfound arrogance a sharp contrast to his earlier humility.

As the party erupted with cheers, Kristine seized the moment to quietly brief the women about Silky's deteriorating mood—a direct result of his heavy gambling losses to Red. "He's mad, ladies. Real mad!" she whispered urgently. "Red took him for a lot tonight."

Before Kristine could elaborate, Silky burst into the room, his frustration boiling over. "Kristine! These girls ain't working the room. Looks like I'm gonna have to pop some ankles!"

The puzzled looks from some of the newer girls prompted Kristine to quickly explain. "When he gets like this, he takes that cane of his and gives a sharp rap on your ankle bone—hurts like hell!"

Kristine immediately ushered the women out, her voice low but intense. "Move it, ladies—he's not joking tonight! Better put dem ankles up." The urgency in her tone left no room for hesitation.

Meanwhile, Silky's rant continued unabated, his frustration spilling into every corner of the room. "All these high rollers up in here, and y'all are laughing it up with the cute, broke ones. We're spent! We need this money!" His voice echoed sharply, his emotional turmoil evident to everyone but himself.

Red, on the other hand, remained absorbed in the glow of his performance and the night's financial windfall. Surrounded by new admirers, he flaunted his earnings with a casual arrogance.

"Hold up, ladies. This here is my OG. I got too much respect for the old gangster," he quipped, his tone both playful and pointed.

Despite the laughter that erupted around him, Silky's expression remained stony, his disdain for Red's antics clear. Red, ever the provocateur, tried to smooth things over with a teasing grin.

"Silky, don't be like that. How about I do you a solid—what do you say we run it back? Well... I mean, if you've got any scratch left."

Red punctuated his words with an irritating, high-pitched laugh that echoed through the room like a hyena's squeal, drawing a few nervous chuckles from the crowd. With a mischievous glint in his eye, he added, "You know where to find me once you put your pennies together, Daddy."

Fuming, Silky was about to respond when Bell tapped his shoulder. "I ain't ever heard that boy talk like that before," she remarked, her tone laced with amusement.

"That's my point!" Silky spat back. "That little punk caught me off my game 'cause I'm full of that yak and sweet tea. I could bend that arrogant twerp over my knee right now."

Bell fixed her attention on the fur coat draped over Red, her eyes narrowing as she took in his exaggerated strut. With a scoff, she said, "I'll loan you some of Frankie's money if you can break him." A smirk danced across her lips. "I want a pair of $3,000 white gold diamond and sapphire earrings that Frankie won't buy me." He says I don't need any more accessories," she added, flipping her hair dismissively. "As if a girl like me could ever have enough."

Silky's face lit up, his interest piqued. "Here's the deal," she continued smoothly. "I'll loan you the money, and you give me forty percent of the winnings. We call it slick. If you lose, well, that's between you and Frankie."

Silky grinned, trying to play it cool. "Make it twenty percent. It's hard out here for a pimp, baby."

Bell shot back instantly, her voice firm. "Stop it. Thirty percent, final offer."

Silky rubbed his neck thoughtfully, then conceded with a sly smile. "Alright, give me that damn money, Bell. I'm about to bleed his lil' narrow ass dry."

With newfound determination, Silky approached Red, who was casually leaning against the bar, surrounded by admirers. Masking his intentions behind a veneer of nonchalance, Silky gestured to the bartender. "Top-shelf cognac," he requested with a sly grin.

The bartender shook his head. "Sorry, sir. The special reserve is saved for midnight. Only Frankie has access."

Unfazed, Silky leaned forward. "Shit, I'm drunk now, and I'm trying to keep it that way!" Without hesitation, he stepped behind the bar and grabbed the bottle himself. Pouring a generous shot, he added, "Tell my nephew if he's got a problem with me drinking his birthday juice, he can come get it from me."

Silky poured a second glass, sliding it toward Red. The two clinked glasses, the moment charged with an undercurrent of rivalry. "To wealth and health," Silky toasted, his voice carrying a subtle challenge. Red drank without hesitation, his ego swelling under the attention of the crowd.

Setting his full glass down, Silky struck. "Come on out back if you've got time for a broke old pimp like me," he coaxed, his tone dripping with mock humility. "I've scraped my pennies together, so let me try to win my dignity back."

The dice game quickly turned one-sided as the small entourage gathered out back for a nightcap. Silky dominated Red, methodically cutting him down with each roll of the dice.

"Once you're out of cash, I want that coat back. It looked better on me!" Silky boasted, rolling the dice and hitting his number again. He barked with a grin, "Throw in that watch while you're at it—I don't want you watching your downfall tick by!"

With each win, Silky's voice grew louder, piercing the cool night air. "You should've stopped while you were ahead—now I gotta embarrass you in front of your lil' basic bitches."

As Silky's relentless taunts continued, some of Red's lady friends began to drift away, their laughter fading into the shadows. Red, his face a mask of frustration, watched helplessly as his fortunes—and his company—vanished roll by roll.

Silky hit his number again and let out a triumphant shout. "Look at you, losing more than just money tonight, huh? I thought you were a big dog!" His words were cutting, his tone dripping with mockery. "Hand over that belt! You're gonna have to hold 'dem pants up with your hand—I might take those too if you're not careful!"

Doctor Williams, Kenya, and Chubbs stood on the sidelines, smirking and occasionally pointing, clearly entertained by the spectacle of Silky reclaiming his stature and leaving Red thoroughly exposed.

Inside, the party roared on, the atmosphere electric as the new year approached. With the clock ticking down, Frankie, Bell, and their guests gathered in the main room, glasses in hand, anticipation buzzing like static in the air.

Bell raised her glass high, her voice cutting through the final seconds of the countdown. "Happy Birthday, Frankie!" she exclaimed as the clock struck twelve, her words met with an eruption of cheers.

"And a Happy New Year to us all!" Frankie added, his voice resonating over the jubilant roar.

The celebration hit its peak as the guests exchanged well-wishes, hugs, and bursts of laughter. For a fleeting moment, the room was alive with unbridled joy, a crescendo of shared excitement marking the turn of the year.

As the night wound down, Frankie and Bell moved through the dwindling crowd, bidding farewell to the remaining attendees. Together, they walked the last of their friends to the door, the early hours of the new year creeping in quietly behind them.

When the final guest disappeared into the night, they stood hand in hand, savoring the newfound silence.

In the stillness of their empty home, surrounded by the remnants of celebration, Frankie and Bell shared a look. It was a quiet moment of contentment, a shared relief. Finally, peace had returned.

# CHAPTER 5

# STAY SCHEMIN'

"I've got to remind him who's really in charge." —Jimmie

In the early morning hours, Frankie felt a growing restlessness as his twenty-ninth birthday faded into memory. Lying next to Bell, he let his mind wander, cluttered with what-ifs and if-onlys. Since diving deeper into the bootlegging world, darkness had crept into his life, dulling the music that once fueled his soul.

"Bell, you awake?" Frankie's voice broke the silence.

A soft rustle came from beneath the covers. "I am now," Bell whispered, her voice heavy with sleep.

"I'm thinking of getting away for a bit," Frankie confessed, his tone carrying the weight of his thoughts.

Bell propped herself up, her silhouette framed against the faint glow of the early dawn. "Running from your ghosts or from me?" she asked, her words tinged with sentimentality.

"It's not like that," he sighed, shifting slightly. "It's just… Everything is piling up. My tunes are stale, and the fans are craving something new. You saw how much they loved Red. He stole the show."

Bell responded with a theatrical yawn, a gentle reminder of Frankie's enduring star power. Her calm tone softened the room. "You said you've been working on new music. Hit the road with it. Test it in the wild."

To lighten the mood, she attempted an exaggerated lion's face, baring her teeth and scrunching her nose. Her performance broke with a laugh as her serious expression cracked.

Frankie responded with a soft smile, his mood lifting slightly. "I would, but if it stinks, I'm afraid you'll run off with Red…"

"Might," she teased.

Rising from the bed, Frankie leaned down and kissed Bell's forehead. "You are always right. The road. That's the answer. If it flops, at least I tried," he mused aloud, determination threading through his lingering uncertainty.

Bell rolled over, her voice barely audible in the quiet. "I know."

In the bathroom, Frankie stared into the mirror, searching for signs of aging—a growing source of insecurity. He turned on the warm water and took a sip, violently swishing it around his mouth before spitting it into the sink. The cold splash of water to his face that followed jolted him awake, momentarily shaking off his doubts.

Needing a change of scenery, Frankie stepped outside, drawn to the calm of the early morning. He kicked off his slippers and walked barefoot into the yard, the cool dewy grass beneath his feet grounding him in simpler pleasures. For a moment, it felt like enough.

But the peace didn't last. Frankie pulled out a stick of reefer, lighting it despite knowing how much Bell despised the habit. Her voice echoed in his mind, calling it "disgusting" every chance she got. Even out here, surrounded by the quiet stillness of dawn, her disapproval lingered, making it impossible for him to fully unwind.

Chubbs poked his head out the door, pulling Frankie from his thoughts. "You down for company?" Frankie hesitated but waved Chubbs over.

"What's on your mind, superstar?" Chubbs asked, noticing Frankie's distant expression.

"Just life, Chubbs. Life and its endless cycle." Frankie took a drag of the reefer and exhaled, smoke curling into the morning air. Their conversation meandered from the mundane to the serious—the business and the risks they took daily.

As dawn crept over the horizon, Frankie and Chubbs stood silently in the backyard for what felt like hours, a muted camaraderie between them. With the stick of reefer dangling from his lips, Frankie finally broke the silence, his voice low and mellow.

"Didn't know you crashed here last night. Everything smooth?" Frankie asked, his gaze fixed on the distant treeline.

Leaning against the weathered bench, Chubbs said, "I didn't crash. Just swung by early to talk to you about Jimmie—he's pressing us for more product; he wants it tonight."

Frankie's sigh was heavy. "Just a few months back, he told me we were overloading him and that he had all he could handle." Frankie began to pace. "Something is off."

Chubbs silently agreed and said, "I feel the same, but let's not raise any concern. We'll weigh his payment first." Chubbs's voice was steady, but Frankie caught the flicker of concern.

"We are swimming in risk, but our pockets aren't getting any deeper," Frankie commented, taking a slow drag as his mind raced. "We need Silky on this drop—he's got an eye for trouble," Frankie suggested.

"Spot on," Chubbs agreed. "I'll loop him in. What's the play?"

Frankie paused for a moment, the chirping birds momentarily filling the space. "Tell Jimmie to meet us at Russo's restaurant at nine p.m.," Frankie directed. "And we get there early to scope the place out. After the way you manhandled Ralph, we can't be too careful."

Chubbs laughed, a rumble in his chest as he flexed his muscles. "Ralph doesn't have the guts to step to me. He knows I will break him."

Frankie was serious. "Never underestimate a desperate man."

Chubbs sighed and threw his hand up in surrender. "Fair enough. I'll smooth things over with Ralph tonight. We don't need bad blood."

Their conversation was interrupted by Ms. Ida, a well-respected, motherly figure within Frankie's close circle. Her tone was playful yet pointed. "Y'all are up early. Did the bar run out of booze last night?"

Chubbs quickly retorted. "Real funny, Ms. Ida."

She smiled as she stood in the doorway. "That wasn't a joke, baby. I'll have breakfast soon. Hope you boys are hungry."

Frankie's focus returned to the smoke, his thoughts rampant. "Chubbs, I've been doing some thinking. I want out, brother."

Chubbs turned to him, sensing the gravity in his words. "I'm tired.

We're not kids anymore. The games are getting too risky," Frankie confessed, his voice soft.

Chubbs started to speak, but Frankie cut him off. "Just hear me out. It's time to expand the music and go legit. We've got Red, but we need fresh talent. New blood to mix in."

Chubbs understood the significance of Frankie's decision. "We need to ditch the drugs and the booze. I know, easier said than done."

Frankie continued, his plan unfolding like a map. "Don't change a thing yet. Keep this under wraps. We need the element of surprise and a lot of cash to secure our freedom. Chubbs was solemn, his loyalty unwavering.

Frankie's voice grew firmer. "It's a long road, Chubbs, but it's the only one worth taking."

It was a gamble against the life they knew, a leap into a world of uncertainty. But for Frankie, the chance to rewrite his story was a risk worth taking. The path to redemption was scary, but the promise of a new future, free from the chains that had shackled them, was all he needed to move forward.

Under the morning sun, Frankie and Chubbs shared a moment of understanding. After a brief pause, Chubbs leaned in and openly spoke his mind. "Look, Frankie, stepping away from the business is bold, and I agree—it's time. We've been rolling far too long, but remember: the streets funded our dreams. That dirty money greased palms and opened doors for us."

Frankie gave a brief, confirming look, then continued, "I know, Chubbs. But it's that very life I can't stand anymore. The fear of getting caught up, the constant looking over our shoulder—it's no way to live. We've got the talent, and soon, we'll have a new sound that'll change everything. We just need to be smart, gather resources, and prepare for a clean slate."

His plan was clear. "We're going to squeeze every last drop out of this life—money, influence, and connections. This next year is critical.

We accept no limits and turn down no opportunity to stash away cash." Chubbs listened closely and said, "You've got my support, Frank. Let's clear the board and start fresh." As they closed the conversation, a sense of brotherhood enveloped them, their shared history and hopes for the future binding them together.

They embraced before Chubbs replied, "I'll leave you with your thoughts. I'm about to eat and sort things out." Chubbs stepped away, leaving a trail of his cologne behind.

Frankie's mind drifted back to the meetup with Jimmie; loud tidal waves of negativity and paranoia crashed around his head. His plan to leave the game made him wary of taking chances, and he questioned the meeting.

Shaking off the dread, Frankie made a swift decision. "Chubbs!" he called out, stopping him in his tracks. "Change of plans. We're not doing Russo's. It doesn't feel right. Have Jimmie meet us at the Phat Kat and tell Silky to secure the back alley—no one gets in or out without our say. I want extra security and undercover women on the lookout. Make it lively, undetectable."

Chubbs turned, a flicker of approval crossing his face. "Smart thinking," he said, his voice carrying a note of respect for Frankie's cautious leadership.

As Chubbs disappeared into the house, Frankie remained outside, the breeze scraping across his skin. Although illegitimate, his decision to leave behind a life of certainty was fraught with risk. Was he prepared to lose the fast money, street fame, and power for a chance at legitimate success?

His answer was yes. The promise of freedom from constant anxiety and fear was all he needed to guide him forward.

Across town, an impatient series of knocks shattered the silence of an otherwise quiet apartment. *Bam! Bam!* "Boss, you there?" Ralph's voice rang out with an urgency that echoed through the space.

Inside, a disheveled Jimmie called out, "Yeah, yeah, I'm here. What's the deal, kid?" His voice carried a mix of annoyance and curiosity.

Ralph replied, "I wanted to go over the plan for tonight one last time."

Jimmie, barely concealing his frustration, grumbled to the woman in his bed, "Fuck, this kid is slow. The elevator doesn't go to the top floor, ya know?" Then, yelling out, he added, "Hold your horses, will ya? I'll be there in a minute."

Ralph's lack of wit was apparent. "Got my horses in check, Boss. I'll wait in the living room."

Jimmie began to drift back off to sleep before he was jolted awake by more banging. *Boom! Boom!* "Is waiting in the living room a good idea, boss?"

Fuming with irritation, Jimmie snapped back, "Yeah, man! Yes! Fuck!" He glanced at the woman under the satin covers. "Listen, baby, let me go straighten this out. I'll be right back."

Oblivious to Jimmie's irritation, Ralph settled into the living room, his mind racing with the details of the night's plan.

Jimmie finally emerged, taking a moment to collect himself as he dragged his feet through the luxurious apartment. Despite the splendor, the disorder in the apartment symbolized Jimmie's chaotic approach to maintaining power. Cigarette butts littered the floor, dishes piled up in the sink, trash overflowed, and empty bottles of hooch were scattered everywhere.

Jimmie made his way to the kitchen for old coffee and then finally to the cluttered living room. As he pushed aside clothes, his demeanor was one of forced patience. "Alright, let's go over it once more," he sighed, bracing for Ralph's explanation.

Eager to understand, Ralph asked, "Why do we want them to get pulled over again, boss?"

Jimmie dropped his head in exasperation, rubbing his temple. "For the fiftieth time, Ralph, I need him to know he's not as untouchable as he thinks. You've seen how he's been strutting around like he owns the town. I've got to remind him who's really in charge. Once someone from his circle gets popped, I'll have the charges dropped, and Frankie will owe me a favor."

Ralph stood a little taller, admiration plain in his voice. "Damn, you're a smart man, boss!"

Jimmie lit a cigarette, the glow illuminating his sharp features as he motioned for Ralph to get started. "Spit it out, kid. Let's get going—I have company."

"First, I'll pay Sheriff Whitaker a visit and tell him we'll tip him off about a car loaded with contraband. Then, I'll hand him the envelope with the cash," Ralph replied excitedly.

Jimmie stood and slapped Ralph on the back of his head, his voice laced with frustration. "No, you nitwit! Give him the envelope first, then tell him we'll phone him with the plates."

Ralph took a deep breath, recalibrating. "Right. Cash first, then the tip-off. Got it." He paused, running the plan through his mind again before speaking. "We start with a visit to Sheriff Whitaker. Slip him the cash, then tell him about the plate number. Cash first, then the tip-off. Got it!"

Jimmie sucked his teeth and replied, "Go on." Ralph smiled and continued, "Then tonight at the meet with Frankie and his troops, I'll load up the car and act irritated, a little jumpy even. We want them to feel like something is off, right?"

Jimmie puffed his cigarette and said, "Attaboy! Now go on."

Ralph said, "Then I'll 'slip' and say, 'Boss... this is too much. We still haven't sold the rest of it.'"

Jimmie's face darkened as Ralph asked, "What do we do if he forces us to keep the extra product?"

For a moment, doubt flickered across Jimmie's face as he debated the risks of his plan. His need for control had driven his vendetta against Frankie to such extremes, and now it gave him pause. He pulled on the cigarette and rocked slightly, fidgeting with his pinky ring as his thoughts spiraled.

Internally, he questioned whether to call it all off. Involving the cops—even the ones on his payroll—felt riskier than he'd initially considered. But Frankie ran the business, and Jimmie needed to run Frankie.

Dragging his feet back to the kitchen, he poured a small shot of brandy and topped it with a splash of old coffee. He threw it back in one swift motion, bracing himself, before returning to Ralph.

"Good question, kid…" Jimmie began, his voice carrying the weight of calculated decisions. "It's fine if we have to keep it. It's a win-win. Either we get extra booze and drugs, or they get popped with the extra. Get it? Win-win."

He grabbed Ralph by the sides of his head, his grip firm but not aggressive. "This part has to be convincing! You know Frankie's posse. They're not easily fooled. Your job is to make them believe the load is too much. We want them to keep the extra. Got it?"

Misunderstanding Jimmie's critical tone for praise, Ralph grinned widely. "Then, I'll find an excuse to use the phone, call in the plate number, and bam, we've got 'em!"

Jimmie shouted in excitement, clapping his hands and pointing at Ralph. "Bingo! You got it. Let me know if anything comes up."

Ralph saluted him and said, "Will do, boss."

Jimmie patted him on the back as he walked him to the door. Before Ralph left, Jimmie added with a knowing smirk, "You've been a good boy. Just remember, if there are any slipups, we're toast."

As Ralph left, buoyed by Jimmie's approval, the quiet of his apartment underscored the fragility of their plan. Meanwhile, as Jimmie pondered the potential fallout, the line between hunter and hunted blurred. Was this vendetta and power play worth the risk?

Jimmie paced his living room, barely able to contain his anticipation for the night. The woman stepped out, nearly naked, with only his silk robe draped over her body. The robe fell open, revealing her smooth, glistening legs and the alluring curves of her hips. The morning light filtering through the half-drawn blinds made her skin shimmer.

She noticed a hint of anxiety in Jimmie and asked, "Is everything okay?"

Jimmie took a look at her and felt the blood and lust rush through his body. His mind was covered in sin. He composed himself and replied, "Yeah, yeah. It's good. Go back in the room. I'll be in shortly."

On the surface, Jimmie tried to play it cool, but he couldn't help but wonder about the consequences of his plan. Beneath his hardened exterior, a sliver of doubt lingered.

Several miles away, Ralph navigated his car through the bustling streets of New Port. Making an impromptu stop, he parked near the Phat Kat to scope out the night's venue. His eyes lingered on the facade, taking in every detail as a prelude to the evening's scheme. Leaning his head against the seat, Ralph found himself momentarily wrestling with the moral aspects of the plan. But his resolve hardened quickly—fear wouldn't stop the show.

Ralph's arrival at the precinct was anything but subtle. He stormed into Sheriff Whitaker's office, his bravado masking the weight of his underworld connections. The envelope of cash hit the desk with a decisive thud, echoing Ralph's bold declaration.

"Listen! I'm here on behalf of Jimmie C. You know who we are!"

Without missing a beat, Ralph leaned in, his voice low but menacing. "We know your pretty little daughter plays tennis every Sunday with that lovely wife of yours. Don't make us do something that'll scar you for life…"

He stared the sheriff down and aggressively asserted, "We will phone you later with the plates of a car you are to pull over. No questions! Hold him. We will tell you what to do next."

Before Ralph could say another word, the unmistakable sound of a shotgun froze everyone. *Chik-Chik.*

"You getting a little rambunctious with my sheriff, ain't ya, boy?" The voice, rich with a Creole lilt, belonged to Judge Kincaid, who emerged alongside Hogg, the muscle he kept close.

"Now, you thought it wise to wave ya' little money and influence around in my parish, hmph?" Kincaid's tone was casual, almost amused, but carried an undercurrent of menace. "I feel *very* disrespected... Now whatcha say 'bout dat, Hogg?" He turned to his top man.

Hogg nodded, his voice rumbling low. "Yessah, he came right on..."

Hogg barely got the words out before Kincaid interrupted, his voice rising. "You right, Hogg! He came right up into my place and spit in my face."

Ralph's initial confidence faltered under the weight of Kincaid's scrutiny. Crossing his arms with a weary sigh, the judge leaned in, his eyes narrowing. "Look here, son. You're gonna tell me everything about your Boss and his little business. Or I'm gonna have you arrested for bribery, trafficking, threatening an officer of the law, and whatever the fuck else I can come up with."

Stepping into Ralph's personal space, Kincaid backed him into the corner of the small office. His grin turned sinister as he added, "Oh, I don't know... Those charges, with my signature... That'll probably get you thirty up there on the Angola Plantation."

Kincaid seemed almost entertained by the idea and called to Hogg for affirmation. "Whatcha say 'bout dat, Hogg?"

"Oh, yessah," Hogg replied, his tone thick with grim delight. "He's a little ole buck, but they'll sho' love to have him swangin' a hammer."

The judge's grin widened. "You sho' is right, Hogg!" He locked eyes with Ralph, his voice turning ice cold. "Sounds like you better get to talking, bucko."

Ralph puffed out his chest in defiance, his voice rising with misplaced confidence. "Do you know who I work for? Be smart. Jimmie reports directly to the Santoro family, and they won't take kindly to you threatening to disrupt their operation."

His words hung in the air for a moment as he leaned forward, his tone hardening. "Think about it, Judge—you put me away and the streets dry up. Nobody makes money."

Ralph's confidence swelled as he added, "Now, you're gonna let me walk out of here because you, nor that big ogre, is gonna do a damn thang to Ralph."

Kincaid, stroking his unkempt beard, burst into a wheezing, almost sinister laugh. He gathered himself and retorted, "Is that right?"

The judge's lighthearted banter evaporated, replaced by a cold, commanding tone as his demeanor shifted. "Son, your threats mean very little in my court. I've put away criminals three times scarier than you and your little Boss." He sucked his teeth, tapping his fingers rhythmically on the desk beside him. "The big bad Mafia and Santoro family are gone come get me in my parish. Do I got dat right, Hogg?"

Ralph opened his mouth to reply, but the judge's stern voice cut through his attempt. "Shut… up," he commanded, signaling to Hogg. The enforcer stepped closer, the cold, unyielding metal of the shotgun pressing against Ralph's chest.

"Now, since you're so confident in your connections," Kincaid sneered, a twisted smile playing on his lips, "tell them to come see 'bout ole Judge Kincaid. I ain't hard to find!"

Hogg punctuated the judge's statement with a swift body blow from the butt of the shotgun, sending Ralph reeling. The defiance drained from Ralph as he crumbled, pleading for mercy.

Kincaid leaned down, his voice a venomous whisper in Ralph's ear. "If that's all you can take, you won't last a week in Angola."

Standing upright, the judge yanked Ralph to his feet by his shirt and gave Hogg a curt nod. "Tighten him up, Hogg!"

Hogg delivered two punishing body blows, one to Ralph's rib cage and the other to his stomach. Ralph collapsed to his knees, spitting saliva and gasping for air as the judge watched with detached amusement.

"Cuff him to the chair," Kincaid ordered, his voice cold and devoid of pity.

The judge strode to the window, closing the blinds with a deliberate snap. Turning back to the room, he directed the sheriff to keep watch. "Make sure we're not disturbed. Ralph and I still got a lot to talk about."

As Ralph found himself restrained, the oppressive silence began to stir panic. The room, bathed in the dull tungsten glow of an overhead light, felt more like a cage with each passing second. Ralph's earlier bravado had evaporated, leaving a sheen of sweat and a voice trembling with raw fear as he desperately pleaded to be let go.

Judge Kincaid loomed over him and shouted, "Stop it! The whimpering makes you look weak." He pulled up  a chair, placing his hand on Ralph's shoulder and glancing over at Hogg, his voice dropping to a low, threatening growl. "Boss Hogg, if I don't believe he understands me, use that shotgun to open him up." Hogg offered a grunt of agreement, his hand resting ominously on the shotgun.

Kincaid focused on Ralph, probing for cracks in his resolve. "You're going to work for me now," Kincaid declared, his tone casual. "You'll report every little secret and every dirty deal to me. Understood?"

Any resistance Ralph had left crumbled under Kincaid's menacing posture. Ralph began to spill the details of Jimmie's plan for tonight, revealing the immediate threat and the precarious state of Jimmie's standing within the Mob. He spoke of sloppy operations and dwindling influence—information he had gathered because Jimmie thought him too stupid to comprehend. But Ralph had always been listening and observing.

Now fully ensnared in Kincaid's game, Ralph saw no way out but through total cooperation. Kincaid's response was a light tap on Ralph's cheek, almost paternal. "Good boy. You're going to keep everything set for tonight. But instead of your little call to the sheriff, you'll call Hogg. Are we clear?"

Ralph silently signaled, cementing his new role as Kincaid's informant. The judge's strategy was clear: leverage Ralph's fear and Jimmie's overreach to tighten his grip on the city's underbelly.

As Ralph was released, his betrayal bore down on him. The dynamics within New Port had silently shifted. Ralph, once a confident player, was now a pawn in Kincaid's broader scheme to control the city's power, wealth, and influence.

# CHAPTER 6

# VICE GRIPS

"You might never play another tune. Just kiss it goodbye."
—Judge Kincaid

The soft lights of the Phat Kat cast a warm, hazy glow, wrapping the room in secrecy. The squad gathered, their whispered conversations blending with the faint notes of jazz. Each moment brought them closer to the night's event, the anticipation apparent as Frankie and his friends tried to keep busy.

Silky leaned against the polished mahogany of the bar, his voice overriding the soft sounds of scattered patrons. "Yo, Frankie, you gotta hear Chubbs out. Man's got a point. You oughta listen," he said, a hint of intrigue in his tone.

Frankie, suddenly interested, turned toward Chubbs and took a few steps closer. "Lay it on me," Frankie prompted, his voice inviting. Chubbs took a breath and began. "You're looking to bleed the city dry, right? Jimmie's ripe for the taking, and he's out there thinking he's untouchable!"

Frankie's face scrunched in confusion. His mouth tightened as Chubbs continued. "I know what we discussed earlier, but the moment is too perfect to pass up." Chubbs addressed the small group of trusted men, making direct contact with each of them. "Jimmie's gang? Soft as they come. Haven't seen a real threat from his side in months."

Silky chimed in, "He ain't lying, Frankie. It's been quiet on our end. If any real mobsters were lurking around, they'd have come knocking by now. I think the lions have left the jungle."

Frankie couldn't believe what he was hearing. "So what are you suggesting?" he asked, incredulous.

Chubbs, filled with confidence, continued to pitch his audacious plan. "We take his shit! We push Jimmie out, take over his operation, and run New Port completely," he declared, a fire burning within him. "We run in and seize everything. We do that, and it's completely our city!"

Frankie was speechless at the boldness of the plan. Sipping his drink, Silky posed a question that hung in the air. "We've got the means to pull it off, but are we ready to step into those shoes? The pressure, the risks—it's not just about the booze anymore."

Before the conversation could gain momentum, Frankie called out for Kenya, seeking the familiar comfort of whiskey. "Kenya, a stiff one, please!" His request provided a brief break from the intensity of scheming.

Turning back to Chubbs, Frankie spoke up, "Chubbs, let me talk to you solo for a second." With Silky and the others excusing themselves, Frankie and Chubbs dove into an intense conversation.

With practiced ease, Kenya gracefully slid a glass down the bar. Drink in hand, Frankie locked eyes with Chubbs and spoke just above a whisper. "This morning we talked about laying low, and now you wanna rob Jimmie? It's a gamble I'm not willing to take. If we hit him, we have to finish it. You understand what that means?" Chubbs's resolve didn't waver. "Absolutely! Candy from a baby, far as I'm concerned." Frankie's face soured as he took a sip of his whiskey. "That's reckless. We're not doing it. End of discussion."

The moment shattered as Chubbs burst into laughter, revealing his true intent. "I'm just stirring the pot, brother. Testing the waters to see where your head is at. It's all about strategy, Frankie." He tapped his index finger against the side of his head. "Chess, not checkers, brother."

Frankie couldn't help but laugh, the absurdity and depth of Chubbs's act not lost on him. "Bell is right. You play too much." Their laughter was a brief interlude to the night ahead. Frankie drifted to the piano, lost in memories of past nights at the Phat Kat, while Chubbs stepped away to handle business. Kenya made her way from behind the bar and slowly approached Frankie.

Her presence reminded Frankie of his ambitions. "The first night you performed here... it changed everything," she said, reflecting on their shared history. Frankie smiled and replied, "The first night I knew I loved you." Kenya sighed deeply. "Cut the charm. We were kids back then. It's time to face reality."

Frankie brushed off her admonishing tone and continued to stroke the piano. "Let me play you a song—let's reminisce about the good times." Kenya remained unyielding. "I don't want a song, Frankie." He began to grow irritated as he continued on the keys. "Well, tell me what you want, baby. Use your words."

Kenya, her voice steady, obliged his request. "I want a future, Frankie; I want my club. One that's mine, away from here."

Frankie fumbled on the piano, her words striking a chord deep inside him. He stopped and turned to her, his voice defiant. "This again… Why leave Kenya? Your life is good here."

Kenya's resolve was firm. "A chance to be more than just a footnote in your story." Her vision blurred, and her voice grew shaky. "Frankie… I want to find myself and make a life for myself. One outside of you."

Frankie's anger flared. He abruptly banged the piano with his clenched fist, startling the patrons, who began to whisper amongst themselves. He looked up at Kenya and softly spoke. "Tell me you are joking, K. Tell me you're not trying to leave again."

Kenya stood there, committed to her cause. "So what, Frankie? You want me to be your mistress forever? I wanted out of New Port before you ever came into the picture all those years ago, but you made me forget that. You showed me this life of luxury, and I became hooked. But maybe the lifestyle has started to fade. Lately, I've been living for myself and wanting my own."

Frankie was anguished, old fears of abandonment resurfacing from his younger years. Seeing his downturned face, Kenya's voice softened, though her words remained firm, "Lift your head. I ain't got no patience for a pouting man."

Their exchange was interrupted by Chubbs's return. Oblivious to the storm he'd walked into, he said casually, "Yo, Frankie… Let's throw that last riff out before the tour." Frankie snapped back, his voice agitated, "Maybe focus on better ideas for our exit plan."

Frankie's veneer of indifference was gone. He could no longer mask his hurt as he added, "Oh, and Chubby... You're right. It's a shit riff. I got the idea from Kenya."

Frankie was in a mood. "Think of a better one next time! And get me another drink while you're at it." He gestured dismissively toward the bar, signaling Kenya to get back to work.

As she turned to walk off, Frankie abruptly grabbed her wrist. "Let's finish talking about that bright idea later." Kenya snatched her wrist from Frankie and replied with a solemn, "Sure."

With Kenya gone, Chubbs immediately addressed the issue. "What's going on, Frankie? You seem off tonight." He tried to feel Frankie out, "And what's with Kenya? What y'all got going on?"

Frankie looked at Chubbs with a straight face and replied, "It's nothing. She's on the rag. I said something that rubbed her the wrong way and she tripped out on me."

However, Chubbs knew something was off. Frankie tapped him on the shoulder before turning his head to yell across the bar. "Kenya! I want that drink neat. Three shots!" Frankie looked back at Chubbs. "Go get Silky. I want to discuss the plan."

The evening marched on, and the club quickly filled up, intensifying with every passing moment. Frankie was spiraling as he continued to drink heavily, drowning himself in liquor and thoughts of Kenya's earlier revelation. He brooded alone at the bar's shadowed end, watching the patrons dance and jive along the walls.

Caught up in his thoughts, Frankie snapped back to reality when Chubbs approached, his voice barely audible above the crowd noise. "Frankie, it's time."

Acknowledging Chubbs, Frankie downed the shot he was sipping and held the glass in the air, signaling to Kenya for another. It was a demand, not a request. She approached him with a shot, concern etched on her face. "Frankie, maybe you've had enough, hon."

His reply was sharp and bitter. "I'm not your hon, remember?" He downed the shot and slammed the glass on the bar before snapping, "Another one!" His voice was heavy with pain.

"Fine! If you want to be an idiot, be my guest," Kenya retorted, walking away.

Chubbs nudged him again. "We need to move, Frankie. Time's wasting." Frankie pushed himself away from the bar, his steps unsteady. He was determined to have the last word with Kenya. He caught up to her and spoke sternly from behind. "This is my city! I decide when I've had enough," he declared, his words slurred with a misplaced pride.

Unmoved, Kenya countered, "Frankie, grow your married ass up. We're done playing these games. It's time for you to face reality; I ain't your mistress anymore, and I haven't been for a few months." Just as Frankie was preparing to respond, Silky's voice cut through. "Frankie, come on! My clock's ticking louder than this doggone music. Let's go, baby. I only got 'bout ten years left on my life, and you using one right now. Shake something, Daddy!"

Frankie turned back to Kenya and said, "We're not done. I want answers." He stumbled out the back door into the alley, the smell of whiskey clinging to him. Jimmie's impatience was evident in his restless movements and forced smile.

Ralph broke the silence, his voice teeming with confrontation. "What's the deal, Frankie? You don't still don't trust us? Ya' know, my old man used to say, 'When people change the location, they're either planning to whack you or rob you.' So which is it, Frankie?"

Ralph continued, "Nobody's dying tonight, boss!" He glanced at Jimmie before finishing, "I'll be damned if I get robbed by these guys."

Frankie's inebriation made him bluntly dismissive. "Jimmie! Please put a muzzle on your damn dog. I'm too drunk for this right now."

Ralph retorted, "You too drunk to fight, tough guy?"

Chubbs chimed in and said, "White boy, remember the party?"

Undeterred, Ralph stepped up, his stance aggressive. "You think I forgot the party? I owe you a good ass whipping. I'll teach you some manners—then we can do business!"

Jimmie's frustration boiled over. "Enough! Ralph, shut the hell up. I already halfway think this is a setup. We're here to do business, not settle old scores."

Frankie brushed off Jimmie's concerns. "Relax. Nothing's gonna happen to y'all, but I don't trust handing off a haul this big to your side. You Italians have sticky fingers."

Choosing to overlook the insult, Jimmie pressed on. "Tonight's a landmark for us. A re-up this big is a win for everyone involved."

Silky cut through Jimmie's enthusiasm. "Enough with the smooth talk, Jimmie. Pop the trunk. Let's get this party started."

Jimmie paused, caution on his face. "You boys seem jumpy tonight. How about I scout the area first? What do you say, Frankie—join me for a drink to mark the occasion?"

After a moment's contemplation, Frankie acquiesced. "Alright, Jimmie. A celebratory drink does sound good." Jimmie saluted Silky and Chubbs with a content smirk before following Frankie inside.

Chubbs cracked his knuckles, the tension easing from his shoulders. He muttered something unintelligible, watching Jimmie closely. Silky chimed in, "That man is slick; he knows how to move people. And Frankie…what's with Frankie tonight?" he asked Chubbs. "He's got the whole place on edge."

Ralph took his time stubbing out his cigarette on the concrete, double-checking the plate number as he did so. As he made his move inside, Chubbs called out, "Hey, hold up…"

Ralph paused, his body tensing. Adopting a conciliatory tone,

Chubbs added, "Relax, man. I shouldn't have pressed you that hard at the party. You knocked over our girl, and I just reacted. Let's put it behind us. What do you say?" Offering a handshake, Chubbs waited.

After hesitating, Ralph accepted the gesture and said, "Fine, I got no problems. Let's get the money."

Chubbs smiled and replied, "My man, let's stack it."

Silky, impatient, interjected from the background, "You lovebirds done? I got Too Tall, Remy, and Byrd inside waiting to throw craps, and you fuckers got the alley closed off."

With a half smile, Chubbs said reassuringly, "Give us a minute, Silk. Just squashed some drama here. We'll clear your alley soon enough."

Exasperated, Silky threw up his hands. "Fine. But hurry it up!"

After a round of drinks inside, the group moved back to the alley behind the Phat Kat. Frankie, slightly unsteady on his feet, attempted to assist in loading Jimmie's trunk. His coordination failed him twice, crates slipping from his grasp, an occurrence he blamed on the wood's slickness rather than his tipsy condition.

In the midst of loading the car, Ralph ignited a fuse. "We're swimming in booze, boss. Haven't cleared out the last batch yet. I thought you said this was going to be more snow." Jimmie grimaced, his response sharp. "Zip it!" he whispered, commanding silence from Ralph.

But Frankie had already caught on and halted the operation. "If you're sitting on a stash of booze, Jimmie, why the push for more?" he pressed calmly, his voice edged with suspicion.

Jimmie attempted to smooth things over. "Let it go, Frankie. I always make good on the payments. What's it matter if I still have a little booze and a few bricks left around?"

His words did not move Frankie. With decisive action, Frankie slammed the trunk shut, cutting the exchange short.

"I heard your man," Frankie responded, his voice firm. "This is excessive, even for you. We'll hold on to the extra at our place until you sort things out."

Jimmie's anger peaked; his fist came down hard on the car's hood, a sharp pain shooting through his hand as it split open, blood beginning to drip. In a moment of rage, he lashed out at Ralph, his bloodied hand striking Ralph's face in a violent backhand. The men stood shocked.

"You fucked this up! You talk too much," Jimmie said, chastising Ralph in front of those present.

In the charged silence that followed, Frankie wavered. Jimmie's actions sent the night spiraling along with Frankie's mind. He thought that perhaps monitoring the surplus himself was the smarter play. If he took it, he could ensure it wouldn't end up in the wrong hands. With this in mind, Frankie announced, "We need to ensure everything is square, so I will run the load. I'll make sure we're not walking into a trap."

Frankie positioned himself in the car, and the entire group immediately approached the vehicle, signaling their genuine concern. Chubbs was the first to try to lighten the mood. "Boy, stop. Get from behind that wheel. You ain't drove no load in years." His deep, resonant laughter failed to mask his underlying stress.

Frankie was in no state to appreciate the humor. "Who are you playing with? I pioneered this game for us," he snapped back, the edge in his voice cutting through the night. "Give me the keys!"

Silky intervened next, hoping to quell the escalating drama. "Calm down—this isn't the play, nephew. Get ya' ass out of that car." Yet, Frankie's anger was undeterred, his demand for the keys echoing in the alley. "Stay out of this, Silk! *Keys!*"

Jimmie, desperate to keep Frankie out of direct involvement, approached next. "No, Daddy, listen. You can't drive this load," he pleaded, his motives concealed.

Ralph, aware of the actual stakes, added his caution. He laid his hand on the car and said, "Frankie, think about it. You're too big of a celebrity to be driving this much work. Let one of your men handle it."

Jimmie persisted. "He's right, Frankie. How about you step out of the car?"

Laughing, Frankie waved them off with a dismissive glance. "Your advice means nothing," he said, his focus narrowing on Jimmie as he looked him up and down. "Step away from the fucking car!" he yelled louder, "Chubbs! *Keys!*"

Chubbs approached the car window. "Frankie, get ya ass out of the car and stop being a brat." Frankie put his head on the steering wheel as Chubbs continued. "You talking 'bout Kenya; you must be on the rag too. Get out of the car—you know you ain't driving this load." Chubbs tapped the vehicle twice. "Stop putting on a show; let's get back inside."

The exchange grew heated as Frankie asserted his dominance, yelling, "Chubbs, you work for me! Give me the keys before you're out of a job." Finally, Chubbs tossed the keys to Frankie with a resigned acknowledgement of his role. "You got it, boss. I'm just a worker. Handle the load yourself." Chubbs stormed back into the Phat Kat.

As Frankie drove off into the night, those left behind were stunned. Their concerns for his safety and the operation's secrecy were momentarily overshadowed by his defiance.

In the inky cloak of night, the city seemed to retreat into the background as Frankie navigated the streets. His car, filled with contraband, was a ticking time bomb on wheels. Yet, Frankie drove with a cavalier disregard.

The glow of a red light in his rearview mirror cut through the darkness, an unwelcome intrusion. Still, he greeted it with reckless nonchalance, pulling over without a hint of concern. The wait felt interminable, a silent standoff between Frankie and the unseen officer.

Finally, the car door eased open. Frankie watched through his mirror as a muscular figure approached him, the officer's hand pressing against the car in a practiced motion. Three knocks on his window, a clear, imperious command, one Frankie could not ignore.

Rolling down his window, Frankie stared into the stern face of law enforcement. "Good evening, sir. License and paperwork, please," the officer requested, his tone absent any recognition of the man before him.

Frankie couldn't help but laugh silently at the absurdity. Years had passed since he'd been subjected to such a mundane inquiry. "Excuse me?" he said, feigning ignorance, his voice incredulous.

The officer, undeterred, repeated his request, prompting Frankie to play his hand. "Shine that light on me. Do you know who I am?" Frankie challenged, arrogance coloring his words.

The flashlight beam washed over him, and for a fleeting moment, Officer 457 was starstruck. Unfortunately for Frankie, he was a rookie still clinging to the rulebook.

Despite the officer's hesitation, duty prevailed. "I still need to see your paperwork, sir. It's protocol," he insisted, though the awe of encountering Frankie Keys lingered.

Frankie's patience, already frayed by the evening's events, snapped. "Listen, I don't care about protocol! I'm having a rough night, and you're not making it any easier."

Officer 457 was caught off guard by Frankie's sudden outburst. He stood there, stunned, as Frankie continued. "You know what... Here! Take this hundred, and let me be on my way."

The officer stared at Frankie, processing his slurred words. Taken aback by the bribe, he demanded Frankie step out of the car. Frankie's refusal only made things worse.

"It's not that important, kid. Let it go," Frankie sneered, underestimating the officer's resolve. "That money I offered you is a month's salary compared to what that corrupt badge is paying you." His voice dripped with privilege—the kind granted by influence, not color.

He continued, "Why are we still here? Let me go. This ain't that important. But I am!"

With a clenched jaw and dwindling patience, Officer 457—still green and visibly fed up with Frankie's cocky attitude—yanked the car door open. His grip was firm as he hauled Frankie out with a force that left no room for resistance. The cold concrete met Frankie's body with a harsh reality check as he was handcuffed and slammed against his own vehicle.

"You should've cooperated. I would've let you go! But you had to push my buttons." Officer 457 stared at Frankie, debating his next move. "You're drunk!" he shouted. "Tell me the truth, and I might help. So long as you calm that attitude down."

Frankie's head hung as he sat propped up against the car, ignoring the officer. 457 continued, "You're all over the place. You know I can have this car towed!" Something about that statement snapped Frankie out of his rebellious funk. He began to sober up and tried to negotiate, his mind returning to the significant cache in his car's trunk.

"Wait a minute, brother. You can't tow this car—let's work something out," Frankie pleaded.

Officer 457 replied, "Why not? I smell the liquor on your breath, and you refused to comply. You ain't driving this car. You could kill someone and end your career!"

Frankie pleaded louder, "Just hold the hell on! Let's talk about this. Shit! Calm down and listen to me for a second, Jack!"

The standoff was interrupted by the glare of approaching headlights blinding Officer 457. He gripped his service weapon as Frankie spoke up frantically, "Did you call for backup? Please tell me you didn't!"

Officer 457 snapped back, "No! It was a routine stop. I don't know who this is."

Frankie's plea for leniency turned desperate. "Help me, kid. Please! I'll pay your house off. Hell, I'll buy you a bigger house! There's too much at stake," he implored, but the officer was unmoved.

As the bright lights dimmed, Officer 457 quickly recognized a familiar face through the glass: Sheriff Whitaker. The sheriff's arrival was an unforeseen twist for both of the men. Frankie's fate hung in the balance, his earlier bravado evaporating as he faced the potential for ruin.

Sheriff Whitaker stepped from the truck, arriving with an air that shifted the dynamic of the standoff. Officer 457, momentarily relieved, stiffened as Hogg emerged from the vehicle alongside the sheriff.

"I have this under control," Officer 457 stated, attempting to assert his authority.

With a dismissive glance, the sheriff countered, "Good job, son… But this scene is now under our command. Step aside, Officer." Confusion marred 457's features, his adherence to protocol clashing with this unexpected turn.

"But Sheriff, I was on the scene first. It's my responsibility to see this through," he protested.

Sheriff Whitaker's response was cold. "Interfere, and I'll have you arrested for obstruction," he threatened, pulling rank in a manner that left no room for argument. "Remember why you were hired… Don't meddle in matters above your pay grade."

The sheriff looked at Hogg with a smirk and said, "And to think… They want us to hire more of these spooks." He looked back to 457. "Step aside now. I got work to do!"

The sheriff's remark stung Officer 457, revealing the murky corruption of New Port policing. Despite his anger, he had no choice— this job was his family's lifeline. 457 exchanged a glance with Frankie, knowing instantly that the night had taken a terrible turn.

Sheriff Whitaker and Hogg approached Frankie and his car with a predatory calm. 457 shouted, "I've already searched the car, Sheriff. Nothing is out of place." The sheriff silenced him with a single motion. Something about the exchange didn't sit right with Frankie; he began to sense a setup.

The sheriff and Hogg closed in on the car with purpose, their search leading them to the trunk, where they uncovered the goods. Frankie was left speechless.

The sheriff shouted, "Hot damn! You must be planning to supply the whole state!" Frankie didn't reply.

"Well… no need for talking. You're coming with us," Hogg declared, gripping Frankie's arm with an ironclad hold as he escorted him to the truck.

Feeling ignored and left out, Officer 457 watched in disgust as they drove away and Frankie's car was towed. This was not the law he'd sworn to uphold. His loyalty to the badge was long gone, a bitter lesson learned under the harsh streetlights of corruption and power.

Frankie couldn't help but feel defeated. How could he be so stupid and emotional tonight? He listened as the sheriff and Hogg cracked jokes at his expense. He knew he was in trouble.

As Frankie walked down the cold hall toward the jail cell, he couldn't help but think about how his life had turned for the worse. As they approached the cell, Frankie was greeted by a familiar voice.

Judge Kincaid spoke up. "Oh, Frankie…how did a man like you get yourself into such a mess? Have a seat, my boy."

Frankie was surprised, but he knew he was in for more trouble. He sat down across from the judge. They were both silent for several minutes before the judge finally spoke.

Looking at Frankie with an evil smirk, the judge said, "You're in a world of trouble, son. If I put my signature on top of all dem' party supplies you got pulled over with, that'll get ya' at least a decade in Angola. Maybe more."

Frankie's heart sank as the judge continued. "You might never play another tune. Just kiss it goodbye."

Frankie knew that Angola was one of the worst plantations in the country. He couldn't imagine spending a decade of his life in that place.

"You look scared, son," the judge said with enthusiasm, leaning forward. "But you shouldn't be. You know why? Because I like the way you run New Port."

Frankie took a deep breath and quickly understood where

this exchange was headed. The judge went on, "You are a clean businessman, except for whatever the hell is going on tonight. But you know, I can make all of this go away."

Frankie sat with his head leaned back against the concrete wall and said, "In exchange for…?"

The judge stroked his dirty beard and said, "Oooh, I don't know. I'm a modest man. What do you say to thirty-five percent of everything you make? Tour, booze, bricks, everything. Let's call it my monthly retainer to keep this little folder sealed."

The judge stood and began to pace before adding, "Yeah, that sounds good. Ya see…as long as I get my retainer, you will never have to worry about those charges ever seeing the light of day."

Kincaid made eye contact with Frankie and extended his hand. "Do we have a deal?" he asked with a grim grin.

Frankie knew that he was in no position to negotiate.

"And one more thing," the judge added with a smirk. "I plan to hand over the seized product to ya' friend Jimmie. We don't need to keep that much in the precinct. It might walk away. You get me? Good…"

The judge used Jimmie as a pawn and decoy to throw Frankie off, knowing Frankie would immediately suspect Jimmie as the orchestrator of the whole ordeal.

The judge left the cell, leaving the bars behind him open. Frankie was startled by the jailer's words. "What the hell are you waiting for? Move it! Unless you wanna stay."

As Frankie exited the police station, Judge Kincaid's demands loomed large in his mind. From a parked car, Detective Marlow approached him. "What the hell are you doing here?" he asked, his face curious.

Frankie was about to reply when he spotted Officer 457 across the lot. Anger boiled inside him, and he stormed over to the officer. "You son of a bitch! You ruined my life!" he screamed.

Marlow quickly intervened, restraining Frankie. "Frankie, what are you doing? You're losing it, man!" He pushed Frankie away from 457.

"I fucked up, Marlow. I messed up bad. How could I be so stupid!" Frankie punched the air in frustration. "The judge has me. I'm screwed! I can't see a way out." Frankie slammed his fist into the palm of his hand.

Marlow looked weary, torn between his duty as a detective and his loyalty as a friend. "Crap, Frankie. What did you do? Under the Judge's thumb is the last place you want to be. This is bad, Frankie. Real bad."

Frankie wiped away the tears, his voice cracking as he spiraled. "I'm falling apart, man. My life, my business, everything is going downhill."

Marlow, feeling empathetic but stern, spoke sincerely. "Listen, brother. I'll help you figure something out to get from under the judge, but you've got to clean up this illegal shit. I'm not going down for you. Got it?" He nervously scanned the building windows and parking lot, aware of the risks and the need to keep his involvement under wraps.

"Get out of here. You're about to make this worse for yourself," Marlow warned.

Frankie replied, "Get me something on the judge and I'll owe you a huge favor."

Marlow scratched his head. "Really... A favor?" he echoed.

Frankie's face was stone cold. "Remember this, Marlow. In the underworld, favors are better than money."

Fueled by his drive to expose the crooked judge and bolster his reputation as a top detective, Marlow accepted the proposal. Frankie knew he was in deep, the stakes higher than ever before.

As Marlow turned to leave, Frankie felt a glimmer of hope, but his predicament remained heavy. This was just the beginning of a long, treacherous path.

# CHAPTER 7

# BREAKING POINT

"The real burden is the truth we hide from ourselves."
— Detective Marlow

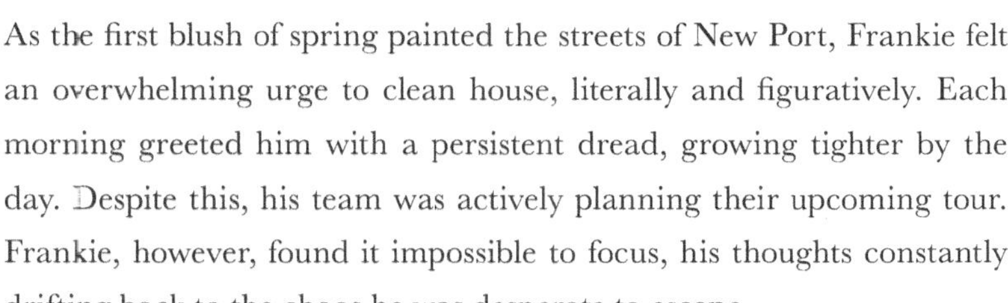

As the first blush of spring painted the streets of New Port, Frankie felt an overwhelming urge to clean house, literally and figuratively. Each morning greeted him with a persistent dread, growing tighter by the day. Despite this, his team was actively planning their upcoming tour. Frankie, however, found it impossible to focus, his thoughts constantly drifting back to the chaos he was desperate to escape.

Lately, Frankie refused to leave home. Bell tried coaxing him out with promises of fresh air and sunshine. At the same time, Chubbs would show up unannounced, hopelessly trying to reignite Frankie's passion. Despite their efforts, Frankie stayed stubborn in his solitude. But today felt different. With a deep breath, he decided it was time to bring order back to his life.

Stepping out to run errands, Frankie felt hope as he watched the city come alive. Freshly bloomed flowers lined the sidewalks, their colors contrasting with the still-damp pavement from the morning dew. He cherished these drives into the city, the way the light danced through the leaves, casting shadows that played like jazz notes. Neighbors exchanged greetings as they tended to their gardens, and shopkeepers opened their doors, ready to start the day.

After visiting a few familiar spots, Frankie emerged from Rhythm & Reeds, a local music store. He took a moment to appreciate the crisp air, the birds chirping, and the bustle of the city around him.

A familiar voice interrupted his thoughts, piercing his introspective fog. Turning, he saw Officer 457, whose messy appearance and evident distress cut through Frankie's initial irritation.

"What do you want?" Frankie's attempt at calmness belied the surge of anger he felt toward the man who had cost him so much.

Officer 457, on the verge of tears, looked down. "It sounds strange, but I followed you today. I've hit rock bottom, Frankie. I'm about to lose everything. I need your help," he pleaded, his voice cracking.

Frankie crossed his arms; his skepticism evident. "Why should I help you? After everything you did?" He waved the officer off dismissively. "Man, get on. I ain't got the time."

Officer 457 took a shaky breath. "We both made mistakes that night, Frankie. I tried to help you, but you threw your influence around, acting untouchable. It messed with my head and made me feel like less of a man. But you need to know… I didn't call for backup that night. I swear." His voice was earnest as he looked away, ashamed. "The badge was all I had. I didn't know anything else. They fired me, Frankie. Said I couldn't be trusted."

Frankie's look intensified. "And you think that's my problem?"

The ex-officer slumped. "I don't blame you for not trusting me. But I'm in a tight spot." He hesitated, then took a step closer. "I have a wife and two young kids I can't provide for. A man is supposed to provide!"

His voice broke as he continued, "I'm begging you, Frankie. Please!"

Frankie's instinct was to distrust, but the sight of his old adversary so vulnerable stirred something within him. He saw the tears in Officer 457's eyes, his struggle apparent. Officer 457 clung to Frankie, his heavy body causing Frankie to buckle. "I don't know where else to turn."

For a long moment, Frankie said nothing. Then, with a deep sigh, he looked away, wrestling with his inner conflict. "Alright," he finally said, his voice low. "I'll hear you out. But this doesn't mean I forgive you."

Officer 457 eagerly asked, "What do you need? I am willing to do anything to make myself useful." Without waiting for an answer, he grabbed Frankie by the shoulders with a firm grip. "I'll work for you and protect your life with my own," he promised, gratitude and relief evident in his tone.

Frankie scratched his head, the ex-officer's desperation making him pause. "First. What's your real name?" Frankie asked, his tone softer but still cautious.

"Cal," the officer replied. "Cal Anderson."

Although irritated, Frankie gave in, realizing how much he could benefit from having a former cop in his back pocket while on tour. "Alright, I'll help you, Cal Anderson. But you're now in my debt, and I expect your loyalty," Frankie stated firmly, setting the terms of their unexpected alliance.

Frankie outlined the role he envisioned for Cal: a driver and bodyguard for his upcoming tour. "I'll pay you double what the force did." Cal smiled as Frankie continued. "You'll start by getting acquainted with Detective Marlow. He's my homeboy and knows how I like to operate." As the statement left Frankie's lips, he began questioning his decision. But the agreement was solidified, and he couldn't turn back now.

As Cal departed, Frankie contemplated the complexity of their new relationship. It was a gamble, but Frankie felt it was better to dance with the devil he knew.

* * *

Several days later, moments before sunrise, Detective Tony Marlow and his trainee Junior convened at the police station. The only light came from scattered desk lamps, where a handful of detectives, either too busy to go home or starting early, worked quietly.

"Hope you caught some z's," Marlow began, noting Junior's grogginess, "because we're in for a marathon, not a sprint." Tingling with nerves and anticipation, Junior's imagination was running wild.

Their first stop was a local diner, a pillar of the community and a place of warmth in the predawn chill. The smell of fresh coffee and baked goods wafted through the air as they stepped inside.

"Two hot glazed, and make it two blacks," Marlow ordered.

Junior chimed in, "One cup is fine." He whispered to Marlow, "I don't drink coffee."

The senior detective brushed off Junior's protest. "Today, you're a coffee drinker." He looked back to the cashier and reiterated, "We'll take two cups of black coffee."

Junior's first encounter with the bitter brew was less than pleasant, his grimace drawing their first shared laugh of the day.

As they settled into the worn booth, Marlow laid out the day's agenda, turning the small space into an impromptu classroom.

Marlow polished off his doughnuts, brushed the crumbs from his hands, and stood up. "Alright, Junior. Let's get moving—there's a lot to see."

The city awaited them, a living textbook of human behavior. Marlow's guidance served as both a compass and a map. They spent the morning riding through town, each stop and encounter revealing lessons in empathy, observation, and the unspoken language of the streets. Marlow navigated through various neighborhoods, highlighting the nuances of detective work—from reading the environment to understanding the community's dynamics. Each moment allowed Junior to learn, ask questions, and witness the broader impact a good detective can have beyond solving crimes.

As the day wore on and the afternoon sun climbed high, Marlow's tone grew more serious. He guided the car into a neighborhood of vacant lots and weathered houses, slowing before pulling over by the curb.

Junior scanned the surroundings, his nerves on edge. "What are we doing here?" he asked.

Marlow turned to him, his expression serious and intent. "Junior, it's not just about seeing; it's about understanding. People live their lives out here, facing challenges you might never experience. A good detective knows the streets and feels the pulse of all parts of the city—not just the nice ones."

He stepped out of the car, motioning for Junior to follow. "Walk with me," he said.

As they wandered through the neighborhood, Marlow's stride caught Junior's eye. There was a sway in Marlow's step, his feet turned out just enough to make his stride look unhurried and distinct.

Junior nudged him, "Why do you walk like that, anyway?"

Marlow shrugged with a grin. "Maybe I'm just struttin'. Or maybe my mama was right when she said I was bow-legged."

They shared a laugh and continued down the block as Marlow pointed out small details that spoke volumes: the faded paintings on brick walls, children playing stickball in the streets, elders sharing stories on porches.

"Look at these murals, Junior. They tell the history of this place, the pride and pain of the people who live here."

They passed a small community garden, a thriving oasis amidst the concrete, where residents carefully tended their plots. Marlow greeted a few of the gardeners by name, exchanging friendly banter. "This garden is a lifeline for many. It's more than just vegetables; it's hope and self-sufficiency."

Marlow introduced Junior to locals, shaking hands and sharing a few words. "This is Mr. Rodriguez. He's lived here for many years and has seen it all. And this is Mrs. Thompson. She runs the local youth club for the kids." Junior noticed the admiration in their voices as they spoke to Marlow.

"Trust and respect are mutual currencies in this line of work. They're earned, never given. You have to show that you care, that you're here to help, not just to police," Marlow said to Junior while they headed back to the car.

The sun began to dip, casting warm hues across the sky. Marlow glanced at Junior, his tone carrying a newfound respect. "I misjudged you," he said. "I thought you were soft, but now I see you're just inexperienced. There's a strength in you, Junior. My job is to help you find it and mold it."

As the late afternoon turned to evening, Marlow continued to share his wisdom with Junior. "Curiosity is your greatest tool," he advised. "Ask questions, and don't stop until you get answers. But at the same time, you need to be quiet. Listen more than you talk. Let people think you know nothing, and they'll tell you everything. In my long experience as a detective, I have learned that there are no coincidences and criminals always leave a trail."

Junior leaned back, absorbing the insights before inquiring, "So, how did you end up in New Port?"

Detective Marlow sighed. "Truthfully, I was reassigned here as punishment for digging too deep into a public official. The establishment wasn't ready for a Black man to expose the truth, even if I'm pale enough to pass. Sometimes I wonder—were they afraid of exposing one of their own, or just afraid of a Black man doing it?"

He focused on the road ahead, adding, "One day, my commander just announced I was being shipped off to this obscure little town. I was livid!"

Junior empathized, "Damn, that's harsh."

Marlow offered a wry smile and continued. "No… That's life." He glanced at Junior, then casually adjusted the dashboard dial, his thoughts seemingly elsewhere. "Always remember: If you go digging in the toilet, you're likely gonna find some shit…or at least get some on you."

Looking at the seasoned detective, Junior playfully added, "I don't know what that means, but I know this. At least moving to New Port got you the best sidekick money can buy."

Marlow cast a brief, measured glance at Junior before responding, "Wrong again, Junior. The best sidekick is no sidekick at all."

He let the words hang in the air, watching as Junior absorbed the lesson. After a moment, he checked the rearview mirror, his expression unreadable.

"Alright, that's enough work for today," Marlow said.

Feeling the need for a break, Marlow ushered Junior to a dive bar nestled on the fringe of town. The bar's murky interior, steeped in the aroma of aged bourbon and stale cigarettes, provided a place to disappear. Neon lights flickered against the cracked walls, casting a dim, shadowy glow over the patrons.

Marlow ordered shots, their amber liquid catching the faint reflections of the neon signs.

As they sipped their drinks, the relaxed ambiance softened Marlow's usually guarded demeanor. He began to share tales of a case from years past—a case that had never quite left him.

Junior listened closely, his fascination growing with each revelation. Yet, as Marlow continued, a sense of dread began to creep in, the weight of the detective's story settling heavily in the young trainee's mind.

"Junior..." Marlow's voice was heavy, the whiskey amplifying his introspection. "This job shows you humanity in its rawest form, the best and the worst." He stared into the glass before taking another sip. "But do you know the hardest part of the job?"

Junior replied, "Arresting bad guys?"

Marlow shook his head in disbelief. "No, rookie... The hardest part is letting go." He swirled the whiskey in his glass, his eyes distant. "We spend so much time chasing criminals that the cases get under our skin. They linger with us, even after they're closed."

Junior sat and hung on every word Marlow uttered. "I'm ashamed to admit how many files I hoard. Cases I won't let anyone see or touch because they might ruin my progress."

Sensing a rare vulnerability, Junior asked, "What about family? What about joy? Does happiness ever find its way into a life like this?"

Marlow laughed cynically, dismissing any notion of contentment in their line of work. "The files I keep are my family," he confided. "And the only joy I see comes from uncovering the truth."

He looked at Junior with a rare honesty. "I'm obsessive; I'm consumed by this job, Junior. It's not healthy." Marlow's voice cracked as he continued, pouring his heart out. "Strive to be a great detective, but don't lose yourself like I did. Promise me you'll find a balance. That's all I want for you."

The conversation stalled, but the tone had shifted irreversibly. Junior realized the heavy burdens carried by those who seek justice. This pivotal lesson was not found in any manual but in the lived experience of a mentor whose own demons were laid bare.

The darkness in the bar grew, mirroring Detective Marlow's spirit. His demeanor continued to shift, his defenses eroded by the alcohol. The toll of his career, marked by loneliness and sacrifice, became more apparent with each passing moment.

Marlow leaned in and slurred, "You see, kid, this job..." He let out a hiccup. "It demands everything from you: your time, energy, and love."

Junior didn't know what to say. He looked up to Marlow as the epitome of what a detective should be. But now, seeing him like this, Junior realized that even the best detectives could be broken.

After a long pause, Junior hesitated, then asked, "How do you keep this side of your life a secret? It's too heavy. I would have to let it out."

Marlow smiled, gently squeezing Junior's arm. "It's not about the secrets we keep from others, Junior. The real burden is the truth we hide from ourselves. That's heavy."

As the night drew to a close, Marlow paid the tab and left a generous tip. When they stood to leave, his parting advice was both a warning and a wish. "You have a bright future, Junior. Ensure it doesn't lead you here."

With a clumsy embrace, Marlow staggered away into the night, leaving the rookie to ponder the meaning behind their conversation.

*　*　*

Sunday arrived, and the day swiftly drew to a close. A soft, golden glow enveloped the sprawling mansion as the evening settled in. Tonight, the house pulsed with anticipation. The warm light of chandeliers bathed the rooms, ready to welcome the select guests invited for Bell's pre-birthday dinner—an evening destined to be memorable.

The grandeur of the mansion was unmistakable. Large hedges sculpted into classical nudes flanked the entryway, inviting guests into the vast living area. Under the long winding stairwell, a marble bar commanded attention. To the right, the lavish dining room awaited, centered around a large oak table with a turtle shell finish, elegantly set with fine china and crystal glasses that sparkled under the soft light.

The air was rich with the aroma of southern cuisine prepared by Ms. Ida. The smell of golden fried chicken, crispy catfish, macaroni and cheese, candied yams, greens, peas, and cornbread filled the room, complemented by fresh lemonade and sweet tea to wash it all down. The bar was open to all, with the bartender instructed to pour only top-shelf spirits. The spread set the stage for an evening where the comforts of home cooking blended seamlessly with the luxury of their surroundings.

Despite the elegant setup, the vibe was relaxed and reserved for Frankie and Bell's close circle—no pretenses, just genuine friends celebrating his wife. Bell's radiant silk red dress perfectly matched the evening's luxury, hugging her figure tightly.

Chubbs, with his easygoing nature, was the first to arrive. He immediately went to steal a piece of chicken but was caught by Ms. Ida. "Fat boy, I know you ain't bout' to eat! You ain't washed not one hand." He relented, returning a goofy grin before excusing himself.

Kenya arrived shortly after, her striking presence catching everyone's attention. Bell noticed a sudden intensity in Frankie's demeanor as he spoke from across the room. Trying to brush off her resentment, Bell turned her focus to the arrival of her own guests.

She was thrilled to see her old friends, Claire and Danielle, whose presence reminded her of who she was before Frankie. They added a personal touch to the evening and helped ground her in her past.

Bell's face lit up as she greeted them, "Well, I'll just swan. I haven't seen you girls in a month of Sundays."

The three women embraced, their laughter filling the room and momentarily lightening Bell's mood.

Frankie pulled Bell to the side and presented her with a gold bracelet as her first gift of the evening. She beamed with appreciation and thanked him warmly, but her bliss was short-lived. In a moment of distraction, Frankie made a slip. "Kenya, could you—" he began before the realization of his mistake dawned on him, the name hanging in the air like a note out of tune.

Bell's smile faltered with irritation as she corrected him. "It's Bell!"

Ms. Ida, sensing the discomfort from afar, approached the pair with a soothing presence. While she calmed Bell, Silky arrived in his usual manner—brash and flamboyant. He stepped in, filling the room with his booming voice. "Mama! It sho' smell good in here!"

Kristine, quieter but always observant, took in the scene, her sharp eyes noticing Kenya's dazzling appearance, Bell's coldness, and Frankie's jitters.

Frankie attempted to steer back to safer waters, but the damage was done. Bell's demeanor changed subtly; her interactions now carried a distant edge. Frankie, realizing the severity of his slip, tried to compensate with heightened affection. Still, the initial harmony of the evening had been irrevocably disturbed.

"In case you forgot," Bell scolded, "I come from an aristocratic family. I know what I signed up for. Rich men have mistresses. But you call me her name hours before my birthday? I'm over it."

She waved her hand dismissively and walked off, leaving Frankie to stand in the shadow of his mistake.

Bell's mind flashed back to her roots. Her grandfather had been a respected teacher, one of the few Black men trusted to educate less advanced white children in their small town. That legacy of respect and education ran deep in her family.

Bell, however, had taken a different path. Though formal work as a therapist was rare for a Black woman, she had become known as the town's listener—people from all walks of life came to her with their troubles, gossip, and secrets. Frankie's wealth allowed her the freedom to do what she loved. But despite all her advantages, Bell was still vulnerable to the sting of Frankie's careless words—a reminder that even with all her lineage and achievements, she was still just another woman in his orbit.

As drinks flowed, the room filled with laughter and casual banter, though a slight edge still lingered. Guests made their way to the dining room for a royal feast, momentarily masking the earlier discord.

Bell's friends, Claire and Danielle, shared knowing glances and hushed comments.

"This place is stunning," Danielle whispered, admiring the elegant decor.

"I know! You can see why she stays," Claire replied with a hint of sarcasm.

Silky grabbed a drink from the bar before swaggering to the table. "A toast to the chef!" he declared, raising his glass and drawing a few smiles from around the room.

Frankie tried to regain control of the evening as everyone settled into their seats. He stood and raised his glass. "To Bell, the heart of our home," he said, his voice betraying a hint of anxiety.

Kristine noticed and offered to bless the food as a distraction. "Dear Lord, protect, keep, and guide us through this maze we call life. Thank you for this food we are about to receive and Ms. Ida for preparing it. May it all be nourishment to our bodies. We pray to you and only you. Amen."

The group echoed, "Amen." Laughter and conversation gradually resumed, the earlier strain receding into the background as plates were filled and glasses clinked in celebration.

Frankie made his rounds, ensuring everyone's glass remained full as if trying to wash away the awkwardness with each pour. Bell donned a mask of composure, her smile gracious but guarded as she engaged in light, aloof conversation.

The group could feel something brewing but couldn't quite pinpoint it. Sensing the undercurrent, Kenya treaded carefully, although for Bell, she didn't tread carefully enough. Every laugh from Kenya, a tad too bright, and every glance she stole toward Frankie stoked Bell's simmering annoyance.

Kenya's affection for Frankie clashed with Bell's desire for respect and acknowledgment in this precarious love triangle. The not-so-secret affair was now teetering dangerously close to the surface. In a rare display of vulnerability, Kenya made an innocent attempt to pander. However, it turned out to be the moment that broke the fragile peace.

As she passed a dish down the table, she remarked, "Frankie knows how to make an evening memorable, doesn't he?" While cryptic to others, this line was as loud to Bell as the clinking dinnerware at the table.

Bell reacted swiftly, her brewing irritation now focused squarely on a clear target. "Oh, Kenya... I imagine you have had many memorable evenings with Frankie." Her voice dripped with sarcasm, slicing through the jovial chatter. The table fell into an uneasy silence.

Kenya faltered under Bell's glare, her usual confidence wavering as she sought to backtrack. "Girl, it's nothing. I'm just saying y'all..." she stammered.

But Bell, discarding her aristocratic poise and slipping into something more raw, interrupted Kenya mid-sentence. "You're not my girl. *You!* You are my husband's mistress," she declared, the words hanging heavy between them.

The guests exchanged awkward glances before Kenya rose to her feet. "You know, I think I should go."

Seething with anger, Bell commanded, "Sit! It's bad etiquette to leave in the middle of the evening. You should know that. I thought you wanted to be a little bar manager."

Kenya snapped with an angry glint in her eye, "Club owner!"

Bell smiled. "Hmph… Same thing."

Frankie, torn between the two women he cared for, felt the pressure of his decisions pressing down. "Enough, Bell!" he interjected, his voice betraying his turmoil. He wanted peace, but the dinner was quickly unraveling.

Aware of the brewing storm, Chubbs regaled the table with old tales meant to lower the heat. His booming laughter filled the room, breaking through the tension. Ms. Ida nodded in amusement at his antics, her presence a comforting constant amid the shifting moods.

As the rocky evening continued, the conversation naturally drifted from casual banter to more reflective dialogue. The guests began discussing birthdays and other milestone events, which led them to contemplate the passage of time. This introspection gradually steered the discussion toward life and its inevitable end.

They exchanged heartfelt stories of loved ones lost too soon, each tale a poignant reminder of life's fragility.

Frankie hesitated, his throat tightening as he struggled to find the courage to speak. "Lately, I've been pondering my legacy," he confessed. "I yearn to leave a mark on the world that transcends my music." His words lingered in the air, heavy with the weight of his desire for change and purpose.

The group remained quiet, moved by Frankie's earnestness. Their silence carried a shared understanding, a quiet acknowledgment of his vulnerability. Bell, however, seized the moment, her voice cutting through the somber mood. "Perhaps that journey begins with embracing the role of a better husband," she suggested, her tone sharp but honest.

Ms. Ida, clearly taken aback by Bell's bluntness, couldn't contain her reaction. "Bell!" she exclaimed, her tone an uneasy mix of surprise and disapproval. "Your manners!"

Bell didn't flinch. Instead, she leaned back, her smile carrying a mischievous glint that betrayed her intent. "Sorry…just thinking out loud."

As the table grew quiet, each person grappling with their thoughts, Danielle leaned in, speaking softly to Claire. "It must be miserable to know your husband is cheating."

Claire replied with a dismissive hair flip, "I highly doubt this lifestyle is miserable. Honey, if a man provides, he can do whatever he wants. Think about it like this—my grandmother used to say, 'All dogs cheat. Even the ones that come home wagging their tail.'"

They shared a quiet smile before Danielle's expression grew serious. "But do you think she's happy?"

"Does it matter?" Claire retorted.

"Uhh, yeah," Danielle replied, clearly unsettled.

Claire patted her friend on the thigh reassuringly, "I don't know about her, but I know a girl like me couldn't live off love and happiness alone. I need diamonds and champagne!"

This brief interlude, marked by Bell's audacious observation and the whispered conversation between friends, underscored the depth of their discussions and highlighted the complex web of personal desires and societal expectations.

Silky broke the silence, leaning back in his seat with anguish etched on his features. "Y'all need to hear this," he started, but Kristine tapped him.

"Not now, Silky."

Silky shook his head. "Nah, nah, Kristine... They need to hear this." His voice carried both wisdom and fervor. "I've been quiet, watching the lot of you squabble over what? Petty grievances? You're missing the bigger picture."

He scanned the room, assessing each person at the table. "Look around," he urged, his voice gaining strength. "We're here, living as Black folks with freedom most don't have, pockets full enough to forget our ancestors' dreams. And yet, here we are, stressin' and bickering like children."

He rose to his feet, emphasizing his words: "Let me tell you what it means to endure, to really survive."

Silky's story unfolded from there, shaped by the harsh realities of his Mississippi upbringing amid poverty and racial division. "My childhood," he began, "wasn't just tough; it was a trial by fire."

He described a life marred by abuse, with a father lost to addiction and a mother to prostitution, painting a vivid picture of a boy forced to grow up too soon.

"The day I lost my parents," Silky continued, the pain evident in his voice, "I was left with nothing but questions and a world that seemed intent on breaking me." He took a moment, lost in thought. "I was only eleven when I met Ruby Buono Sr. He was a major player known as Sweet Red, with a charisma that hid the darkness of our trade."

Silky grew distant as the memories played in his mind. "Sweet Red saw something in me, a potential I didn't know I had. He introduced me to a life that promised escape—but I often look back and ask... at what cost?"

Silky recounted his rise in the underground world, leveraging his charm and cunning persona to draw women in with promises of a better life. "I convinced myself I was offering them a way out, just like I was looking for mine. But the truth?" He let the words linger. "It was just another chain, another cycle of exploitation. And sometimes... another muse for my selfish pleasure."

Silky's story laid bare the complexities of survival and ambition. "I made choices," he admitted, "that I thought were my only way out. It took losing someone I cared about, watching my world nearly crumble, to realize the cost of my so-called success."

Silky's journey through the dark corridors of the pimping business had come at a high cost. "I've seen too many good women go young because of me," Silky confessed, his voice heavy with regret.

After a moment of silence, he felt the sting of unshed tears as painful memories resurfaced. "Prison was a crucible for me. It forced me to confront my actions, to truly see the harm I was causing. That's when I vowed to change my approach—less coercion, more choice, ensuring a semblance of dignity for those under my wing."

He continued, "Ruby taught me you got to love yo bitch hard, but you gotta work her harder," he added, his words reflecting the harsh lessons learned from his mentor. "But as I grew wiser, I decided to stop riding my girls so hard and to let them be free… as long as I got a small portion for connecting them with high rollers."

Silky gave an exaggerated wink, offering a quick and much-needed laugh.

Bell, however, couldn't mask her skepticism. "And yet, you continue in this line of work. Why?" she probed, her curiosity tinged with criticism.

Silky met her gaze squarely. "It's not just what I do; it's who I am. Pimpin' is in my blood, but that doesn't mean I haven't evolved. I've moved past the brutality that once defined this life," he explained, his tone earnest. He gestured smoothly, a visual flourish that underscored his words. "Now, I offer a choice. My role is more of a connector than a controller. Believe it or not, some women find empowerment in the independence it brings."

Kristine gave a brief sign of agreement. "He's changed. It's not the same game with Silky anymore."

Bell was unconvinced. "It still doesn't change the facts. Pimps want the benefits without any of the work," she retorted, her words slicing through the air.

Silky didn't flinch, but the subtle shift in his expression suggested the comment had hit its mark.

Overwhelmed by the memories, Silky sat down abruptly, his usual composure slipping. "Enough of this gloom," he declared, wiping away a stray tear. "Frankie, bring out that whiskey. Let's toast to better days ahead!"

His call for a drink marked the end of his story, bringing him back to the present.

A pensive hush enveloped the dining room. Each guest pondered the gritty realities of life that Silky had laid bare. Moved by the moment and Silky's request, Frankie retrieved a bottle, pouring generous amounts for Silky and himself before passing the bottle around the table.

When the bottle reached Kenya, she politely declined. The stories of hardship and endurance resonated with her, amplifying her anxieties about the future.

"Come on, Kenya, just a sip," Chubbs urged, pushing the bottle toward her.

Kenya shook her head, her voice soft but firm. "No, really. I can't."

Seeing an opportunity to needle her, Bell leaned in with faux sweetness. "Oh, come on, Kenya. It's my celebration. Don't be such a spoiled brat. Be a good sport."

Kenya's hands trembled slightly as she picked up the bottle before putting it down again. "I'm so sorry, Bell. I'm just not in the mood for it. Silky's story has me all emotional." Kenya put on a fake smile, hoping to deflect the attention.

Claire whispered to Danielle, "She is a bore. Can't imagine what Frankie sees in her."

Danielle smirked. "Good in bed, I suppose."

Kenya was furious, the insult clinging to her.

The room fell into an uncomfortable silence, the pressure mounting. Trying to lighten the mood, Silky joked, "What's the deal, Kenya? We get loaded all the time. Take a swig and let's get this party started."

The room began to spin, everyone's voices echoing in her head. Kenya's composure broke as she stood and banged the table. "I said no! I'm pregnant!"

The words tumbled from her lips, each syllable heavy with consequences, swiftly followed by her tears. "And I'm terrified!" she confessed, her voice cracking as she continued to break down.

The room erupted in shock, guests exchanging glances of surprise and disbelief. Bell's face twisted into a look of stunned outrage. What had started as a night of celebration had devolved into an evening of revelations, each guest now bracing for the fallout of Kenya's unexpected announcement.

Kenya searched Frankie's expression, desperate for any hint of understanding or reassurance. But Frankie's face became a canvas of shock and confusion as he struggled to process her words.

Bell rose in a flurry of rage, her movements swift and decisive. Her hand connected sharply with Frankie's cheek, the slap cracking through the room like a gunshot in the quiet forest. Before anyone could react, she seized a glass of iced tea from the table and dumped it over his head, the cascade of cold liquid punctuating her fury. Her silent accusations of his failures echoed louder than any words.

Frankie reeled, the sting of the slap and the icy shock of the tea leaving him momentarily frozen.

Bell's icy glare shifted to Kenya, her voice a venomous whisper. "You're carrying my husband's child?" The rhetorical question was laced with disbelief, underlining the depth of her pain.

Frankie finally found his voice, albeit shaky. "Bell, I—"

"Don't," she snapped, cutting him off before he could finish. Her silent command was clear: she wasn't ready to hear any justifications.

The men sat quietly; the moment was too charged for their input. Ms. Ida, wise and maternal, offered a comforting hand to Bell once again, though words of solace were hard to find.

Silky shifted uncomfortably, his story of change and redemption now overshadowed by the present drama.

Quiet but observant, Kristine watched the unfolding scene, her sympathy with Kenya evident. Yet, she understood the pain etched on Bell's face. "Life's never straightforward," she said softly, a sentiment that seemed to encapsulate the evening's events.

Caught in the storm's eye, Frankie felt his world unravel.

Suddenly, the doorbell rang, drawing everyone's attention to the entrance. Ms. Ida made her way to investigate and quickly announced Detective Marlow's unexpected arrival.

Still reeling from the slap, Frankie hesitated but instructed Ms. Ida to let Marlow in. The room seemed to hold its breath as Marlow entered, his presence adding another layer of intensity. He took in the scene. "Sorry to interrupt. Frankie, I need a moment with you."

The dining room was a mosaic of reactions. Bell's focus narrowed, her irritation still simmering beneath a composed facade. Her friends, Claire and Danielle, exchanged uneasy glances, visibly uncomfortable. Kenya seemed to shrink back, hoping to avoid any further conflict. Ms. Ida stood quietly beside the detective, her face reflecting cautious concern.

Frankie, however, was done with the surprises. Rising from the table, he strode to Marlow, his patience threadbare. "Have a seat, detective," he instructed, the strain in his voice barely contained.

Marlow shook his head, his demeanor respectful but firm. "This is a bit of a delicate matter, Frankie. I think we should discuss this in private."

Frankie was in no mood for discretion. "Whatever you've got to say, do it here, in front of my family," he insisted.

Marlow's hesitation, coupled with a cautious glance, only heightened the room's attention. "It's about the judge," he whispered, a statement that cemented Frankie's resolve to keep the conversation public.

As the others looked on, Frankie said commandingly, "Say it, or get out!"

Compelled by Frankie's firm stance, Marlow reluctantly opened up about his ongoing reconnaissance. "I've been quietly investigating the judge. Quietly! That's the key word here," he said, lowering his voice and scanning the room, betraying a hint of fear that someone present might compromise his cover. "I think we're on the brink of exposing him,"

Marlow revealed, his tone measured.

"That's a relief," Frankie replied, though his words were subdued, burdened by the evening's turmoil.

Marlow quickly interjected. "Not so fast. This is far from over. I've had to poke some big bears to get this information, and those bears don't like being poked. This could come with serious blowback."

Frankie poured another shot and motioned for the detective to continue.

"You need to keep your head on a swivel," Marlow warned, his tone grave. "The judge isn't the kind of man who takes people probing into his background lightly. He will start asking hard questions if he catches wind of this."

Frankie sighed deeply and asked, "So what are you saying?"

"Stay vigilant and deny any involvement," Marlow advised, his eyes sweeping the room to caution everyone present.

"We understand," Frankie uttered in response before adding, "Thank you for the warning, Detective."

Marlow nodded. "I'm going to be out of pocket to dive deeper into Kincaid's background. I'm leaving Junior in charge. He can reach me if necessary."

The news hit the group hard, casting a somber pall over the room. They knew Marlow was a skilled detective but understood the judge's power and connections. The group feared for Frankie's safety and the well-being of anyone else involved.

Bell broke the silence, her tone sharp and bitter. "Really, Frankie? Are you willing to let him keep digging into the judge and risk everything? This is just another disaster the rest of us will be stuck cleaning up when it all blows up in your face." She shook her head, too angry to think clearly. "But you do whatever you want, Frankie. Clearly, you're great at making decisions without thinking about anyone else."

Frankie turned to her, his frustration evident. "Bell! I know you're mad at me—I get that. But I have to do this. I can't let Judge Kincaid keep exploiting me. It's not right."

Before Bell could respond, Chubbs tapped the edge of his glass, his expression calm. "Everybody just relax. We're with you all the way, Frankie. Even Bell. What she's trying to say is we just have to be smart about it."

Bell glared at Chubbs, her words cutting. "Don't speak for me! I said what I said, and I meant it."

Silky sighed, leaning back in his seat. "This shit is messy, baby boy."

Frankie exhaled heavily, the weight of it all pressing down on him. "I know," he said, his voice strained. "But I can't back down now. Too much is at stake."

The party fell silent once more, each guest lost in their own thoughts. Kenya's pregnancy and the progress of the judge's undoing had cast long shadows over the evening, marking a significant turning point. As the night wound down, the group exchanged subdued goodbyes before heading to their respective homes.

Frankie was relegated to the guest room, left alone with his thoughts. In the stillness, a deep sense of unease took hold. The road ahead was fraught with danger, and he couldn't shake the feeling that his life was on the verge of irrevocable change.

# CHAPTER 8:
# SOUTHERN HOSPITALITY

"Whispers carry wisdom—listen, and you'll learn." — Eli

The year was off to a turbulent start, but Frankie found solace in the upcoming tour. The thought of traveling across America and performing lifted his spirits. This tour, running from late spring through summer, promised an escape. Frankie eagerly anticipated trading his broken reality for the freedom of the open road. Bell, however, remained on edge, her mood icy and her words scarce.

With his home life in shambles, Frankie buried himself in the one thing that still made sense—the tour. Bell had been distant since learning about his unborn child, and their steady communication had all but collapsed. To escape the chaos in his mind, Frankie fixated on tour logistics: the car service, the venues, the train tickets. Everything had been confirmed a thousand times, but he needed to hear it all again. His insistence was wearing on his close circle, yet Frankie called everyone to the house for one final meeting. Reluctantly, they agreed, gathering later that afternoon with growing frustration.

Cal was the first to arrive, nearly an hour early. His casual attire and relaxed posture marked his transition from badge to civilian. While waiting for the others, he walked the grounds, taking in the surroundings. Chubbs was next, his presence as steady and reassuring as ever, unfazed by Frankie's obsessiveness. Silky, as always, made his entrance with effortless fl air.

"Why all the fuss over this meeting? I got better things to do!" Silky grumbled, his voice sharp with irritation.

A beat later, Mississippi Red breezed in, full of swagger. "What's shaking, fellas?" he called out, tipping his hat to the room. His look settled on Silky. "Silk! Where's Kristine? You two are tighter than shoelaces."

Silky shot back, his voice smooth as ice, "Do I come to your place asking about your woman?"

Chubbs stepped in, taking control of the conversation and steering it toward the heart of their assembly. "Just relax, Silky. Frankie is just being careful." He outlined the shifting dynamics of their terrain—marked by the judge's blackmail and Jimmie's unchecked ambition—painting a vivid picture of the covert threats looming over them.

Silky remained unmoved, his defiance clear. "I don't give a damn 'bout no unchecked ambition or no phony blackmail. I'll take care of it if they bring any drama," he asserted, his stance unyielding.

Chubbs redirected him toward caution, emphasizing the need to avoid unnecessary attention.

Frankie, weary of the bickering, called for Cal and Bell to join the group. Cal entered with his usual enthusiasm, a stark contrast to Bell, who lagged behind. Her footsteps were heavy and deliberate, her arms crossed tightly over her chest. She kept her eyes fixed on the floor, offering nothing more than silence to anyone around her.

Frankie rubbed his jaw nervously, his eyes darting around the room as if searching for reassurance.

He hesitated momentarily, thrown by Bell's dramatic entrance, but quickly shook it off. After a steadying breath, Frankie took charge, outlining the tour's framework with a tone that was clear and focused.

"Bell," Frankie began, "you'll continue as our money manager, keeping the books balanced and ensuring everything lines up." Bell stayed silent, offering only a reluctant nod.

Silky draped an arm over the back of his chair, a smirk playing on his lips. Frankie continued, "Silky, your connections and network make you perfect for handling our day-to-day operations." Silky gave a casual wave. "What's new, baby boy?" he said, oozing confidence.

Frankie continued, "Chubbs, you'll oversee the entire tour and keep a pulse on New Port." Chubbs remained steady, his calm presence grounding the room.

Frankie moved to Cal. "Your job is simple: protect, serve, and keep us moving." Cal lit up, his eagerness bringing Frankie a rare smile.

Red shifted anxiously in his seat, eager to hear his role again. "Red," Frankie said, "you'll be talent scouting and performing alongside me to ease the load." Red's grin stretched wide, his excitement evident.

Kenya's uncharacteristic absence stirred uneasy glances around the room. Bell shifted to lean against the wall, her presence effortlessly drawing attention. Frankie took a deep breath and pushed forward. "Anyway... Kenya will run the bar while we're gone and keep the cash flow operation in check."

A tense silence followed. Everyone knew why Kenya wasn't there. Chubbs nervously squeezed his knee, Silky's smirk disappeared, and Red stared at the floor, his foot tapping restlessly.

As the meeting adjourned, a collective understanding settled over the group, each member clear on their role. Though the plan seemed airtight, Frankie was still uneasy. Kenya's absence weighed heavily on his mind.

Late that evening, Frankie found himself standing outside Kenya's door, his heart racing with apprehension. Their last conversation—marked by her revelation that she was pregnant and terrified—had been buried under the avalanche of tour preparations. He knocked softly, feeling the weight of his neglect.

The door swung open, and Kenya stood before him, her expression a mix of hope and weariness. Without hesitation, she stepped forward and wrapped him in a warm embrace.

"Frankie," she whispered, her voice calm but tinged with longing. "I thought you'd come sooner. We need to figure this out together."

Frankie stiffened in her arms and stepped back, the space between them more than just physical. "Why weren't you at the meeting? We needed you there. The tour is coming up, and there's a lot we have to get in order."

Kenya's confusion briefly masked the pain in her eyes. "The meeting?

Frankie, we have more pressing concerns—about us, about the baby." Her hopes for a shared future hung in the air, unacknowledged.

"I know, but I have to focus on the tour. It's not just about me or you—people depend on this. I need you to keep the Phat Kat running and make sure the income stays clean. Can you do that?"

His focus on the tour and his request that she manage the club felt like a betrayal—both to Kenya and to the part of himself that wished he could handle things differently.

Kenya took a step back, the hope in her eyes fading. "Is that all you see me as now? A caretaker for your ventures?" Her disappointment cut deeper than any confrontation. "Is that all you came here for? To remind me of my duties?"

Frankie's resolve wavered, but the weight of expectation kept him steady. "I'll check in on you when I can. We'll figure this other little thing out. I promise."

"*Little thing?* Frankie…" Kenya's voice trembled, her pain evident as his casual dismissal cut deep. Realizing his mistake, Frankie scrambled to recover. "You know what I mean," he muttered, but the distance between them had already crystallized.

"Listen, can you do what I asked or not?" Frankie pressed, his tone firmer than he intended.

Kenya stared at him in disbelief, her voice low and solemn. "Sure, Frankie. I'll do my job, like always."

As Frankie turned to leave, a profound sorrow gripped him. He couldn't shake the feeling that this rift might be too great to mend. In that moment, he felt the weight of his choice—choosing the tour over reality. It felt like an empty victory. With every step away from her door, the looming sacrifices became harder to ignore.

The following day, as dawn broke, Frankie awoke to the familiar solitude of his bed. He quietly tiptoed to the guest room, where a sliver of light revealed Bell sleeping peacefully. He lingered in the doorway, hesitant to disturb her, then quietly stepped away.

As he made his way downstairs, the house creaked with life. Chubbs was sprawled on the couch, snoring softly. Outside, Cal was already in the middle of a light workout, the rhythmic beat of his skipping rope setting the tempo for the day.

Frankie nudged Chubbs awake with a knee. "Time to roll, brother."

Still shaking off sleep, Chubbs muttered with a quiet but determined smirk, "I been up... Let's ride."

The aroma of breakfast wafted through the house, grounding them in the comfort of familiarity. As they ate, the kitchen buzzed with quiet energy, a pause before the world outside demanded their focus.

Mississippi Red arrived, bags in tow, breaking the calm. "Is there still time for a quick bite? I need to load up the tank before we hit the road."

Chubbs motioned toward the kitchen. "Grab yourself a plate." Red tossed his bags aside and went to work.

The brief interlude of small talk among the guys swiftly dissolved as Bell summoned Frankie. Each step toward the impending confrontation was heavy with anticipation. Inside, the morning light barely seeped through the thick blackout curtains. The air was heavy with unspoken grievances and the remnants of past arguments.

"Frankie, we need to talk," Bell's voice called out from the darkness. Frankie followed the sound into the room, straining to see. "It's too dark in here, Bell. Can I turn on a lamp so I can see you?"

Bell hesitated before pulling back a curtain, revealing her silhouette against the soft glow. She wore a silk gown that hugged her natural curves, instantly arousing Frankie. He couldn't help but step closer, his voice softening. "You look so good," he whispered, scanning her face for a sign. "I'm sorry for everything."

Bell's smile, once full of ambition, now mirrored her fatigue. She blushed briefly as he stepped into her personal space, their proximity reigniting a spark of intimacy. She allowed herself to lean into him momentarily, her guard lowered. But as reality set in, she tightened up, gently pushing him away.

"Stop," she said firmly, regaining her composure. "Don't play with my feelings. That! That ain't happening no time soon."

When she spoke again, her voice was steady, each word deliberate and infused with frustration. "I'll play my role for the sake of the business and what we've built. But this is not over. Don't mistake this truce for a resolution!" Her stance wasn't just about asserting her role in the business; it echoed deeper, unhealed wounds. This wasn't simply a failed business arrangement. It was the unraveling of years spent building something together—dreams and struggles, now on the brink of collapse.

Frankie started to respond, but Cal's impatient knocking cut him off. "We gotta roll, boss!" Cal reminded him of the travel schedule. Frankie called back, "Give me a few, Cal! I'll be right out."

"Yes, sir! Just remember, you told me to keep us on a tight clock," Cal replied, his urgency unmistakable.

Turning back to Bell, Frankie sighed. "We'll talk more about this later. I promise."

Bell waved him off in frustration. "Just go, Frankie. We'll deal with this when you get back." But as he turned to leave, she called him back, her voice barely a whisper. Pulling him in tightly, she held on as though willing him to stay. "I love you. Please… be careful," she murmured, her voice faltering, a trace of the anger lingering beneath the worry.

Frankie paused at the hallway's edge, Bell's words still weighing on him. He exhaled deeply, steadying himself, but the dread remained. At the front door, he glanced back one last time before stepping outside. The echo of the closing door lingered, a stark reminder of his fragile personal life.

Chubbs broke the silence with a playful jab. "Ready to leave the drama behind and hit the road, Superstar?" Frankie managed a slight smile in response.

With that, they set off, each man grappling with his thoughts as New Port faded into the distance. They rode silently beneath the blazing southern sun, and soon, the blurred pulse of New Orleans engulfed them. The city vibrated with low jazz notes and the heady mix of Creole spices, pulling them into its depths.

That night, Frankie and Red took the stage. Their sound flowed like an undertow—dark, raw, relentless. The venue was alive, colors and sounds bleeding together in a dizzying haze. Mississippi Red's trumpet cut through the chaos, igniting the crowd in a feverish frenzy. They had left their mark on the Crescent City and set the tone for the tour.

The next morning, they sluggishly packed their belongings, New Orleans having drained their energy. The road to Mississippi stretched ahead, and the thrill of last night's success pushed them to keep moving.

Red couldn't contain his elation. "Did you see that? We set the night on fire!" he exclaimed, the joy in his voice almost masking the sourness of his breath.

Frankie laughed, cracking a window. "New Orleans always knows how to party. But trust me, Jackson's got its own magic," Red said, taking in the rolling hills and landscapes that bridged the cities.

Frankie glanced back at Red with a smirk. "Red, you're right. We lit up the stage last night. But next time? Do us all a favor and brush those teeth—it smells like a dumpster in there."

The car erupted in laughter as they rolled toward Jackson.

The conversation shifted naturally as Chubbs glanced at Frankie in the rearview mirror. "Speaking of Jackson's magic, you plan on pitching the product to the locals?" Chubbs prodded gently.

Frankie was indifferent. "I'm not sure, but I doubt it. I could use the extra cash with the judge blackmailing me, but are new clients worth the risk?"

Chubbs leaned up to the front seat and said, "Smart thinking. We have more than enough risk in New Port. Let's focus on the music."

Red chimed in, "That's it, baby! Focus on the music! Keep the music front and center. The rest will follow. Just believe, baby!"

Chubbs replied, "You need to believe in brushing yo teeth."

Frankie laughed, cracking the window even further. "Listen to Chubbs, Red." Frankie smiled, but his mind was focused, his ambition clear.

Jackson radiated warmth as fans gathered, their cheers bouncing off the brick buildings. Nearby, the irresistible scent of soul food drew the men into a local diner. They stopped for a quick plate of fried chicken and collard greens, each bite steeped in rich flavors.

Embracing the city's heartbeat, they decided to walk down Farish Street, where the soulful strains of jazz and blues spilled from the midday venues, enveloping them in the afternoon's jubilant atmosphere.

The locals offered handshakes and heartfelt greetings, their faces as familiar as the weathered signs above the row of shops. This was the Farish Street of lore—alive, thriving, and the cultural backbone of Jackson.

Afterward, they returned to the hotel, where Frankie found a quiet spot at the bar to unwind. Eli, the bartender, recognized him right away. "What'll it be, boss?" he asked, reaching for a glass.

"Double bourbon on the rocks," Frankie responded confidently.

Eli selected a top-shelf bourbon, pouring it smoothly into the glass. He slid the drink across the counter, casting a knowing smile in Frankie's direction. As he wiped down the bar, he remarked casually, "Just holler if you need anything else."

As Frankie took a sip, he overheard two patrons nearby discussing a local underground club. Intrigued, he called out to Eli for more details. "Eli, Jackson is swinging today. Know any spots where the night keeps going?"

Eli threw the towel over his shoulder and leaned closer to Frankie, lowering his voice. "The city is swinging every day, Daddy. I can hook you up with some after-hour recommendations if you like."

Frankie slid a generous tip across the bar, adding, "I'd appreciate that. Send me off right."

Eli pocketed the tip with a smile and offered some local wisdom. "Keep those ears open while you're here. In Jackson, whispers carry wisdom—listen, and you'll learn," he advised, glancing around the room meaningfully. "This city keeps its secrets tight, and still always has something to say."

"Thanks, Eli. I'll remember that."

Eli responded with a wink. "Any time. Let me get you those recommendations." Frankie tipped his glass in a silent toast before turning away, ready to dive into the night.

As the evening settled in, Frankie rallied his band. "Today, Jackson bared its soul to us," he declared, his voice alive with passion. "Let's respond in kind. Tonight, we shake 'em down. Leave it all on the stage. Be focused—no mistakes!"

Their journey to the venue was electric, the city's rich musical legacy giving them a sense of belonging. Inside the cozy club, the place was brimming with energy. Frankie thrived in these settings, often slipping away to observe his surroundings. He found joy in watching people, absorbing their enthusiasm and eagerness.

As the ensemble warmed up, Frankie noticed two locals casting furtive glances his way, whispering nervously among themselves. Curious, he edged closer to the bar to order another drink, subtly eavesdropping on their conversation.

One of the men eventually mustered the courage to speak. "You're Frankie Keys, aren't you?" he exclaimed, his voice tinged with awe. "We've been excited to catch your show. Heard you really light up the stage, Daddy."

Grateful for the warm welcome, Frankie flashed his trademark smile. "Appreciate that. Let me get you fellas another round," he offered, signaling to the bartender.

The men accepted the drinks with evident gratitude, their voices rising to compete with the background music as they resumed their conversation. Frankie, drink in hand, leaned in to listen as the topic shifted to a mysterious figure in South Louisiana.

They spoke of a shadow broker offering top-shelf liquor at a steal. "Just imagine—fifty bucks a crate!" one of them mused. "It's risky to fetch it, sure, but that kind of come-up will get you rich!"

Frankie's interest was piqued—not just by the tantalizing lead but by the implications. He pondered the risks and who might be behind such an operation, his mind racing with possibilities.

"I couldn't help but overhear," Frankie interjected, masking his shrewd intent behind a veil of casual curiosity. "Where might one run into this deal? I've got a bar at my place and would love to meet this connection."

The men exchanged a wary glance but eventually relented. "South Louisiana is where you start. Just ask around, and they say he'll find you."

Grateful for the tip, Frankie signaled to the eclectic torcedor. "Take care of these gentlemen. Craft them two of your finest cigars."

The men lit up with surprise and delight. "Now that's class, Frankie!" one of them exclaimed.

Energized by the exchange and the valuable information he'd gathered, Frankie felt a surge of confidence. Tonight, Jackson had transformed from just another stop on their tour into a pivotal source of information.

As the evening progressed, Frankie took his place on the conductor's stand, ready to channel the local energy into his performance. The melodies began to weave through the smoky air, his presence commanding atop the bandstand. Suddenly, the stage went dark.

A wave of murmurs rippled through the crowd, filled with anticipation. Moments of uncertainty passed before the lights blazed back on, revealing Mississippi Red center stage, dramatically seizing the spotlight.

"Listen up, Jackson," he declared boldly. "Now that I've got your attention. Let's shake it!"

Caught off guard, Frankie's initial shock quickly turned to anger. He stormed onto the stage, yanking Red as the band played on, seemingly unfazed by the unfolding chaos. "What the hell do you think you're doing, Red?" Frankie demanded, his voice barely containing his fury.

Red's retort was sharp, fueled by his own frustrations. "It's my turn to lead!"

Frankie shot him a glare that could slice through steel. "You're not leading anyone, especially not with that attitude."

As Frankie turned to leave, Red's voice cut through the tension. "You're scared of my talent, Frankie!"

Frankie retook the stage, seamlessly turning the disruption into part of the act. "Jackson, dear, give my stuntman a hand," he quipped, his voice dripping with charm. The moment of discord transformed into an electrifying performance. Initially jarred, the audience erupted into cheers, their admiration a testament to Frankie's skill as both a musician and a showman.

As Frankie stepped off the stage, he leaned close to Red. "That's how you win them over," he whispered, his tone laced with triumph.

In the aftermath, fans lingered, their animated chatter filling the air. "Did you see that stunt? Pure genius!" one exclaimed. Another chimed in, "They're not just talented—they've got real drama. Makes you wonder what they'll pull off next." The incident didn't tarnish their image; it only heightened the audience's sense of intrigue and admiration.

Frustration simmered on the drive back as Frankie fumed over Red's stunt. "I can't believe this kid. I give him a chance, and he's jeopardizing everything," Frankie grumbled. Chubbs, seated beside Red, nodded in agreement. "Might be time to cut ties with him," he suggested firmly.

From the backseat, Mississippi Red's voice cut through the tension, tinged with humor. "Y'all do know I'm in the car, right?"

His remark earned a momentary pause but did little to ease Frankie and Chubbs's irritation. Despite his immaturity, neither could deny the kid's undeniable talent—a fact that only made their frustration more complicated.

Frankie brought up the bootlegging rumor to shift the conversation, expressing concern about its potential impact on their business. After briefing Chubbs on the new information, the group rode in contemplative silence. Breaking the calm, Frankie proposed, "We should head back to Louisiana in the morning so I can ask around myself."

Chubbs quickly countered, "We can't let rumors distract us. Let's finish this leg of the tour first, then deal with it." Frankie nodded reluctantly, acknowledging Chubbs' point, though still uneasy.

Chubbs added, "We'll get to the bottom of this. I'll contact Silky when we hit Rolling Fork and see if he's heard anything. But we're not cutting this tour short. Got it, Frankie?"

Frankie sighed. "Yeah, I got it. The show must go on."

Chubbs cracked a smile. "Exactly. This will give us time to think up a strategy."

Days passed as the quartet lingered in Jackson before finally setting off for Red's hometown, Rolling Fork, Mississippi. Still, Jackson's revelations clung to Frankie, even in the quiet moments between shows. Sensing the tension, Red approached Frankie to make amends. "I messed up, I know. I'll dial it back."

Frankie nodded, the weight of leadership on his shoulders. "Good to hear, Red. Stick to the music, keep the show tight, and we're square. Just focus on that, and we'll be fine."

As they settled into the Delta, the slow pace and the weight of unresolved issues began to wear on Frankie. Increasingly impatient with Chubbs' delay in contacting Silky, he decided to take matters into his own hands. Finding a phone at the local general store, Frankie dialed Silky, his voice tight and urgent as he navigated the call.

The line crackled with static, punctuated by Silky's slow, measured breaths. Frankie broke the silence, "Silk, it's Frankie. I need you to find out who's behind this rumor."

"Talk to me," Silky replied.

"I met some cats back in Jackson. Cool cats. We were talking, one thing led to another, and they gave me a lead. Apparently, there's a mysterious dealer in South Louisiana selling premium crates for fifty dollars, and—"

"That's Jimmie's work," Silky cut in. "No need to dance around it. Why do you come calling me on this government-tapped phone like you don't know it was Jimmie? Trust your gut, nephew."

Frankie absorbed the betrayal in silence, his mind racing with strategies. "I'll figure out how to handle this. Still, could you keep your eyes and ears open for me?"

"Sure thing, baby boy. Kristine needs me now, but I'll get some eyes on Jimmie. Don't worry, we'll handle him," Silky assured, his tone quickening as he ended the call.

With the conversation behind him, Frankie shifted his focus to the looming show in Rolling Fork. That night at the venue, he spotted Red perfecting his latest dance move, "The Stiff Leg," pulling himself across the stage while stiffening one leg rhythmically. Though Frankie despised the move, he couldn't deny its appeal to the crowd.

Red's taunt—"You can't learn this, Frankie. It's in me. It's all me"—only added fuel to his irritation. Frankie's patience wore thin. "Keep up that talk, and you'll be on your own," he snapped, the threat hanging heavily in the air.

As the tension simmered, Chubbs proposed a bold idea. "Why not let Red headline tonight? It's his hometown; let's see if he can handle the pressure."

Frankie, taken aback, felt his anger give way to strategic curiosity. "You might be onto something," he replied, his tone thoughtful.

Chubbs grinned. "If he falls on his face, you can go out and save him."

Backstage, the moment was charged with nerves and exhilaration. Tonight, the band had made a unanimous decision: the stage belonged to Mississippi Red.

"This is your shot, Red. We're all behind you, but take this seriously," one band member urged, his voice a blend of urgency and support.

"I've got this," Red responded confidently, his assurance rallying the others.

As they gathered around, setting aside their usual routine for a night filled with risks and potential rewards, the unity and resolve of the performers were evident. Red stepped into the spotlight, fully supported by his bandmates.

Settling into his seat, Frankie took a deep breath, wrestling with the possible outcomes of Chubbs's bold suggestion. "Alright, Chubbs. Let's hope you're right," he murmured, his eyes fixed on the stage. After grooming Red for over a year, it was finally time for him to prove himself to the world.

From the sidelines, Frankie watched as Red took over the stage with uncontainable energy. Dancing with abandon, Red partnered with anyone nearby, regardless of gender. Frankie could see the intense focus in him and knew he had made the right decision. The audience responded wildly, cheering and clapping in rhythm with Red's every leap and primal scream. Drenched in sweat, Red seemed almost possessed, completely surrendering to the music's grip.

As the performance wound down, Mississippi Red approached the microphone with a wide smile. "Rolling Fork! I gotta head out soon— they're gonna call the cops on me for murdering this stage tonight!" The crowd roared, their applause thunderous, feeding into his exhilaration.

Red's voice rose over the din. "Y'all wanna see the stiff leg?"

The sea of faces yelled back, "Yeah!"

Holding center stage with a mischievous smirk, Red teased them further. "Aww now, y'all know Mississippi Red can't hear! I said, do y'all *really* wanna see my move?"

They erupted as the pianist executed a dazzling glissando, his hand sweeping from one end of the piano to the other, perfectly accentuating Red's show-stopping move. Red stiffened his upper body and slid backward effortlessly, his stiff leg dragging in a rhythmic, almost mechanical motion. The seamless glide and his rigid posture created an illusion of floating across the stage. The crowd went wild, and even Frankie and Chubbs were floored by what they witnessed.

As the applause dwindled and the stage cleared, Frankie approached Red backstage. Patting him on the back, he offered a warm smile. "You did great tonight, kid. Really proud of you."

Red's face lit up, his eyes shining with gratitude. "Thanks, Frankie. I'm just grateful for the chance to prove myself. Couldn't have done it without you."

Frankie suggested, "How about we hit up the Delta Dive and grab a few cold ones to celebrate. What do you say?"

Chubbs interjected, "I say that sounds perfect!"

Red hesitated for a moment, then smirked. "I'm in, but I wouldn't pay a nickel to get into the Delta Dive. The music's dead, and there aren't any dolls worth scoping in that joint. We need to hit the Rocking Chair—that's where it's happening tonight!"

Frankie chuckled. "Alright, the Rocking Chair it is."

With that, the two performers returned to their dressing room to gather their things. The excitement of the show gradually ebbed as they prepared for a quieter end to the night.

When they stepped inside the Rocking Chair, they were immediately enveloped by its rustic charm. The scent of aged booze mingled with the occasional whiff of cigarette smoke, a familiar aroma that evoked memories of countless nights spent unwinding just like this. Laughter and spirited exchanges floated above the jukebox's melodies, filling every corner of the bar. The beer-stained floors clung slightly to their shoes with each step.

Mississippi Red, still riding the adrenaline of his performance, stumbled slightly as he made his way toward the stage. Once there, he signaled for Frankie. As Frankie approached, attention naturally followed him. Both women and men seemed captivated by his commanding presence. He reached Red and wrapped an arm around him.

"What's the play, Red?" Frankie asked, unsure if Red was emotional, drunk, or both.

Red started, his voice thick with sentiment. "I used to stand right there, Frankie. It was my childhood dream to come back to this city and perform. Thanks to you, that dream is alive. I'm forever indebted."

With that, Red hopped up onto the stage, throwing his arms wide. "Little Red done came on home, y'all!" he shouted, his voice ringing out over the room.

Frankie retreated, shaking his head in amusement. Returning to Chubbs and Cal, he hoisted his glass. "A toast to Red… Looks like we've got ourselves a budding superstar."

The music boomed, and libations flowed freely as the Rocking Chair lived up to its name. The festive atmosphere, however, was abruptly shattered—*Thud! Clang!* The doors swung open, drawing all eyes to a woman storming in, flanked by her three imposing brothers.

One was a towering brute, the second lean and athletic, and the third shorter but quick to temper. The woman's voice pierced through the room. "There he is! That guy owes me money!" she wailed, her finger stabbing the air toward Red.

The brothers zeroed in, their glares locking on Red as they cracked their knuckles. Kenny, the towering brute, stepped forward. "Sissy says you owe her money. Looks like you're doing well for yourself. Time to settle up."

Red's denial was vehement. "Hell, no! Your sister's a liar. I ain't paying her shit!"

The second brother was quicker to anger and wasted no time. He stormed up to Mississippi Red and hoisted him off the ground by his shirt. "Sissy says you owe, so you do!"

The situation escalated as Frankie intervened, his voice slicing through the mounting tension. "Gentlemen, let's sort this out calmly. What's the debt?" he asked.

The woman stepped forward, her anger blazing. "Ten dollars!" she demanded, her voice trembling with intensity.

Frankie, drink in hand, nearly choked mid-sip, caught off guard by the minuscule amount. "Excuse me… ten dollars?"

"Yes, ten dollars!" she yelled, her frustration spilling over. "Red knows it. We were together once. I stole it from my father, and he promised to pay it back!"

Tears welled in her eyes, resentment breaking through her anger as she continued. "How could you just leave me like that, Redmond? You said you loved me!"

The third brother stepped forward, fists clenched tight. "Enough talk. I say we rough him up. You hurt my sister, and now I'm gonna hurt you!"

Red reacted swiftly, grabbing a drink off the table and splashing it into the biggest brother's face as he yelled, "Run!" Instantly, the club erupted into chaos. The biggest brother swung wildly but missed, and Red, realizing he was outmatched, bolted for the door.

Frankie seized the moment, flinging a wad of cash at the woman. "That should cover it!" he shouted, ducking as a punch whizzed past his head. Chubbs, quick on his feet, grabbed his beer and coat, knocking over stools to create obstacles for their pursuers.

The bar descended into a frenzy. Patrons shouted and scrambled as furniture toppled, adding to the pandemonium. Cal bulldozed through the crowd, his focus unshaken as Frankie and Chubbs struggled to keep up, navigating through the stampeding bodies with their hearts pounding.

By the time Frankie and Chubbs burst outside, Cal was already behind the wheel, revving the engine. "Come on! Move it!" he yelled over the roar of the car.

Suddenly, Red dove headfirst through an open window. Chubbs scrambled into the passenger seat, while Frankie, with one foot still dragging on the ground, managed to yank himself inside just as the rear door slammed shut.

The tires screeched, leaving clouds of smoke across the parking lot as they sped away into the night.

Frankie couldn't help but laugh as the club faded into the distance. "Tonight will make for one hell of a story," he said, the adrenaline still coursing through him. The tale of their daring escape was bound to grow into legend.

Despite the chaos in Jackson and the near brawl in Rolling Fork, the next shows in Memphis and New Orleans unfolded smoothly, restoring a sense of normalcy to the tour. By the time they returned to New Port after the first leg, the group was in high spirits.

But for Frankie, the triumph felt hollow. Professional success only magnified his inner conflict. Torn between his wife and the woman carrying his child, Frankie felt trapped in a web of responsibilities where every choice seemed like the wrong one.

One evening, the group gathered to strategize, but Frankie was distant. His thoughts frequently drifted to Kenya and the mess he'd left behind. The room fell quiet, all eyes on Frankie as they waited for direction.

Finally, he broke the silence. "We need to talk about Jimmie," he said, his tone heavy with resolve.

Silky leaned back, swirling his drink thoughtfully as he crossed his legs and started the dialogue. "That rat Jimmie has been undercutting us with those cheap crates, costing us money and credibility."

Frankie pondered aloud, "But why?" He seemed to be questioning himself and the group.

Bell, usually quiet, spoke up. "Maybe we're too concerned with the cheap crates. We need to figure out Jimmie's endgame. Why sell them so cheap?"

Silky leaned forward, a memory clicking into place. "One of my girls mentioned Jimmie is hoarding cash. He wants to run things his way, answer to no one."

Frankie's face tightened. "If money's his focus, we can turn that against him."

Chubbs interjected, "You know...I was joking that night at the Phat Kat. But what if—big 'if'—we picked the right time and hit Jimmie. We could crush him… And clear him out."

Silky picked up the thought. "That might not be a bad idea. We can arrange it and keep our hands clean."

Bell inquired, "Use outside men?"

Frankie shrugged. "That's an idea." They continued to brainstorm, meticulously crafting a plan to confront Jimmie.

"Let me think on this for a few weeks. I'm not sure I trust anyone else to handle the job better than I can," Frankie said.

Silky nearly choked on his whiskey. "A few weeks! You're just gonna let him keep moving these cheap crates?"

Frankie stood and walked over to Silky, giving his shoulder a reassuring squeeze. "Yes, we need to gather intel. When we move, he'll have no choice but to bend."

Turning to Chubbs, Frankie added, "Combine the Midwest and East Coast leg of the tour. I want to stay on the road—that's our alibi. As long as we're moving, Jimmie will think we're oblivious. It also gives us time to tail him and better understand his actions."

Chubbs accepted. "Got it. I'll start tomorrow." With that, the meeting adjourned.

Left alone, Frankie felt the heavy and isolating weight of leadership.

His thoughts drifted to Bell and Kenya, their faces a reminder of the delicate balance threatening to unravel in his personal life. Despite the looming storm with Jimmie, it was the turmoil in his marriage and with Kenya that haunted him most.

# CHAPTER 9

# MIDWEST MOTION

"You'll rent the car from me, or not at all." — Bill

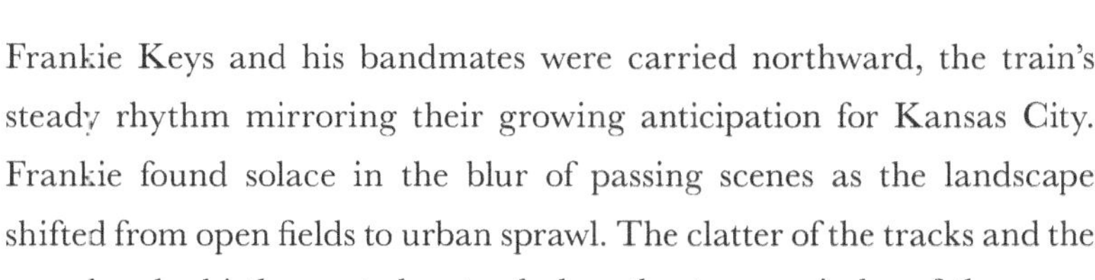

Frankie Keys and his bandmates were carried northward, the train's steady rhythm mirroring their growing anticipation for Kansas City. Frankie found solace in the blur of passing scenes as the landscape shifted from open fields to urban sprawl. The clatter of the tracks and the occasional whistle created a steady heartbeat, a reminder of the eager audiences awaiting them.

Across from Frankie, Chubbs sat with his briefcase open, his brow furrowed as he meticulously reviewed schedules and venue details. His focus was unyielding, each document a crucial piece of their tour. Red, on the other hand, was a bundle of energy. Unable to sit still, he paced the narrow aisles, his voice bouncing off the walls as he practiced vocal riffs. Each note revealed his relentless drive to improve. Meanwhile, Cal, ever the silent guardian, observed quietly, his presence a reassuring constant in their journey.

Their morale soared as they arrived in Kansas City. The show was nearly flawless, with Frankie's melodies captivating the crowd's heart and soul. But as the night came to a close, Red couldn't resist adding his own flair. Overcome by overzealous ambition, he attempted a new dance move, only to trip and tumble across the stage.

Frankie, unable to suppress a smile, extended a hand to help him up. "Damn it, Red, just stick to the script," he teased. "Next time, let's focus on the music, yeah?"

Red nodded, a sheepish grin spreading across his face. "Got it, Frankie. No more surprises." Dusting himself off, he adjusted his coat and, with a playful bow, ended with a high hop and click of his heels.

As the train carried them toward St. Louis, the shared stories of Kansas City lingered in their minds. America's heartland unfolded outside the windows in golden hues, fields stretching endlessly into the horizon. The comforting aroma of roasted coffee and warm pastries mingled with the crisp morning air.

As they stepped off the train, St. Louis was everything Frankie had anticipated. The streets buzzed with energy, people moving with purpose, their hustle sparking a sense of drive in Frankie. He absorbed the city's rhythm, lost in thought, until Cal nudged him. "The car," he reminded, pulling Frankie back to the task at hand.

When they arrived at the car rental service, the mood subtly shifted. A collective tension settled over the group, their chatter fading into an uneasy silence.

From the back, a stout man emerged, his scowl deepening as he peered over the counter at them, his eyes sharp and scrutinizing.

Chubbs immediately sensed something was off.

The owner's voice carried an unwelcome edge. "I'll need to see identification from each of you boys before we proceed."

Frankie, taken aback by the unexpected request, exchanged a quick, uneasy glance with his companions. He pulled out his information and asked Cal for his. "We are the only two who will be driving the vehicle, sir," Frankie said, extending their paperwork toward the man.

The owner grew more critical as he assessed each of their faces. He snatched the papers from Frankie and looked him square in the eye. "You must be hard of hearing, son. I need paperwork on every one of you."

The demand felt excessive, but Frankie tried to stay diplomatic, his voice betraying only a hint of frustration. "This seems unusual. We've rented cars before without this requirement."

The owner was unmoved, his stance rigid, and his expectations clear. "Well, son, that wasn't my town, and them wasn't my cars. Now, like I said, if you and your cronies want to get in one of my cars, I will need to see paperwork on the other two knuckleheads."

As they reluctantly complied, the owner sat to review their paperwork.

His chair gave a loud, protesting creak as he leaned back. After a few moments, he grabbed the armrest to stand. "Louisiana! Creole capital, huh?" he said with an almost accusatory tone. "A long way from home. What brings you boys to St. Louis?"

He sat the paperwork on the counter. His curiosity felt more like an interrogation, an unwelcome prying into their lives.

Frankie's patience waned. Renting a car had spiraled into an awkward encounter of thinly veiled disrespect. His responses, though polite, now carried an edge, a defense against the unwarranted scrutiny. "We're here for a show. We'd appreciate it if we could finalize this and be on our way," Frankie managed, his tone assertive.

The owner reacted as if Frankie had just cussed him. "Whew! The mouth on this one. Son, you should be glad I'm progressive and that these are different times…"

Frankie replied with a bite, "And why is that?"

The owner replied coldly, "I would have taught you a thing or two about manners."

Across the room, Cal's hands clenched into fists at his sides. Frankie hissed back, "Maybe you should teach yourself a thing or two."

Chubbs stepped forward, hoping to smooth things over. "Sir, with all due respect, you don't know who you're speaking to. This is Frankie Keys, frontman of one of the most popular bands in the country. We don't want trouble. We just want to rent a car and get up the road."

The owner sneered, clearly unimpressed. "Oh, really? A star, huh? Well, why don't you put on a little show for us, then?"

Frankie was taken off guard. "We're not here to perform for you. We're here to rent a car."

The owner's eyes narrowed, "In my establishment, you'll do as you're told. Now, let's see if you can sing and dance as well as you run your mouth."

Frankie maintained his composure as he walked to collect the papers.

"We'll take our business elsewhere," he said, grabbing the paperwork from the counter. "Come on, y'all. We don't have to deal with this."

As they turned to leave, the owner's voice rang out. "Gentlemen!"

They looked back to see the old man leaning on the counter. "The Midwest is like a tight-knit family. You'll rent the car from me, or not at all. One phone call and you won't get a rental for 150 miles. Gimme 'bout an extra hour, and I can make that about 250. You ain't nothing special around here."

Chubbs quickly pulled Frankie aside. "Frankie, we need that car. If we have to re-plan transportation, we might have to cancel shows. It'll mess everything up."

Before Frankie could respond, the owner's voice boomed through the tense air. "Maye! Get in here!" His shout echoed through the cramped space.

His wife, Maye, shuffled in, her movements slow and deliberate, a noticeable hunch curving her back. "What's all the commotion, Bill? I was right in the middle of my stories."

Bill's enjoyment bubbled over as he gestured at Frankie and his companions. "Babe, we've got celebrities in our midst."

Maye's response was indifferent. "And? So what, Bill?"

Frankie exchanged quick, knowing glances with his entourage, each one a silent conversation about their next move. Bill broke the silence, "These fellas," he said, pointing toward Frankie, "are gonna put on a little show. Right here, right now."

Frankie's jaw tightened, "That's not going to happen," he replied firmly.

Bill's response was equally stern. "Well, if you want the car, it will."

Frankie and Bill exchanged looks, each man sizing up the other. Determined to resolve the issue, Frankie reached for a practical solution. "How about we make this easier? We'll pay double the rate," he offered, his tone calm but firm.

The owner glanced at the money and smirked, his voice dripping with condescension. "Oh, son, it's not about the money."

Frankie's frustration mounted as Bill's stare remained unyielding. With a smug motion toward an open area of the office, Bill added, "Right over there is fine."

Maye, seated in a squeaking chair, rocked idly, her disinterest contrasting with the tension in the room.

Frankie took a deep breath, the pressure building as he measured his words carefully. With a tight smile, he leaned forward. "Alright. Red and I will perform. We're the only musicians here."

Frankie scoffed. "This is nonsense… I'm a band leader, sir. I don't perform solo. I book musicians in each city. We don't even have instruments."

The owner's mocking grin stretched even wider. "Well, there is a first time for everything."

Red looked at Frankie with a submissive glint. "You know I keep my trumpet close; I can lay you some background."

Bill excitedly interrupted, "That's the spirit!"

Frankie frowned and looked at Bill. "But in return, we need that car, no strings attached."

Bill teased Frankie's lack of trust, "My word is bond. Have a little faith… Impress my wife, and the car is yours. No strings attached."

As Frankie and Red prepared to turn the rental office into a stage, the air bristled with anticipation and disbelief. However, before they could begin, Bill made one final claim.

"But…if Maye isn't impressed, we will need an encore."

Frankie's anger simmered beneath the surface, but he knew he had to swallow his pride for the sake of the tour. With a heavy sigh, Frankie turned to Red. "Alright, let's do it."

As Red played each note, accompanied by Frankie's impassioned dancing and vocals, it was clear this was a forced show of defiance against the owner's unfair demand. The trumpet and Frankie's voice intertwined, filling the office with a raw, unrelenting melody. Frankie poured his frustration into every note and step, determined to leave an impression the owner wouldn't forget.

As the final note reverberated in the air, the room fell silent. Frankie's chest heaved as he fought to steady his breath.

The owner's expression softened, a hint of begrudging respect creeping onto his face. "Son, you are a talented man. I've seen enough. The car is yours."

Frankie's bitterness was evident as he regarded the owner with barely concealed disgust. The backhanded praise stung more than the humiliation of the performance, each word a sharp reminder of the injustice he had just endured.

When they finally received the car keys, they vowed to put the ordeal behind them and continue their journey, united by their music and resilient spirits. Determination burned brighter than ever as they drove through the streets of St. Louis, a renewed sense of purpose fueling them.

Upon arriving at their living quarters for the night, Cal pulled a small book from his shirt pocket. "After today… it's a good thing I got my hands on this." He held up a copy of *The Negro Motorist Green Book*. "One of my old police friends got me a copy. It lists all the places we can and can't go. Which cities along the route are sundown towns, and what hotels and restaurants will accept us."

The book was a sobering reminder that not every place welcomed change.

Cal, ever aware of the dangers ahead, spoke with calm resolve. "We've got to be careful out there. This isn't just about music—it's about making it back home safely."

Frankie nodded, his voice carrying the weight of shared understanding. "Thank you, Cal. It's unfortunate that we even need such a book, but I'm glad you have it."

Chubbs chimed in, his tone serious. "Absolutely. We can't afford to take unnecessary risks. We'll follow the guide and stay aware of our surroundings at all times."

Mississippi Red, usually quick with a quip to lighten the mood, stayed uncharacteristically quiet.

Frankie reassured Red, his tone steady and supportive. "Hey, Red, we've come this far, and we won't let anything—or anyone—hold us back. We'll face the challenges head-on and keep making our music. You and I are here to create. And this? This is what the creative process looks like."

Red met Frankie's gaze, a spark of determination igniting in his expression. "You're right, Frankie. Nothing's gonna stop us. We'll put the country on notice. The movement is nonstop!"

The following evening, Frankie and his team arrived at the venue in St. Louis, ready to give their all on stage. Yet, the weight of the previous day's racial encounter lingered in Frankie's mind, dampening his usual enthusiasm. Bitterness and frustration simmered within him, casting a shadow over his focus.

As they stepped onto the stage, the spectators cheered wildly, eager to witness the brilliance of Frankie Keys. But as the music filled the air, it became clear that something was amiss. Frankie's voice lacked its usual fervor, and his movements were stiff and mechanical.

The audience, initially swept up in the show's anticipation, began to sense the change. Whispers rippled through the crowd—a mix of confusion and disappointment. This wasn't the magnetic Frankie Keys they'd heard about.

Chubbs exchanged a worried glance with Cal, both recognizing the need to act quickly to salvage the night.

Mississippi Red seized the moment. Stepping forward with unwavering energy, he took center stage. The spotlight traced his every move as his voice surged with passion. Red ripped through trumpet notes with precision, his soulful vocals blending seamlessly with his dynamic movements.

He danced with unrelenting energy, tapping and spinning across the stage, his performance charged with the kind of charisma that left no room for doubt. The crowd, captivated by his intensity, erupted into cheers.

Red, a true showman, now commanded the stage, carrying the night with a presence that was impossible to ignore.

As Red neared the end of his performance, he threw a wink at the audience. With a sudden, flamboyant flair, he spun around and slid backward, flawlessly executing his signature *Stiff Leg*. The crowd erupted, their cheers growing louder until the entire venue rose to its feet in a thunderous standing ovation for the band and Mississippi Red's electrifying performance.

With the applause still roaring, Red stepped to the front of the stage, pausing as though to take a bow. Instead, he raised his hand to quiet the crowd and called out, "Let's get my brother Frankie back out here! This man went through hell to make sure this show happened."

The crowd erupted into even louder cheers, and Frankie couldn't help but feel a wave of gratitude. Red's acknowledgment of his efforts warmed him, and as they took their final bow in St. Louis, Frankie felt a renewed sense of purpose.

Backstage, Frankie approached Red with a mix of humility and pride. "Red, you saved the show. I don't know what got into me, but you brought the magic back."

Red, his face still glistening with sweat, flashed a cheeky grin as he patted it dry with a towel. "No problem, Frankie. We're a team, right? We lift each other up when we need it."

Frankie snapped his fingers and pointed at Red, a genuine smile spreading across his face. "I couldn't agree more."

With that, Frankie let go of everything that had weighed on him in St. Louis. His focus shifted back to what truly mattered—the music and the journey ahead.

At dawn, Cal loaded their bags into the car, and they set off for Cincinnati. The drive was uneventful, the steady hum of the engine a backdrop to their quiet reflections.

Upon arriving, the Queen City unfolded before them, showcasing its rich cultural fabric. Early skyscrapers stood proudly alongside stunning Art Deco designs, while the streets buzzed with life. Each neighborhood reflected the unique identities shaped by its immigrant communities, adding to the city's vibrant charm.

The venue awaited, and the group eagerly prepared for their performance. As the stage lights illuminated their faces, Frankie and his unit poured everything into their set, captivating the audience with every note and move.

The following days passed in a blur of travel and brief stops, the rhythm of the road becoming second nature. With every passing hour, their focus sharpened, and the excitement for the next stage grew steadily.

Leaving Cincinnati behind, they approached Detroit, the city's storied history drawing closer with each passing mile. Known as the heart of the American automobile industry, Detroit thrived as a bustling melting pot. The city pulsed with the energy of its residents—Black people, Eastern Europeans, and Southern migrants, all contributing to its rich culture.

Factories dominated the skyline, their smokestacks billowing under the endless hum of industry. The streets thrived with life, and the lively sounds of jazz and blues echoed through every corner, breathing soul into the heartbeat of the city.

After freshening up, they immersed themselves in Detroit's low-key groove. They sampled dishes at local eateries and mingled with fellow musicians, tapping into the city's thriving community spirit. As evening fell, Detroit morphed into a bustling hub of glamour and rhythm. The streetlights illuminated the setting, enhancing the sparkle of diamonds, the sheen of silk dresses, and the quiet confidence of women adorned in their finest. It became a place not just to see, but to be seen.

Backstage, Red was a whirlwind, his body in constant motion as he fine-tuned his high-flying dance moves. He couldn't sit still, transitioning from his energetic choreography to trumpet practice. The blasts from his trumpet echoed against the walls, high notes screeching through the halls as he emptied the air from his lungs. Mississippi Red ran the musical scales, his fingers dancing up and down the instrument.

Meanwhile, Cal stood guard, shielding the band from a steady stream of eager admirers. Chubbs deftly navigated a sea of salesmen pitching partnerships and slick record executives angling for a piece of Frankie's rising star. The backstage hustle was a chaotic ballet of ambition and excitement.

As the bustle gradually settled, the anticipation in the venue peaked. The lights dimmed, and a hush fell over the crowd. The first notes filled the air as Frankie and Red took command of the stage. At the piano, Frankie was a portrait of focus and passion, his fingers gliding effortlessly over the keys to weave melodies that spoke straight to the soul. Beside him, Red's trumpet added depth and grace, echoing the joy and sorrow intertwined in their music.

The audience swayed and moved to the rhythm, captivated by the magnetic synergy onstage. Each note drew them deeper into the shared experience. Detroit wasn't just listening—it was feeling every moment.

Suddenly, the bass drum thundered to life, punctuated by crisp rim shots. The snare drum snapped sharply as the hi-hat ticked out a steady tempo, inviting the patrons to catch the beat. Frankie pushed himself away from the piano with a dramatic flourish, his hands hovering in the air before he strode purposefully to the bandstand. The saxophones blared at his signal, the trombones sliding in sync, igniting the room. Instantly, everyone was on their feet, dancing to the rhythm. At center stage, Red played his trumpet with unrelenting intensity, each note sending chills through Detroit.

Two women in the audience drew Frankie's attention, their presence sent Frankie's thoughts into a swirl of sinful temptation.

The first, with a smooth caramel-toned complexion that gleamed under the lights, wore a gold satin gown that clung to her slender frame and long legs, exuding refined elegance. Her almond-shaped hazel eyes scanned the room, eventually locking with Frankie's. She moved with luxurious fluidity; every step and gesture was a silent, enticing invitation, though Frankie tried to play it cool.

Beside her stood a woman whose bold sensuality was impossible to ignore. Her dark, radiant skin and deep brown eyes paired with a mysterious smile that hinted at both charm and danger. The midnight blue dress she wore hugged her voluptuous curves, her every motion deliberate and seductive. She swayed her hips with confident ease, each step a dance of allure.

With Frankie's intense direction, the band soared. He stole glances at the two women, drawing their presence into his performance. It was a moment suspended in time, a celebration of life, lust, and art.

As the show reached its climax, Frankie and Mississippi Red left everything on the stage, driving the crowd into a frenzy of awe. Frankie, drenched in sweat, soaked in the moment, relishing the electric energy of the audience. Meanwhile, Mississippi Red, feeding off the attention, pulled the trumpet away from his lips and shouted, "Y'all wanna see my move?"

The assembly erupted in unison, "Yeah, Daddy! Hell yeah!"

Red stiffened his body and slid backward, nailing his famous "Stiff Leg." The crowd roared as he galloped to the front of the stage, hopping off to kiss a woman flirting from the crowd. Without missing a beat, he executed a flawless backflip, landing with dramatic flair. He gasped for air theatrically, hands on his knees, his tongue lolling out like a winded dog, drawing laughter and applause. After catching his breath in this exaggerated fashion, he tipped his hat to the woman and seamlessly jumped back into the performance.

As the final notes echoed through the venue, the resounding applause and fervent demands for an encore confirmed the impact of their performance. That night in Detroit wasn't just a show—it was a euphoric high.

Frankie and the performers took their final bow, their connection with the audience clear. A deep sense of accomplishment filled them as they exited the stage. Without pausing, Frankie immediately sought out Chubbs. Once found, he pulled him close. "Chubbs, find those two women from the front row. Invite them to En Passant. Let's celebrate, baby."

Chubbs' face lit up with a wide smile. "Gotcha, brother... I'll ensure they get the message."

Chubbs approached the two women who had intrigued Frankie during the show. With a charming smile, he extended an intriguing invitation. "Ladies, Frankie Keys would love for you to join him tonight at En Passant in Paradise Valley. It's a low-key speakeasy where we like to unwind."

The tall woman tilted her head slightly, intrigue dancing in her eyes. "Remind me—who are you again?"

Chubbs, undeterred, confidently replied, "Think of me as his right hand. I manage the company around Frankie, ensuring he meets only the finest people." His grin widened a touch. "He was quite taken by your elegance this evening and hoped to enjoy more of your company."

The shorter woman's eyes sparkled with a hint of mischief as she turned to her friend. "Evie, this is our chance! Let's see what En Passant is all about," she urged, her tone low and enticing. Seeing her friend smile, she looked at Chubbs and said, "We'd love to join. We've always heard whispers about En Passant. It's tempting to finally step inside."

Chubbs extended his hand. "I'm Chubbs."

She blushed faintly before replying, "I'm Lorretta."

Chubbs lifted her hand to his lips with a touch of old-world chivalry. "A pleasure, Lorretta. I look forward to seeing you there. Your energy is exactly what we need tonight."

Upon arrival, the doors of En Passant swung open, unveiling a low-lit haven of clandestine charm. Nestled within a quiet alley, the speakeasy was a time capsule of the roaring twenties, adorned with plush curtains, antique wood paneling, and the soft, golden glow of wall-mounted gas lamps. The air, rich with the aroma of tobacco and aged spirits, carried the sultry tunes of a jazz band through the room.

Frankie and his group settled into a secluded corner, offering privacy and a panoramic view of the space. Lounging with his shirt slightly open, Frankie absorbed the mellow tunes drifting through the air. The arrival of Evie and Lorretta shifted the atmosphere, their presence adding a magnetic energy that seemed to elevate the room.

Frankie watched them closely, a stick of reefer pinched between his fingers. "You two made quite the impression at my show. Caught my eye. Was that the plan?" He took a slow drag, then flicked a stray piece of tobacco from his tongue. "Well, intentional or not, it doesn't matter nohow. You're here, and I'm all for good company—especially when it's as beautiful as you two."

Lorretta batted her eyes, a playful smile tugging at her lips. "This place feels almost like… euphoria."

Frankie exhaled a smoke ring, a slow grin forming. "I'm glad it impresses. This is my hideaway when I'm in Detroit. Figured you'd appreciate it, too." Leaning in, his voice dropped to a low, seductive purr. "So, what's your story? I invited you here to get to know you better, and…"

Evie cut in; her tone was full of skepticism and curiosity. "Do you really want to know, or is this just your routine?" She continued, her voice inviting. "I am an honest woman, Frankie, so I hope you can appreciate this. We dressed up tonight to get some attention because being desired feels good. But don't mistake that for availability. We're both spoken for."

Frankie leaned back, his interest deepening. "I don't believe I caught your name."

Evie met his eyes, her expression tantalizing. "That's because I didn't offer it," she replied, her voice smooth and measured. After a charged pause, her demeanor softened just enough to reveal a hint of vulnerability. "It's Evie."

Standing, Frankie raised his hands in a gesture of peace. "Easy, Evie. No schemes here. I'm tied up enough at home and don't need more complications. I thought you and your friend looked interesting. I asked Chubbs to come find you because I wanted some female company—honest enough? Relax and enjoy the night. No pressures, no expectations. You're free to leave whenever you wish."

Evie's cheeks warmed with a rush of embarrassment. "I'm sorry, Frankie, I can be too forward sometimes."

Frankie smiled, waving off her concern. "No need to apologize," he reassured her, signaling to the waiter. As he ordered a round of drinks, he gestured towards the comfortable seating area. "Let's sit and enjoy each other's company. Now, I asked about your story. Care to share?"

As they settled into the velvety chairs, Evie adjusted her hair, her movements more relaxed. Turning to face Frankie, she shared, "You know, I've always wanted to be an artist, but my family and friends constantly tell me that 'women should make babies, not paint.'"

She continued, "I yearn to create and express myself through my art. I just need someone to believe in me, to tell me I can do it, that I'm talented enough. All I want is to be seen and to be remembered."

Frankie offered her a sympathetic look, his tone earnest. "These are the times we inherited, not much we can do about that. But I'll tell you this—don't let that stop you. That's outdated thinking, Evie. You should pursue your passion relentlessly. Art is about expressing your true self, and you have every right to chase that dream—barriers be damned."

Evie's expression brightened, a spark of hope igniting in her eyes. Overwhelmed with gratitude, she leaned in and gave Frankie a quick, heartfelt hug, planting a kiss on his cheek.

Frankie gave a mock gasp, feigning shock. "Easy now. We agreed to keep things strictly platonic tonight, didn't we? Or should I start calling you my muse?" His flirtatious tease drew laughter from the group, a mix of camaraderie and relief, lightening the atmosphere as they all basked in the moment.

Lorretta chimed in, inspired by the openness of the conversation. Her voice carried a mix of defiance and aspiration. "Well, since we're sharing, I've always dreamed of being a business owner. But my partner doesn't see me as capable. He thinks a woman's place is solely in the home."

Chubbs took her hand, his grip gentle but firm, conveying respect and support. "Lorretta, don't ever doubt your capabilities. The world needs strong women like you to challenge and change these outdated ideas."

Her initial tension eased under Chubbs' supportive gesture. "You're right. I know so many influential people here. I just need to take that first step," Lorretta acknowledged, her voice growing steadier.

Frankie leaned in, his tone warm, recognizing the opportunity to uplift. "Ladies, both of you have dreams worth chasing, and you've got the determination to make them happen. Don't let anyone's narrow views box you in. If you ever need support—or just someone to believe in you—you've got us."

The women exchanged grateful glances, feeling genuinely encouraged by the men. As the night wore on, Frankie and Chubbs' initial conversation faded into the background. Under the subdued glow of the speakeasy, the mood was about to shift.

Chubbs, the contemplative soul of the group, broke the silence first. "You ever think about how far we've come, Frankie? But somehow, it still feels like we're just treading water," he said, his words cutting through the smoky haze with a quiet intensity.

Frankie wrapped his arm around Evie, absorbing the impact of Chubbs's words. He knew this side of Chubbs—the one that veered into deep, unfiltered reflections without warning. Their conversation took on a gravity that silenced the room in Frankie's mind, leaving only the weight of shared history and the burdens they carried as Black men navigating a divided America.

Chubbs broke the stillness, his voice steady but charged. "The racial divide has been heavy on my mind. Especially lately, with everything going on. I keep wondering—will we, as Black people, ever experience true freedom?"

His eyes searched Frankie's for understanding, the unspoken bond between them evident in the pause. "Think about it. Silky always goes back to the Constitution, how it counted us as three-fifths of a person. So, tell me, Frankie—with that kind of history hanging over us, what does freedom even look like?"

The question lingered, filling the space between them with an ache that demanded acknowledgment.

Frankie leaned in, his voice laden with resolve. "Freedom's a long road, Chubbs. But every note we play and show we give is a step forward. We can't let history break our spirit—we've got to keep pushing, keep inspiring."

Chubbs nodded, the weight of their reality settling in. "You're right, Frankie. It's just tough sometimes, not seeing the end of that road."

Their conversation, though heavy, underscored their shared commitment to endure and excel.

Lorretta and Evie listened intently, drawn into the depth of the discussion. Frankie continued, "It's a tangled history we carry, but look at us now. Just over sixty years ago, our ancestors faced unimaginable hardships. Today, we're here, making a mark, traveling the world, earning our way. That's Progress we can't ignore.

Chubbs scoffed, skepticism etched deep in his voice. "Progress, huh? Sure, we travel the country and make money, but that's not normal. You, Frankie, are an exception. The stars aligned for you, but for most, they don't. Remember, the same folks who enslaved us are still in power. They control the wealth and the opportunities."

Frankie, searching for words, responded with frustration and conviction. "You're right, Chubbs. What we have is rare. But don't underestimate the strength of our collective voices. The next decades will be tough, but change can come faster than you think."

Chubbs cut in, unconvinced. "Sounds naive, Frankie."

"Just hear me out," Frankie insisted as Chubbs leaned back, a sign of reluctant patience. Lorretta, sensing the tension, leaned into him to provide comfort. Frankie pressed on, "Our resilience will break barriers. Together, we can claim what's rightfully ours."

Laced with sarcasm, Chubbs retorted, "Preach all you want, Frankie. But sometimes, you avoid reality."

Frankie's frustration simmered to the surface. "Well, what the hell is the truth then, Chubbs? Tell me! I'm all ears."

The women exchanged wary glances, the weight of the conversation beginning to sour the air. Chubbs, noticing the shift, casually slid the ladies $50 for another round. "Why don't you two grab us something to lighten the mood?" he suggested with a forced smile.

As they walked off, their scent—a delicate mix of citrus and lavender—lingered in the air momentarily, a fleeting trace of their presence. Once they were out of earshot, Chubbs turned back to Frankie, his expression serious.

"You sure you want to hear this, Frankie? The raw truth?"

Frankie sat unfazed, "I asked, didn't I?"

Chubbs shrugged and continued his spill. "I hear all that preachy talk, Frankie. But let's get something straight. The same folks you expect to integrate with are the ones who are afraid to concede power. If they wanted us as equals, they would've made it happen by now."

Chubbs sighed, his words heavy, "Progress, they say, creeps slower than a cop looking for trouble. You seem to think this thing is going to happen quick. But the weight of oppression doesn't lift overnight, Frankie. Generations have carried these chains, and those clutching the reins aren't looking to let go.

Just as Frankie was about to respond, the women returned, their curves brushing against the men as they sat down. Chubbs acknowledged them with a nod. "Thanks, ladies."

With the drinks now on the table, Chubbs wasted no time diving back into his argument. "All this money might blur your vision, but that's where I come in—to keep you grounded in the truth." He took a deliberate sip, his eyes fixed on Frankie.

"Money can't buy our freedom, brother. And no amount of success will ever change how they see us. A rich Black man is still just a Black man to them—and sometimes, that's all it takes to find yourself at the end of a rope. Don't you forget that."

He set his glass down with a quiet finality. "So save that 'together we stand, divided we fall' jive for someone else. I ain't buying it."

Leaning back, Chubbs draped an arm around Lorretta, who crossed her legs and settled in beside him, a subtle smile betraying her pride in his unfiltered honesty.

Frankie's tone hardened, frustration creeping into his words. "So what's your solution, Chubbs? Pack up the piano and head back to Africa? You can't just dismiss the movement that's building. It's gaining momentum. Soon, we'll have leaders preaching and organizing, bringing the changes we need to finally move past this dark history."

Chubbs started a slow clap, his laughter sarcastic and cutting. "Y'all hear this? Still preaching! Someone needs to splash some water on him—wake him up from his dream." He took another drink, his tone laced with cynicism. "Leaders, huh?" Chuckling, he added with a sneer, "Let me enlighten you about what's gonna happen to your precious leaders."

Frankie, his interest piqued, demanded, "What?"

"They'll be killed," Chubbs declared bluntly.

He leaned back, his posture relaxed but his expression unyielding—a mix of resignation and defiance. "Mark my words, Frankie. We'll be having this same conversation for a hundred more years. America is built on division—power and greed shaping a land of the haves and have-nots.

But let's be real. We're part of the problem too. As long as we stay divided, tearing each other down, we're doing their work for them. Playing into the hands that built the shackles we're so desperate to escape."

Frankie attempted to soften the mood and end the evening on a lighter note. "Man, this is getting deep. Came here to relax, not to dive into the heavy stuff," he half-joked, trying to redirect the conversation.

Red barged into their bubble with his usual flair. "Damn! Y'all still on about saving the world and preserving Africa?" Red continued unapologetically, "I'm glad y'all fighting for the people, but listen here. That dark thang over there wants me to take her by the hotel to teach her 'The Stiff Leg.' Time to call it, boys. I've got a cat to scratch."

Red's antics cracked up the entire group, lightening the mood instantly. Frankie waved Cal over, leaning in to give him a quick directive. "Make sure the ladies get home safely," he said, his tone firm but appreciative.

The following day, they boarded the train from Detroit to New York, still carrying the echoes of last night's revelry. Nestled in their compartment, soft sunlight filtered through the windows, casting warm, shifting patterns on their tired faces.

Frankie reclined, waving off Red's enthusiastic suggestion for a poker game with a weary smile. "Not today, Red. I just want to sit back and enjoy the ride."

Cal nodded in agreement. "Let's take it easy. We've got a big show ahead. Some rest will do us good."

The cabin hummed with quiet conversations and bursts of laughter, underscoring their collective anticipation for the upcoming shows and the promise of New York's vibrant energy.

As the train barreled through the darkened countryside, a restlessness crept over Frankie. The rhythmic clatter of the tracks failed to soothe his thoughts. Rising from his seat, he wandered down the narrow corridor, his footsteps echoing softly as he made his way to the front of the train, seeking a moment of solitude to untangle his mind.

In a secluded corner, Frankie discreetly pulled out a wad of cash, handing a bill to the conductor. He then retrieved a small piece of paper containing communication frequencies from his pocket and gave it over. A knowing glance passed between them. With practiced precision, the conductor adjusted the portable device to the correct frequency and handed it to Frankie.

Rising to his feet, the conductor stepped away, affording Frankie the necessary privacy. As static crackled from the speaker, Frankie brought the cup to his ear. A voice came through, faint but discernible—it was Silky.

Frankie spoke softly into the receiver, "Hey, it's me. I need an update. Confirm what you have found on Jimmie."

The voice on the other end of the line crackled with assurance. "Nephew, I've had a tail on Jimmie's operation. He's been playing both sides—selling to his loyal clients while undercutting the market everywhere else. Looks like he's been running dirty behind your back."

Frankie's jaw tightened as his grip on the transmitter grew firmer. The revelation stung, a betrayal cutting deep. He knew it but didn't want to believe it. He issued clear instructions, his voice firm and resolute. "Keep this under wraps for now. I need time to think about what to do with this information. It's not something I'll let slide."

Silky replied, "understood." As the call was about to end, Silky switched topics and added, "Nephew, I know you're juggling a lot, but don't forget about Kenya. She's been handling everything on her own, and that ain't easy, baby boy."

Frankie paused, guilt flickering across his expression. "I hear you, Silk. I'll check on her. Thanks."

Frankie terminated the call, his mind racing with thoughts, plans, and possibilities. He carefully stowed the radio transmitter, leaving no trace of his conversation before returning to the cabin, his demeanor unshaken.

Mississippi Red, brimming with eagerness, leaned over the moment Frankie sat down. "Hey, Frank, I've been thinking. I've been killing it on stage, and the people love me. I need more time to showcase my talent. Hook me up!"

Frankie barely registered Red's enthusiasm. Forcing a smile, he waved a hand dismissively. "You're doing great, Red. We'll talk about it later. For now, just enjoy the ride."

Red took the hint and leaned back with a slight frown, letting the matter drop—for now. The rhythmic clatter of the train lulled the cabin into a calm quiet. Surrounded by the soft snores of his companions, Frankie allowed himself a rare moment of reflection. As the train gently swayed, it pulled him into a restless sleep filled with dreams of music and revenge.

CHAPTER 10:

# EASTERN STAR

"Chase dreams, not women." — Chubbs

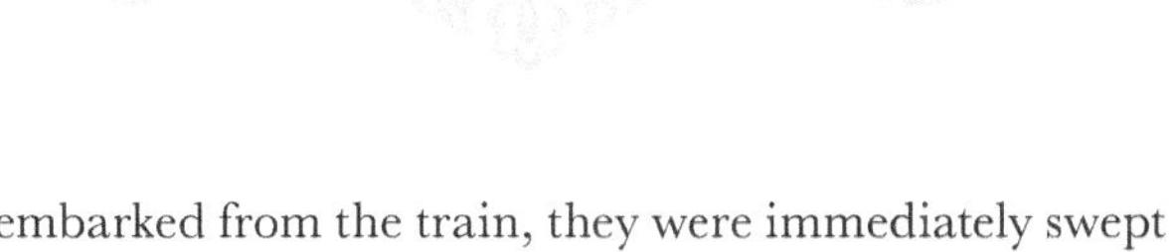

As they disembarked from the train, they were immediately swept up by New York's rapid pace. Skyscrapers towered above, symbols of ambition and progress, while the city's soundscape—honking cars, background chatter, and occasional shouts from street vendors—filled the air. Every corner thrummed with movement, the city pulsing like a living organism.

Their overnight journey led them to New York just before 7:00 PM on a Wednesday. Despite the fatigue from the previous night and their travels, they were invigorated by the prospect of their upcoming performance. The Velvet Note awaited them—a renowned Harlem venue that stood as a cultural cornerstone where jazz and blues magically intertwined.

The lounge was a sanctuary for musicians—a place to push creative boundaries. Its smoky interior, with glowing lamps and walls adorned with classic posters, provided the perfect backdrop for the intense feelings the club stirred. It possessed an intangible aura that drew influential figures from various industries like moths to a flame. In this place, connections were forged and legacies were written—or undone.

As they approached, profound respect filled them, aware they were about to add their southern roots to the club's illustrious history. Their stride quickened as they neared the neon-lit marquee, flickering an invitation to an unforgettable night.

Pausing at the entrance, they took a collective breath. Beyond those doors, they were not just musicians but conduits of emotion, ready to create unforgettable experiences for everyone who walked into The Velvet Note.

Just then, the owner, Verse, stepped out to greet them. At 54, he was a well-traveled musician, having played with, written for, and produced some of the biggest artists of the time. His presence was magnetic, witty, and versatile—masculine to men and feminine to women.

"Which one of you is Chubbs?" Verse asked, scanning the group.

Chubbs stepped forward.

With a wink, Verse continued, "You had me worried, baby. Didn't know if you guys were gonna show. We're tight on time, and that ain't how I operate, Daddy." He stepped closer, shaking Chubbs' hand and pulling him into a friendly hug. "But I'm glad you're here. Listen... The band's seen the sheet music you cats mailed over, but they're not feeling it. That tune? It ain't gonna move nobody around here. So, get inside and sync up with the band—help 'em catch what you're laying down. We've got a big crowd tonight. Can't afford any mistakes."

Chubbs showed respect to Verse. "Yo club is big time! Trust me, my guys are gonna bring the house down."

Verse's smile widened. "Damn right! And listen... This ain't just a club. It's a place for our people. You see, the white man done left us nothing but the underworld, but that's where I thrive," his voice took on a serious edge as he leaned in closer. "Our folks? We're the main attraction at those other big-name joints, but they won't let us through the door unless we performing. Ain't that something?"

He quickly glanced over to the line, noting it was starting to pick up. Verse continued, "And don't you know... Back in its heyday, mixed couples couldn't even get through the doors at those other Clubs. But here? At The Velvet Note, I run things differently. I'm a man of the people, ya see? I'm not Black, I'm not White—I'm Verse, baby. As long as you've got money in your pocket, you're welcome here."

Verse's attention shifted as he called out to his bouncer, "Let dem girls in, Tiny, they good people," Verse said, gesturing at three women in line." Then, he yelled out again, "But check him, Tiny! Yeah, him! The one in that silly-looking hat. He still got a tab from last week." Verse threw his hands up in exasperation, "You thought I forgot? I want my money, joker! You keep playing with me, ya hear? Trust me, next time your wife asks if you've been at the club, my memory will be much clearer!"

Verse turned back to the group with a charming smile, focusing on Red. "This one looks tired, is he up for this?" he said, giving Red a side-eye. "You know what, don't answer that. Just ask for Shayne when you get to the back; he's my stagehand and will get you cats anything you need. Now, get on! Time to practice."

Verse then walked off to catch up with the three ladies. "Ladies, I'm glad y'all showed up... Follow me."

With hearts full of resolve, Frankie and Chubbs pushed through the club's heavy doors, stepping into a realm of opportunity. As the first night's performance in New York unfolded, it was magical. Bathed in the soft glow of stage lights, the men tapped into a deep well of skill, delivering a show that left the audience spellbound. Their flawless execution, honed through countless hours of practice, resonated throughout The Velvet Note, captivating every soul.

The thunderous applause that followed was a surge of appreciation, sending waves of affection cascading back to the performers.

In the aftermath of their triumph, with the echoes of their music still lingering in the air, Mississippi Red found himself cornered by Shayne. Between drags of his cigarette, Shayne dropped a tantalizing piece of gossip that set Red's heart racing.

"Daddy, you were on fire tonight! Can't wait to see what you've got planned next... Heard Johnny Dash will be in the building Friday night, and he's bringing the house!" Shayne said, his words laced with excitement and smoke.

The mention of Johnny Dash, a titan in the music industry, sent a jolt through Red.

"Johnny Dash! *Thee* Johnny Dash? Here, to see me? I mean, us..." Red stammered, disbelief and ambition clashing within him. The prospect of performing in front of such a legend humbled him and ignited a relentless desire for recognition.

Red was jittery. "You got an extra cigarette?" he asked. Shayne pulled one from his pack and handed it over, then struck a match, shielding the flame with his hand as he lit it for Red.

Red puffed it nervously, his eyes darting around. He leaned in closer, lowering his voice. "Can I trust you?"

Shayne laughed lightly, "Verse only hires the trustworthy boss. What's on your mind?"

Still buzzing from the thrill of the night and the anticipation of meeting Johnny Dash, Red shared more, "I met this girl in Detroit—she was something else. I'm usually more of a drinker myself, but she introduced me to something called 'caine.' It was a ride, daddy." He paused, glancing around before continuing, "You know where I can find more? I ain't hooked or nothing... just curious, that's all. But this city, man—New York's alive! It never sleeps, and I don't wanna miss a second of it."

Shayne smirked. "You talking about cocaine? It's been around a while." Reaching into his pocket, he flashed a small packet before quickly tucking it away. "Listen, Red, I know you musicians are always on the move. If you're tired, let me get you some bennies."

Red tilted his head. "What's that?"

Shayne flicked his cigarette aside. "Benzedrine. You must be new to this business? Performers and veterans use 'em to stay sharp and keep going."

Red replied quickly, "You can keep the bennies. I'm looking for the 'caine.'"

Shayne contemplated for a second before conceding. "Be careful with this; you only need a bump. It's the real deal. Verse will kill me if you don't show up Friday."

Red puffed out his chest, "I'm a grown man, daddy. I'll handle myself." He pocketed the small bag from Shayne and rejoined the group inside.

The night stretched into the early morning as the squad explored New York, still riding high from their performance.

The following days blurred together, in a mix of relaxation and hurried meals, all set against the backdrop of the city's relentless energy.

Friday arrived quickly, heightening the anticipation for their second night at The Velvet Note. As the group approached the entrance, they were immediately recognized by Tiny, the bouncer, whose stern demeanor softened as he stepped aside.

The line of patrons froze, amazed as the men bypassed them. Whispers of their previous performance circulated, adding to their mystique.

At the entrance, two women dressed in elaborate corsets adorned with feathers and jewels gracefully pulled back the heavy purple curtains. With a practiced flourish, they motioned for the men to enter, their open hands and welcoming smiles adding a touch of elegance to the moment.

The Velvet Note was alive, a mosaic of colors flowing across the dance floor. Women in dazzling dresses swirled gracefully, their laughter blending with the music. Men, decked out in tuxedos, tried to match the performers, their moves punctuated by dramatic splits that drew cheers from the onlookers. Dollars and coins discreetly changed hands, tipped to women whose figures were accentuated by their sumptuous attire.

The room was a parade of fashion—tailored suits, shimmering pearls, and sparkling diamonds set against the soft, intimate glow of the club. Each ensemble told its own story, contributing to the unfolding drama of the evening.

The air was rich with the scent of perfume and tobacco, embodying the essence of the night's indulgence. Showgirls moved in perfect harmony alongside the Prince of Hi-de-ho, whose performance elevated the night's prestige. The dance floor, worn from countless tap dancers, bore witness to the many nights of celebration that The Velvet Note had hosted.

In the elevated high-roller booths where Johnny Dash and his entourage sat, heavy curtains occasionally drew closed, casting a veil over the private world within. Above the main floor, these booths offered an optimal view of the stage, a vantage point reserved for those with the means to command it. Business mingled with pleasure here, the secretive discussions as intoxicating as the drinks that flowed freely. Men and women alike moved in and out of Johnny Dash's booth, but it was the women—dressed in silk and shimmer—who truly captivated, their beauty uncontainable and their presence undeniable.

Modest tables were nestled along the lower level, catering to guests from all walks of life. The large dance floor, alive with movement and rhythm, welcomed all who dared to step into its embrace. This was The Velvet Note—a world where the ordinary faded away, leaving only the extraordinary.

As Frankie and his men took in the scene, they knew that tonight, amid the splendor and spectacle, they had to rise to the occasion and leave their mark on this legendary venue.

Backstage, there was a whirlwind of focus and preparation, with the aroma of brass cleaner lingering in the air. Each member dedicated themselves to perfecting every detail of their appearance, from the sleek lines of their outfits to the polished shine of their shoes. In the corner, Eddie Banks, the bass player, tuned his instrument, each pluck echoing his deep focus.

A medley of notes filled the air as fingers flew over strings and keys with practiced ease. Cal meticulously polished Red's trumpet, the soft cloth gliding over its surface. Anxiety and suspense coursed through the performers like twin currents.

Feeling the moment pressing down on him, Red glanced around, then quietly slipped away from the group. Finding a secluded spot, he took a *bump* to calm his nerves. Meanwhile, Frankie found solace in the curling smoke of his cigarette, the familiar burn a grounding force.

He exchanged a meaningful look with Chubbs, whose steady presence was a reassuring anchor amid the pre-show jitters.

"We're on the edge of magic hour," Frankie remarked, a smile tugging at his lips.

Chubbs returned the smile, his demeanor understanding. "It never gets cld, does it?"

"Never," Frankie replied, the thrill in his voice unmistakable.

Frankie and Chubbs bumped into Red as they made their way from the side stage to the prep area. Frankie immediately noticed something off—Red was overly amped, his eyes bucked and restless, unable to stay in one place.

"Red! You good?" Frankie asked, trying to keep his tone light but failing to mask the concern in his voice.

Red flashed a quick, nervous grin. "Yeah, Frankie, I'm just… ready to kill it tonight," he replied, his voice a little too fast, his movements too erratic.

Frankie pulled Chubbs close as Red wandered off, unable to settle down. "Chubbs, you reckon Red's cut out for a night like this?" he asked quietly. "Wednesday was one thing, but tonight, there was no room for error."

Chubbs looked at Frankie, his demeanor calm and reassuring. "Frankie, Red's got this. Sure, he's wound up, but it's not without reason. The boy lives for the spotlight, and all those hours we've heard and seen him practicing are about to pay off."

Reassured, Frankie watched as the stage came alive, the curtain lifting to unveil an eager collection of fans. Red stepped into the spotlight, his presence electric, captivating everyone in the room.

He transcended expectations, and his performance seamlessly blended skill and passion. Each note from his trumpet and each movement drew the listeners deeper into the world he crafted. This was his domain—under the bright lights, captivating hearts, and claiming his place on the stage.

At first, Frankie stood back with a swell of pride, admiring Red's natural charisma. However, as the performance wore on, it became apparent that Red's appetite for the spotlight knew no bounds. Gradually straying from the planned performance, he infused each moment with his personal touch, escalating his showmanship to new heights. What started as admiration for Red slowly morphed into concern.

Red, however, seized the moment to electrify The Velvet Note, diving into his signature move, 'The Stiff Leg.' His dance, bold in its precision and audacity, brought him to the forefront. He didn't merely perform; he commanded the stage, his voice booming as he shouted, "Tell me ya love me! Tell me ya need me! Tell me I'm incredible!" The cheers surged around him as he reveled in the moment.

Red called out to the audience once more, "Y'all wanna see my move again?"

The room erupted, "Yeah, man! Hell, yeah!"

Red pushed even further, feeding off the roar, yelling, "I can't hear ya! I said, do you wanna *seeeeeee* it again?"

The response was deafening, "Yeah, man! Hell, yeah! Hell, yeah!"

Red spun, dropped into a split, and popped back to his feet, hitting the infamous Stiff Leg once more. The atmosphere exploded, their enthusiasm matching his intensity.

Red's performance was a bold declaration, proof of his unstoppable drive to be the center of attention. For Frankie, this was a double-edged sword. On the one hand, he was witnessing the birth of a star, but he could also feel his own light beginning to dim. As Red soaked up the adoration, Frankie couldn't shake the thought that Red's brilliance might be the very thing that unraveled the magic they had built together.

As the last note reverberated through the room and the curtains fell on an unforgettable performance, the unit gathered backstage, breathless from the exhilaration. Verse was quick to approach Frankie and Red, his praise effusive.

"Frankie, your crew is always welcome at The Velvet Note, especially Red," he said, his admiration clear. Turning to Red with an impressed look, he added, "Red, you were magic tonight! Keep that up, and you'll be talking about a residency in New York before you know it."

After a final nod, Verse excused himself to attend to other guests, leaving just as Johnny Dash approached Frankie. A warm, calculating smile played across Johnny's face as he extended his hand.

"My man, you've got an eye for talent. That Red of yours is pure showtime! Keep grooming him," Johnny remarked, his tone intriguing. He gripped Frankie's shoulder. "You've got him locked down in a contract, yeah?"

Johnny paused, his eyes narrowing slightly as he scanned for a reaction. "Because if you haven't, you'd better handle that fast. Don't let him slip through your fingers, ya hear?"

His laughter echoed faintly, adding a sinister tone. "You see, I'm a businessman and always keep my lawyer close by." He gestured casually toward a quirky man with large glasses lurking in the background. Leaning closer, his voice dropped to a persuasive murmur, "For a talent like that... We could have something drafted in thirty-five minutes. If you catch my drift..."

Johnny's candor reminded Frankie that the industry was teeming with wolves. However, Frankie was already steps ahead—secretly, he had secured Red under a contract known only to Chubbs.

The validation of Red's raw talent by an industry legend affirmed Frankie's instincts. Yet, beneath his pride, Frankie recognized an emerging truth: Red's thirst for the spotlight was unquenchable, and managing his desire would be challenging.

As the night wore on, The Velvet Note transformed. Chandeliers cast a golden hue over the room, and the quartet's syncopated rhythms kept everyone swaying. The club became a melting pot—pretty girls, gangsters, businessmen—all mingling, each adding their voice to the evening.

In one corner, intellectuals debated politics and poetry; nearby, tap dancers in spats launched into an impromptu encore, their rhythms echoing through the floorboards. Women in sequined dresses and feathered headbands moved gracefully to the beat, while men in tailored suits held court, their glasses raised as they swapped stories.

Verse made his rounds with a wide grin, assuring everyone with his signature line: "You might leave broke, but you sho' gone be happy!"

Eddie Banks, the bass player, embodied grit and soul as he worked overtime, his hat flipped upside down to catch tips that overflowed the brim. Stripped down to his undershirt and suspenders, ash from his cigar dusted his chest while his bass lines kept the club pulsating.

Despite the sweat pouring off him, Eddie played on, fully committed to fueling the night. When the last note finally rang out, Eddie casually flipped his hat back onto his head, now heavy with tips, and disappeared out the back door.

That night, The Velvet Note was more than a club; it was a celebration of Black culture, a dynamic intersection of history and hope. Amid the bustling energy, Frankie, Red, Chubs, and Cal savored their achievements, each reflecting on the path that brought them to this moment. They understood they were part of something significant—not just in their careers, but in shaping a cultural legacy.

As their time in New York came to a close, the men packed their belongings and boarded a train bound for their next destination: Washington, DC. Stepping off at Union Station, they were met with the imposing grandeur of the city's architecture. Washington's unmistakable aura seemed to amplify the weight of their arrival.

Navigating through the bustling station, the strain between Frankie and Red was palpable. Though no words were exchanged, the tension hung heavy in the air. It revealed itself in quick glances and curt exchanges—a subtle undercurrent of unease threading through their camaraderie.

Upon exiting, Chubs said, "Our accommodations aren't quite ready. We've got some time to kill."

Clearly irritated, Red rubbed his temples and sighed, "I could use a bed right now."

"Yeah, I bet," Frankie muttered, his tone sharp.

Hoping to shift the mood, Chubbs made a suggestion. "Why don't we take a walk? Might as well see the sights while we're here." With little else to do, the guys agreed. They set off toward the National Mall, with the city's iconic monuments standing tall against the backdrop of the afternoon sky.

They began at the Washington Monument, its towering presence sparking quiet reflection. As they approached the Lincoln Memorial, the serene setting along the Reflecting Pool gave them a brief escape from the weight of the day.

Frankie lagged behind, captivated by the stillness of the water. As he stood alone, thoughts of Bell and Kenya crept in. He wondered about their well-being and felt an urge to reach out, to hear their voices. But with the tour nearing its end and so much still to accomplish, he sighed deeply and let the impulse fade just as quickly as it had come.

Noticing his delay, Chubbs called back, "Frankie, you're dragging. You good?"

Frankie offered a faint smile that masked his inner turmoil, saying, "Yeah, keep moving. Don't worry about me."

Their exploration of Washington, D.C.'s monumental sights left them both inspired and exhausted. They made their way to the hotel, a historic building whose old-world charm hinted at countless stories. The moment they stepped into the tasteful lobby, they were enveloped by its impressiveness—high ceilings and polished floors dominated by a tranquil quiet.

The check-in process was seamless, and while they found a split second to unwind, the looming rehearsal kept the group on edge.

When it was time to leave, they gathered in the lobby, ready to head to the venue. The ride was filled with small talk, primarily driven by Chubbs, who did his best to keep things civil. At the rehearsal, an irritable Red, eager to prove himself, proposed fresh ideas and new moves. Frankie, in no mood for distractions, dismissed the suggestions without a second thought.

Red whipped his jacket to the floor, the fabric landing with a dull thud. Neither man seemed willing to let the evening end without saying their piece. Frankie headed toward his dressing room, his posture rigid. Red followed a few paces behind, frustration bubbling over. The footsteps echoed through the corridor, each step amplifying the unspoken friction between them.

The late summer sun sliced through the dressing room window, creating sharp lines of light. Red stormed in, his demeanor defiant. "Frankie, we gotta hash this out. I'm not just some side act; I'm a headliner," he declared, his voice urgent. "I had this dream, see? The universe is screaming at me… It's my time to shine!"

Frankie's response was icy but controlled, a steely edge to his tone. "Dreams are just that—dreams. Real success is earned over time. Sure, you've had some strong performances, but that doesn't mean you can skip the grind. You still have to pay your dues."

Red, fueled by a cocktail of ambition and impatience, pushed harder. He stepped closer, his fists clenching as his voice edged higher with anger. "To hell with waiting! I'm the one carrying this band and writing the hits. It's time I took the lead!" His posture stiffened, embodying his turmoil, daring Frankie to push back.

The confrontation hit a boiling point when Frankie snapped. He hurled a crystal vase across the room. "Hold your tongue!" Frankie roared as he blazed with fury. "You owe everything to this band—to me! Don't forget who pulled you out of the Delta. Show some respect!"

Pacing like a caged animal, Frankie's voice dropped to a menacing whisper. "You've got no idea what I'd do to protect what's mine." He took a step closer, his focus pinned on Red. "You want to push me until I break… Is that it?"

Stunned by Frankie's intensity but unwilling to back down, Red stepped closer and shot back, "You think I wouldn't do the same? I'd kill for my shot at fame."

Frankie leaned in, his voice chilling. "Well, here's your chance. Go on—kill for it."

For a brief moment, Frankie's words hung in the air. Red's bravado faltered as he realized just how far this had gone. The line had been crossed and couldn't be undone.

The room fell into a tense silence, broken only by both men catching their breath, their anger and exhaustion visible in their heaving chests. Frankie, his voice steady but firm, broke the quiet. "We're done here. We've got a show to pull off, and we can't let this mess up our chemistry."

Without another word, they turned away from each other, retreating to their respective corners. Yet, as Frankie tried to focus, Red's words continued to echo in his mind, a haunting reminder that Red had meant every word he said.

As the next day unfolded, the focus naturally shifted back to the task at hand. Chubbs, playing peacemaker, pulled Frankie and Red aside, urging them to cool off for the sake of the performance. After exchanging a few uneasy words, they shook hands and agreed to set their differences aside. Resolved, they returned to the venue, each determined to deliver a flawless set.

Before taking the stage, Frankie gathered the band. "Tonight, we're not just playing another gig," he declared, his voice steady and intense. "We're making history in the heart of our country. Miss a note, and you might as well retire. I won't have anyone embarrass us in the nation's capital."

His words resonated deeply, underscoring the gravity of the evening.

As the call to the stage came, Frankie and Red walked side by side. This wasn't just another tour stop; it was a defining moment. Their performance was a seamless display of talent and teamwork, solidifying their place in the city's cultural scene.

After the final note, a sense of satisfaction filled the performers. Backstage, Frankie allowed himself a rare moment of humor. "Well, that one went off without a hitch. If only they all did," he quipped, drawing laughter from the group. The glow of success clung to them as they returned to their rooms, ready to rest before the final stretch.

When they entered the hotel, they were enveloped by quiet luxury that felt worlds apart from the high-octane performance. The plush furnishings invited them to release the adrenaline still pulsing through their veins.

Gradually, they parted ways, each retreating to their rooms, moving slower now but buoyed by the fulfillment of an exceptional show. The hallway was scented with fresh linen and the faint traces of room service, guiding them to their doors. Frankie's room awaited like a sanctuary— quiet, with the twinkling city lights below.

Alone at last, Frankie wandered to the tour schedule pinned on the wall, a silent testament to how far they had come. He exhaled deeply, his relief mingling with reflection. The glamour and chaos of the stage seemed distant now, leaving him alone with his thoughts and the daunting task of confronting the neglected corners of his personal life.

He edged closer to the phone, his mind occupied with thoughts of Bell and Kenya. Yet, he didn't allow his hovering hand to lift the receiver. Instead, he laid back, staring at the ceiling, fully aware he was delaying the inevitable.

"When I get back, I'll make things right," he whispered.

As Frankie drifted off to sleep, his thoughts turned to their final show in Charlotte. With the tour nearing its end, he realized the future would hold even greater challenges.

The next day, they traveled from the District to Charlotte's cozy embrace. The group's mood shifted as dense cityscapes gave way to rolling farmland and serene horizons. This reflective journey brought them closer together, drawing them toward the finale of their tour with each passing mile. On the train, the soft churn of the wheels lulled them into deep contemplation, their conversations weaving through topics of love and life.

Clutching the armrest as if to steady himself, Frankie's voice carried a weighty confession. "You know, boys," he began, his gaze distant, "my heart truly belongs to my wife—she's my anchor, my calm in the storm. But this life... it's draining. Some days, it feels like I'm wrestling with something primal as if being with just one woman defies a part of me. But I try, because she's worth the fight."

Maintaining a relaxed posture, Chubbs listened intently, his presence steady and unfiltered. "I hear you, Frank. Being a man ain't easy— always walking that fine line between what you want and what you know is right," he said, his tone reflective.

The sentiment resonated around the cabin, and everyone murmured in agreement, "Ain't that the truth..."

The mood lightened, and Chubbs spoke with conviction. "But let me tell y'all something—a man focused on his purpose don't have time for lust." He grinned, clearly pleased with his own insight. "I know y'all aren't philosophers like me, so here's the simple truth: chase dreams, not women." His laughter filled the cabin, the delight in his self-proclaimed wisdom evident.

Feeling reflective, Chubbs leaned forward, his tone shifting. "Enough about that, fellas. What's next for us? We've toured the country and seen everything—from the peaks to the pits. But what now? Family, chasing more money, settling down?" His questions lingered like a challenge, prompting each man to consider his own path forward.

As the train rolled closer to Charlotte, their compartment became a confessional. Looking out the window, Red broke the silence. "I'm not just here to play; I'm here to leave a legacy. To be remembered as one of the greats and clear a path for others to follow." His words, filled with ambition and hope, struck a chord with the others, prompting them to share their aspirations.

Cal spoke next, his voice resonant with purpose. "Being around you dreamers has been an inspiration. For me, it's all about keeping my house in order and ensuring I can provide for and protect my family. That's where I find peace."

With a spark in his eyes, Chubbs added, "I hear you, Cal. Me? I've got business in my veins. It's not just about making it in music; it's about making it, period. Building something from the ground up. If that's with Frankie, even better."

Frankie, his voice heavy with conviction, concluded, "I'm chasing a life that's real—where my actions align with my values. A life of honesty. That's what I'm after."

A contemplative silence settled over them as they leaned back in their seats, each man lost in his own thoughts. As the train drew closer to Charlotte, they remained in quiet contemplation, pondering the future that awaited them beyond this journey.

A bittersweet feeling accompanied their arrival. After settling into the comfort of their lodging, the men embraced a much-needed pause before the final night of the tour. The soft linens and the quiet stillness of the evening offered fleeting solace, giving them a moment to gather their thoughts and rest.

Morning arrived in a blur, the hours slipping away as anticipation mounted. By the time the afternoon gave way to night, they were readying themselves for their final performance—a show that would not only close this chapter but define their careers.

The club buzzed with life as patrons crowded in, drawn by the allure of the band's final performance. Laughter wove through soft jazz notes, a harmonious backdrop to the camaraderie forged over countless miles. Frankie and Red, their drama set aside, seemed at ease amidst the festive atmosphere. The evening exuded unity and celebration.

Red's eyes roamed the crowd, soaking in the energy that seemed to feed his ego. He leaned back, basking in the adoration swirling around him, until something—or rather someone—pulled his attention. She entered quietly, her arrival unannounced but undeniable.

Her beauty wasn't loud, but it demanded recognition. Red's usual smugness slipped as he tracked her movements, mesmerized by the way she glided through the room.

She wasn't tall, yet her presence towered, commanding attention with quiet authority. The soft glow of the lights kissed her skin, perfectly complementing the deep crimson gown that hugged her frame. A high slit revealed a toned leg with each deliberate step, her effortless grace captivating all who glanced her way. Her hair—a sleek braid flowing like a ribbon of midnight—draped over her shoulder, swaying with her movements. Confidence radiated from her in waves, while delicate gold jewelry—necklaces and bracelets—caught the light, their subtle shimmer amplifying her magnetic charm.

Red was no longer the center of his own universe. She had now taken up real estate in his mind. He had to have her.

Red sauntered over to her with an effortless swagger, his steps bolstered by the liquid courage in his glass. He began his introduction with a charm that had wooed many before. "Darling, darling! Where did you come from—Heaven or Hell? Doesn't matter, though; I'd follow you anywhere."

He extended his hand and said, "They call me Red, short for Mississippi Red." He watched her reaction closely.

She laughed, not just amused but intrigued. "Oh, Daddy! I've never met a man like you!" she teased, her voice carrying a playful challenge. She stepped closer, allowing Red to catch the warm scent of amber and vanilla emanating from her neck.

Rather than basking in his attention like so many before her, she posed a question that caught him off guard. "You seem like a man with layers, Red. Tell me—what really drives you?" Her inquiry, filled with genuine curiosity, signaled she was not just an admirer but a woman of substance, interested in understanding the man behind the persona.

Sensing he had her attention, Red played up his confidence. "You ask what turns me on, huh?" Red's vibe gradually shifted, becoming more suggestive. "I write, I dance, I freak—I does it all, baby."

But the woman didn't bite. Instead, her look grew suspicious, her smile becoming more calculating. "I'm intrigued by you, Red. You clearly pour your soul into your work. But beyond the stage and the applause, what are you really chasing?"

Red, brushing off the question, kissed her hand. "C'mon, babe, let's skip the dreamer talk. Tell daddy what you like, and I'll get with you after the show."

Her amusement faded, giving way to a calm, appraising look. "Oh, Red," she began, her voice cutting through the ambient chatter, "there's not much to like about stale conversation. You're quite the performer—I'll give you that."

Annoyed, Red cut in, "So what's your point?"

She stepped back, her demeanor relaxed but still commanding respect. "You reek of liquor and smoke—hardly the scent of sophistication. And let's be honest, you're not that cute, and I'd bet you struggle with reading anything beyond a menu."

Red's confidence wavered, but before he could react, she continued, "Here's the thing—a real man knows his strength lies in his mind and his respect for himself."

After a deliberate beat, she added, "You might want to invest in a comb, some mints, and maybe learn how to hold a real conversation."

With a graceful ease, she checked her reflection in a small mirror she pulled from her purse. After a moment, she snapped her mirror shut, scanning over Red. "Still here? There's more to this world than the shallow end you swim in. Dive deeper next time you approach a real woman, and you might catch a fish."

Red smiled, brushing off the slight with a cool hand. "I see how it is—I'll step back." He turned on his heel and walked away, returning to the guys with a hint of humility.

"She's off-limits, but it's her loss."

The men laughed as Frankie teased, "What happened, Cat Daddy? I saw your wink—I thought you had her in the bag!"

Red slicked back his hair, trying to reclaim some of his dignity. "She wasn't sophisticated enough to handle a man like me, that's all."

The group burst into even louder laughter, teasing Red until he threw his hands up. "I'm going out back for a smoke! I can't let these ladies stress me—I got too many waiting for me back in New Port. Hell, I'm ready to end this tour and ride my ponies!"

He stormed off, muttering under his breath as Frankie called after him, "We're on in thirty—don't stay gone too long!"

Frankie turned to the others, shaking his head. "Always has to make a scene," he said with a half-smile.

Chubbs chuckled, adjusting his hat. "You know Red—he's gotta blow off steam. He'll be back, all fired up and ready to go."

As the curtains lifted, they owned the stage with a sound refined by months on the road. Each selection wove together the threads of their journey, brought to life with a passion that stirred the soul of every listener.

The final note lingered in the air, a perfect conclusion to a journey full of struggle and triumph. For a brief moment, there was silence—then the crowd erupted, rising to their feet in a thunderous ovation. It wasn't just applause; it was validation, a testament to the miles traveled, the sacrifices made, and the dreams shared.

Leaving the stage, their hearts swelled. The tour had been more than a series of performances—it was a proving ground that shaped them as artists and men. This wasn't an ending; it was the beginning of a legacy.

# CHAPTER 11:
# TIES THAT BIND

"I'll kill you before I stay trapped in this loveless cage." — Bell

The days grew shorter as September settled in, bringing a breeze of change. The summer tour was over, and now it was time for the hard conversations that had been avoided for too long.

Frankie and Chubbs sat on the worn couch under the faint light of their old hideaway, a place Silky had secured for them years ago. It was a hidden sanctuary, steeped in memories and off the radar from the world outside.

Frankie's fingers drummed on the armrest as he spoke. "It's time," Frankie said, his voice full.

His focus shifted to an old photo hanging on the wall—him, Chubbs, and Kenya as teenagers, a snapshot of simpler times. He lingered on Kenya, regret gnawing at him.

"You're thinking about her, aren't you?" Chubbs's voice broke the silence.

"I am," Frankie admitted, his voice barely audible. "I've been dodging this for too long, Chubbs. She deserves better."

Chubbs inquired, "And Bell? She's your wife, Frankie. She's entitled to know what's in your heart."

Frankie sighed, frustration evident in his tone. "I've been a coward, hiding behind the music, letting distance do the work for me. But you're right—it's time to face it."

He rose from the couch and walked to the window, staring out at streets that had seen the best and worst of their years.

"I start tonight. No more running. I'll go to Kenya first. It's a conversation long overdue."

Chubbs watched the determination settle in Frankie, a resolve he hadn't seen in months.

"And after that?" he asked quietly.

"Then I go home," Frankie replied, the words feeling like a vow. "To Bell. No more secrets, no more lies. We need to figure out where we go from here, together or apart, but it has to be honest."

With a final nod to Chubbs, Frankie went out into the night. Each step reflected his decisions, guiding him toward a reckoning.

Not long after, Frankie approached Kenya's door, dread gnawing at him as he silently rehearsed his apology. His hand trembled slightly as he knocked three times.

When the door creaked open, Kenya's surprise quickly hardened into a cold glare as he stepped inside uninvited. The air was tense, burning with betrayal and disgust.

"So you disappear for months and then just randomly show up?" Kenya's voice was steady, each word edged with contempt. "You really think you can just barge into my house like nothing's happened? You are so arrogant!"

Frankie reached for her, desperate to bridge the gap between them, but she recoiled as if his touch burned her skin.

"I know I messed up," he stammered, his voice cracking under his guilt. "I'm here to fix—"

"Fix it?" Kenya's words were like shards of ice. "You think a few tears can erase what you did? You left us behind, Frankie! You vanished like we didn't even matter."

Overwhelmed, Frankie's voice frayed, each word soaked in emotion. "You're crushing me, Kenya. I'm here, trying to make things right. I'm begging you. Please, just hear me out."

Kenya's anger erupted, her pain raw and fierce. "Who do you think you are, Frankie? You don't get to waltz back into my life and smooth things over with empty words. You walked away—from me, from us!"

Crushed, Frankie sank to his knees, his plea silent but notable in his quivering form.

Kenya's tears began to flow, undercutting the strength she tried to project. "While you were running from the mess you made, I was stuck here, carrying the weight alone," she whispered, her voice weak. "I lost the baby, Frankie."

The words were slow, heavy with sorrow, unleashing a wave of grief she had long suppressed.

The revelation hit Frankie like a sledgehammer, severing the last shreds of hope he clung to.

Kenya wiped away her tears with the back of her hand, her resolve hardening. "What we had is dead. You hear me? Leave in the past. That kind of love don't live here anymore."

Before Frankie could respond, Kenya's voice cut through the silence like a blade. "Get out! And don't ever show up at my door unannounced again."

She pointed toward the exit, her voice cold with finality. "If you need me, I'll be at the Phat Kat until I can save enough money to get out of New Port and away from you."

Frankie stood there, paralyzed by his mistakes. The magnitude of his neglect and the cost of his procrastination settling in. The door slammed shut behind him, a resounding end to what they once shared.

As Frankie walked away from Kenya's door, her words echoed in his mind. The cool evening air did little to soothe the turmoil within him. Rather than finding closure, he experienced a profound sense of loss—a bitter realization that offered no peace, only a deeper understanding of his pain.

The ride home dragged, each mile stretching endlessly, mirroring the distance he had created in his relationships. A heavy silence settled in the car as his house came into view.

The conversation with Bell could either pave a path toward healing or shatter whatever remained of their marriage. Yet, he recognized that confronting this truth was unavoidable.

Stepping inside, Frankie found Bell in the living room, her presence both familiar and distant. With sweaty palms, he took a deep breath, steadying himself for the conversation ahead.

"Bell," he began, his voice carrying a rare vulnerability, "we need to talk."

Bell looked up, her fingers tightening around the murder mystery in hand. She set the book aside, a silent gesture for him to continue.

Frankie moved closer, sitting across from her. "I've been reflecting," Frankie said, his voice steadier than he felt. "About us, the choices I've made, and the pain I've caused."

He watched her closely, each word more deliberate than the last. Bell remained fixed on Frankie, her demeanor calm, her attention unwavering.

"I went to see Kenya tonight," Frankie confessed, pausing as he struggled to find the words. "She, um... she lost the baby," the pain in his voice unmistakable. "It was a wake-up call, Bell. A harsh reminder of the reality I've been avoiding."

Bell's posture stiffened, her demeanor controlled. She tilted her head slightly forward, silently urging him to continue.

"You've been my rock, even when I didn't deserve it. You've stood by my side, never giving up on us, on me. I took that for granted, and I'm here to say I'm truly sorry."

Frankie took a deep breath and exhaled slowly.

"But there's something else you should know," he began, his voice laden with regret. "When we got married, I was still in love with Kenya. It's not easy to admit, but it's the truth. We can only move forward if you know everything."

He straightened slightly, gathering his thoughts before continuing.

"My relationship with Kenya was a rollercoaster of highs and lows, passion mixed with constant breakups and makeups, leaving me unsure about our future."

As he reflected, Frankie interlocked his fingers and stared at the floor.

"You brought stability and discipline into my life, qualities I desperately needed. Marrying you seemed like the right decision—a business move, a way to start anew. It was more about what I thought I needed than what my heart truly wanted."

Tears streamed down his cheeks as he searched Bell's face for a sign of understanding.

"With you, I found strength. With Kenya, I found a novelty," he let those words hang, heavy with meaning, hoping she could grasp the depth of his realization.

He concluded, "But you, Bell, are my confidante, my partner. You are the love of my life."

Finally, Bell found her voice, her words measured.

"Frankie, this is a lot to take in. You've just told me our marriage wasn't built on a foundation of love but instead strategy. And while I appreciate your honesty, it doesn't take away the sting of knowing you saw me as a 'business move.'"

She took a moment, fighting to stay composed. "Do you know the pain I feel right now, realizing you loved another woman more than me? How can I trust our memories? Every happy moment—is it tainted? How do I cope with that?"

With a heavy heart, Frankie reached out and clasped Bell's hands. "I chose you, Bell, because I see my future with you. Despite my flaws, I believe our bond is worth fighting for. I love you, Bell, from the deepest place in my heart."

Bell yanked her hands away, tears rolling down her face.

"Love isn't enough, Frankie. It doesn't erase the years of lies and betrayal. I can't trust you," she screamed, her voice breaking with anger.

"For years, I tolerated your infidelity, thinking it was just the way things are, hearing my mother's voice in my head, 'Men keep women around—that's just the way it goes, baby girl.' But no more!"

Bell was frantic. "I can't pretend anymore. The truth is tearing me apart," she said, her voice edged with despair.

Overwhelmed, she lashed out at Frankie, her movements erratic and charged with desperation. She swung her tiny fists wildly, each strike a manifestation of her pain. Frankie, towering over her, caught her wrists to stabilize her.

Her efforts intensified, fueled by a rage she could neither contain nor understand. Snapping like a cornered animal, Bell tried to bite his hands. With a sudden movement, she thrust her knee towards his midsection, trying to push him away. Undeterred, she lunged forward, attempting a headbutt—all in a frantic effort to make him feel even a fraction of the pain consuming her.

"Please, calm down, baby. I'm so sorry," Frankie pleaded, his voice full of hurt.

Bell, her breathing labored, momentarily ceased her struggles.

"I understand the pain I've caused, and I'm desperate to make things right," he continued, his voice sincere.

Bell screamed in his face as she remained pinned. "Screw this marriage, Frankie! I'm leaving you!"

As Frankie tried to steady her, his grip inadvertently tightened, briefly mirroring the intensity of his own feelings. But as Bell continued antagonizing him, his self-control slipped, and he forcefully repositioned Bell against the wall.

"Woman, you ain't ever leaving me, and don't you even think about it. Till death do us part!"

Bell shrank away, fear clearly etched on her face. "Let go! You're scaring me," she cried, her voice breaking, deeply piercing Frankie's heart.

Realizing his mistake, Frankie released her and stumbled backward, beginning to apologize. But before he could finish, Bell's hand struck his face sharply.

The slap cracked through the room like a whip, knocking him off balance and onto his knees. He clutched his face, the room spinning around him.

Bell's words were chilling as she now towered over Frankie, who knelt defeated at her feet: "I'll kill you before I stay trapped in this loveless cage."

Regaining her composure, Bell stood firm. "Frankie, I think it's best if you leave," she said, her tone quiet but unyielding. "And stay away. I need time to sort this out."

She gestured towards the door, her face unreadable.

Without a word, Frankie calmly stepped out of his home, the door closing softly behind him. This heartache shadowed him into the darkness, setting the stage for the unraveling that awaited.

In the passing weeks, Frankie's descent into the darker corners of his world made a confrontation with Jimmie inevitable. Flanked by Silky and Chubbs, Frankie entered Jimmie's office, a utilitarian space situated in a rugged old warehouse surrounded by dense woodland. The scent of aged wood mingled with traces of tobacco and liquor. Sparse light filtered through grimy windows at the top of the room, creating a gloomy ambiance.

As they faced Jimmie, an uncomfortable silence settled over the room. Unbeknownst to Frankie, Vincent "The Viper," one of the Santoros family's most trusted lieutenants, observed the unfolding drama with a stony calm.

Despite his precarious position, Jimmie maintained a façade of complete control. He knew the importance of his outward appearance— neither side could see him sweat.

Jimmie lit his cigar, the flame briefly illuminating his face in an orange glow as he stood from the desk.

"You know I've got love for you guys," he began, his smirk lingering despite the stern faces before him. "We started this together, like a pack of wolves, right?"

His attempt to lighten the mood was met with silence.

Silky interjected sharply. "Cut the smooth talk, Jimmie. What's your point?"

Jimmie shook his head and took a few thoughtful drags from his cigar. "Ralph, can you believe these guys? Coming here unannounced, acting like they run things. They must be sampling their own stash."

His joke drew muffled laughs from his men, but Frankie and Vincent remained stone-cold.

As the room quieted down, Frankie stayed locked on Jimmie.

"Frankie, what's this about? What brings the trusted trio here without warning?" Jimmie asked, his tone casual.

Frankie's response was direct. "Jimmie, I know you've been moving half-priced hooch—and I know you've been doing it outside of our arrangement."

Jimmie pointed his cigar at Frankie in response. "Those are hefty accusations. You storm in here throwing around claims of skimming?"

Unfazed, Frankie pressed on, one hand casually in his pocket, the other wagging a finger at Jimmie.

"I know about the trucks you hijacked—my trucks," he openly accused. "You flip the stolen liquor by selling it cheap to anyone willing to take on the risks of transportation. It's clever, keeping your hands clean and minimizing exposure," he said sharply, his frustration evident as he sucked his teeth. "That's exactly how I would've done it, too."

Jimmie's slack-jaw tightened, his teeth grinding, the smoldering cigar forgotten in his hand.

"But here's what I don't get—why do you need that much cash? What are you really up to, Jimmie? Or what do you need to get out of?"

In response, Jimmie slammed his hand on the desk, sending ash scattering across the polished mahogany.

"Shut your mouth! That's ridiculous!"

Frankie had struck a nerve and ended his theory with a slight smile. "It all leads back to you, Jimmie."

As Ralph shifted his weight, Jimmie's glance flicked nervously between Frankie and The Viper, his composure cracking.

"Frankie, let me explain—"

Frankie cut him off. "No, Jimmie. I want the truth," he demanded. "You've been stealing from the business. From me. Why?"

Jimmie let the smoke from his cigar cloud around him, a feeble shield against the reality of his predicament. "Look… Frankie, Silky, Chubbs," he began, focusing on each of them in turn. "We've come a long way together. But the game's changing, and I did what I thought was necessary to survive."

Silky stepped closer, his posture a physical challenge to the man he once trusted.

"Opportunities, Jimmie. That's what we gave you. And you repay us by sneaking behind our backs?" His words were a direct accusation, his disappointment apparent.

Chubbs interjected with a flat, ominous tone, "You're gonna make this right, Jimmie, or we'll take what's ours. Believe that…"

Vincent finally spoke, his voice smooth but serious, "Let's keep this professional; we don't make threats here."

Chubbs shot a glare at Vincent, sizing him up.

Reassessing the situation, Vincent realized he had underestimated Frankie. His confrontation with Jimmie revealed Frankie's deep influence within New Port's criminal underbelly. The Viper was forced to reconsider the balance of power in the city.

Frankie was taken aback by the difference between the ambitious partner Jimmie once was and the man he had become.

Standing there, a rush of memories took him back to the night it all began at an unassuming steak house in New Port. Waiters paraded meat selections before them, hinting at the feast to come, while the gleam of shiny cutlery promised a communal dining experience like no other.

Frankie and his future wife were seated next to Jimmie and his soon-to-be ex-wife. Under the soft glow of candlelight and white tablecloths, their destinies intertwined over shots of strong liquor and intimate chatter.

With its relaxing ambiance, the steak house became their partnership's cradle.

That night, as if by fate, they met—two young bulls in a world ripe with opportunity and danger. Amid the clinking of glasses and shared laughter, they forged a bond over the remnants of their meal, a handshake that would reshape New Port's underground. Together, they expanded their reach, influence, and profits.

However, as their empire grew, so did the rift between them. With his natural charisma and knack for negotiation, Frankie gradually became the preferred contact, a development that gnawed at Jimmie. He grappled with a growing sense of insignificance, feeling increasingly diminished by Frankie's rise.

This subtle shift marked the onset of a fracture in their partnership, a gap that widened over time, fueled by unspoken grievances and simmering jealousy.

As they stood opposite each other in the warehouse years later, Frankie could hardly believe how far they had strayed from the unity and shared aspirations that once defined their relationship. Those early days now felt like a distant memory.

Extinguishing his cigar, Jimmie leaned back in his chair—a gesture that resembled a silent white flag. The room fell mute as he stared at the ceiling, seemingly searching for answers in its blank expanse.

"Alright, Frankie, you've got it," Jimmie said. "I'll pull back, and we can keep our business going. You need me, and I need you... Just remember, my eye is always on my profit margins," he conceded.

Ralph cleared his throat, indicating that Jimmie had revealed more than he intended. Hastily, Jimmie added, "We're talking about profits for the organization here. Times are changing, and I've got to look out for the family."

Frankie nodded slowly, his face giving away nothing. "So, I expect we'll discuss how you plan to make this right when there aren't so many ears around?" he proposed.

Jimmie stood and approached Frankie, offering his hand.

Frankie looked from Jimmie's face to his extended hand. "After we square things away," he replied coolly, his voice measured.

He let the moment linger, studying Jimmie's expression before stepping back. Slowly, Frankie adjusted his hat, a subtle gesture that carried more weight than words. With a terse nod to Silky and Chubbs, he turned and strode toward the door, his mind already racing with calculations and plans.

As they retreated to the car, Chubbs broke the tense silence. "Just like that, we let it slide? After he's been bleeding us dry?" His voice was tight with disbelief and anger.

Frankie glanced over at Chubbs. "Not quite, brother. Let's just say the tax collector has Jimmie on his schedule."

His words were cryptic, a quiet promise of retribution that needed no further explanation.

Meanwhile, back at the office, Jimmie's frustration boiled over. He ranted about dividing territories and managing Frankie's influence. His tirade continued unchecked until Vincent intervened, silencing the room with a commanding bellow.

"Shut up!" he roared, his voice resonating with frightening authority—a clear signal that negotiation time had ended.

Vincent chastised Jimmie for even considering a conflict with Frankie, highlighting the foolishness of such a move. Striding back and forth with evident frustration, Vincent scorned the notion of conflict.

"Going to war! Over what? A few dollars?" he scoffed. "You'd risk everything, all for greed."

His words left the room stunned. "Jimmie, you're an idiot," he added, looming over Jimmie like a predator to its prey.

Jimmie's earlier confidence evaporated under Vincent's scathing reprimand. His resolve crumbled, replaced by panic as Vincent issued another command.

"Sit down! I'm calling Salvatore on this one. Where's the fucking phone?" The Viper hissed.

It became clear to everyone present that Vincent, not Jimmie, held the reins. Deciding to involve Salvatore—the revered Don of the South's most powerful Mafia family—was scary business.

Jimmie's men and a few of Vincent's associates exchanged glances, some shifting nervously from foot to foot. They were fully aware of the severity of involving Salvatore—a figure who could dramatically alter their life expectancy.

Visibly deflated, Jimmie reflected on his overreach and ambitions. The room held its breath, everyone bracing for the verdict.

When Vincent returned, his presence darkened the mood of those assembled. He approached the still-seated Jimmie and yanked him closer, the chair scuffing the floor.

"The Don says you will peacefully work with the nigger. Got it?"

Jimmie squealed in agreement. "Not a problem!" he responded quickly.

Vincent lightly slapped Jimmie's cheek, seemingly satisfied. "Good," he murmured, walking away before abruptly spinning back, his face darkening ominously.

He grabbed Jimmie by the collar and yanked him close. "I forgot! Let's discuss that extra money you didn't report to the family."

With a forceful shove, Vincent commanded, "Get him on his knees."

Before Jimmie could react, he was pushed to the floor, his eyes wide with fear as they locked with Vincent's in a desperate plea for mercy.

Vincent's voice was deceptively soft, laced with lethal intent. "Sal's not pleased about you pocketing money without paying your fair share to the family."

Panic surged through Jimmie as Vincent drew his weapon. "You know what Sal said to me? 'I don't like it. You should put him to sleep.'"

The room turned ice cold, every heartbeat seemingly suspended by Vincent's declaration. He cocked the hammer on his revolver and pointed it at Jimmie.

"Are you ready?" Vincent's question caused Jimmie's heart to palpitate.

As Jimmie knelt on the cold floor, a torrent of memories flooded his mind—choices made, alliances broken, and a relentless climb for power that now teetered on the brink of oblivion. He wondered, not for the first time, if the pursuit was worth the price of his soul.

Just as despair seemed to grip him, Vincent stepped back, offering a sliver of hope.

"But lucky for you, Angelo reminded The Don that your father was a good man, a loyal man, a made man."

Jimmie exhaled and dropped to all fours, gasping for air, his vision blurred, heart fluttering.

Vincent snapped his fingers to reel Jimmie back to reality. "Angelo wanted me to relay a message…"

As Jimmie was still on edge, Vincent grasped his chin, his iron grip unyielding. "Don't mistake his mercy for weakness, capisci?"

Fervently, Jimmie affirmed his understanding, "Got it! Got it!" as he was helped to his feet.

Vincent leaned in close, his presence imposing. "The Don wants a luxury tax. Twenty thousand dollars for your little stunt. You have four months, Jimmie. Four months…"

He let the threat hang in the air, his tone a sinister promise. "If you don't make good on the payment… I just hope I get the call to do it."

As Vincent slithered away, stillness filled the room. His absence was a chilling reminder that enforcers like him came and went, but the decisions of bosses lingered long after.

Three weeks later, under the muted gleam of a single lamp, Frankie, Chubbs, and Silky gathered in secrecy. The blueprint of Jimmie's warehouse sprawled before them on the table, its worn edges and intricate lines resembling an artifact from another era.

Frankie's hand swept over the aged construction plan with surgical precision. "Gentlemen, every door and window, we need to know of it," he said, his voice low but firm, as his finger traced potential entry points.

Chubbs, absorbing every detail, tapped his pencil on the map. "Right here and here—these are our sweet spots. We caught the guards slacking during recon. Our window is tight; between 2:15 and 3:00 a.m. is best," he noted.

Silky leaned in with an alternative angle. "Before we commit ourselves to doing this, hear me out," he began.

Frankie and Chubbs sat back to let him take the floor.

"I've got two guys who are experienced in robbery. Creepy and Sneaky, brothers, out-of-towners. They're sharp, they're clean, they're hungry. Perfect for getting in and out without a trace."

Frankie's mind was racing, interested in Silky's alternate approach.

Silky stroked his chin, "If we are talking fewer than five guards, they can handle this job no problem. And that lets us keep our hands clean."

Frankie raised an eyebrow, intrigued and cautious. "And the catch, Silky? There's always a catch with guys named Creepy and Sneaky."

Silky laughed, acknowledging the point. "Creepy's got a bit of a temper, sure."

Frankie probed, "And Sneaky?"

Silky smirked, "Sneaky... The boy can charm venom from a snake. But sometimes his smooth talking leads to too much talking." Silky quickly reassured Frankie, "Trust me. They're professionals. With the right prep, they're golden."

Frankie mulled over the scenario and said, "Alright, set up a meeting. I want to meet them in person before we go all in."

"As for the plan," Frankie continued, standing up to emphasize his words, "this heist is more than a payday. It's a statement. It's about karma and showing Jimmie what having his back against the wall feels like."

Silky added, his voice smooth but edged with grit, "We hit fast, and we hit hard."

Frankie's lips curved into a rare smile, the strategy clear in his mind.

As the meeting concluded, the blueprint rolled up like a scroll of destiny, and each man left the room fueled by adrenaline and purpose. Successfully pulling this off would force Jimmie into a position of reliance on Frankie. In turn, this would offer Frankie the perfect opportunity to shift his focus entirely to the music, handing Jimmie the reins of their illegal operations.

Such a final move would provide freedom from the life that had been both a curse and a boon.

While Frankie felt the tumultuous circumstances of his world, Bell found herself wrestling with her own unresolved issues. Intent on finding some resolution, she arranged a dinner with Kenya at SinTika, a venue bathed in romantic light and adorned with decor that spoke elegance.

The gentle melodies of a quartet in minor softened the ambiance, creating the perfect undertone for the evening's sensitive conversation.

SinTika, a serene spot cherished for its tranquility and seldom frequented by men, offered a comforting haven tucked away from the public. Here, women could relax amid plush chairs and fine cutlery, surrounded by dark flooring alive with twinkling gold flakes and walls graced with fresh bouquets, all contributing to a sense of renewal and beauty.

In the restaurant's most secluded corner, Bell had secured a table that afforded privacy. The flicker of candlelight set the stage for an intimate exchange. Both women, seated in this carefully chosen spot, showed signs of apprehension, their mannerisms reflecting the burden of past grievances and the hope for understanding.

With a nervous sip of her wine, Bell's leg twitched rapidly as she broke the silence. "So... How are you?"

Her words, opened the door to a conversation that promised to be as revealing as it was necessary. This was not just any dinner; it was a rare opportunity for both women to speak and, more importantly, to listen.

Kenya hesitated, the question awkwardly hanging in the air between them. After a moment, she offered a brittle smile. "I've been better," she admitted, allowing her guard to lower just a fraction. "And you, Bell? How are you handling everything?"

Bell paused, considering her words carefully. The directness of Kenya's question caught her off guard, compelling her to confront her feelings.

"I'm surviving," she finally said, the words heavy with unspoken grievances. "Surviving in a reality I never imagined would be mine."

The conversation faltered, each woman acutely aware of the other's pain.

"Kenya, I need to talk to you about this thing you have with Frankie." Bell scrutinized Kenya with a thorough glance. "It's time for it to end. I can't keep living like this, sharing him with you," she said with a touch of compassion.

Kenya looked away briefly, collecting her thoughts before taking a deep breath. "Bell, let me be clear. My intimate relationship with Frankie is over. I work at the club, and that's the extent of it."

Bell smiled sarcastically. "Of course it is…"

Kenya's response was quick, her tone earnest. "It's not so simple, Bell. Things with Frankie were always complicated."

Bell let out a low, catty purr. "Honey, he's married, yet he was with you because of your history. Perhaps you satisfy him in ways I don't. It's painfully simple, not that complicated."

Kenya replied with a wry smile, "Oh, Bell… We've broken up so many times before. I know it seems like we always end up back together— like there's this magnetic pull neither of us can resist."

Bell listened, nodding slowly as she clenched the knife's handle.

"Look. I get it, Kenya. But you're worth so much more. Move on.

There are plenty of successful and powerful men out there who would truly value you and treat you like the queen you are," she said compassionately.

Kenya glanced at Bell, a pleading look crossing her face. "Bell, you know Frankie better than most. You know how persuasive he can be."

Bell's patience snapped, and she slammed her fist on the table, knife in hand. The sudden noise drew startled looks from nearby tables, but both women flashed reassuring smiles to diffuse the onlookers.

Bell leaned in, her voice softer but filled with intensity. "Sorry. But listen, Kenya, you're a beautiful, intelligent woman. You deserve more than to be someone's fallback. Why settle for less than you deserve?"

Kenya sighed, the sound carrying both honesty and vulnerability. "Being with Frankie has its perks, Bell. The lifestyle, the glamour—it's more than most girls could dream of. But it's not all roses; there are plenty of headaches and heartaches," she confessed.

Kenya gathered her thoughts before delving deeper into her tangled history with Frankie.

"You know, Frankie and I were on a break when he married you." Kenya drifted, lost in the memories. "I should've walked away then, I know. It wasn't right, but...I loved him. His world was enticing, and somehow, I fit perfectly within it. I never intended to take your place."

Kenya's voice grew softer, more reflective. "Frankie made me feel wanted, loved in an intoxicating way. I tried to break it off, knowing deep down it was wrong, but my heart just wouldn't let go."

A brief, humorless laugh escaped from Kenya's lips. "I even tried dating, looking for someone to help me move past him. But Frankie, he was possessive, told me I'd never find anyone better, that I shouldn't even try. And I listened."

Kenya looked up, her eyes meeting Bell's. "But here's the thing, Bell. Amid all the luxury and the illusion of security, I wasn't truly happy. It took me a long time to admit that to myself. Frankie's assurances and declarations of love kept me tethered, making it hard to imagine a life without him. Yet, here I am, realizing I don't want a life with him anymore. Not like this."

Kenya's confession was a raw, unvarnished glimpse into her soul. "His only rule was to never let you know the depth of what we had. I honored that, out of respect for you, and maybe out of fear, too. It wasn't until recently I realized that being the 'other woman' isn't a badge of honor, but a chain. And I'm ready to be free."

Her words carried hope—a desire for redemption and a new beginning.

Bell took a deep breath, her words deliberate. "Kenya, I know about you and Frankie—about your history, about how intertwined your lives have been. And I know about the baby," she said, her voice steady, the soft guitar strumming in the background enhancing her words.

At the mention of the baby, Kenya flinched, the pain of the loss still fresh. "I never meant to hurt you, Bell. Or to embarrass you," Kenya whispered, her confession testing their fragile connection.

"I understand more than you think, Kenya. And I don't want us to be enemies, or rivals, or whatever this twisted situation has made us," Bell said, her voice gaining strength. "I want to move past this, for both our sakes."

Kenya smiled, a sign of understanding. "I know it's not easy for you either, Bell. We're both caught in circumstances that are complicated and draining. But we need to figure out what's best for ourselves," she said.

Their conversation had taken a positive turn, one marked by mutual respect.

Bell swirled her red wine. "I admire your ability to dream, Kenya. To own your club, to start fresh somewhere far from New Port and this mess." She paused, gauging Kenya's reaction.

Kenya appeared surprised.

Bell leaned back, "I want to help you make that dream a reality. If Frankie won't give you the money to help you fund your dream, I will."

The offer hung in the air, leaving Kenya speechless. She finally mustered a response, "Why would you help me?" she asked, her voice filled with genuine confusion.

"Because," Bell replied, "it's time for all of us to find some peace. And this—this is a step toward that peace. For you, for me, and yes, even for Frankie."

CHAPTER 12:

# FRANKIE'S INTERLUDE

"You can't control everything, and you'll regret crossing me."
— Mississippi Red

In the days that followed, Frankie greenlit the heist. This was their golden opportunity to reclaim the cash siphoned by Jimmie.

Silky's connections in the underground circuit provided them with critical intel: Jimmie had grown careless, stashing both the money and the booze in the warehouse. It was the perfect setup for a clean sweep. But robbing a man with mob ties came with deadly risks, so they meticulously planned every step to ensure the hit couldn't be traced back to them.

As the night drew near, Sneaky and Creepy meticulously tracked the rhythms of the warehouse. With adrenaline coursing through their veins, they advanced under the cloak of darkness; their figures blending into the night—movements sharpened by years spent perfecting the art of theft and deception.

Jimmie's warehouse was a fortress that had taunted many but bowed to none. But tonight, it would face a challenge unlike any before.

Creepy, true to his name, loomed like a ghostly omen, the jagged scar carving down his face a chilling reminder of his ruthless past. Sneaky was finesse—the scalpel to Creepy's hammer, his mind a maze of plans and contingencies.

Their first encounter was with a lone guard caught on a smoke break.

With the suddenness of a southern storm, they descended upon him—Creepy's imposing figure blocking any escape while Sneaky's words cut through the silence. "How many are inside?" Sneaky's voice was cold and sharp.

"Two!" The guard's reply came out choked.

But Creepy sensed deceit. "He's lying," he growled, the click of his gun slicing through the stillness.

"I swear to you—it's only two, and me," the guard stammered, desperation driving the truth out. "I'll give you whatever you want. I have a family. I'm not ready to die."

They took him at his word—satisfied by the fear-stricken honesty.

Using the guard, now tied and silenced, they breached the entrance with lethal precision.

Inside, they clung to the walls, their presence undetected as they navigated the corridors with ghost-like efficiency.

It wasn't long before they found the others—Ralph and his nephew, all unsuspecting pawns in a game they didn't know had begun.

The takedown was swift, and now, all three men were bound, their fates sealed by the brothers' unyielding grip. Creepy, the looming watcher, ensured order while Sneaky searched the premises for the elusive loot.

Each step was measured, every creak in the floorboards sending their hearts racing.

In the room where the hostages were held, Ralph's nephew was the first to shatter the silence—a mix of bravado and ignorance in his voice. "Do you thugs have any idea who you're robbing? We'll find you, and we'll make you pay."

Creepy, reacting swiftly to the challenge, struck the boy with the butt of his gun. Yet, the young man's spirit remained unbroken. Seething with anger, he spat out,

"You motherfuckers are going to wish—"

Before he could finish, Creepy delivered a series of brutal blows. He cracked him three times before kneeling in front of him, placing a finger over the boy's mouth.

"Shhhh..." Creepy whispered, his voice a low threat meant to silence the young man.

Yet, Ralph's nephew felt untouchable under his uncle's protection. Blood streamed from the gash on his forehead as he spat into Creepy's face.

"You're a dead man! Ya hear me? Dead!" he yelled defiantly.

It was then, in that charged moment, that Creepy decided he had heard enough. Rising slowly, he loomed over the boy and his uncle, a shadow darkening the space. Without a word, he drew his gun, aiming it squarely at the boy's head—his finger wrapped around the trigger.

"Nooo! Please, no!" Ralph's voice cracked, desperation and fear slicing through the room as he begged for mercy.

For a moment, time itself seemed to hang in the balance—the cold metal of the gun and the rebellious boy locked in a standoff of life and death.

Then, like a lifeline, Sneaky's voice cut through the intensity. "Brother! Put it away. I found the stash.

Creepy's grip on the gun relaxed, though he stared at the boy, a silent warning not to push further.

Ralph's breath came in ragged gasps, his face marked by the realization of how close his nephew had come to death. He strained against the ropes, urging the young man to stay quiet.

With the standoff resolved, the brothers returned to their true objective—the cash.

Without a word, they moved swiftly, their faces lighting up in awe at the shelves stacked with bundled bills. Sneaky grabbed the first bag and began stuffing it, his hands a blur as he worked quickly.

Creepy returned to the tied men, keeping watch while Sneaky focused on the task. Once the first bag was packed to the brim, Sneaky zipped it shut and tossed it into the next room.

One by one, the bags were filled. The men worked in near silence, broken only by the rustling of bills and the dull thump of each bag hitting the floor, marking their progress like a steady drumbeat.

The pile of cash that had once seemed endless now fit snugly inside four tightly packed duffel bags.

Sneaky wiped his brow and flashed a sign to Creepy, indicating it was time to move. He hefted the first two bags over his shoulder and headed out to the car parked in the darkness. Sneaky moved with purpose, his steps quick and deliberate. He loaded them into the trunk, then returned for the final two, repeating the process with the same speed.

Once the last bag was secured in the car, he slowed to catch his breath. But something inside the warehouse caught his eye—the sight of aged bourbon.

"How about we celebrate our little victory?" Sneaky suggested, his interest fixed on the crates of top-shelf booze. "It's not just cash that can quench a thirst."

Creepy's brow furrowed, a silent reminder of their unspoken rule for this job: cash, not booze.

But the lure of the bourbon, coupled with Sneaky's infectious enthusiasm, was hard to resist.

"Just a few crates, I promise," Sneaky added. "This deal is too good to pass up. It's practically free."

Creepy relented with a sigh, the corners of his mouth betraying a reluctant smile.

As they prepared to load the crates, Ralph found his voice. "This smells like Frankie. You're working for him, ain't ya?"

Sneaky turned, flashing a crooked smile. "Frankie? Never heard of him. But since I take pride in my work, let me set the record straight."

He knelt down, greeting Ralph with a smirk. "Word travels fast, and rumor had it there was a warehouse in New Port stuffed like a treasure chest—but no one was brave enough to try and take it."

Sneaky smoothed his eyebrow with a sly grin. "But that was before I got wind of this little treasure trove. My daddy always said, 'If you're gonna be a bear, be a grizzly.' So, hearing about all this cash just lying around, we had to come and take a look."

He leaned in closer, his tone almost playful. "You see, my brother and I, we're takers. It's the family business. And just so ya know, before you pour your resources into tracking us down, here's a tip—start the search in Mexico. Plenty of places to hide out there. See you boys later."

He stood up with a mocking salute and smirked, "Actually, we won't.

So to you, sir, I bid farewell!"

As they vanished into the night with one hundred thousand in cash and several crates of booze, they left behind a scene that would echo through New Port's underworld.

Frankie, Silky, and Chubbs huddled together, patiently waiting for confirmation that the job was done. Suddenly, the crackle of tires on gravel broke the silence. Creepy and Sneaky rejoined the group, confirming what the others had been waiting to hear.

Frankie wasted no time—he reached into one of the bags, peeled off $30,000, and handed it over to the brothers. "Your cut. Job well done."

Sneaky, satisfied, glanced at Creepy, who grunted in approval as he pocketed the cash. "Pleasure doin' business," Sneaky quipped as they turned to leave.

With no need for drawn-out farewells, the brothers slipped back into the night, their work here finished.

Silky's voice carried a note of caution about what was to come. "Jimmie and his men won't just lick their wounds. They'll be hunting, sniffing for any trail that leads to us. We've made our move; now we brace for theirs."

Chubbs leaned in, a confident look on his face. "If they come knocking, we ain't seen nothing, we ain't heard nothing."

The trio shared a moment—a silent oath of solidarity in the face of looming threats.

"We've danced with danger before," Chubbs intoned, "and we'll do it again. Together."

As they dispersed, the thrill of victory mingled. They had outsmarted their foe today, but tomorrow was a new battle.

With the heist behind him, Frankie turned his attention to Judge Kincaid. Trapped in a web of debt and blackmail, Frankie fought to break free—only to find the grip tightening with every move he made.

One evening, Frankie decided to confront the judge and end his suffocating hold over him.

When they arrived, Judge Kincaid's mansion loomed like a fortress at the end of the cul-de-sac, its towering facade a monument to the power within. Marble columns guarded the entrance, leading into a lavish foyer adorned with antique vases and paintings that whispered of old money and deep-rooted influence.

Hogg escorted them through opulent corridors, leading to the judge's office—a cavernous room where luxury and intimidation mingled seamlessly. Behind an enormous mahogany desk, the judge presided over his domain, surrounded by bookshelves that held more secrets than law. The grand window behind him cast his silhouette in a halo of moonlight, framing him not just as a man, but as an empire unto himself.

Frankie greeted him with forced politeness, masking the simmering anger beneath the surface.

Judge Kincaid welcomed him with a chilling smile, exuding arrogance and superiority. "Ah, Frankie, my boy. I've been expecting you. Sit down, won't you? To what do I owe the pleasure?"

Frankie took a seat, fighting to steady his quivering hands while Chubbs positioned himself near the door. Frankie knew he had to tread carefully; the judge held all the power, and any misstep could have dire consequences.

Taking a deep breath, Frankie mustered the courage to speak. "Judge, I'm done with the underground hustle. It's time for me to step away," he said firmly. "My music's taking off, and the risk isn't worth the reward."

The judge's expression hardened as he leaned forward, gleaming with a predatory glint. "Step away? You forget, you owe me—and I always collect what's owed," he replied, his voice dripping with menace.

Frankie's frustration boiled over. "I've paid my dues, Judge. I've done everything you asked. It's time to clear my slate."

The judge leaned back in his chair, a twisted smile creeping across his face. "Oh, Frankie, I do have a soft spot for you. Truly, I do. But you don't seem to grasp how this works," he said, stroking his beard, his tone cold and deliberate. "Son, I'm the only thing keeping you out of prison, and it's about time you recognize that. As long as you're in debt to me, you'll be dancing to my tune and feeding my streets."

He paused, letting his words sink in. "Is that clear enough for you?"

Frankie shoved his chair back and planted his hands firmly on the judge's desk, leaning in close until they were face to face. "No more, Judge. I won't be your puppet any longer," he declared, his voice sharp with defiance.

"If you don't release me from your grip, I'll expose everything—your dirty dealings and your ties to organized crime. A scandal like that would send shockwaves through the city, shredding your reputation."

His anger boiling over, Frankie continued, veins bulging from his head. "I'll go to the papers, and I don't care if I go down with you. In fact, I've already spoken to a journalist known for exposing corruption. Once I make the call, the whole city will know who you really are. The cat will be out of the bag, and there's not a damn thing you can do to stop it."

Throughout the tense exchange, Chubbs stood by the door, a silent pillar of support for Frankie. His eyes remained fixed on the unfolding scene, body tensed, ready to react at any sign of danger.

Opposite him, Hogg maintained his calm and imposing presence, a stoic sentinel for the judge. His face was impassive, revealing nothing, while his broad-shouldered stance served as a clear reminder of his role as an enforcer.

The judge's laughter echoed through the room, sending a chill down Frankie's spine. "Such bravado, my boy. But remember, crossing me is not a path you want to take."

He locked eyes with Frankie and added, "Your debts will catch up to you, one way or another." His voice dripped with twisted certainty, his fingers casually brushing a stack of papers.

"If you ever pull that stunt, I'll reopen your case file and have you and your posse shipped to Angola so fast, you'll think you got hit by a hurricane. Your pretty wife and that mistress of yours too! I'll have your whole family put away for racketeering."

The judge's hand flicked in a dismissive wave, a sneer curling his lips. "And these ain't threats, son. These are promises."

The judge reclined, his tone dripping with smug satisfaction. "Oh, I don't know... Given your little stunt, adding an extra five hundred to your monthly tab seems fair. Just a small price to pay for my silence on that shiny new extortion charge you earned tonight."

He tapped his fingers rhythmically on the desk, his smile malicious. "Whatcha say 'bout dat, Hogg?"

Hogg grinned, savoring the moment before responding, "Yessuh, boss. It sounds—"

The judge cut him off by slamming his fist on the desk. "You right, Hogg! It sounds like Frankie's gonna have to come up with some extra cash to keep me off his ass. Now get out!"

The moment Frankie stepped out of Judge Kincaid's mansion, trepidation gripped him as he prepared for his next move. He silently berated himself for misplaying his hand, his mind racing through scenarios, searching for a way out of the web that trapped him.

As they got into the car, Frankie looked at Chubbs and said, "We've got to dig something up on this man. And we have to do it quickly."

After his alarming conversation with Judge Kincaid, Frankie seemed to vanish. He deliberately isolated himself from the familiar comforts of family, friends, and the world.

For an entire month, he embarked on a journey of introspection. This period of solitude wasn't a retreat but a fearless confrontation with his inner demons and fears.

One night, the weight of his thoughts left him pacing the edge of his sanity.

In his home studio, Frankie paced like a caged animal, the rhythm of his steps clashing against the moody strains of jazz that filled the air. Each note echoed his personal conflict, a soundtrack to his distress. The room, usually a sanctuary of creativity, now felt like a witness to his unraveling.

With a glass of bourbon in hand, its contents swirling with every unsteady movement, Frankie found no solace in the amber liquid—only a bitter reminder of the escape he sought but couldn't find.

The music crescendoed, mirroring the storm inside him—a clash of euphoria and regret. Frankie threw the window open, letting the cool air slap against his face as he shouted into the void, a primal release of all his pent-up frustrations.

"Is there more?" he bellowed, his voice lost in the sleeping city.

As the music dipped into a somber melody, Frankie's thoughts spiraled. Cleaning up his life felt impossible, like navigating a minefield blindfolded. His relationships were no better; the very fabric of his world was frayed and worn.

With Bell, there was a fragile thread of improvement, a glimmer of hope. Kenya's pregnancy—and its tragic end—had stretched the distance between them into a valley filled with regret. Frankie's heart ached for what could have been, for the pain he had caused each woman.

Despite the chaos, Chubbs still looked to him for direction, relying on Frankie as a compass for the future. That responsibility felt like both an honor and a shackle around his neck.

Amid the storm that consumed him, Judge Kincaid was the thorn that bled Frankie dry—a relentless parasite draining his resources and spirit. Frankie's resolve to break free from the judge's grip had never been stronger; he was desperate to reclaim his life from a man who saw him only as a path to profit.

As Frankie sat in the silence of his studio, a newfound clarity settled over him. His mind was sharp, his heart renewed, and his purpose reforged. In the depths of his solitude, he had stumbled upon a sound that resonated deeply with his core—a musical gumbo of jazz, blues, and soul. This experimental sound was a raw reflection of his struggles and triumphs, a sonic embodiment of the complex emotions that had shaped his journey.

After a month of isolation, Frankie felt transformed, ready to face the world with a new sense of direction and a unique sound.

Now reconnected with reality, Frankie's resolve was unmistakable. Once a place of unraveling, the studio now felt like the launchpad for his rebirth.

"This sound... it's more than music. It's my truth," he said, sharing his vision with Silky, Chubbs, and Bell.

Silky's admiration was evident. "It's bold, Frankie. I love it!"

Chubbs clapped him on the back. "You've always had the gift of turning chaos into art. Let's shake things up."

"Chubbs," Frankie added, turning to his friend. "We need to bring Red into this. Book a session for us."

The agreement was immediate, and a shared eagerness filled the room.

Bell, though still nursing some resentment, couldn't hide her pride. She kept her words measured but genuine. "I couldn't be prouder, Frankie," she said softly, a subtle reminder that while the past wasn't forgotten, healing was underway.

This wasn't just a change of direction; it was a declaration of growth. Frankie's isolation had been a metamorphosis, and through this new sound, he was ready to share his evolution with the world.

With everyone assembled, the studio pulsed with creativity as Frankie and Mississippi Red dove into crafting what promised to be an unforgettable hit. The air crackled with the electricity of creation as they immersed themselves in every note and lyric.

Hours passed, but soon the contours of a hit single took shape.

"Hot shit, Daddy!" Red exclaimed, a grin splitting his face. "Even a deaf man could hear this is a hit. What are you gonna call it?"

Frankie stepped back from the mixer with a contemplative look. "Midnight Blues."

The room erupted in cheers, with Chubbs's loud howl cutting through the noise. "That's sweet, Daddy. Real sweet!"

*Midnight Blues* wasn't just a song—it was the culmination of Frankie's journey, filled with the rawness and vulnerability that had defined his path. The enthusiastic praise echoed a shared sentiment.

Yet, as the session wound down, triumph gave way to an unexpected twist.

Red poured out his heart to Frankie. "Listen, Frank—that song is all yours. You wrote it, produced it, recorded it. It's your truth," he began, sincerity etched in his voice. "But Frankie… I've paid my dues. I'm ready to carve out my solo career. I'm giving up all credit on this song in exchange for my freedom."

But Red's declaration of independence clashed with Frankie's vision for their partnership. The very control Frankie had fought to reclaim from the judge was now something he refused to relinquish.

His voice remained steady, almost cold. "Red, our contract says otherwise."

Red's expression darkened, frustration simmering just beneath the surface.

But Frankie pressed on, his tone coaxing. "Look, I know you're capable of great things, Red. We've got a once-in-a-lifetime shot here, something special. And there's no one I'd rather do this with."

He reached to place a reassuring hand on Red's shoulder, but Red shrugged it off.

Unfazed, Frankie delivered the final blow, his voice softening just enough. "I'm sorry, Red. I really am… but the hits you make, the records—they come to me first."

The irony hung heavy in the air: Had Frankie really changed, or was he simply repeating the very cycle he sought to escape?

His threat to chain Red's talent to his own ambitions marked a shift from mentorship to tyranny. The fallout was immediate and intense. Mississippi Red clenched his jaw as he processed Frankie's words, resentment flashing across his face.

"Frankie," Red began, his voice strained, "I've been with you every step of the way, pouring my heart and soul into your music and your tour. But trapping me in a bad contract? That's cold. I have my own aspirations, my own path to walk—one that's not tied to yours."

Frankie remained steady, unwavering. "I understand that, Red. I do. Being at the top comes with pressure. It's better to be shielded by me so I can protect you."

Red's frustration simmered, his fists clenched at his sides. "I don't need protection! What about my dream, Frankie? I won't let anyone dictate my path, not even you."

A charged silence hung in the room.

Frankie ended the quiet standoff. "Is that a threat?"

Red burned with intensity. "Maybe it is, maybe it ain't."

Frankie stood still, choosing his words carefully. "You're at a crossroads, Red. You can walk your path alone, but how far will you get without my resources and name—hell, without me?"

Red's chest heaved with each breath, but Frankie pressed on. "Think about it, Red. I'm the star here, baby; you're just background talent."

The words cut Red deep, and after what felt like an eternity, he finally spoke, his voice brimming with disgust. "Fine… but fuck you! I'm out!"

Red stepped closer, his shadow swallowing the space between them. He paused for a second, his eyes cold. "You can't control everything… and you'll regret crossing me."

As the session ended, Frankie found himself staring at Chubbs, searching for validation but finding only concern.

"I thought you were changing, brother," Chubbs said, his voice low and serious. "You're holding on to Red, but maybe it's time to let go."

Frankie opened his mouth to argue, but deep down, he knew Chubbs was right. In that moment, the pain of transformation and the fear of loss collided, exposing the delicate balance between ambition and integrity. Frankie's confrontation with Mississippi Red wasn't just about music or fame; it was a struggle between the man he was and the man he was trying to become.

With the studio finally empty, Chubbs's words echoed in Frankie's mind, refusing to fade. With nothing left to say, they parted ways quietly, each lost in their thoughts.

Frankie sank deeper into the merlot leather of the backseat, Cal guiding the car through the New Port streets. The world outside seemed suspended between the tangible and the abstract.

The pressure from all sides was suffocating, and Frankie felt like he was drowning. This simple car ride was his lifeline, a momentary escape from the chaos closing in.

Frankie enjoyed the passing cityscape, each landmark a reminder of memories, each light a distant star in the constellation of his life.

In a fleeting spark, Frankie decided to debut "Midnight Blues" at his birthday party—at midnight, for dramatic effect. "We're all just passing through, aren't we?" he mused quietly.

Cal caught Frankie's distant reflection in the rearview mirror. "Everything good, boss?" His voice pierced Frankie's thoughts.

"Yeah, Cal. Just taking it all in," Frankie replied, a smile barely touching his lips.

There was no room for regrets, no space for what-ifs—only the road ahead.

As Cal steered the vehicle into the familiar quiet of Frankie's neighborhood, the solitude of the streets was soothing. "Things are about to change, huh?" Frankie whispered, more a statement than a question.

Cal's response was simple. "Change is the only constant, boss."

Stepping out into the early morning, Frankie paused, looking up at the dark sky above.

This ride, a metaphorical voyage through the chapters of his life, had brought him to this moment of solace—a pause before dawn.

With a deep breath, Frankie turned toward his home, the air around him alive with the silent anticipation of tomorrow's mystery.

# CHAPTER 13:
# EYE OF THE STORM

"He's skilled at deflecting, but he's hiding something." —Junior

Chubbs stood frozen, his mind a whirlwind as the reality of murder settled over the room. With Frankie gone, an ominous dread filled the space, each heartbeat amplifying the silence.

Detective Marlow moved subtly through the gathering, his questions sharp and probing. Kenya, visibly shaken, cast nervous glances around, deliberately avoiding eye contact. Across the room, Hogg propped himself against the wall, arms crossed, while the restless Judge Kincaid paced nearby.

Junior circled the crowd, keeping containment, his eyes tracking every movement.

Bell sat stiffly by the piano, clutching Frankie's gift, her expression vacant. Beside her, Doctor Williams leaned thoughtfully against the polished edge, his eyes watchful. Near the door, Cal stood on guard while Silky and Kristine exchanged wary glances in a quiet corner. Jimmie lingered by the tall window, isolated yet attuned to the room's charged atmosphere.

With a deliberate clearing of his throat, Marlow commanded attention. "I understand the magnitude of tonight's events," he began, his voice steady, "and your cooperation is invaluable. We're here to uncover the truth behind Frankie's untimely demise. Let's proceed with some questions."

Bell immediately spoke up, her voice measured. "With all due respect, Detective, I don't think you have the right to interrogate us. You're just as much a suspect as anyone here."

Junior jumped in, defending his mentor. "Detective Marlow's as straight as they come—no shortcuts, no drama. Just a lame by-the-book cop." Junior gestured confidently toward Bell before catching

Marlow's eye. "No offense, boss."

Marlow offered a slight smile, his focus unbroken. "None taken," he replied calmly. "Given the situation, I understand the suspicion. But I'm here to find the truth." He looked at Bell. "If I were in your shoes, I'd feel the same way. But if you let me do my job, I'll bring you the killer."

At that moment, bristling with intensity, Chubbs could no longer contain himself. "What's there even to question?" he burst out, his voice thick with grief and accusation. "Frankie was my brother, and now he's gone. If anyone's behind this, it has to be Judge Kincaid!"

Judge Kincaid abruptly halted and fixed his glare on Chubbs. "You're out of your mind if you think I had anything to do with this!"

Sensing the strain, Detective Marlow smoothly interceded. "Gentlemen, let's keep our heads. Every angle will be examined, rest assured."

Turning his focus to Kenya, he probed gently, "Now, Kenya, you were close to Frankie. Did you notice anything unusual before his death?"

Kenya hesitated, her expression troubled. "No, I didn't. Frankie and I... we've had our issues recently, but nothing that could lead to this. I never wanted any harm to come his way."

Marlow filed away Kenya's mention of "issues," his mind racing. "Bell?" he spoke softly. "Are you okay?"

Bell flashed a look sharp enough to cut glass, venom lacing her words. "What do you think? My husband is dead! Of course, I'm not alright!"

Marlow took a cautious step back, continuing his questioning with care. "Did Frankie ever confide in you about any specific threats or unusual concerns?"

Bell's voice softened as she brushed away a tear. "He's been tense, more so than usual. Something was deeply troubling him, but he never divulged the details. We haven't exactly been on the same page."

With each of Marlow's questions, the tension in the room mounted, weaving a tighter web of doubt. Junior kept a vigilant watch on the proceedings, piecing together the puzzle from the sidelines.

As the light questioning continued, fatigue wore down everyone's composure. Sensing the tipping point, Marlow decided to be more direct.

"Ladies and gentlemen," he announced, his voice empathetic. "I understand the discomfort this investigation brings. But I need to be transparent with you…"

He gathered himself before continuing. "The next few hours will be difficult, but we need each of you to stay until we've made meaningful progress in understanding tonight's events."

A heavy hush fell over the room, each person absorbing his words.

Detective Marlow and Junior conferred quietly in the corridor, consolidating their thoughts and strategizing. Junior, offered his insight. "Given the gathering size and the alibis we've checked, the perpetrator must be one of those we just left. It's a chilling thought."

Marlow ran a hand along his jaw, concern etched on his face. "Indeed," he replied. "Our next move is to separate and question them one by one. Focused interrogation is our best shot at uncovering the truth."

When the detectives returned, all eyes shifted to Marlow and Junior as the group awaited direction. Detective Marlow took the lead, his voice unwavering with authority. "Folks, here's the grim reality—we believe Frankie's killer likely stands among us." He scanned the room, watching for the faintest hint of guilt or evasion, but instead found a sea of shock and bewilderment staring back.

Undeterred, Marlow continued, outlining their next steps with clear resolve. "To unravel this crime, we must speak with each of you individually. It's crucial we understand the sequence of tonight's events and where you all stand in relation to what happened."

Silky's voice reverberated through the room as his feelings poured out. "Like hell you will! Not on my watch!" he declared, the force of his conviction undeniable. "You think you're going to split us up, Detective? Not a chance. We're dealing with this right here, right now!" His actions mirrored his words, punctuating his defiance by hurling his cane to the ground.

"If there's a snake among us who struck down my nephew, then believe me, we're digging it out together. No beating around the bush, no whispers in the dark," he proclaimed, his voice boiling over with frustration.

Silky's demand was unwavering. "Everyone's going to pop out, one by one, and tell us what they know and what they saw… including you, Detective." He stepped forward, arms crossing as he shot a hard look around the room. "I'm putting my eyes on each of you so-called suspects, and there ain't no two ways about it!"

Silky's chest heaved, his words hanging in the air. Kristine moved toward him, her presence calming as she attempted to soothe the storm within him. It was then that Bell stepped forward, her voice unwavering. "Silky is right. As Frankie's wife, I hold the right to dictate how we proceed. We will face this ordeal together. That's what my husband would have wanted."

Without hesitation, Chubbs reinforced their unified front. "You heard 'em, Marlow." Fueled by grief, loyalty, and determination, the group's resolve was cemented, binding them together in their search for answers.

Momentarily caught off guard, Detective Marlow looked at Junior, his slight shrug signaling resignation and agreement. He murmured to Junior, "Unconventional, but it might just work in our favor."

Internally, Marlow sifted through the implications of Silky's demand, his intuition kicking in. "Silky's willingness for a public trial nearly clears him," he thought. "That's not the move of a guilty man."

Shaking off his internal analysis, Marlow turned to address the room. "Alright," he announced, his voice steady and inviting. "Who's first?" This approach gave Marlow control and insight while respecting the group's demand for involvement.

Cal stepped forward. "I'll start," he said. His willingness set a trend of cooperation as he stood at the center, facing the room.

Marlow's tone was firm. "Cal, tonight's timeline is crucial. Can you walk us through your activities and whereabouts leading up to the incident?"

Without hesitation, Cal began his narrative. "My evening started routinely, with an interior patrol to get an accurate count of the attendees. After my count, I walked the home's perimeter." His narrative was smooth and detailed. "Following the perimeter check, I remained inside, mingling and maintaining vigilance for the next few hours until it was time for another exterior patrol."

The listeners, drawn into the unfolding testimony, evaluated Cal's words against their own observations of the night. Many noted Cal's consistent presence and professional demeanor throughout the evening, subtly shifting their suspicions elsewhere.

Cal's story took an unexpected turn when he described checking the perimeter and spotting an open window in the Cashmere Room— strange given the evening's chill. "As I headed inside to check it out," he explained, "I heard a loud crash." He paused, glancing at the group. "It turned out a vase had fallen, so I stopped to help clean up. Once we took care of it, I went straight to the Cashmere Room to inspect the window."

Cal looked at the faces before him, ensuring they felt the impact of his words. "It was then that I found Frankie on the floor, gasping for air. I quickly called for help, drawing Kenya to the scene, followed by Detective Marlow and Chubbs."

Concluding his detailed account, Cal rejoined the group. A collective sigh of relief swept through the room, silently affirming his apparent disconnection from the crime.

Attention then shifted to Kenya, who stepped forward with poised confidence, ready to unveil her own account of the evening.

Standing before the attentive group, Kenya began. "I'll be honest with you, Detective. My evening was straightforward. I mingled, mixed drinks, and danced. Aside from a few breaks, I was always in the mix—a fact many here can confirm."

Yet, in pursuit of truth, Marlow revisited the undercurrents of her relationship with Frankie. "Earlier, you mentioned some issues between you and Frankie. Would you care to elaborate?"

A brief struggle swept across Kenya's face, her words gathering momentum. With a deep breath, she leaned into her truth. "The reality is... Frankie and I were more than friends. We'd been having an affair for years. It was a complex chapter of our lives."

Kenya's revelation shed light on her connection with Frankie and introduced a nuanced layer to the ongoing investigation. She concluded with a clear statement to the audience, "I had no motive to harm Frankie. My love for him was true."

As Kenya spoke, all eyes turned to Bell for her reaction. Without hesitation, she replied with cold sarcasm, "Oh, surely you all knew I was aware of Frankie's affair. Do I really look that foolish? I'd better touch up my makeup if so."

Caught up in the moment, Bell threw out a charged accusation. "Frankie's absence during your miscarriage—that would have driven you to the brink, no?"

Kenya's expression tightened, hurt flashing in her eyes. "That's a low blow, Bell. That's my personal pain you're talking about."

Unmoved, Bell's voice turned colder. "Frankie is dead, Kenya. We're beyond the personal. Everything is under scrutiny now."

The air between them crackled as Kenya, anger rising, snapped back. "Fine! If everything's on the table, let's talk about your secret affair, then."

All attention shifted to Bell. She shot back, "You're one to talk, homewrecker! It eats you up that he chose me, doesn't it?"

Bell accused Kenya, "You probably did it out of revenge...or fear of never escaping him." Kenya, her fury peaking, lashed out. "You pretend to care, offering me help one minute and accusing me the next." Her voice rose as she said, "And don't you dare bring up our child again. You wouldn't understand what it's like."

The two women began to move toward each other, the room electric with the intensity of their confrontation. Before things could escalate further, Silky and Junior stepped in, separating them.

Sensing the urgent need to steer the chaos back to order, Detective Marlow raised his voice, demanding silence. "Enough!" His authoritative tone sliced through the turmoil. "Bell, we need clarity. Is there truth to the allegation of your secret affair?"

Bell, caught off-guard, struggled to maintain her composure. "What kind of question is that? My husband has just been murdered, and you're scrutinizing my personal life?" She moved to exit the room, but Cal, though empathetic, blocked her path. "I'm sorry, Bell, but we need the full truth here."

Cornered and visibly shaken, Bell's admission came out in a near-whisper. "Yes... I was involved with someone else." With a defiant flip of her hair, she set her boundaries. "I'll say no more until it's my turn to speak."

Marlow gestured for Bell to take center stage, his eyes scanning the room for reactions.

Bell reluctantly stepped into the spotlight, her anger simmering beneath the surface. "Alright," she declared bitterly. "You're so eager to know my whereabouts? Fine." Her words, both bold and theatrical, captured the room's attention.

"I was out on the town, away from this house, and away from Frankie," she began, daring anyone to challenge her. "I was downtown, trying to find something—anything—for Frankie's birthday that might bridge the gap between us." She held up the gift she had clutched earlier, a symbol of her honesty. "I spent time choosing it, hoping it might mean something." Her eyes drifted across the room as she continued. "Afterward, I sat in a café, thinking about our entire charade."

Detective Marlow cut in, his tone skeptical. "Can anyone confirm this?"

Bell forced a smile. "You can check with the boutique where I bought the gift. The café staff saw me too—the loving wife, buying her husband's last birthday present." Her words dripped with irony.

"And what about your...affair?" Marlow pressed.

Bell's glare hardened. "Yes, as I said...I was seeing someone else. But that doesn't make me a murderer." Her voice softened, a hint of sadness breaking through. "I admit, I was contemplating leaving Frankie. But not like this...never like this."

The room fell silent as they measured her alibi against their doubts. Detective Marlow made a note and then looked up. "Thank you, Bell. We may need to ask more later." Bell stepped back, her posture remaining rigid as Marlow motioned for the next person.

Silky's entrance brought a wave of anticipation, his demeanor broadcasting the night's toll. With Kristine by his side, he was ready to share his observations.

"Look, Marlow. Before we get started, let me address something," Silky began, commanding the room's attention. Marlow responded with an open-handed gesture. "Take as much time as you need, Silky. The floor is yours."

Silky cleared his throat, the room hanging on his every word.

"I'm a pimp, I'm a thief, I'm a gambler—you know it, and I know it. I'm scum." He let his words hang in the air as the crowd shifted, trying to read his intent.

"It's no secret I'm kept around because I manage the finest women in New Port—ladies soft as cotton, with charms that'll make a man forget his name." He glanced around, a sly smile playing on his lips. "I spread my money around, and I keep company with the right people—the ones throwing the real parties, the ones with the secrets."

Silky's eyes gleamed with a hint of mischief.

"But let's get one thing straight: outside of keeping my girls in line, they'll tell you—Silky's a lot of things, but he ain't no killer."

Confident he'd made himself clear, Silky began recounting his night. "My evening went as usual, keeping an eye on our esteemed guests, making sure everything was smooth," he said, his tone casual but sharp.

"Most of the time, I was watching a card game. Jimmie over there seemed to be on a real lucky streak."

Jimmie's reaction was instant and heated. "Whoa! What the hell, Silky. You know I had nothing to do with this. I wasn't even supposed to be here tonight, and now you're saying I'm a killer?" His voice rose, panic edging into each word. The room watched him closely, unsure if his outburst was guilt or desperation.

Silky's eyes narrowed. "Calm down. You're about to show your hand, and I can think of a few reasons you might want my nephew gone."

The detective cut in, "Silky!"

Silky raised his hands in surrender, "I'm cool, Detective, I'm cool. But Kristine told me she heard something." With that, all eyes turned to Kristine, waiting for her to speak.

Kristine brought a new dimension to the investigation, her calm demeanor a stark contrast to the storm swirling in the room. "While I spent much of the night by Silky's side, there were moments I stepped away to attend to the girls," she began, her voice steady, her gaze sweeping the room as if replaying the night's events. "It was during one of those times, near Frankie's room, that I overheard a tense exchange. The voices were muffled, so I couldn't make out the words or tell who was with Frankie."

Judge Kincaid's skepticism rang out, his Southern accent stretching each word. "Are you kidding me? This is preposterous! It's clear these two are in cahoots," he scoffed, his voice laced with disdain. "They'll say anything to keep each other's hands clean. Marlow, you can't be serious."

Silky snapped back with equal force, "Listen here, don't cut my lady off while she's talking. Show some respect! With the night I'm having, I don't care about your fancy title."

Hogg stepped forward, his deep voice reverberating off the walls. "Calm it down, hoss."

But Silky held his ground, sneering at the judge, "Control your lackey!"

Detective Marlow's patience was wearing thin as he pleaded for calm. "Will everyone please just fucking relax!" His frustration with the group's dynamics was starting to show, and he began to wonder if agreeing to the joint testimonies had been a mistake.

Refocusing on the investigation, Marlow redirected his attention to Kristine, probing for more details about the argument she had overheard. "Kristine, did you get a chance to identify the voice? Male? Female?"

She shrugged. "No… I'm sorry. If I had to guess, I'd say it was a man."

Though vague, her uncertain response added a piece to the puzzle. Marlow pressed further. "Anything else you two observed tonight that might help us?"

Silky nodded, ready to reveal more. "Yeah, there was something else," he began, holding everyone's attention. "I saw Red at the bar, mumbling to himself before he started spilling his frustrations. He was clearly upset, going on about feeling trapped by Frankie—tied down by some contract." Silky paused, letting the weight of his words settle. "He kept saying he wanted more out of life. I think the boy's at his wit's end. It wasn't just the liquor talking—you could feel it."

Then, as if backtracking, Silky added, "But listen, while he sounded fed up, Red is soft—the boy can't kill a roach."

As Silky and Kristine receded into the background, Marlow turned his questioning to Jimmie. "What did you mean when you said you weren't supposed to be here tonight?"

Jimmie stepped forward, confidence evident in his demeanor. "I'll cut to the chase," he began, his voice tired. "I came here tonight to confront Frankie about robbing my warehouse. After piecing things together, it all pointed back to him." Moving closer to the window, cigarette in hand, Jimmie recounted, "He didn't just admit it; he made me an offer I couldn't refuse. I won't get into specifics, but believe me—I needed him alive. After our talk, he was worth much more to me breathing."

He left the details vague but clear: Frankie's survival served his interests.

Chubbs unexpectedly vouched for Jimmie, adding weight to his story. "I can confirm that conversation, Marlow. I know the details, and Jimmie's telling the truth."

Jimmie looked around the room, addressing the silent judgments forming around him. "Yeah, I won big at the card game—that's just luck. As for Frankie, we squared things up. I had no reason to hurt him." He framed their last interaction as moving toward mutual benefit rather than conflict.

Still skeptical, Marlow pressed further. "That sounds very diplomatic. But did you leave the card game at any point?"

Jimmie sighed, admitting, "For a few minutes, yeah. Just needed some fresh air and a smoke. But plenty of people saw me at that game; they can tell you I didn't stray for long." His story, backed by witness accounts, offered an alibi—albeit a porous one.

Mississippi Red staggered slightly as he stepped forward. "Silky thinks I'm losing it. Maybe he's right..." His usual flamboyance was dulled by the night's events. "You want to know what's driving me mad?" he began, his voice rough. "I've been haunted—consumed by fantasies of breaking free from Frankie."

His confession darkened, painting a chilling picture of his inner turmoil. "I thought about strangling him in his sleep once while we were on tour," he murmured, his expression distant. "Another time, I imagined pushing him down a flight of stairs. I was sure I could make it look like an accident." A twisted glint flashed in his eyes as he described his desperate need for independence.

Red's demeanor shifted sharply, and he started hitting the sides of his own head, each blow punctuating his words. "Frankie was controlling behind closed doors... but damn, he was good at what he did," he muttered, his agitation growing. "All I wanted was a mentor, not a manager!"

His voice rose, his actions growing erratic under the weight of his admission as the onlookers watched with mounting concern. "The truth is, I wanted him gone. I needed to be out of that suffocating contract. I wanted to make music on my terms," he shouted, his voice reaching a crescendo. "The only way I saw… was by ending Frankie."

A tense hush blanketed the room, leaving everyone frozen as they absorbed the shocking turn.

"I hear it. I feel the music—the beat, the sound, the rhythm!" Red's voice trembled as he became absorbed in his own trance. *"Rrrrrrrrrrr, rrrrrrrrrr… tuh tuhtuh tuhtuhtuh. Bum, bummmm… chatchatchatchat, tuhtuhtwo!"* He seemed possessed by the music pulsing through him, each sound reverberating like an unspoken truth. "But none of it's mine," he sighed, his face twisting with frustration. "To the world, I'm just the backup—the shadow. I was never gonna be a star while Frankie was alive."

Red's eyes burned with something fierce, and the room held its collective breath, caught in the intensity of his confession.

Then, as though the weight of his words finally broke him, he softened, his voice dropping to a murmur. "They're just thoughts, you know? Thoughts that come and go." His eyes fell to the floor. "I ain't no killer, Detective. I don't have the heart for it," he added, his tone wavering between bitterness and defeat. "I was just drinking, too much maybe, wondering about my future… but it was only ever thoughts."

Detective Marlow, taken aback, studied Red closely. "Did you share this with anyone?"

Red shook his head. "Nah, it was just me and my bottle." His words slurred slightly as his inebriated confession continued. "Well… I told Silky once a while back that I wanted more freedom, but let's be real—Silky's influence is fading. Kristine practically runs his whole operation now. Everybody knows it."

Silky flared, raising a finger to respond, but restrained himself, his expression holding back deeper frustrations. As Red shuffled back to his place, the room held onto his words—a man yearning for freedom but seemingly incapable of violence.

Detective Marlow scanned the room before signaling to Dr. Williams, inviting him to share his side. The doctor, embodying the calm and precision of his profession, adjusted his glasses, a gesture marking the transition from observer to key witness. "Thank you, Detective," Dr. Williams started, his voice steady and clinical. "As Frankie's physician, I was called tonight to assist in a dire situation, only to find my patient—excuse me, my friend—beyond help."

His next words introduced an alibi, anchored by his entanglement with Cyn. "My personal life is my own, but I will share my business simply out of respect for what has happened." His tone was agreeable, that of a man with nothing to hide. He continued, "For most of the evening's drama, I was occupied in the last bedroom on the right, far from the immediate scene of the crime."

Acknowledging the doctor's alibi, Marlow shifted his questioning toward the medical angle. "Thank you, Doctor. I understand you were occupied during this critical time. But could you offer your medical insight into what transpired with Frankie?"

Dr. Williams, now in his professional role, answered promptly.

"To be fair, Detective, that's a loaded question. It's nearly impossible to determine without proper testing," Dr. Williams replied cautiously.

Marlow rubbed his temple, his frustration was evident. "Could you at least give it a try?"

Nodding, Dr. Williams recounted his arrival on the scene. "When I first saw Frankie's condition, I suspected an acute choking episode. I immediately attempted back blows and abdominal thrusts to clear the obstruction." His voice wavered as he continued, "But soon, it was clear we were dealing with something far more sinister."

He adjusted his glasses, a nervous habit, and explained his next steps. "I rushed to retrieve my medical kit, which I'd left here for emergencies just like this. To my shock, it was missing." He snapped his fingers rapidly—a nervous tick betraying his anxiety. "Oddly, I later found it in a different location." He let the point linger before adding, "This might seem minor, but to me, it's critical. "Frankie's death wasn't an accident—it was deliberate. In my professional opinion, there's no doubt something malicious occurred."

The suggestion of foul play gripped the room, prompting Marlow to urge Dr. Williams for more details. "Could you elaborate, Doctor?"

Dr. Williams crossed his arms, his professional demeanor unwavering. "Frankie's symptoms and sudden decline suggest something insidious, like poisoning," he theorized, his foot tracing small circles on the floor as he spoke. "I can't prove it without tests, but it's the only explanation that fits under the circumstances."

Frustration flashed across his face. "Had I reached my medical kit sooner, there might've been a chance to counteract the effects."

Seizing on this, Marlow inquired about potential suspects. "And who, in your opinion, could have done this?" he pressed further.

"The person responsible would have to know Frankie's routines and the location of the medical kit—someone who could move unnoticed," Dr. Williams said, his eyes fixed on Bell. "You knew where the kit was stored, allowing you to interfere or remove it to prevent its use…"

This revelation steered the investigation from mere motive to the intimate knowledge and access needed to execute such a crime. The idea that Bell might have orchestrated the act shifted the narrative dramatically.

Bell's reaction to Dr. Williams's insinuation was immediate and visceral; her face flushed with shock and anger. "Doctor! Are you accusing me of poisoning Frankie?" she demanded, her voice laced with disbelief and frustration.

Dr. Williams, unflinching, maintained his composure. "I'm merely presenting the facts as I see them," he replied calmly. "The missing medical kit raises questions, and given your access, it's a point that cannot be ignored."

Shifting his scrutiny, he continued, "And Judge Kincaid, your contentious history with Frankie is well known. With your resources, orchestrating something like this wouldn't be out of reach."

Judge Kincaid scoffed, quick to deflect the mounting suspicion. "You're weaving a story from guesswork and coincidence," he retorted. "These implications are baseless."

Undeterred, Dr. Williams held his ground. "I can only offer my observations and medical expertise. How they're interpreted is up to the investigation," he said, unwavering. "But remember, poison is often the weapon of those who prefer subtlety over brute force."

As Dr. Williams stepped back, whispered theories swept through the room. Detective Marlow, absorbed in his notes, wore a look of perplexity. His head was starting to spin. Junior's attention shifted between Bell and Judge Kincaid, his mind racing to connect the dots.

Bell, visibly shaken by the accusation, seemed to shrink into herself. Across the room, Judge Kincaid's frustration grew, his frown deepening as Dr. Williams's words hung over him like a cloud.

Detective Marlow snapped his notepad shut and refocused his attention. "Judge, your perspective on these events could be invaluable," he said, extending an implicit invitation for the judge to address the suspicions surrounding him.

Judge Kincaid stepped forward, adjusting his suit, ready to defend himself.

"It is with a heavy heart that I stand before you under such somber conditions," he commenced, his words imbued with his Creole accent. "Indeed, Frankie and I had our share of discord. Let's just say I kept certain files from reaching the wrong hands—for his benefit." Judge Kincaid paused, fixing his cuffs before continuing, "In truth, Frankie recently came into possession of sensitive information…information that, if revealed, might cast a shadow over my reputation."

His declaration was measured. "But to insinuate that I'd murder him to resolve our differences is absurd," Kincaid asserted, his stance stiffening as if to fortify himself against the wave of skepticism he faced.

"I have built my life in the public domain, where integrity and reputation are my bedrock. The notion of endangering my career over personal grievances is unthinkable," his voice trailing off.

Silky seized the moment, pressing further. "Rumor has it you're aiming higher in politics, Judge. The governor's chair, maybe?" he quipped, slicing through the judge's air of superiority with his inquiry.

The question struck a nerve; Kincaid's composure faltered briefly, replaced by a flash of annoyance. "My career trajectory is irrelevant here, Silky. Our focus should remain squarely on uncovering the truth behind this tragedy," he countered, skillfully deflecting the insinuation.

Judge Kincaid's demeanor hardened as he addressed the room, his voice layered with disdain. "This gathering, eclectic as it is, hardly aligns with my usual circles," he remarked, clearly delineating his social standing. "Let me be clear: my career is built on years of dedication. I certainly wouldn't throw it all away for some bootlegging, drug-dealing singer."

Silky, unimpressed, shot back, "That's a half-baked alibi if I ever heard one."

The judge chuckled to himself, but his laughter did little to ease the strain. Instead, it amplified the accusations against him and underscored his disrespect for Frankie's lifestyle and profession.

Sensing the growing suspicion, Kincaid decided to address his political aspirations. "I'll say this to get you all off my back: I spent most of my evening discussing my upcoming campaign. Yes, I stepped out occasionally—for some fresh air and private conversations that don't concern any of you, unless you're planning to vote," he declared.

Detective Marlow questioned Kincaid's alibi. "Is there anyone who can corroborate your account of the evening?" he asked, his inquiry pointed and direct.

Kincaid's response was swift. Adjusting his jacket, he presented himself as a man frequently seen but not closely monitored. "Of course, I was in plain view throughout the evening. As for an exact record of my movements, I'm afraid I don't keep a ledger cataloging my social interactions," he replied, dismissively waving a hand.

Marlow's patience wore thinner with each evasive answer, and his frustration with Kincaid was now evident. "Judge, could you elaborate on the state of your relationship with Frankie at the time of his death?" he asked, his irritation barely concealed.

Kincaid exhaled heavily. "Son, you, of all people, should know that Frankie was no simple character. Yes, we clashed at times, but there was mutual respect. Our business dealings, though sometimes bending the rules, were fruitful. Recently, we'd even made efforts to mend fences, reaching what I believed was a mutual understanding," he explained.

Marlow pressed further. "And the nature of these disagreements?"

Kincaid's demeanor stiffened. "Those were private matters, Detective. Not relevant to this unfortunate event," he replied curtly.

Undeterred, Marlow touched on a theory that had piqued his interest. "Dr. Williams introduced the possibility of poisoning. What's your take on that?"

Kincaid's humorless laugh underscored his dismissal of the idea. "I'm a judge, not a chemist. I lack both the knowledge and the inclination for such... clandestine methods. And for the record, I didn't prepare a single drink for Frankie tonight—hell, I haven't even prepared my own drinks. So, this notion that I could orchestrate such a scheme is far-fetched at best. Y'all using my status against me, and frankly, it's laughable," he asserted.

The detective's words cut through the stillness with precision. "The doctor never specified how he was poisoned," Marlow pointed out, directly challenging the judge.

Caught off-guard, Kincaid stumbled momentarily and began to fidget, now avoiding eye contact. Regaining his composure, he retorted, "A guess,

Detective! How else does one poison?" His attempted recovery, however, was undermined by a quick, telling exchange of looks with Bell—a gesture that did not escape Marlow's meticulous observational skills.

Bell, for her part, shook her head nervously under the judge's glance, her discomfort evident to all present.

Marlow seized this moment, focusing on the exchange between Kincaid and Bell. "And your engagement with Bell tonight?" he inquired, noting how Kincaid adjusted his tie, perhaps a sign of his growing unease.

Kincaid's response was too swift to seem entirely genuine. "Our interaction was minimal," he quickly added, "and our paths didn't cross until now."

Marlow shot back, "So you do keep a ledger of your interactions?"

Detective Marlow concluded his interrogation, allowing the judge to withdraw. Kincaid stepped away, his performance having done little to dispel the implications that now hung heavier than before.

Junior whispered to Marlow, "He's skilled at deflecting, but he's hiding something."

Marlow stayed fixed on the judge, his focus unwavering. "Agreed. There's a story he's not telling. Keep close tabs on him." Junior's steady surveillance of Kincaid underscored the rising doubts in the room, reinforcing the shared belief that Judge Kincaid's polished exterior masked deeper secrets.

The focus then shifted to Chubbs as Detective Marlow addressed him. "Chubbs, it seems you are the last one to speak. Please, tell us what you know." As he moved forward, grief was evident in his posture. The impact of the loss was apparent as he neared the brink of tears.

"I've known Frankie for over a decade," Chubbs began, his voice heavy with sorrow. "What happened to him… it's tearing me apart." He cast a sympathetic glance toward Bell. "Yes, the rumors of Bell's infidelity were known, and their relationship was complicated. But despite everything, her love for Frankie was undeniable." His tone softened, expressing his faith in Bell's character. "The idea that she could harm him contradicts everything I know about her."

Chubbs's heartfelt statement challenged the others to look beyond surface suspicions and consider the deeper connections that bound them to Frankie.

He took a steadying breath before continuing. "I was around all night—dealt a couple hands in the card game, served some drinks, stepped out for a few smokes to clear my head, but I was always around." His presence, subtly woven through the evening's events, offered him a silent alibi.

Chubbs paused, then revealed, "There's something else you all need to know. Judge Kincaid's been blackmailing Frankie for some time now." A wave of tension rippled through the room, shifting suspicion to Kincaid, whose face had turned noticeably pale.

Marlow pressed on. "Did you see or hear anything specific tonight that felt… out of place?"

Chubbs shook his head slowly. "Nothing specific. Just a feeling. Frankie seemed worried, like he knew something was coming." He looked around the room, resting briefly on each face. "We were supposed to leave the illegal business and start fresh. Frankie was ready to go legit, but his past caught up with him first."

As Chubbs stepped back, his words left a lingering impact. Frankie's death was no longer seen as a random act of violence but as the culmination of hidden struggles. This wasn't a straightforward crime; it was a complex puzzle of rumors and secrets, drawing everyone closer to a chilling truth.

# CHAPTER 14

# SLEIGHT OF HAND

"The truth hides in plain sight." — Cal

The room fell silent as Detective Marlow stepped forward, his presence alone enough to extinguish the chatter. "At Silky's request, I'll present my timeline for the night," he announced, his voice steady. "We must account for every detail—my movements included, along with Junior's." Standing tall with calculated precision, Marlow continued, "To be candid, my evening was uneventful. I mingled, exchanged pleasantries with the guests, and kept a watchful eye—nothing more."

He clasped his hands together, holding firm as he continued. "Earlier in the evening, Frankie confided in me about personal matters, later thanking me for handling them discreetly—Chubbs can verify those details."

The audience absorbed every word. "I watched the card game for a while, even joined in to avoid appearing standoffish. But duty called; I have a problem sitting still. During a quick smoke break outside, I noticed Hogg slipping away from the premises." The mere mention of Hogg triggered a wave of gossip.

Marlow paused, letting the murmurs die down before proceeding. "While outside, I also spotted Chubbs through a window, deep in conversation. Despite my obvious observation, he didn't seem to notice. The person he was speaking with was hidden behind a partially drawn curtain."

Before Marlow could continue, Chubbs cut in, his voice sharp. "It was Kenya. I've got nothing to hide, Marlow."

Judge Kincaid followed with a dry chuckle, laced with arrogance. "Indeed… Seems you're chasing ghosts, son."

Detective Marlow maintained a steady focus on both men. "I'm simply recounting what I observed, giving my account of the evening," he resumed, demonstrating his methodical approach. "Out of habit, I conducted a quick perimeter check. That's when I spotted Jimmie lurking amongst the trees, consistent with what he mentioned earlier." Marlow noted, his tone reflective.

He paused, methodically piecing together the sequence in his mind. "After re-entering, I grabbed a fresh drink and continued to mingle. Eventually, nature called, leading me to the bathroom. It was during that brief moment of solitude that the vase incident occurred. By the time I collected myself and emerged, the commotion had mostly died down. But shortly after, Cal's scream drew us all to the grim discovery of Frankie."

Marlow concluded his statement, leaving a heavy silence hanging in the air.

Junior's demeanor indicated readiness to share his experience. "Compared to our top cop, my night was less structured," he began, lightening the mood with a few laughs. "It's tough not to enjoy the company of a musical legend," he added, his voice tinged with regret.

"I made myself quite visible—mingling at the bar, dancing, and maybe flirting a bit more than necessary," he continued, his smile self-deprecating as he rubbed his hands together—a sign of his underlying anxiety. "Despite how it looked, I was observant. I noticed curious glances and caught snippets of conversations that seemed off, especially from those who thought they were unnoticed."

Concluding with a confident nod, he took control of the narrative. "From where I stood, the night seemed free of trouble. As for any loose details, we'll address those only if they become relevant to the investigation. Everyone deserves their privacy until then."

With a clearer picture of everyone's account, the suspects were now left to wrestle with one question: Who done it?

Detective Marlow regained everyone's attention. "I know it's been a long night," he stated, his voice heavy with fatigue. "But we're close— closer than ever—to revealing the truth behind Frankie's demise. Let's reexamine the evidence carefully."

The room quieted, each suspect refocusing as Marlow began to untangle the web of motives and alibis. Junior opened his notebook, prepared to capture any new revelations.

"Let's review what we know," Marlow continued, his tone firm. He first addressed Mississippi Red. "Red, your desire for independence from Frankie's control gives you motive, but your demeanor today doesn't suggest premeditated violence." Red nodded, his expression a mixture of relief and sorrow.

Turning to Chubbs, Marlow observed, "Chubbs, your close relationship with Frankie makes it hard to see you as a suspect, despite your intimate knowledge of his life and business. Could you have seen yourself leading the business better than him?"

Chubbs replied with firm conviction, "I could never harm him."

"Your loyalty stands out, Chubbs," Marlow acknowledged, giving him a brief nod.

He then quickly cleared the others based on the night's disclosures. "Silky, Kristine, Kenya, and Doctor Williams, after reviewing your statements and behaviors, I find no motive or opportunity linking you to the crime. You're all cleared."

Quiet amens rippled through the room.

"As for you, Cal," Marlow continued, "your consistent presence tonight and corroborated accounts show you were merely performing your duties without any ill intent towards Frankie. You're also clear."

With these assessments, a subtle sense of relief permeated the tense atmosphere.

With most of the group now exonerated, Marlow's attention turned to those still under suspicion. "Let's focus on Bell and Judge Kincaid," he announced, facing them directly. "Bell, your strained relationship with Frankie and access to Dr. Williams's medical supplies place you high on the suspect list."

Bell's response was silent, her hands trembling slightly.

"However, we're at a standstill without concrete evidence linking you directly to the crime," Marlow admitted. Bell maintained her stoic facade, though her discomfort was apparent.

Marlow then addressed Judge Kincaid, his approach measured. "And then there's the judge," he declared, his eyes narrowing.

Kincaid scoffed in disbelief. "You can't be serious!" he snapped.

Marlow stood firm. "Your political ambitions, the leverage you'd gain from Frankie's silence, and the blackmail all suggest a strong motive," he countered sharply.

Kincaid simmered silently, fists clenched, offering no rebuttal.

Marlow continued, "We must also consider the method—poisoning, a tactic requiring both forethought and access. Both you and Bell had the opportunity, but who stood to gain the most?"

As the room pondered this, Junior interjected, "We can't overlook Jimmie either. His financial ties to Frankie and knowledge of the robbery make him a prime suspect."

Marlow nodded in agreement. "Indeed, Jimmie's recent dealings with Frankie are suspicious, but the precision of this crime seems too calculated, too professional for someone like him." He turned to Jimmie. "Or... are you just playing a part?"

Jimmie's voice wavered. "You really think I killed Frankie? That's absurd. After everything I've seen and heard tonight, I think I'm the only sane one here."

Whispers spread as everyone processed Marlow's revelations. Silky, leaning against the wall, stroked his chin thoughtfully. It was then that Kenya spoke up. "I didn't speak earlier because I was shaken and didn't want to make a hasty accusation," she admitted, her expression reflecting her fear. "But earlier tonight, I overheard Judge Kincaid talking to Hogg. He was demanding, almost desperate, saying, 'I want it done tonight.' He was impassioned, but I couldn't catch the full context."

All eyes turned to Judge Kincaid, whose face flushed red with anger. "This is outrageous! I will not stand here and be slandered by criminals and lowlifes!" he barked.

Silky quickly retorted, "Did she hit a nerve, Judge?"

Before the tension could escalate further, Marlow intervened. "Is there any truth to this, Kincaid?" he demanded.

Kincaid, furious, snapped back, "Y'all are trying to set me up!"

Marlow, raising his hand to quiet the room, countered, "Judge, if you're innocent, you have nothing to worry about. We're just following every lead. What orders did you give Hogg tonight?"

Still bristling with anger, Kincaid admitted reluctantly, "Yes, I gave orders—but they were unrelated to tonight's incident. He had other business to handle for me."

Marlow turned his attention to Hogg. "And what was this 'business,' Hogg?"

Hogg's response was cryptic, his voice deep and unsettling. "Well, I'm afraid I can't say... That's a secret."

Marlow's brow furrowed as he pieced the puzzle together. "The judge," he muttered under his breath. The subtle shift in his demeanor didn't go unnoticed—Kincaid stiffened defensively, his arms crossing tightly over his chest.

Marlow's voice cut through the tension, sharp and commanding. "Cal, cuff him."

Kincaid's composure shattered. "You're out of your mind! Don't you dare lay a hand on me, boy!" he roared, his self-control unraveling.

Sensing his imminent arrest, Hogg made a sudden move. Before he could act, Chubbs, Silky, and Dr. Williams lunged, tackling him to the ground. The room flinched, startled by the sudden burst of action. Junior swiftly cuffed Hogg's wrists while Cal restrained a thrashing Kincaid.

With Judge Kincaid slumped against the wall and Hogg fuming on the floor, Detective Marlow pressed on. "Interesting choice of words,

Hogg. They cut straight to the heart of this matter," he said confidently, his mind already spinning with the triumph this case could bring.

Marlow turned sharply toward the judge. "Secrets!" he declared, his voice slicing through the tension. "Secrets push people to desperate lengths. And Judge Kincaid, you've been hiding a significant secret—one that could ruin your political career." The atmosphere in the room thickened as Marlow continued, his words deliberate and damning. "I know what you and Frankie talked about. And I'm convinced it's the reason you needed him silenced. Permanently."

Kincaid's fury erupted, shattering the fragile silence. "Uncuff me now! What the hell are you getting at? Say it!" His voice thundered, reverberating through the room. "I won't dignify these baseless accusations with a response!"

Marlow stood firm, his focus unwavering. "Judge, your secret is out—you've been passing as a white man, but the truth is you're just like us." His words sliced through the room like a blade. "Considering your run for governor, this revelation is particularly damning. A mixed man in the governor's office? Unthinkable. So, Judge... How far would you go to keep this buried?"

Judge Kincaid began to hyperventilate, his face flushed deep crimson. He bellowed, "It was you! You dug up that information and handed it to Frankie. How did I not see it coming? You're the one out to destroy me!" His voice swelled into a feral roar. "You bastard! Ohhh, motherfucker..." The growl that followed was raw, unhinged, the sound of a man unraveling.

Silky fanned the flames. "All this drama, and he still hasn't denied a thing. He's guilty!" Silky shouted.

"When I'm free of these cuffs..." Kincaid hissed, his voice venomous, "I'll crucify you!" The room froze under the weight of his threat. Kincaid seethed, spitting the words like poison. "Get these damn cuffs off me!"

Amid the chaos, Cal shifted closer to Dr. Williams, catching his attention with a quiet whisper, his head shaking in disbelief. "The truth hides in plain sight, buried beneath what you think you know. I can't believe it. It was him the whole time. "

Dr. Williams's gaze shifted from Cal to Judge Kincaid, who continued to rage, his threats ricocheting off the walls. With a subtle, almost resigned motion, the doctor adjusted his glasses, his lips pressing into a thin line. "You never really see it coming, do you?" he murmured, his words carrying an eerie weight.

For a moment, the two stood in a shared silence, grappling with the shock of what was unfolding as the room descended further into chaos.

Silky stepped forward, his movements swift and deliberate, driving the heel of his boot into the judge's face. "Shut up!" he snarled. The blow stunned Kincaid, who spat blood as his head thudded against the wall, his breaths deep and ragged.

"Enough!" Marlow commanded, his authority instantly restoring order. "Let's lay out the facts that point to Judge Kincaid," he began confidently.

"First, the blackmail," Marlow continued. "Judge Kincaid had been extorting Frankie for months. The pressure he applied was relentless. When Frankie cut off the payments, it may have jeopardized the judge's campaign fund."

He paused, scanning the room as the weight of his words settled. "Next, consider the motive tied to his secret of passing. Frankie knew the truth—a truth that could shatter not only his political dream but also his social standing. With everything at risk, Kincaid had every reason to silence Frankie."

Rumbles of agreement rippled through the room as the theory took hold.

"Now, let's consider the method of murder—Dr. Williams suggested poisoning," Marlow stated, his accusation pointed and precise. "It's discreet, calculated, and exactly the kind of plan one would expect from someone of the judge's stature. Someone who wouldn't dirty their hands but needed a sure way to silence Frankie once and for all."

Marlow zeroed in on Judge Kincaid, his certainty evident. "And we can't ignore Kenya's testimony. She overheard you instructing Hogg that something needed to be done tonight. You claim it was unrelated, but the timing—mere hours before the murder—is highly suspicious."

Judge Kincaid remained silent, his earlier defiance drained by the accusations.

Marlow turned to address the room, his voice firm. "All evidence points to a man desperate to protect his reputation and future—a man willing to do whatever it takes to keep his secret buried and his path to power clear."

His intensity grew. "Tonight, Frankie confronted you, Judge. Caught off guard, you panicked. That's when you ordered Hogg to act! Frankie pushed you into a corner, and you reacted in the only way you knew how—by making your problem disappear."

Marlow delivered his conclusion with unwavering certainty. "The evidence is clear—Judge Kincaid had the motive, means, and opportunity to orchestrate Frankie's murder. All paths lead back to him, whether directly or through his orders."

As Judge Kincaid sat restrained, glaring at the detective, Marlow allowed a subtle smile to surface. "We've got our man," he declared, his voice steady with relief.

But as the others absorbed Marlow's words, a flicker of doubt crossed Junior's face—brief but unmistakable. Silky leaned in, his curiosity piqued. "What's on your mind, Junior?"

Junior hesitated, scanning the faces around the room. With a deep breath, he made a choice that felt like stepping into an abyss. "There's just one thing that's been bothering me," he admitted, his voice wavering with hesitation and fear.

"Marlow, you mentioned you were in the bathroom during the vase incident, but something doesn't quite add up," Junior began, his voice steady. "When I casually questioned Dr. Williams earlier, he mentioned sticking his head out of the back bedroom when he heard the crash. That's not suspicious in itself, but here's the catch." He let the moment linger. "The doctor said he looked because he thought it was Cyn returning—from the same bathroom you claimed to be in."

The room froze, confusion rippling like a shockwave as everyone processed the revelation. All eyes locked on Marlow, the man who had just expertly cornered Judge Kincaid with seemingly irrefutable logic. Now, the tables were turning.

Emboldened, Silky stepped forward, his voice sharp and cutting. "And another thing, Detective. Your composure tonight—it's been... off. Too smooth. Every move you've made, every word you've said—it's like you've been a step ahead of us the whole time. Almost like you knew exactly what to expect." His tone turned accusatory. "You're not just calm under pressure—you're rehearsed. Like you've been playing a part."

"Are you two suggesting..." Chubbs began, his voice trailing off, unable to complete the thought.

"I'm a detective! Keeping composure is part of my job," Marlow snapped, his tone taut with irritation. Yet, the faint tremor in his voice betrayed a crack in his usual control. "Junior, this is a serious accusation. Are you sure you want to go down this road?" His tone shifted, the edge of defensiveness creeping in. "It's easy to mix up times on a chaotic night like this," he added, his words laced with subtle doubt.

"And Dr. Williams," he continued, his voice smoothing into practiced confidence, "you must be mistaken too. It was likely a different moment—or maybe even a different bathroom."

Junior persisted, steadying himself. "I'm saying we should consider that the killer might not be Judge Kincaid, but someone else here—someone who knew too much, secretly had access to everything, and guided our suspicions flawlessly." The room plunged into an even deeper silence.

Kristine, who had been quietly observing, suddenly found her voice. "There's something else," she began. "I didn't mention it earlier because I thought it was too trivial, but now... now it feels important." She paused, her hands gripping the edge of her chair as if for support. "Around the time we're discussing, I saw someone slipping into Frankie's room. I couldn't see their face, but the walk—it was unmistakable."

Her eyes flickered toward Marlow, then quickly away, as if afraid to confront him directly. "Detective Marlow is bowlegged," she said, her words slicing through the tense air. "It's pretty distinctive. We don't talk about it, but I know what I saw."

Jimmie spoke up, his voice low but deliberate, fueling the mounting suspicion. "Yeah, I was outside earlier and heard a thud from Frankie's room. Then there was rustling in the bushes. I glanced back, but I didn't see anyone. Thought nothing of it at the time, but now..." He let the sentence hang, his words trailing off.

Bell's face pinched in concentration as she worked through the details.

Junior quickly cut in, his theory solidifying. "That makes sense. He slipped out the window, spotted Jimmie, and cooked up that story about 'sweeping the perimeter'—just in case he had to explain away any noise."

Junior's pacing intensified, his thoughts coming together into a pointed accusation. His voice grew more assertive as he spoke. "Earlier, you described the method of murder—poisoning—as 'discreet, calculated.'" He twirled his pen absentmindedly, his expression unreadable. "When I heard that, the first person I thought of... was you."

The room tensed as Junior's conclusions morphed into direct accusations. "A crime scene this clean—it's textbook, like someone knew exactly how to cover their tracks. Someone with your experience," he concluded, his eyes fixed firmly on Marlow, daring him to challenge the mounting evidence.

Judge Kincaid erupted, his voice a mix of outrage and vindication.

"He's the real culprit! He knew too much, too quickly. It's obvious now—I was the easiest scapegoat." He gestured sharply toward Marlow, his movements abrupt. "This man listened to all our stories and crafted his own to fit seamlessly. He chose his suspect based on who seemed most likely to be guilty, selling his theory as if it were fact. This wasn't detective work—it was masterful manipulation. Now, uncuff me!"

Gasps filled the room as a restrained Kincaid continued to plead his case, his voice rising over the increasing clamor. "Search him! There's enough for probable cause. I'm here, cuffed like a common criminal, based on nothing but circumstantial evidence. At least check him. Who knows what he's holding!"

After a brief hesitation, Silky stepped forward. "He's right, Marlow. You need to prove your innocence like everyone else."

Marlow's response was steely. "No! You're not searching me. I've done nothing but work to solve this case. I won't be treated like a suspect!"

With a sly tone, Judge Kincaid interjected, "Well then, if you've done nothing wrong, what's the harm in a quick search?"

Silky signaled to Cal, who advanced with a determined stride. "Sorry, detective, but this is how it has to be. We're all under the same pressure."

Reluctantly, Marlow consented to the search, nervously scanning the room as Cal's hands methodically patted him down. One by one, Cal emptied the contents of Marlow's pockets onto the table: a wallet, keys, and some loose change.

Then, Cal's hand paused inside Marlow's jacket. Slowly, he pulled out a small, neatly folded handkerchief. The room fell deathly silent as he unfolded it, revealing a tiny bottle that tumbled onto the table with a faint clink.

Silky stepped closer, picking up the bottle and examining it with a skeptical eye. He raised a brow, his tone sharp. "What's this, Marlow?"

Grasping for control, Marlow quickly replied, "It's personal. Medication for nerves and anxiety. It's experimental—you wouldn't recognize it."

Dr. Williams stepped forward, his professional curiosity piqued. "May I take a look?" he asked, extending his hand. Silky handed him the bottle without hesitation.

The doctor examined the mysterious vial carefully, uncapping it and taking a cautious sniff. His expression shifted rapidly as he looked up. "This isn't medication; it smells like almonds..." He scrutinized the bottle a moment longer. "You know, that's really odd. It could actually be cyanide."

Marlow's composure cracked as the implications of the moment settled over him. His attention darted from wall to wall, searching for an escape that wasn't there. After a tense pause, he lifted his head and locked eyes with Junior.

Marlow drew a shaky breath, his resolve crumbling at last. The words slipped out, quiet but undeniable. "Yeah... I did it."

Judge Kincaid, still handcuffed, growled in anger. "You set this up... to frame me?" he seethed, his voice thick with resentment.

Accepting the inevitable, Marlow adjusted his coat and brushed past Junior. He casually pulled a stick of reefer from his pocket, lit it, and swaggered to the center of the room. Marlow's lips twisted into a sinister smile as he exhaled a cloud of smoke. "I guess the game is up... I killed him, and I'd do it again!"

Overcome with emotion, Chubbs lunged at Marlow, his punches fueled by raw fury landing with solid thuds. After a flurry of relentless blows, Cal and Junior intervened, dragging Chubbs away.

Marlow, now handcuffed and bruised, was pinned against the wall. Despite the chaos, he remained eerily calm. Silky stepped forward and used his cane to lift Marlow's chin, forcing their eyes to meet. "It's time to talk, Detective."

# CHAPTER 15:
# THE SUN
# WILL RISE

"In times like this, the less you know, the better." —Judge Kincaid

The room fell silent. Detective Marlow, handcuffed and seated on the floor, looked utterly defeated—his eyes hollow, his posture slumped.

Silky, leaning heavily on his cane, loomed over him. "Let's hear it, Marlow. The floor is yours," he demanded, his face stern.

Marlow slowly lifted his head. "Alright," he conceded, his voice as steady as a slow drumbeat. "Perhaps it's time you all knew the truth."

With a pained look, he shifted against the wall. "In grief, closure helps us heal. But without it, the pain only deepens." He left his words to linger in the air. "This… this wasn't just about justice. This was personal."

Junior's face twisted in disbelief, a portrait of betrayal and utter shock. "Personal? What exactly are you saying, Marlow?" he demanded.

Marlow let out a weary sigh. "This has been brewing for a long time," he began, his confession spilling out. "Over a decade ago, in Chicago, my life took a turn that forever scarred me." His tone was distant, a single tear running down his cheek. "I know Frankie killed my father, and I promised my mother I'd stop at nothing to find him."

As Marlow spoke, he swayed slightly as if caught in a trance, his mind lost in the memories. "He could have survived…if only Frankie had called for help. But he didn't. He left him to die alone, in a cold, forgotten ditch."

With each word, Marlow's voice grew sharper, his despair morphing into simmering anger. Suddenly, he began to bang his head against the wall, each thud echoing around the room. "I was just a kid but swore I'd avenge him. No matter how long it took."

Marlow's composure shattered, revealing the depths of his dark obsession.

Silky's voice was icy as he demanded more context. "So, you were setting my nephew up all this time?"

Marlow's lips curled into a twisted smirk. "Set him up?" he repeated, his tone dripping with malice. "Oh, Silky, you have no idea." His voice grew cold and menacing. "I stalked him—I haunted him. For seven years, I followed Frankie's every move, unnoticed but always present."

He gestured toward himself with cuffed hands. "I was there, lurking, observing, learning... Weaving my way into his life, sinking my fangs deeper into his soul."

Chubbs had heard enough. He stepped forward calmly and knelt beside Marlow, bringing his face close to the detective's, and whispered, "Cut the act... Spill everything or Hogg and I will drag you out back and beat it out of you."

His hard fist lifted Marlow's chin, forcing the detective to look directly at him. "It's your choice," Chubbs added with a dangerous edge.

Clearing his throat, Marlow dropped his voice to a low, haunting timbre as he began his tale. "So you want the details?"

He briefly surveyed the room. "I'm not sure this group has the stomach to handle the grim reality of my actions, especially the ladies, but since you insist..."

Detective Marlow began, "My plan started many years ago. My mother was battling illness, in and out of the hospital constantly. As I sat beside her bed in that cold, sterile room one day, I overheard some staff members raving about a new music act. Needing a distraction from reality, I joined the conversation."

He took a moment to reflect. "Funny, isn't it? How fate plays its hand. I might never have found Frankie if I hadn't talked to them that night. But as luck would have it, I did."

"One of the nurses had just returned from visiting family in the South, where she met this rising star. She was clearly enamored. When I asked her to describe him, she went a step further. She eagerly pulled a flyer from her bag. As she gushed about his talents, I took one look at the paper and froze—it was him. It was Luckey! Now masquerading as Frankie Keys."

His voice grew darker, tinged with a fervor that bordered on obsession. "I showed it to my mom. She was too weak to speak, but her eyes... they told me everything I needed to know. It was time to act."

Detective Marlow struggled against the cuffs as he fought to stand. "After finding that flyer, everything became a blur. I left the force, not just quitting my job but erasing my past existence. I meticulously crafted a new persona. One perfectly suited for the task ahead. Relocating to New Port was easy; nobody questioned it. I walked into the local police precinct, threw around some jargon, and they hired me on the spot," he explained, standing tall, his posture exuding pride and ruthlessness.

"In reality, after a year of digging, I had tracked Frankie to New Port," Marlow revealed, his tone both cruel and candid. "Joining the local force was merely the first step in my plan."

"As he toured, I tracked him—always there, blending into the background. I managed to stay under the radar until my resourcefulness got me backstage. That's when I came face-to-face with the monster and knew it was time to advance the plan. I put on my best mask and introduced myself," Marlow recounted, his voice lowering, drawing the room into the depths of his past espionage.

"Chubbs was naturally suspicious—understandable, since gangsters don't trust cops. But Frankie saw the value in having a detective on the inside. Little did he know, I was orchestrating his downfall, feeding his paranoia, and subtly manipulating him."

He stopped momentarily, relishing the impact of his words, a faint smirk tugging at his lips. "One pivotal night set everything in motion. Shortly after meeting Frankie, when his career was starting to soar, I saved him during a random police raid at a jazz club. He nearly caught a major possession charge. I stepped in as a concerned friend, flashed my badge to the arresting officer, and with a few private words and some discreet dollars, I defused things. That night, my silent loyalty didn't just clear Frankie's record—it cemented my place in his inner circle."

"In the following months and years, we grew even closer. Silky and Chubbs began to trust me. Then, one night, I got Frankie out for drinks. Unbeknownst to him, I had arranged with the bartender for his drinks to be stronger than usual. As the alcohol loosened his tongue, he spilled the secret I'd long suspected. Years ago, he fled Chicago and took refuge in New Port. He never said why, but the pain in his voice was telling. That night, I began plotting my revenge, waiting for the perfect moment to strike."

The room hung on his every word, horror and fascination etched on their faces. Junior, visibly shaken, barely managed to whisper, "And the night of the murder? How did you do it?"

As Marlow recounted the scene, his smile faded, replaced by a cold, detached expression. "It was elementary—it barely required thought. I waited in his room, hidden in the darkness. When he entered and saw me, he joked nervously about needing a drink. So I offered to pour his favorite," Marlow said with icy clarity. "As I laced his drink, he suspected nothing. With cyanide, it only takes a light touch to bring a man down."

Kenya crossed her arms defensively, her face a mix of hatred and fascination as she absorbed the grim narrative.

Marlow's eyes darkened. "I watched for the signs. First, his laughter turned to coughs. Then his voice grew weak. When he clutched his chest, I knew it was working."

He leaned forward, his stare cutting through the room. "That's when I pulled Frankie close, my lips near his ear, and whispered, 'Officer Trammel had a son, Frankie. Me. I'm Anthony Trammel. Remember that name in hell.'"

His tone sharpened, colder now, as though savoring the memory. "Frankie tried to grab me, but the cyanide had already done its work. He was too weak to fight. I pushed him to the floor and left him—just as he left my father all those years ago."

Bell was frozen, horrified by the reality of the confession.

Marlow's tone turned somber as he described his escape. "I spent too much time watching him struggle in his final moments. I was forced to think fast, so I swiftly exited through the window, my only option to ensure I was never seen in the room. As I fled the scene, a dark satisfaction took hold, a grim pleasure in knowing that justice, however twisted, had been served."

He sat down, this time in the heart of the room, his tone filled with satisfaction. "I slipped back into the house unnoticed during the vase commotion—a perfect diversion. Luck seemed to be on my side, or so I thought. Once I rejoined the group, I just had to wait. I knew it was only a matter of time before someone would find him. All I needed to do was play the part of the committed detective one last time."

Bell's voice faltered as she asked, "Why frame the judge?"

Marlow let out a bitter laugh, infuriating the judge. "Kincaid was a convenient scapegoat. His own ambitions and the secrets he held made it easy to point the finger at him," he explained, his voice dripping with disdain. "When I discovered he was *passing*, that gave me a personal reason to steer the blame his way. Plus, seeing him fall would have been another victory for me. He was a win-win scenario—a target whose downfall served me on multiple fronts."

Judge Kincaid, his anger momentarily subdued by the revelation, stared at Marlow with a mixture of revulsion and relief. "You're a monster," he added hoarsely.

Marlow shrugged, embodying the demeanor of a man with nothing left to lose. "I did what I had to do," he declared, his tone unapologetic.

"I studied him, learned his habits, his vulnerabilities. When the time was right, I struck," Marlow resumed, his voice cutting through the uproar. "I never planned to kill him on his birthday—that would be too cruel, even for me. But when I learned the party would be small and intimate, I knew it was my best opportunity to carry it out. I knew how to cover my tracks and make the deed untraceable. It was almost the perfect crime."

The man they had known as a dedicated detective was, in reality, a vengeful murderer.

Silky spoke into the heavy quiet. "You played us all like pawns in your twisted game."

Marlow, unflinching, met Silky's gaze. "Not just pawns, Silky. Necessary elements. Every one of you added credibility to my story. You all made it painfully easy to get close to Frankie and, later, to frame the judge."

Junior added, "We all trusted you. You were supposed to protect and serve, not manipulate and murder." His voice cracked under the toil of his disillusionment.

Marlow let out a mocking laugh. "Protect and serve? That's the idealistic motto they feed to rookies and the masses. The world isn't just black and white, Junior—it contains shades of gray. Sometimes, you need to step into the darkness to bring about what you believe is justice," he explained, his tone philosophical. "To me, justice required drastic measures."

Chubbs spat out, "Justice! You call this justice? You're a murderer, Marlow. A cold-blooded killer." His words resonated with each person in the room.

"Call it what you want, Chubbs. But let's be honest! How many people have you and Frankie put in the ground over the years? Do you have the balls to stand here and answer that in front of all these people? No, you don't!"

Slowly, Marlow worked his way back to his feet, his movements deliberate. "I got my revenge. That's all that mattered to me! Frankie took something irreplaceable from me, so I simply returned the favor."

Bell interjected, "And what about us? What about the lives you've ruined on your quest for vengeance? Does that mean anything to you?"

Marlow glanced around at the faces of those he had deceived and replied, "Collateral damage," his tone cold and devoid of empathy.

Judge Kincaid, now uncuffed and standing, stepped toward Marlow, his body tense. "You ruined my life, my career, all for your personal vendetta?"

Unperturbed by the judge's anger, Marlow answered, "You were just a means to an end, Kincaid. Nothing personal." He paused, a sardonic smile forming. "Think of it this way: now you're free to walk your true path. Your secret stays buried with these people, as long as you let it lie."

After a deep breath, Junior faced the others and insisted they turn Marlow over to the authorities. "We need to call this in. He has to answer for what he's done," he declared firmly.

Judge Kincaid was quick to interject, his voice booming. "Now hold your horses, Junior. Let's not jump the gun here." He cleared his throat, straightening his posture as he reclaimed his authority. "As the highest-ranking official present, I'm assuming control," he announced, his tone commanding."

"First, everyone out! We need to have a private discussion. Chubbs, Bell, Silky—stay put." His demand left no room for debate. Turning to Junior, he instructed, "Take the detective outside with the others. Keep a close watch on him."

Once the room had cleared of all but the chosen few, the small group stood in silence, somber reflections on their faces.

Judge Kincaid's voice, though low, held a distinct significance. "We have a decision to make. Marlow's confession changes everything. What he did to Frankie... it can't just be brushed under the rug," he stated, scanning the faces before him.

Silky was solemn, leaning on his cane. "He's destroyed lives, not just Frankie's. We need to ensure he doesn't get the chance to harm anyone else," he asserted, bitterness evident in his voice.

Chubbs cut in sharply, his jaw clenched tight. "He took Frankie from us. Justice won't come from the system that let him be a detective in the first place. We handle this our way," he declared, leaving no room for disagreement.

Bell's voice quivered with grief as she added, "He followed Frankie for years, waiting for the perfect moment to strike. He's not just a murderer; he's a calculated monster." She hesitated, her thoughts tangled. "He needs to pay, but… are we really considering…?"

Judge Kincaid added, "If we do this, it's final. No turning back. We ensure Marlow disappears. No one will ever find him," he concluded, his voice heavy with finality.

Silky grimaced before adding. "We have the means to make it happen. It's the only way to ensure this ends tonight."

After a moment of internal struggle, Bell gave in. "I hate it, but… it's what Frankie would have wanted. For us to protect each other," her voice was filled with sorrow.

The group shared a heavy silence, each member grappling with the imminent actions.

Judge Kincaid finally ended the discussion. "Then it's settled. We do this quietly and efficiently. Marlow's reign of terror ends tonight."

Kincaid stepped out and gestured for the two men to follow him back inside. "Let's join the others. It's time we put this matter to bed," he said, his tone urgent. As they reentered, Marlow scanned the group, noting the range of emotions etched on their faces.

Approaching, Judge Kincaid radiated a cold intensity. "Marlow, you thought you were clever, but you underestimated us. You're going to find out just how cruel we can be," he said, his tone edged with malice.

Junior stepped forward and addressed Judge Kincaid, his voice marked by a sense of duty. "Judge, I know what he did is unforgivable, but we can't—"

Judge Kincaid cut him off, his voice stern and resolute. "Junior, you've grown tonight, more than most do in a lifetime. But this is a family decision."

Junior's line of sight traveled past the judge, locking with Silky and Chubbs.

The judge placed a firm grip on Junior's arm. "Son, did you hear me? It's best if you stay out of this."

Understanding there was no room for debate in the judge's tone, Junior stepped back reluctantly.

He watched the scene unfold with a heavy heart, the night's revelations draped over him like a suffocating cloak. He had entered the evening as a green detective—eager and somewhat naive—but tonight had stripped away any illusions he held about the world.

As he looked around the room, Junior's attention moved from one face to another, absorbing their shared burden. Every one of them had been shaped by Frankie's life and now, irrevocably altered by Marlow's betrayal.

In that moment, Junior realized that the world of law and order he had once believed in was far more complex than he'd ever imagined. He understood that justice wasn't always served in the well-lit halls of a courtroom; sometimes, it was delivered in the dark corners of the night by those who felt wronged and saw no other way. Whether it was morally right or wrong, this truth of human nature could not be ignored.

Despite the inner turmoil churning within him, Junior felt compelled to play a part. "I understand what needs to be done. But let me help. I can make sure everything goes smoothly, with no loose ends."

Judge Kincaid turned to him, his eyebrow lifting in surprise. "You sure about that, Junior? This isn't police work."

Junior stood firm. "I know. But I've seen enough tonight to understand that some things are beyond the reach of the law."

After a moment's scrutiny, Judge Kincaid relented. "Alright, if you're determined to help, start by getting everyone out of here.

Once they're gone, you go home too." He snapped his fingers sharply, underscoring his words. "In times like this, the less you know, the better. That's your role now—do it right."

Tonight, Junior had crossed a line he could never retreat from, but deep down, he felt it was the right choice.

Junior did his part, escorting the remaining guests out of the house and watching them disappear into the night. After ensuring their departure, he made a final, thorough sweep of the house to confirm it was clear. Satisfied, he returned to the room to deliver his report.

There they stood—Silky, Judge Kincaid, Chubbs, Kenya, and Bell— each reflecting the tension surrounding Marlow's impending fate.

While the room teemed with anxiety, Marlow stood against the wall, disturbingly calm. He looked like a man resigned to the inevitable, unflinching as he faced his final moments.

Junior paused for a final glance around the room, tracing the familiar space they had occupied for hours.

Judge Kincaid interrupted his thoughts, stepping up to him with advice. "Remember this night, Junior. Remember the lessons you've learned. They'll serve you well in the days to come."

Junior stood still, absorbing every word.

Kincaid leaned in closer, his voice dropping to a whisper, "Listen to me... When you wake up tomorrow, act like tonight never happened. Do you understand?"

These words settled in Junior's chest like a stone, but he accepted them nonetheless. As he stepped out of the room, the echo of his footsteps seemed to mark the end of one path and the uncertain beginning of another.

Silky turned to face the group, his voice rich with wisdom gleaned from a lifetime of experiences. "You know," he began, "life's a strange journey. We cross paths with all sorts, carry burdens, and face trials that test us to our core."

He let his words wash over the group. "Tonight, we've felt the sharp sting of anger, plumbed the deep well of grief, and brushed against the cold edge of betrayal. But life... life marches on. It always does."

He shifted his stance, the creak of his cane breaking the stillness. "Frankie's gone; no force on earth can bring him back. But the memories, the music, the impact he had on our lives—that remains. That's eternal."

Silky stepped to the window and took a deep breath, letting the cool early morning air fill his lungs and steady his spirit. "So, we move forward. We carry the scars, the lessons, and the memories. But we keep moving. That's life—an endless journey of learning, loving, and, sometimes, letting go."

Silky straightened as much as his body would allow, his presence commanding despite his reliance on the cane. His voice carried across the room. "It's a shame that such a brilliant mind will go to waste. Let's get to it," he declared.

The judge grew serious. "Any last words? To God or the family?"

When Marlow spoke, his voice was surprisingly soft. "To God... I know I lost my way. My vengeance became my God. Forgive me, though I doubt I deserve it."

Letting out a slow, deep sigh, he continued. "To the family... I can't say I'm sorry because that would be a lie. But I understand your pain—I caused it. The sun will rise, and the moon will set, even on me."

His words hung in the air, a solemn acknowledgment of the end. Chubbs scoffed, his arms crossing tightly over his chest. He leaned back slightly as if putting distance between himself and Marlow's attempt at redemption. "You're right about one thing: the sun will rise, and life will move on. Just not for you."

Detective Marlow, now merely a shell of the man who had once commanded respect, finally resigned to his fate. Judge Kincaid stepped forward, his voice somber. "Marlow, you understand what's about to happen, don't you?"

After a moment, Marlow nodded slowly. "Yeah, I get it. I always knew it might end like this one day."

Together, Silky and Chubbs escorted Marlow through the hallways of the house. His footsteps echoed softly on the wooden floors. Outside, the first light of dawn crept over the horizon, stretching long, jagged lines across the gravel drive.

They approached Frankie's black car, its polished surface glinting in the early morning light. Silky reached out and opened the trunk, which lifted with a slow creak, revealing the dark, cramped space where Marlow's journey would end.

Marlow offered no resistance as his body fit snugly within the tight confines. Bell, standing a short distance away, wiped away tears that ran freely. She whispered a quiet goodbye, her voice trembling with a mixture of grief and relief—a final farewell to the man who had irrevocably changed their lives.

Kenya watched silently, yet her expression revealed the sadness in her soul, both for Frankie and the brutal necessity of their actions.

The trunk closed with a definitive thud, punctuating the conclusion of a night filled with tragedy.

Chubbs finally broke the silence, his voice firm and resolute. "This ends here. We did what we had to do. Now, we go back to our lives, carry our burdens, and honor Frankie the way he deserved to be remembered."

Chubbs and Silky climbed into the car and let the engine rumble to life. Silky rolled down his window and gave the car a solid slap—a final gesture of resolution. With Marlow securely inside, they drove off into the morning light, heading toward the secluded swamps, far from the world's scrutiny.

The final chapter of their tragic tale was drawing to a close, leaving behind a legacy marked by love and betrayal. Kenya, Bell, and Judge Kincaid watched the car until it disappeared from view.

They stood together a moment longer, absorbing all that had

transpired. Though no words were spoken, they shared a silent understanding: life, with all its complexities, mysteries, and drama, must go on.

www.ingramcontent.com/pod-product-compliance
Lightning Source LLC
Chambersburg PA
CBHW051128190726
48290CB00006B/1735